I061162?

the Donkey and the Wall

Book Two:
The Thief

J. L. Lawson

J. L. LAWSON

THE THIEF

the Donkey and the Wall
Book Two: **The Thief**
J. L. Lawson
http://jeffreylewislawson.com
jefrelaw@jeffreylewislawson.com

J. L. LAWSON

No one saves us but ourselves. No one can and no one
may. We ourselves must walk the path.

---Buddha

J. L. LAWSON

Table of Contents

J. L. LAWSON

THE THIEF

1

Sea-Change

"Men do change, and change comes like a little wind that ruffles the curtains at dawn, and it comes like the stealthy perfume of wildflowers hidden in the grass."
--John Steinbeck

The guest reclined in his chair for a moment as his host stared out across the little pond and the long shadows of evening waved in the rising wind. "This is as far as I can go without letting you know how enriching to me both our own talks have become and of course the beginning of this story," said the young man in sincere appreciation. "But I need a little time to let this all really sink into my mind."

"That is perfectly alright," his guest replied, "Will resuming in the morning be acceptable? That is if you wish to continue so soon."

The younger man hesitated only a moment, "Absolutely. I mean... I just need a little pause in the action, you know? It's really a lot to absorb."

"Good then. It has been a pleasure for me as well; you have been a most gracious and inquisitive host," drawled the older man, "I am a little in need of a good rest myself," and with that they stood. The host inclined his head as they shook hands and parted. The young man sat back down and watched the old man stride off down the lane toward town. His steps were steady and sure, his back was straight, and his eyes were upon his destination.

"Remarkable..." whispered the young man as he picked up his notes and reread certain of the passages he'd recorded.

In the morning he went about his usual routine, though he also tried to also keep his shoulders back as long as he could manage attention for them. A tall very beautiful woman with graying hair wearing blue jeans and walking with a strong gait approached his house. He first noticed her as she was just turning up the path to his porch step so he came to the door to inquire if he might be of some assistance. "Surely her car's broken down and she just needs the phone or something," he thought.

Before he formulated his first sentence of inquiry, she settled into a chair on the porch deck and smiled up to him, "Is there any coffee ready yet?" she asked as if this were her usual morning routine.

Somewhat taken aback the young man answered haltingly, "Uh...yes," and then regaining some of his composure he added, "Do you take anything in it?"

"Just black please, if it is good coffee; a dab of milk or cream if it's not."

"Oh...Okay..." he muttered and fetched out full cups for them both. She accepted the proffered mug and took a sip while her host stared on.

She looked at him through the corner of her eye over the steaming cup. "Thank you, this is just lovely," she began.

But before she got any further, he asked, "Are you having car trouble? I can drive you into town, if you need?"

"I don't own a car," she answered simply. That unsettling feeling he'd had days and days ago upon his first encounter with his now anticipated daily guest re-awoke in his stomach. She sensed his disquiet and said simply, "Shall we continue with the story?"

At those words he instinctively reached beside him for his notepad---always at his elbow these days---and caught himself in mid-movement at the realization that this was *not* his story-teller. He looked up at the lady beside him who was gazing across the little pond into the far distance of her thoughts. In that brief but poignant moment he saw her objectively. An immaculate beauty who wore an unpressed oxford shirt, well-worn blue jeans and walking shoes, yet who radiated confidence and invited inexorable trust. Her

10

elegance and poise could not be masked if she had been wearing a potato sack, he thought.

She began, "The reunion on the gangway of the *R.M.S. Britainic* was so contagious that even the few passersby were caught up in the shouts of joy and tears of happiness displayed by the eight travelers and the Captain. That small gathering of strangers added their own applause to the jubilation of the knot of people beside the great steamship. The spring sky which had been looming throughout the early morning at last let go a gentle shower; two porters began loading the travelers' luggage onto trolleys and carting them across the tarmac.

Kaitlyn put her arm in Harry's and turned to face her family and friends all of whom reflected her own immense catharsis. What had been anticipated hungrily was now a reality, and she was instantly greeted with her new title: 'Mrs. Henry Livingson' by Titania and Hipolyta, which they followed with curtsies and embraces. The sprinkles of light rain persisted and the travelers followed the newlyweds quickly away from the gangway across the tarmac. With Kaitlyn on his arm Harry led them to the train station.

Mandy spoke up, "We just came from here and were told that we could not book simultaneous passages to both Redditch and Manchester, and that the Manchester booking took priority since it was paid in full..."

"Yes Miss Hill I apologize for that inconvenience on your part; I booked that passage. I... that is to say... *my wife and I* would like to invite you all to *our* house." replied Harry. That elicited a quick quizzical look from Kaitlyn. He continued, "Where you may witness me carry Mrs. Livingson over the threshold of her new home." He smiled proudly, "So, we are off to Greengate."

The ride to Salford station was less than an hour, and while the showers persisted in turbid spates the companions sat quietly with their own thoughts. The train sped through the urban then rural, and then urban landscapes between the port of Liverpool to the central neighborhood of Salford in Manchester. Upon their arrival at the Salford Station the gentlemen helped the hired drivers load their luggage onto coaches and they were off for the short jaunt to Greengate. Jameson and Titania rode with Harry and Kaitlyn in the forward coach.

"That was the most astounding thing I've ever seen," announced Jameson still evincing an expression tinged with awe at the rapid chain of events. "Had you planned this before our arrival? How have you remained so quiet about this Kaitlyn? All these days and weeks without a hint or a word?"

"Jameson, it was not planned," she responded assuringly.

Titania insisted, "But how did this *just happen* so suddenly? Harry?"

He began to answer, but Kaitlyn answered for him, "Nothing worthwhile *just happens*. That is counter to the laws of nature and to reason..."

Harry smiled broadly and finished, "Real faith I suppose; and being always aware that one's preparations may be called into action at the drop of a hat for that one chance---that glimmering moment of opportunity. Kat is right; nothing worthwhile just happens." And they both recalled nostalgically when they stood in the cloisters of Mont Saint-Michel the first time Kaitlyn elicited those same words from Harry which she'd just repeated. That had been the first feeble launching point toward the path of her own development, and becoming the woman she was at this precise moment.

"So which of you was the one prepared for this?" asked Jameson probingly.

At the same time Mr. and Mrs. Livingson responded, "We were," to the instant amusement of both their companions.

As the coaches stopped at the Greengate address, there was a slatch of fair weather; Harry handed Kaitlyn and Titania out of the carriage. He shock hands once again with Jameson as he stepped down. Harold performed the same service for Mandy and Hipolyta. Chloe handed Hannah to her father, then she stepped out on her own. They all looked up at the town house and were instantly taken by the charming grounds and inviting path to the front entry. Harry helped to unload the baggage and compensated the drivers. "Mrs. Livingson, welcome home," he whispered into her ear; Kaitlyn beamed in beatific rapture.

"Titania, Hipolyta," he called to his sisters, "If you will do me the honor of standing us to the door..." His sisters rushed up to the front door, and stood on either side as an honor guard. Harry lifted Kaitlyn off her feet in a sweep which looked for all the world as if he were simply taking up an overcoat in his arms---not a fully grown woman. She held an arm around his neck, and plucked an antique rose from the stem with her free hand as they passed between the bushes. Hipolyta turned the door knob and gave the door a little push as their brother carried their newest sister into the entryway. With a flourish of laughter and giggles they strode into the house.

Mandy looked at the richly carpeted parquet floors wall-hangings and artwork that complemented the modestly painted and papered walls. She gazed up the grand staircase and said, 'Harry, when did you move in here? The rent must be astronomical!"

Harold and Chloe whistled their approval of the appointments as did Harry's siblings. Kaitlyn looked to Harry for an answer to Mandy's outburst. "One month today actually; it's a perquisite of my employment. Of course I've been adding furniture and other comforts as I go along. It was quite a bare and unfinished residence when I accepted the keys"

Kaitlyn's cheeks were starting to actually cramp from her permanent grin; she held her hands to her face and rubbed them as she toured her new domain. Harry led their guests around the rooms with Kat's hand in his as they walked. Fortunately, he had continued furnishing the other bedrooms so there were comfortable quarters available for all the travelers. As they came to bedroom after bedroom some one or two of the party would claim a room for themselves. At last they reached the master chambers: a suite of rooms still minimally furnished, yet appealing for their openness. Kaitlyn was well pleased.

The traveling party took advantage of their well provided accommodations and set themselves to changing from their damp and dusty clothes. The ladies were not required to vie for bathroom time since there were three commonly available bathrooms upstairs and one downstairs---all adequately supplied for any personal need. Harry showed Kaitlyn to the master suite's private bath; she was very thankful for the opportunity after the long train and coach rides. They all were refreshed and changed inside an hour and met again in the Drawing Room.

"Alright m'lord: show me to the kitchen pantries and the cook stoves so I can take up my duties on behalf of our guests!" Kaitlyn announced still grinning.

"Oh no!" Jameson's voice rose in protest. "There'll be no wives in this house's kitchen tonight!" Mandy and Titania seconded that, and they strode off in the direction they thought they might surely find the kitchen. Harry called after them, "They use coal over here. There should still be some paper and kindling near the fire box..." The disappearing cooks just waved a hand as they turned a corner out of sight.

"Harry I'm sure our ice box and pantry are supplied, what about a wine cellar?" Kaitlyn inquired hopefully, "We should offer our guests every nicety."

"Actually, knowing your approximate arrival date allowed me to have certain preparations made against your arrival." He couldn't help his own indelibly satisfied smile either, "Although I must admit that having you near, sharing the office of hostess is more than I'd hoped or dreamed."

Harold was still bearing Hannah in his arms and turned to Harry as they entered the drawing room. "Hannah this is your Uncle Harry," she looked where her father was looking. "Uncle Harry this is your niece: Hannah Belle Bessamer."

Harry bowed, "I am most honored to have your acquaintance young lady. Shall we dance?" He took Hannah into his arms and waltzed around the room to the silent strains of Strauss or of Dvořák. Her parents were so delighted they just sat down next to each other and watched as their daughter twirled and danced with her graceful partner. Mrs. Livingson was likewise thoroughly enchanted by the scene. Hipolyta came in and put her arm around Kaitlyn, squeezed her close, and whispered, "That's exactly what he used to do with Tania and me until we were big enough to dance on our own two feet." Kaitlyn kissed her sister with tears in her eyes though her face still glowed blissfully.

Titania came in as Harry was just returning his niece to her mother's care. She wore a cherubic expression of near sleep that slowly drifted down her little face. Tania crossed to what she presumed to be the liquor cabinet, opened it, then stood away from it with one of the doors still in her hand, "Harry. I've never even heard of some of these bottles of stuff! Jameson and Mancy need sherry and some white wine for their recipes..."

Harry crossed the room and reached up to a higher shelf. He took down a bottle of sherry from behind some other bottles. "Kat my love there really is a wine cellar. The door in the Butler's Pantry accesses the stairs down to it." She turned to go with Titania to find it as he called after them, "Unfortunately we don't have butler though..."

Hipolyta sat across from Chloe and took little Hannah into her arms without disturbing her. "I'll need to feed her shortly," Chloe announced, "I'll just pop up to the room and fetch a shawl. I don't want to miss a thing this evening!" and she hurried out of the room on her errand.

Harold looked through the open doors after his wife as she mounted the staircase. "What a woman," he sighed aloud. They all nodded in full concurrence.

"Speaking of that," Hipolyta turned to Harry and briefly

recounted their last dinner at Chelsea House; about the hilarious, but also misfortunate episode leading to their mutual promises to Mandy. "She's going to want some answers Harry. I don't know what she imagines, but she has known all of us forever---surely she realizes... I just don't know..."

Kaitlyn returned as Chloe was re-entering from upstairs. "Harry m'lord, that is some wine cellar! Please tell me you didn't stock that too?"

"Oh no," he corrected at once, "That was left by the previous tenants, or owners, or someone. That there was even a wine cellar at all came as a surprise to Mr. Strenhowell, my Director at the office."

Kaitlyn brought her hands from behind her, and in each she carried a bottle of 1875 vintage Château Lafite Rothschild Medoc. "Do you suppose anyone would mind then if we opened a couple bottles?"

"I can't imagine why not," her husband answered easily. "Mr. Strenhowell had a oenophilist, a professional wine surveyor, take inventory. He removed all the bottles for auction that he thought were worth anything." He returned to the cabinet and produced glasses and an opener which Harold employed with great facility.

"...Comes with the job I'm afraid." Harold continued, "All those client dinners and all. I'll just go and share the rest with our faithful chefs," he went to the kitchens. They all sat with their glasses untouched until he returned with Mandy and Jameson in tow.

"Good," he began as he poured a glass for himself, "A toast to our most esteemed sister and brother upon the occasion of their long-awaited nuptials," the room echoed with 'Here, here.'

"Here's to the groom with bride so fair, and here's to the bride with groom so rare!" toasted Harold. They raised their glasses and sipped at that.

Then Mandy had another, "There is nothing nobler or more admirable than when two people who see eye to eye keep house as man and wife---confounding their enemies and delighting their friends. To Harry and Kaitlyn Livingson!" Again they raised a glass and drank.

"Oh I just can't hear it enough!" Kaitlyn announced excitedly, "Mrs. Henry Livingson... Kaitlyn Livingson! I feel as though I have just undergone coronation." They all agreed that it was magical.

Harry blushed and added, "Perhaps not all of you have heard my Kat sing?" She looked at him in surprise, and it was her turn to blush. "Sweetheart I had an upright installed for just such an occasion, and I happen to know that Chloe is a most excellent pianist."

Chloe looked up from Hannah's feeding and glanced around the room for a piano. Harry walked to an ornate quilt hung, as it turned out, between two cabinets that was hiding the instrument. As he pulled the hanging aside he announced, "Tada."

"Oh that's lovely Harry; really lovely," Kaitlyn began, "and you brought it here just on the off chance I might sing?" She was deeply touched.

"Yes. And it has an interesting history," her husband replied, "During renovations at the University in Leeds, next door to our building project, this behemoth was uncovered in a basement room amongst a mess of lamps and chandeliers."

"How did *you* come by it?" Mandy asked.

"I simply inquired of the school administrator in charge of the renovations. I asked to where he'd like a crew to remove it, and he responded by saying 'the rubbish heap for all I care.' It seems he was more of an accountant than music lover and had no interest whatsoever in finding a new home at the university for the instrument. 'Rather ugly piece of furniture isn't it.' he'd said. I offered to have it removed at once to my own residence, and asked if I might compensate the university for their loss." Harry paused and looked around, "He said, 'pay for its removal and we'll call it quits'!" His guests murmured over the good fortune.

"I had it brought here straight away, tuned back up, and 'voila' here she stands," he finished.

"So you have a piano, and a very rich looking piano at that," Mandy replied, "but you haven't a even wardrobe or chest of drawers in your own bedroom. Are there any other curiosities we're to encounter here abouts?" She peered around her suspiciously, "I suppose these pre-Raphaelite paintings are originals?" She couldn't help herself really; she was made to believe by her companions that Mr. Henry Livingson was something of a magician and she simply didn't know what to think after the morning's events.

Harry laughed, "Only those three there and one of those in the parlor; they are on loan from the office, just in rotation---They are not ours." He added this last to Kaitlyn.

"But I was kidding! You mean they *are* the originals!" Mandy was now on her feet and inspecting Rosetti's *Lady Lillith*, and then she moved to where Harold was admiring Millais's *The Two Princes Edward and Richard in the Tower*. Hipolyta stood transfixed by *Take the Fair Face of Woman*, by Sophie Gengembre Anderson. From the parlor Titania and Jameson called, "Mandy your *in* this painting!"

They all rushed to the parlor/drafting office, and there on the wall amidst Harry's technical drawings, hung J.W. Waterhouse's *Diogenes*. They gathered around it and Titania pointed at the woman in the blue striped scarf, "If that's not you; it's your twin!"

Mandy looked at the likeness as the others looked from the painting back to her own upturned face. "That's an uncanny resemblance..." whispered Harold just loud enough for the others to hear, "Remarkable."

"Well this has certainly been an eye-opening day," remarked Mandy obviously flattered that her companions thought well of the likeness. "I'd better check that meat in the oven..." and she nearly trotted back to the kitchen.

Hipolyta looked to Harry and Kaitlyn, and motioned with her eyes to the departing figure of Miss Hill. Then she shrugged her shoulders and raised her brows in an obvious question as to what should be done. Harry asked Kaitlyn if she'd like to stroll the gardens, "The afternoon light is truly kind to my pitiful attempts at planting arrangements." They walked through to the rear of the house and out onto the grounds. After just a few steps with his arm still around her waist, he opened the discussion about their friend. "Kaitlyn, my cherished love, I am uncertain as to what *I am* to do regarding Miss Hill." He made to keep walking, but she stopped at those words. The sprinkles which had briefly abated now commenced once more.

Her face was towards his, but her eyes were unfocused and seemed to not see him at all. He waited for... he didn't know what. Her smile that had so shone all morning and into the day retreated and now only played about the corners of her eyes. When she spoke it was with a directness only a wife may employ. "But *we* promised her hope... *I promised her*," her voice became almost a whisper. Harry held her hands in his and she held on to him as if she were suddenly precariously uncertain of her balance.

His look was the very heart of compassion and he whispered in answer, "Then *you* must fulfill *your* promise."

Her expression nearly yielded to the panicked pounding in her chest as her heart recoiled in the clear understanding of his simple words. In the same low strong tone he promised, "You are stronger and far wiser than you realize. My faith in you is absolute."

Her hands lessened their terrible tension gripping his, and she slipped her arms around him holding her head against his breast listening to his own heart's reassuring throb. "I am not as sure as you are nor as firm in my own confidence, but I have always trusted you implicitly so there's no sense in my questioning your discernment now!" Although her body was still pressed to his, she leaned her shoulders back so that she might still hold him close to her and also look into his eyes. With drops of rain dappling her face and shoulders she asked simply, "How shall I begin?" He kissed her unreservedly, and her soul felt its worth. She decided some questions would take care of themselves.

Harry held his arm out for his Kat, and they continued the inspection of the gardens. "Besides," he began, "Mandy may never mention it again. A person gets a notion into their head and before long another takes its place with equal strength then the previous 'need' is forgotten entirely. Of course our Mandy is a woman of disciplined passions and maybe she's still considering re-approaching the subject of personal transformation, but still---people are people." When they finally rejoined their guests inside, Kaitlyn was ready for anything. She reminded herself: she was Kaitlyn *Livingson* after all--- Wonders are our family's stock in trade.

Harold asked Harry as they came back in, "Is there a telegraph office nearby? I really should let my family and the Allcocks know that we have arrived safely, and that we will be along to Redditch soon."

"I have already taken the liberty of sending those wires as soon as I saw the *Britainic* coming into the docks," Harry replied. "That's why I wasn't at the quay waiting at the gangway when you all disembarked. They shall expect us Saturday evening for dinner at Clive House."

"Brilliant," clapped Harold jubilantly.

Chloe added, "Thank you so much Harry. I know father and Olivia would want to know of our arrival... that is... at least of *Hannah's* arrival as soon as possible."

"Yes. Your father made that quite clear when last we spoke," admitted Harry.

The evening approached and the clearing skies permitted a most magnificent sunset. It filled the large dining room windows even though slightly shadowed by the adjoining house. They dined well on Jameson and Mandy's prepared 'wedding feast.' After they had cleaned away the remainders of the meal and adjourned to the drawing room once more, Chloe asked if they might not play some parlor games once she put Hannah down for the night. Her suggestion was greeted enthusiastically. Hipolyta and Titania went with Chloe to offer any assistance they could, while Kaitlyn explained to Jameson and Mandy how several of the games were played.

By the time Hannah was snuggled into bed and they were all assembled once more, a game of Proverbs had been decided upon by the quorum in the drawing room. It was also decided that there should be a limit placed on the guessing person's time allowance for resolving the clues. They drew lots to see who would be making the first attempt at unraveling the clues and Harold got the short straw. He went to the wine cellar in search of a bottle of brandy while the rest of them chose the initial proverb: *A drowning man will clutch at a straw*. They were ready for him by the time his successful foray was completed, and as he went to the cabinet for snifters he asked Titania, "Would you care for a touch of brandy?"

"Just a touch if you please," she answered nonchalantly. That caused him to look back over his shoulder at her to be sure she was both answering his question *and* at the same time offering the first clue. She looked back at him with an innocent smile which confirmed for him that he should proceed.

"Jameson was there hint of saffron in that wonderful rice dish?" he queried.

"Yes indeed, and I am well pleased that you were able to taste it. Titania helped with the dish so it was drowning in butter," he replied with a smile, and received a quick jab from Titania. Harold thought about that as he poured and delivered a snifter to Titania. As he returned to the cabinet he asked Harry "Would you care for a sip?"

"Good man for asking. I would be remiss however, if did not insist that you first serve the ladies." Harry responded quickly with a wink to Kaitlyn.

Harold reviewed the first three responses in his mind scanning for the possible clues. He began decanting the bottle into another snifter and asked Hipolyta, "Would you care for a glass of brandy as well?"

"Yes please, I will." She replied promptly. Too promptly to

Harold's taste, but at least Hipolyta's answer offered a clearer idea of what the fourth word of the proverb may be. The four simple words of her reply narrowed his mental list of possible choices. He delivered the glass to Hipolyta, and asked Chloe, "Darling, do you think you might could have a sip or two?"

"Sure, as long as it's not poison Hannah won't mind. But if I should clutch at my throat and die---one of these other ladies shall have to take over my feeding duties." She made the statement in full dramatic mode even to falling over onto Mandy's lap beside her when she 'died.' They all laughed, then correctly stifled their outburst.

He delivered the wee draught to his wife, and approached Mandy next, "Miss Hill, a finger or two of brandy?"

"At once? Yes please, thank you Mr. Bessamer," she answered haltingly, and her face was visibly flushed before she'd finished the short reply.

He digested her manner and this response, then continued thinking to himself he must surely be nearing the end of the exercise by now. "Mrs. Livingson, you *will* have a nip. Won't you?

"A nip, yes please," she replied.

Again a very brief reply; his mind raced. He glanced over to Tania and realized her glass was near emptied. "Well Titania, are you in need of a refill then?"

She glanced down at the snifter in her hand, "Ooh I *am* ready. I must have drank that last one with a straw it went so quickly." And then she added, "You may now stop serving... *and* asking questions!"

Harold poured a snifter for himself and went to sit beside his wife on the settee. He muttered; repeating the responses almost aloud while Harry watched the minute hand of his pocket watch.

"Two minutes yet," he said quietly.

Harold acknowledged the signal with a wave, then stood up suddenly, "I've got it! A Drowning Man Will Clutch At A Straw!" He looked around at the others, "That is the *only* one that fits."

Applause greeted his solution and he chose Mandy to succeed him since her response, he explained, was the most ill-formed. Mandy smiled sheepishly; she knew she had been caught off guard. While still replaying her chagrined performance in her thoughts, she rose to check on dessert as the others selected another proverb. A shorter one was decided upon---out of kindness to the novice player. A brief while later, Mandy peeked her head in at the doorway and was waved in with smiles.

She looked first to Harold, "Did you notice that the rain has stopped?" She hoped variations on yes or no questions would offer her the best advantage.

Harold turned to the window and peered out, "Yes, but I think there are still a few clouds drifting across the moon which may bring more showers." Mandy realized at once that her initial strategy might need refining.

She asked Chloe, "Did you have time for a bathe yourself when the rest of us did?"

"No dear; I was uncertain that if everyone used the tap for hot waters to fill the tubs, or have their showers, would there be enough. I know I've asked Harold often enough about that at home," she answered coyly.

Mandy added this bit to Harold's, and searched their wording against the few proverbs she knew. "And your shower Hippolyta? I know you were rushed a bit?" She knew that because it was herself who had knocked on the door often enough to have distracted anyone's ablutions.

"I just let the water run over me briefly to rinse away the train smells," she answered without pause.

'Well that was quick,' Mandy thought, and tried to rerun her answer to glean something from it. "How am I to select the key words from these normal sounding responses?" she asked aloud of no one in particular. The simple parlor game seemed to have taken its toll on her; when Kaitlyn attempted a rescue.

"Look *deep* in your heart and you will uncover the pearl hidden inside..." She intentionally made an inflection where an inflection was not required, "...you may cease all questions," she finished cleanly. Harry looked at his wife with unabashed pride in her and honor for her; she felt gooseflesh rise all over her skin when she looked up at him for his approbation of her response.

"Deep." Mandy repeated the emphasized word, and posed to herself a four word proverb ending with 'deep.' The others in the room smiled knowingly sure that she would have the solution in no time. Then one minute went by, and then another. As the second hand on Harry's watch neared the last tick of three minutes, Mandy exclaimed, "STILL WATERS RUN DEEP!" to the applause of the group now at the edge of their seats in anticipation.

Kaitlyn yawned after the ensuing chatting dwindled. Titania espied her from the corner of her eye, and announced she was ready to turn in. The others accepted that it was a fitting end to a long day which had begun at sea, and retiring a bit early was perhaps wise. Not a few glances to the newlyweds were covertly made as each in turn made some similar declaration. Harry made sure they all were aware that should they need something or other in the night they were on their own to secure for their needs. Those conditions were readily accepted. Only Kaitlyn and her husband remained in the room when the last guest retired.

They walked hand in hand up the grand staircase and into the master suite. "So you haven't yet had even a shower?!" Kaitlyn announced innocently as they closed the door behind them. Their wedding night was an adventure upon which neither had ever embarked. It is enough to say that human instinct and hormones will, when guided by an extraordinary discipline, provide more than mere satisfaction.

Jameson was first to the kitchen in the morning and figured out the proper function of the coffee press on his own. Fortunately for the other early risers there were three of them among the kitchen's inventory. He employed them all, then set up the kitchen to prepare for a 'Tahoe' breakfast. The large kitchen table had enough chairs for more than their company and before the first sausages were ready for serving nearly all the house was around it. No one had bothered with dressing for 'going out' so there they sat: robed or casually attired for a day indoors away from public scrutiny. Kaitlyn and Harry made their appearance at last to the sounds of flatware on dishes as their company cleaned their plates of the first round of the meal.

"How did you sleep?" Kaitlyn asked of her friends and family as she and Harry entered. Harold and Chloe looked at each other and Chloe winked, "We at least slept..."

That sparked a bout of giggles, chuckles, and considerate laughter from the rest. Mr. and Mrs. Livingson did blush, and proudly. They sat down for their meal and Kaitlyn mentioned her desire to see some of Harry's projects for the Waterhouse firm. Harold and Chloe wished to see the newly opened Manchester Museum which got votes from the others as a pleasing destination for the afternoon. Harry said that a visit to the museum would be very worthwhile, and that Kaitlyn would actually have more time than the others to spend viewing his other architectural endeavors whenever she wished. She acquiesced willingly to the consensus. This came quickly on the heels of Harry's confession that he had been involved in the museum's design and construction as well, so it was like getting two birds with one stone.

The weather was brightened from the day before, and it was decided they would walk in the morning, rather than wait for later. Should they tire; they could ride taxis home. "As long as we are about it, we could stroll over to Mosley Street and see the Art Museum and other galleries as well," proposed Harold to nods of agreement.

It was a very lovely day for a walk. The rains of the day before had freshened the city to some degree, and the late spring temperatures allowed for a brisk pace without becoming over-warmed. After the Natural History Museum, and Harry's thorough tour and explanations of its various architectural interests, they found a nice pub for lunch. Just as they entered an unexpected call rang out.

"Hello, Harry!" came a voice only Harry recognized.

"Aaron! what a pleasant surprise. What brings you out on a beautiful day like this? Shouldn't you be in a stuffy library or reading room?"

"I am punishing myself for just the day, and I've promised to cloister myself most thoroughly as a reward for today's suffering," answered his friend candidly. Mandy wasn't sure if she should take him at his word or not.

"Kaitlyn dearest, this is my friend Aaron Backhouse." Harry introduced her with a smile of great pride and satisfaction. "Aaron, this is my beautiful bride, Kaitlyn Livingson, newly arrived from our hometown in Tahoe."

Kaitlyn, also smiling broadly, extended her hand and Aaron held it with an expression of awe upon his face. "Madam, you must be a most extraordinary woman indeed to have captured the exclusive affections and respect of Mr. Henry Livingson. It is a great honor to meet you."

Harry continued, "These are the rest of my family save our parents who are running things in our absence. This is Miss Mandy Hill, famed restauranteur and noted entrepreneur." She nodded and smiled. "These are Mr. and Mrs Harold Bessamer, of San Francisco lately of Redditch and their daughter Hannah." They inclined their heads; any friend of Harry's was someone to properly greet. "This is my longtime friend and near brother: Jameson Connor, and these two elegant and charming ladies are my own twin sisters: Hipolyta and Titania Livingson." Each of them bowed, or curtsied, or shook hands with Harry's friend.

"Twins?" Aaron responded, "I see the family resemblance surely, but twins? Miss Hipolyta is clearly quite distinct from her equally charming sister Titania. I am a twin myself although thankfully no one has yet confused me with my sister. By the same token I can't see how anyone could confuse these two ladies."

Jameson seconded Aaron's sincere observations, "Right?! That's what I've been saying for years. Titania is just so different from Hipolyta. You can see it in her walk, or merest movements." Then he had to admit, "Of course back in Tahoe there isn't a person in the village who is able to consistently distinguish one from the other--- outside our family that is."

"Just so, just so. Do come and sit with me we can most certainly make room here," offered Aaron. Kaitlyn accepted promptly and led the group over to his table. Jameson and Harry pulled up a couple more tables and chairs around as they settled down for a rest.

Aaron interviewed each of them in turn always returning to Harry as the center of his conversations. He was a brilliant conversationalist, and Hipolyta, who was seated closest to him, enjoyed his muttered comments as well. They were generally self-deprecating, sometimes insightful, but always humorous. "I can recommend Greengate personally Mrs. Livingson," he began as they turned to talking of the neighborhoods of Manchester.

"Please Aaron, call me Kaitlyn," she insisted.

"I'm sorry; it's more for my own benefit really. I am trying to fix it in my head that Harry is married. Anyway, I can recommend Greengate as Harry has offered me safe haven there often enough over the last month. It's a quaint and quiet community."

"Aaron you must continue to call and stay at Greengate as is your wont. I wouldn't dream of putting anyone off who has gained Harry's friendship," she persisted with Harry's approval already evident.

"Mr. Backhouse what is your profession? If that is an appropriate question over here?" Mandy queried.

"Oh it's quite appropriate, but I'm afraid it's not so glamorous as say: *architect*." He glanced at Harry and rolled his eyes. "I am an Associate Professor of Histories and Cultures in the Humanities

College over at Victoria University, or rather shall be at the beginning of the Summer Term," replied Aaron proudly at last.

"But that's wonderful Aaron! When did you receive word of your confirmation?" Harry asked excitedly. Aaron had applied to several regional Colleges over the last six months to no avail; so this was great news indeed. "Just yesterday as a matter of fact. Did anything of note happen to *you* yesterday?" he asked with his eyebrows raised.

"Yes. Kaitlyn arrived a single woman to the Liverpool docks and by the time she made it to the streets of that fair city she was a married woman!" answered Harry.

To which Kaitlyn added, "A very fortunately married woman."

Harry related the entire experience omitting nothing. The rest of them listened with relived excitement to the recollection of Harry and Kaitlyn's welcome embrace, but none of them were aware of the interruption---they had missed the Stanley intrusion entirely. Kaitlyn reached into her little purse and set the derringer on the table in front of them.

"It was only a moment's diversion really," she finished. Harry opened it, removed the cartridges, and asked his wife to return it to her purse. Mandy's and Aaron's eyes were wide with intrigue at the disclosure, and at the souvenir as the proof of the encounter.

Recovering himself, and not wishing to appear overly impressed, as the other Livingsons certainly seemed only delighted at the story, Aaron commented, "I *thought* the rain was auspicious and couldn't be for my achievement alone."

Mandy was not so eager to dismiss the tale, "Harry, Kaitlyn... but you could have been killed!"

Kaitlyn replied a little abashed, "No, there was never really any danger. For one thing: Harry was *right there*," as if that fact alone should allay any distresses. "And secondly: there are very few males who are not at least momentarily diverted at the sight of a swooning female. That's all the time I needed."

Their food arrived and they commenced to enjoy the meal. "Mr. Backhouse," Hipolyta began, "Are there any reputable Colleges that admit women over here?"

"Miss Hipolyta, my own university is chartered for conferring degrees upon the fairer sex," Aaron began, "It's just that there is such a small enrollment of women, that most students are unaware of their presence---let alone that Victoria University has admitted women since its charter eight years ago."

"That's fascinating, and are there any women in the Humanities College at present?" she followed.

"Three I believe in a population of three hundred and sixty some odd students," said Aaron with a sigh at the disparity in numbers. "Are you entertaining thoughts of acquiring a British University degree as your brother has, Miss Hipolyta?"

She merely replied, "Perhaps," as if she were choosing between desserts.

The others listened to their banter and looked at each other with raised eyebrows as that last 'perhaps' was admitted. Mandy spoke up, "Hipolyta dear, I'm sure your brother and sister-in-law would enjoy your staying with them during a career at University." To which Harry and Kaitlyn nodded encouragingly. Unfortunately Hipolyta wasn't sure if they were serious or merely taunting her for monopolizing Aaron's attentions.

Before they rose to go and after consulting with Kaitlyn Harry asked Aaron, "We are going to the Art Museum. If you are unattached for the afternoon, please join us and perhaps if possible come along to Greengate. Jameson is occupying your favorite room overlooking the rear garden, but there are two beds there..."

"As it happens I am wholly unattached until the start of Summer Term in early June. Mother and Father haven't exactly given me the boot, but would be pleased if I wasn't underfoot, so to speak. Thank you very much for the invitation Mrs. Livingson." He knew precisely to whom his gratitude should be provided for this generous offer.

"You should be forewarned Professor Backhouse," Harold cautioned, "Even the air of the house has no doubt changed considerably since your last sojourn. So much *amour* about the place..." Chloe groaned at her husband's wit.

"I'll chance it," replied Aaron smiling, with a glance toward Hipolyta.

Aaron Backhouse had Greengate to himself for the next long weekend while the companions visited Clive House Saturday through Tuesday. Harry had to return to Manchester for business reasons and Kaitlyn naturally returned with him. Not to be absented from their brother, Titania and Jameson with Hipolyta returned as well. The Bessamers and Miss Hill remained a few more days at Clive House enjoying the great hospitality of Olivia Allcock. It was during their last evening with the Allcocks that a scheme for a grand tour began to be pieced together. At first they were merely to travel to Bath upon Olivia's recommendation. Next Chloe mentioned a desire to return to Paris, and Harold said he'd always wanted to tour Bavaria. By the time every one was reassembled at Greengate: Florence, Venice, Lucerne, and Vienna had been added to the list. Harold had begun examining train schedules on the continent, and the ladies were assembling books and Baedeckers covering all their desired destinations.

Kaitlyn and Harry had to have a long talk about his responsibilities attendant to Waterhouse contracts. "I suppose I should first apprise them of my new marital status and go from there. Perhaps they have an instituted 'Honeymoon' policy of which I am unaware."

Kaitlyn had been wanting to see where he worked and so she accompanied him to the Waterhouse offices that next day. That turned out to be a stroke of great good fortune. Not only did she singularly charm Mr. Strenhowell, but the other Directors with whom Harry routinely associated as well.

"Mr. Waterhouse will be most disappointed when he returns to find he missed your first visit to our humble offices. " Mr. Strenhowell was saying, "but you *will* return again and grace us with your company in the near future. Well not the too near future, but certainly after your return from Honeymoon at least."

Harry had been skeptical of mentioning all the destinations his family was planning, but Kaitlyn hadn't any compunction about disclosing their itinerary. After Mr. Strenhowell heard her list, he added, "You really should consider a tour of the Rhine Valley from Basal to Amsterdam; it is a *most* picturesque journey Mrs. Strenhowell and myself enjoyed that tour on our own honeymoon, aah a long time ago. We still return every few years or so. I recommend the Köln-Düsseldorfer Steamer Company---highly reputable, been making the passage for ages." As he walked them to the front doors of the offices, his parting words to Harry were, "Many blessings upon your union, Mr. Livingson. We shall manage until your return---say by early June? It was a great pleasure to make your acquaintance Mrs. Livingson. Don't forget: tour the Rhine."

With that impediment out of the way they became as immersed in the tour planning as the others, and they added the Rhine valley. Whether it was the result of coaxing, or just being caught up in the general fervor of the tour, Aaron Backhouse asked if there might be space for him on the journey. To which the ladies assured him most heartily that they wouldn't have considered his *not* accompanying them.

He rejoined, "I am at the present time quite penniless I'm afraid. Of course there is my inheritance into which I am to come on my birthday this very month... when we are to be in... St. Malo is it by then?"

"Your birthday is this month? So is Harry's!" Hipolyta exclaimed, "What day?"

"The twenty-second. Rebecca and I shall be eighteen and awarded the initiation of our quarterly allowance from the Backhouse Trust Funds," replied Aaron.

Harry looked at him curiously, "I would have thought since your father is a partner of Brown and Backhouse that a Trust Fund would not have been necessary."

"But father isn't THE Backhouse of that firm---that's Uncle Silas, and coincidentally that's not the origin of the Fund in any case. It seems there was an advantageous marriage many years ago which both restored the family and resulted in an extraordinarily generous allowance for each of the Backhouse children. Of those children, sadly my sister and I are the last. What was once a one time bestowment, when there were lots of little Backhouses running about, has become a semi-annual allowance over a lifetime. Remarkable really."

Harry listened; fascinated by the brief family accounting, and asked in a whisper, simply, "How much per quarter?" In answer Aaron put his hand beside his mouth up to Harry's ear and whispered the amount to him. Genuinely struck by the impressive sum, Harry nodded as he resumed his previous posture. His expression of incredulity was only matched by his admiration of his friend, "And you have taken up an Associate Professorship? Now *that's* a step toward what I consider: Giving back to the community."

"Thank you Harry. I appreciate that very much coming from you," answered Aaron.

Aaron could afford his own part in the adventure.

A letter and a guest arrived at Greengate just the morning before they'd planned for their departure. The letter was addressed to Mrs. Kaitlyn Spelman Livingson, and was in an official envelope of the White Star Lines---embossed and addressed by hand. She opened it after Harry joined her in the drawing room. "Oh look Harry. Captain Perry has sent us our certificate of marriage: the authorized White Star Lines announcement of his prerogative as Captain having been exercised." Attendant to that the good captain enclosed a note which indicated that he'd forwarded a copy of the same form to the registration agent in Liverpool as his duties required, and they could refer all proper inquiries to that department. In short: they were certifiably wed. "Let's frame this. I would like to put it over the mantle just like MamaBelle does with all her important memories." Harry smiled at the reference. "And that reminds me Harry; we have a good number of niches to fill in honor of those who have made our lives possible." She began to inventory her options for placements when there was a knock at the door.

Harry went to answer, and was shortly ushering Rebecca Backhouse into the Drawing Room. He made introductions. "Please call me Becky, Mrs. Livingson." she requested.

"And I am Kaitlyn. Harry has told me so much about you... at least in his last letter. Thank you so much for your companionship and guidance."

Becky was positive she liked this woman very much indeed. "No, no, it's Harry who has been the truly helpful one here. He single-handedly transformed the Waterhouse attitude toward Construction planning, and it has been himself who offered so many truly key insights into process and staging. So let's agree to have no more said about *guidance*."

"As you wish Becky." Kaitlyn accepted. "We have entertained your brother recently, and he has accepted our invitation to tour with our party. I don't suppose we could coax you as well? You could take as much or as little time away from the office as you see fit; your company will be *greatly* appreciated," proposed Kaitlyn knowing Harry would likely enjoy having a fellow builder with whom to to converse on the journey. "We were made to understand that finances could not inhibit your decision, and even if that were the case, you should understand we would be pleased to have you as our own guest. Please consider it."

Becky looked at her for a moment with an odd expression of: temptation over the offer and confusion at the mention of financial facility. "What has Aaron told you of our finances?"

Harry related the conversation he'd had with her brother just recently. "I hope we haven't been inappropriate in broaching the topic with you?"

Becky reassured them that it was of no consequence at all to speak of money, "Honestly, it seems such an act of hypocrisy for gentlemen to strive so desperately for money and at the same time keep so tight-lipped over the subject. Anyway it wasn't the subject which caught my attention, and you are quite correct---I *can* financially afford the tour that I have so very much looked forward to for so long as Harry knows well. It's the time away from the job; I am in constant fear that any prolonged absence on my part might spell the end of the inroads I've made into this 'men's domain.' As for Aaron, he is not bridled by those limitations. However it is curious to me that he mentioned *only* the *short term* situation of the Trust with regard to *his own* status in it."

"How do you mean?" Kaitlyn was now alert.

Becky paused and pursed her lips unsure of whether it was prudent to disclose the long term arrangements of their family's endowment. "Well for myself it is as Aaron described. On the twenty-second, in just a few days really, I shall begin receiving semi-annual very generous installments from the Trust and they shall continue for *me* into perpetuity. Aaron however has only until our twenty-first birthday. At which time, if he is still unmarried, those installments shall cease absolutely. Totally unfair. More hypocrisy it seems to me. It was a dowager aunt, a female, who established the Trust. Why it should be that *the male* should be so singled out for perpetuating the family line or endure financial punishment I can not fathom. What's in a name after all?"

The three of them sat silent in their own thoughts at this news. "I wonder why he didn't mention that proviso when he so readily announced the boon of the upcoming bestowments," pondered Kaitlyn aloud. Harry remained quiet all through the breaking of the news and to the musings of his wife.

"Silly male pride no doubt." Becky said of her brother, "He has a streak of self-regard which I quite understand. It's that very trait I suppose which gives me the confidence to do what I do." She fell silent again, but this time her brows were knitted in the throes of a decision. Miss Backhouse was quite habituated to making big decisions at a moment's notice---decisions which affected whole projects and the lives of the workmen involved. As she weighed her own great desire to see the places she'd always dreamed of seeing versus the projects currently on the ground and those pending... She began, "If you truly wish my company upon this tour," she took a deep breath, "I shall make all the necessary arrangements to join you. In fact I am now determined to do so. At once!" Harry and Kaitlyn were instantly over-joyed at her declaration. "When were you estimating for your departure?"

Harry went to fetch coffee and cake while Kaitlyn and Becky talked over the grand scheme of the journey. When he returned laden with the tray of refreshments, Becky momentarily grinned in memory of their first encounter. Kaitlyn laughed when she realized the re-enactment that was being played out before her. Becky spoke up, "Of course, it is *your place* to send your husband upon what ever errand you please. I was however mortified at discovering I had sent the *Waterhouse lead architect* off for pastries! Which nobody even ate as it happens..." The humor surrounding that first meeting set the tone of the ladies' planning session which took up a good bit of the morning. When she did rise to leave and make her own necessary preparations, they parted as the close friends they fully intended to become.

Harold had business to attend to in Stratford and London so the Bessamers were taking a separate route to arrive in Bath. The companions took up rooms in Norton Saint Philip at the Plaine House just a short carriage ride into Bath proper. They were to be in the area for four days when the Bessamers would join them, then they would proceed to Weymouth and on a steamship to St. Malo. Meanwhile they enjoyed the Roman Baths and most enjoyable walks in the countryside. While Mandy and Becky were making a return trip to the baths, Harry and Kaitlyn happened upon the canal towpath that meandered through the surrounding bucolic paradise for several miles west of Bath. With Aaron and Hipolyta, Jameson and Titania they strolled the easy path through the pleasant spring morning, and ate a most hearty luncheon at a little village Inn--- strategically situated near where the canal met the river. The return journey was nearly as pleasant although they were very full and walked a bit slower. By the time they reached the Crescent, Mandy and Becky in the company of the Bessamers were just making their own way to the town center. They had enjoyed a brief guided tour of the historical sights with Becky's provocative insights into the structures and layout of the city as constructed by the Woods family. She had also intimated the arcane suspicions of the Woods' ties to secret societies and other such intrigue. It was a very interesting and enjoyable walking tour.

"Well met. How was your stroll?" asked Mandy when they came together.

Harry described the towpath and the charming little Inn, the villages, and flowers they saw along the way. "And your bathe and tour?" he asked in kind.

"I think I could spend a lot of time in those waters; rejuvenating, very rejuvenating," replied Becky in a very relaxed voice.

Mandy and Chloe added how wonderful it was to have a professional builder as a guide for their tour of the white stone city. "Did you know that the angels on the ladders of the cathedral facade came to the bishop in a dream? It was a fascinating tour---just wonderful," they agreed on that point completely.

Becky was only a little embarrassed at the praise, "I thought I was probably boring you silly. I just love buildings..." she admitted innocently.

They rode carriages back to Plaine House and made ready their luggage for the train to the coast. The gentlemen of the party assembled downstairs in the tavern of the Inn for a drink and a huddle over the plans for their travel during the next several days. "The crossing to St. Malo should be uneventful...I hope," Harold was saying, "The issue which keeps dogging me is the arrangement of carriages for our various excursions. We are ten plus little Hannah makes eleven. Two coaches at a time are barely sufficient for any trip longer than several miles, and that is *without* our luggage."

Harry spoke up at that, "We are, as gentlemen, in the minority on that score. But it was personally satisfying to me that each lady has sufficed with merely *one* trunk," he grinned, "It could have been so much more of a logistical nightmare had they not been so considerate."

"Just so, just so," agreed Harold to the nods of relief from the other two. "Yet we are ten with ten trunks. I was most gratified that Hannah's things were so acceptably dispersed through Chloe, Kaitlyn, Titania and Hipolyta's baggage. That was a blessing to be sure."

Jameson and Aaron each spoke up in turn with ideas. "If we set up bases of operations, so to speak, at each of our predominant destinations at least we won't be hampered at every turn in our daily jaunts," offered Jameson.

Aaron agreed and added, "What's the matter with preparing ourselves for a great deal of walking? The stroll along the towpath from Bath and back was certainly pleasant enough."

Harold and Harry both nodded at that, but Harold inserted a caveat, "Hannah *must* begin walking upon her *own two feet* soon, or I shall have to deposit her in the nearest orphanage!" Laughter and another round was forthcoming at that rejoinder.

"The little idler!" Harry chimed in as acknowledgment of their most obvious 'burden.' "I would appeal to your and Chloe's good sense to allow me the privilege of being my niece's personal donkey for the duration of this tour."

"Harry, that is a most gracious offer. She will no doubt be the safest child in all of Christendom should Chloe consent. I shall make known your wishes to her at my earliest opportunity." He stood as he said so, and bowed in genuine and humble acceptance---for himself at least.

"So," began Jameson, "Mont Saint-Michel, a train to Paris and the kitchens of that fair city," he added, "then on the Express d'Orient as far as Vienna. A second train south to Florence, and a northern return through Venice, then on to Basel, Switzerland where we may be parting our company?"

The question was legitimate both for their logistical planning and for the real concerns of insuring some one of them at least with sufficient travel experience to be with each group should there be a parting of ways. Aaron expressed his own inclination to remain with the Livingson family as long as practicable. Even if it meant, "getting cooped up on shipboard for a week or so..."

Harry answered to the concern by saying, "It may be a moot consideration by the time we arrive in the Alps. Kaitlyn and I are only just *considering* the river passage. There might not be any desire to embark upon it once we are actually at that juncture."

"Or," Harold joined in, "We may be able to see the Bavarian country side quite well during sides trips which must surely be offered by the K-D Steamer Company."

"True." They all nodded.

The ladies meanwhile had been occupied with quite different matters. Chloe was in Kaitlyn and Harry's room with the twins, while Becky and Mandy became more acquainted in their own room. Chloe was feeding Hannah as Kaitlyn looked on and attempted to disguise a disconcerting sensation arising within her. When Hipolyta couldn't help but notice her odd expressions she inquired as to whether she was quite alright.

"Oh, I... I hadn't thought it would really come to this... I mean it was only meant as a precaution really..." Kaitlyn deflected, poorly.

Chloe was intrigued, "What are you trying to say dear? Our curiosity is piqued." Kaitlyn blushed and explained how: before they left Tahoe she had asked MamaBelle about any precautions she might offer by way of advice before she would be without her assistance and succor for the indefinite future.

"We got around to her telling me about certain preparations which I could make against any foreseeable difficulties Chloe might have with Hannah..." Who at the mention of her name stopped suckling and blinked at the other ladies. That solicited smiles and giggles from them. "To make a longish story shorter, one of the herbal medicines with which she supplied me is called Hu Lu Ba in Chinese according to George, or fenugreek in English."

Chloe was sincerely touched that her dear friend had made such thorough preparations on her own and her daughter's behalf. "*And...*" she encouraged.

"And it's for increasing milk should distress or other bodily concern curtail a mother's lactation," she explained then halted again.

"That's *very* considerate and far-sighted of Belle..." Chloe agreed, quite pleased indeed. "I assure you that so far at least I have been able to keep up with her demands. Although I admit it is a little inconvenient to stop whatever I am doing every several hours and become a cow." They all smiled or giggled at that. All except Kaitlyn who, though smiling weakly, was determined to finish her response.

"MamaBelle said as much for herself. But even *she* required the help when Titania and Hipolyta came along. Well... after Harry's and my wedding night and during the next few days I began to wonder about 'how did you feel about that very thing.' Since I was suddenly a wife with the possibility of motherhood before me it pressed on my thoughts more and more," confessed Kaitlyn slowly. "Over the last few days, I have been taking a pinch of the herb, and... since I'm just as endowed as yourself... well..." She opened her blouse to expose wet spots on her camisole.

"Oh my goodness!" Chloe gasped. "Oh Kaitlyn! Oh my sweetest friend and sister!" Titania and Hipolyta were equally agape. Chloe passed Hannah to Kaitlyn, and settled her in Kaitlyn's arms. She arranged her little angel just so, and Hannah began to nurse at Kaitlyn's breast. The bride's expression said everything.

Chloe answered the unspoken communication, "Yes it is... uh, quite... well... you see. It's one of the few perquisites, but the novelty does wear off; I assure you."

Hipolyta spoke up before Titania. "Kaitlyn where are you keeping this wonder herb?"

Chloe put her foot down at that course of thought emerging in the twins simultaneously. "Kaitlyn is a married woman and will no doubt have this little chore ahead of her before long on her own account. You two however have neither the immediate excuse, nor... if you don't resent my saying it, the overly generous build for such spontaneous production. Of course when the time comes your bodies will naturally rise to the occasion. I only wish I were fashioned as you each are---so ideal in proportions."

Titania answered that she was correct in her assessment, but they were justly envious of both women---their close friends and sisters. There was a knock at the door and Harold's voice called gently asking if it were alright to enter. "A moment please dearest," Chloe called back and went to the door. She opened it only far enough to squeeze into the hallway with her husband. He related to her Harry's most acceptable offer of becoming Hannah's personal donkey, and Chloe grinned for reasons other than her acceptance of the offer. She gladly authorized her husband to convey her delight, and she went back inside with her sisters.

"I don't know if Harry *knew* about your clandestine supplements, but it appears Harold and I may be able to at last have more than four hours at a time uninterrupted during the course of our tour," she announced with great pleasure and anticipation. "I think that if we apply ourselves to some modest wardrobe alterations no one need know of your and Harry's status as surrogate parents." And the four sisters turned their considerable skills and attention to the task at once.

The crossing to St. Malo was smooth and without incident. So was the transport to Mont Saint-Michel where each of the company was as enchanted upon their approach as were Chloe, Kaitlyn and Harry were on their first encounter with that timeless island enclave.

Their rooms in the hotel were most comfortable, and they gathered for dinner at the same restaurant used so many years before by the early travelers.

"A toast to our enterprise," Aaron raised his glass, "to Harry and Kaitlyn for allowing such a grand entourage to accompany them on their Honeymoon, and to the adventures awaiting us all." They all drank to that.

Mandy and Becky were so rapt with the medieval island already that they were quiet as church mice during the meal. Hipolyta, Titania and Jameson shared the ladies obvious rapture, but were a bit more vocal in their joy. Chloe and Harold were secretly looking forward to their first private night alone without their darling Hannah for the last many months, and so simply maintained expressions of smiling anticipation. Harry asked if anyone *hadn't* researched the island for their personal tours tomorrow. "If not, there are worthwhile tours led by the locals," and their dinners arrived.

When they returned to their room, with Harry still carrying Hannah, he said, "Just let me take Hannah to Chloe, and I'll be back straight away."

Kaitlyn blocked his exit. "My lord I have something to tell you..." By morning, Harry was certain there was nothing so inspiring as the efforts of enlightened women toward improving the commonwealth of humanity.

A person might travel to that little island fortress-village-cathedral every other year and still find themselves transported by its power over their imagination. The company wandered up and down the steep lanes and steps of the monument for two days, and were still planning another foray for the next. Just sitting in the heights of its walls and towers looking out at the world beyond and below inspired their spirits and nourished their wanderlust. At some point each of them made the short trip by boat to Tomberlaine and back. Each had made the full circuit of the island, and plumbed the depths of the edifices painstakingly constructed from the native rock of the island. At last on the fourth morning they readied to say their farewells to the silent stones and buildings which had spoken so poignantly to their hearts.

With Hannah in his arms Harry supervised the porters as they loaded their trunks onto the train for Gare Montparnasse in Paris, and then he settled into a seat next to Kaitlyn. The women had decided that when they were with the company assembled, Chloe would take Hannah for her usual feeding times. The other ladies rotated in tending to her nappies and burping and such. It was when they were re-formed into their separate exploration groups, that Kaitlyn was again able to resume her assistance unnoticed. Paris rose from the fields and vineyards before the on-rushing train as a thriving city of exuberance and energy.

They had already arranged rooms at the Splendid Etoile Hotel. Jameson and Mandy headed straight for the hotel's restaurant to introduce themselves to the staff and management. Without much arm-twisting Jameson was given the rare pleasure of observing the function of a well-run French kitchen. He had to promise not to take notes on the recipes he witnessed in preparation, but beyond that he was generally regarded with acceptance by his counterparts. He even got to assist in minor capacities much to his delight.

It was the current construction of the Eiffel Tower for the upcoming World Exposition which dominated the visit for Harry and Becky. Harry spent hours in discussion with Becky sitting in a cafe across the Seine from the rising tower. They marveled at the vision, the boldness of design, the innovation of the material production and construction. All of which was very interesting for the *first* couple of hours to Kaitlyn. She then focused most of her attentions on Hannah.

As they walked along the Seine returning to the hotel, Becky began to ask Kaitlyn of her and Harry's meeting and courtship. Kaitlyn hadn't needed to formulate that tale until this occasion. She organized her thoughts and experiences and conveyed the most remarkable tale of their association. She tried her best to do the story justice without revealing the 'too much' which would invite some obvious and difficult to answer inquiries regarding her own journey. Becky listened closely while the neighborhoods of Paris melted into the background of the story. "That is a most remarkable courtship," Becky responded when the story was done and they neared the avenue to the hotel.

"You mentioned a 'longing to be more than you'd hoped to be' which you said you worked through during your time in Stratford. How did you go about it?" She paused, "You see I have the self-same personal complaint," and then she said no more for a while.

Kaitlyn looked to Harry whose expression was compassion and confidence personified; she answered meekly, "In what way: the same personal complaint?'"

Becky hesitated to respond at once. Kaitlyn's story had awakened her most feared demons. She gathered her courage and at last began, "I am a successful woman in a field dominated by men. I must wear the mask of a sea captain, the persona of absolute confidence, just to be taken seriously in my daily activities and intercourse with my peers and workmen." She had to gather her strength to confess the next revelation. "I am good at what I do, but sporting this constant mask of conviction has opened my eyes to the realization that I am struggling at every moment to keep up the image I intend. And I am afraid of losing that struggle. I am beginning to have the distinct impression that the mask is wearing me, and it terrifies me..." she began to choke on the emotion welling up at the words, "...that I shall lose the possibility of ever being anything more." She was positively unable to take another step and continue. They sat on a bench looking over the river. "I can't keep this up. I can not abide never being anything more than a mask!" Kaitlyn put her arm around her shoulders in support. Harry paced around the bench with Hannah, rocking and cooing in her ear to calm her.

Becky made a desperate play for hope. "What *exactly* did you do to get you over your own despair and longing? I am desperately in need... will you help me?"

"What do you have in mind?" asked Kaitlyn in an echo of an answer she so long ago received in response to her own despair.

"Teach me. I'll do anything you say. But I can not go on like this. In truth, I came on this tour to distance myself from that mask, but it still hangs upon me like an albatross round my neck," moaned Becky between sobs.

"I can show you the path, but it is you who must make the journey," replied Kaitlyn with absolute calm. She took the handkerchief Harry offered and dabbed at her friend's cheeks. They made the rest of the walk back to the hotel and each returned to their rooms in preparation for dinner.

"Well! You weren't a lot of help back there!" retorted Kaitlyn sharply to Harry's innocent question about a bath and dressing for dinner.

Harry knew he shouldn't laugh just then, but even his own prodigious self discipline was faltering before that urge. "My love," he attempted, "I have watched many times as the most amiable of sweet-natured women---when subjected to their body's transformation into imminent motherhood---become the most quick-tempered and shrewish of she-beasts before the very eyes and ears of their most trusted and faithful family and friends," he said as if offering evidence in court. He added with a shrug, "I suppose what White Feathers told me is true: 'No good deed goes unpunished'."

They still stood in the same postures and attitude they had at Kaitlyn's initial outburst, and Harry made every effort to remain so. After a pregnant pause, Kaitlyn's face allowed a smile, then soon a chuckle erupted until she was nearly beside herself in laughter. She had to gasp for breath before long... Harry relaxed and decided his best course of action was to hug his wife---*now*!

Still gasping, but gaining some modicum of control over herself, she managed, "White Feathers is always right I suspect. You are his star pupil Harry; a most immaculate observer of human nature." She composed herself at last, put her hands upon her hips, and mocking herself in exaggerated tones, said, "*Well! You* weren't a lot of *help* back there!" She laughed again, but then more seriously said, "Harry how will you deal with me when I actually *am* with child? I'll probably tear your heart out everyday and eat it, like that Prometheus character."

"My love, one of the efforts of Conscience is to discern the person from their state. I know you. I know your love for me. That you should slip into a particular 'state' from whatever cause---be it physical, emotional, mental or spiritual---I shall endure it," he said without pause, "I could as easily cut off my own head as abandon you to the whirlwind of a woman's caprice when in the throes of child-bearing."

With tears now replacing laughter, Kaitlyn threw her arms around his neck and whispered, "I am the luckiest woman in the world, and don't you forget it!" She smiled feebly, "I hope I don't do serious harm to poor Becky when she begins her training."

"I'll protect Hannah. Becky can probably protect herself. Yet you introduce a novel point: How shall you effect her training while we are touring?" mused Harry. "This should be interesting to watch!"

"You shall direct me George Henry Livingson. That is how," and she was through with any considerations regarding the notion.

Jameson was learning French---at least enough to tell a pot from a pan, a ladle from a spoon. He helped the company order their meals and offered suggestions for wine selections. Mancy was pleased and most delighted at his facility in so quickly adapting to the new language and styles of cooking. His successes weren't lost on any of the party. Aaron in particular was quite vocal in his astonishment at Jameson's rapid reorientation and adaptation, including the new language. "Mr. Connor are you quite sure you haven't been studying a text or something in preparation for this encounter?"

"Honestly Aaron it's likely just the environment: a kitchen is a kitchen after all. That we use different terms for the same things and actions is just relabeling, not a miracle," replied Jameson innocently. Titania looked to Harry and Kaitlyn with an unabashed smile of pride in her Jameson.

"If you maintain that is all it is, I am satisfied. However it does truly suggest that there is more to our Mr. Connor than meets the eye." Aaron got nods of agreement from his sister and Mandy at that pronouncement.

Jameson's selections and guidance provided for one of the best meals they had eaten on their journey thus far. When the bill was settled, the gentlemen retired to the billiards room of the hotel. The ladies retired to one of the comfortable sitting rooms where they were relatively secluded from the traffic of the hotel's other guests. Mandy remarked to Chloe that she had not, as had been promised back at the Chelsea House, been introduced to any education under Harry's direction since their arrival in Europe.

Chloe looked at her new friend with a look of surprise, "Have you asked?" Mandy balked as an attendant approached; Kaitlyn requested tea and cake for their party. After he left, Mandy resumed.

"Well no; I have not asked. I was under the distinct impression that you all were to arrange the circumstances for me," answered Mandy a little shaken at the notion of her approaching Harry on her own. She had after all nearly watched him grow up before her own eyes, and it was disquieting to think that the same boy she had once---in her mind---'defended from bullies' was to be her teacher. Kaitlyn, Titania and Hipolyta simply looked back at her with the same look of surprise which Chloe had just evinced. "Why are you looking at me like that?" Mandy had to ask. The tea service and cake arrived; they were left alone once more.

Hipolyta was the one to speak, "Mandy, may I pour some tea for you?" Mandy nodded absently, and watched Hipolyta's careful movements. She set a cup and saucer in front of Mandy and proceeded to pour, and pour, and pour. The cup was well filled and over-flowing.

Mandy flinched and said, "Stop Hipolyta the cup is already full."

Hipolyta looked up to her friend and said simply, "I suppose that is why you have not pursued any further your desires proclaimed at Chelsea House. One can not pour tea into a cup that is already full. A person only comes to learn anything, who is already empty and knows it."

Becky watched and listened to Hipolyta's little demonstration, then she looked to Kaitlyn who returned her gaze and nodded imperceptibly. Mandy looked into Hipolyta's eyes to ascertain whether she had heard and understood what the young woman intended. Hipolyta continued, "What you said you desired can not be merely tacked on to your knowledge of things as one would add a new language, or simply learn a new skill. Although it is both those things. The understanding which allows for the renovation of a person's heart and mind must be built upon a new foundation, not pieced together upon the half truths and fanciful notions of an incomplete and dysfunctional personality," she paused, still smiling gently and reassuringly, "Does that make sense to you?"

It made perfect sense to Becky, who kept her eyes on Kaitlyn to watch her responses to Hipolyta's concise explanation. Kaitlyn remained impassive, but for the smile playing at the corners of her eyes as always. In fact as Becky looked from one woman to next, each of them maintained that very same expression.

She had to ask, "I realize I am new to your company, and am not fully acquainted with each of you as I should wish, but how is it that I should find myself in the midst of such a remarkable group of women."

Titania answered easily, "Becky we're not just remarkable women, and thank you for saying so; we are sisters and know each other quite as well as we know ourselves. It's no more mysterious than that." Becky looked from one to the next of the four women, each with that pleasant expression, each seemingly so able to respond to the thorniest of questions. And all with a direct connection to Harry Livingson.

Mandy was still sorting out for herself if she were as full of herself, so to speak, as Hipolyta suggested. Her thoughts ranged, and she could not easily focus them. If she were confronted with a more familiar task, her formidable organizational skills would naturally take up the challenge immediately. But this was a challenge of a nature with which she was quite unfamiliar. This was a question of the workings of her own mind and heart---an inner analysis, an inner contemplation. If there was one thing she did know how to do, it was to recognize when she was the right person for the job or not--- But *this* was a job *only she* could do. No one else could rearrange the habits of her own nature built over years, no one but her alone. In a flash of realization she suddenly made the connection to what Hipolyta had demonstrated. "I am full to the brimming with myself; I can't even conceive of how to approach this. But it seems no one else can reach inside me and do it for me," she blurted, "I need guidance. I can not help myself out of this quagmire alone."

Those four ladies for the benefit of their two dear friends now began to discuss in practicable terms the conditions and circumstances of the general psyche of man, or woman in this case. After a lengthy dialog in which both Becky and Mandy sincerely acknowledged that their own hearts and minds were embarrassingly revealed in the descriptions, Kaitlyn began and each of the Livingson women took up a part of the story in an unbroken presentation:

"There once was no donkey in the Guang, so someone from the Heavenly Court sent one there..."

They continued through to the final invocation, "...in order to be able to unite the machine of man, all his lower centers must be active, strong and willing to surrender to the higher center's will. This must be trained in a man, it can not be left to chance. Otherwise he will be like the discarded Guang donkey, helpless before the forces of nature, and never recognized as the helpmate to mankind he was meant to be. We are the faithful, and humble bearers of truth. The wall around the house isn't only for the thief or the tiger, but to keep honest men from the temptations of riches they can not bear unassisted."

Then it was Kaitlyn who concluded by explaining the state of man's being, and the structure of man's machine; that it is a microcosm of the great world, and how it is supposed to function. Then she detailed the necessary steps which enabled it to perform as intended. At length she sat quietly as the two ladies absorbed as much of the information as they were able. Becky and Mandy responded slowly, each professing a desire to begin. Kaitlyn then recounted, and wondered as she did so how many generations of Harry's family had heard these very words, and how because of MamaBelle she now sat here with these women as their guide.

"Before you can approach any external training, we must assist you in your internal discipline. Titania and Hipolyta were taught this from birth, Chloe and I were taught at the hand of a master. Once you have achieved a new balance internally, you may decide if you wish to continue with external training. But it is not an everyday wish like, 'wishing for more pie,' it is a wish that must command your whole attention. When you decide to begin, there is no turning back. It would waste what you have might have acquired and endanger your future desires---even your grasp of what you now consider to be 'reality'."

She allowed the two women a moment of personal reflection on their own true wishes. Then she added, "This training is a sacred trust. It is not for the ears of those who are merely curious, how ever genuine. Nor is it for those who would use this teaching for their own material gain. I was easily tricked, like the helpless Guang donkey, when I first stepped onto this path. I would not wish that for either of you. It will take all your effort to overturn the habits of a lifetime, but know this: We four sisters, Jameson, Harold and Harry will be here to catch you if you stumble." With that she rose, as did the other Livingsons. Becky and Mandy followed her example. "Your first task is to not believe anything: not yourself, not even me. Verify everything. When you take on an exercise---prove its worth for yourself. When you are offered an answer to a question---verify it as best you can. Only from your own experience and knowledge can you truly understand the reality of the situation in which you find yourself." She smiled then and added, "As I've just told you: we are made of different centers, each with its own function. Over the next few days see how confused your own centers have become. Watch for the leaks I described. Try to uncover their roots and origins."

There were hugs all around as the ladies decided to retire. Interestingly, the gentlemen emerged from the billiard room at about the same time. Harry noticed the expressions on the ladies' faces and quickly realized what had at last transpired. He took his wife up in his one free arm as Hannah was fast asleep in his other. She kissed him and he followed her lead to the front entry and out onto the sidewalk for a stroll. She explained all that had occurred, omitting nothing: what she explained, what was demanded, and with what she'd tasked them. Harry listened and as she concluded she looked to him for some comment, or correction, or praise, or something to reassure her that she had done what was needed. "Kat, MamaBelle would be very proud of her eldest daughter tonight."

Kaitlyn burst into the tears of joy which only decorate the cheeks of the truly victorious after the darkness of a great battle courageously fought. Hannah looked up from Harry's arm at her, and cooed for a moment, then began a pouting little protest. Kaitlyn's camisole dampened slightly at the sound. She pulled her shawl over her shoulders to cover little Hannah as Harry transferred her over. She quieted the infant as, between them, only she could.

The next morning they chose to assail Montmartre and take in the view of Paris from its heights. Kaitlyn made a few suggestions to Becky and Mandy as they began their walk, then she nodded for Titania and Hipolyta to walk with their two friends. Kaitlyn resumed her place beside Harry. Chloe walked with Harold, and Jameson and Aaron strolled side by side. Each little group maintained their own conversations---when conversation was desired at all. Becky and

Titania, who were 'leading' their company, spoke rarely; neither was their much spoken between Mandy and Hipolyta. Each of those women were forcing themselves to watch their machines' reactions to their environment, and to their habitual random thoughts and emotions as they had been directed to do. Surprisingly, they each also began to see the world around themselves and the passersby with a bit more clarity than they had before.

Aaron talked of the history of the streets and neighborhoods through which they passed. He explained the culture which had given birth to the Republic, the imperial dreams and expansion under Bonaparte, the reordering of the city at the direction of Hausmann, and the powerful families who still shaped the politics and commerce of the modern nation. All this as they steadily climbed higher through the winding lanes. For his part, Jameson listened attentively yet every now and again was compelled to redirect Aaron's footsteps to avoid this or that impediment, or carefully herd his friend back toward the path followed by the others of their group ahead. All this was done as inconspicuously as a cat leads her master to the empty food bowl. Aaron at last fell silent for a while---a little while anyway---before he began a new topic. "How do you know the Livingsons? I thought I understood that you are all from Lake Tahoe in California?"

"Yes, we grew up in the same little village and nearly under the same roof for most of our lives," replied Jameson casually.

"But what of your own family that you spent so much time with Harry and his sisters?" pursued Aaron.

"My mother died when I was born; my father followed her several years later. The Livingsons put a roof over my head since White Feathers had always had me under his wing anyway..."

Aaron floundered a bit at the news of Jameson's parents, "I'm sorry to have brought up a troubling subject," he said sympathetically.

"It's not. The only mother I've ever known is MamaBele. My father was a great man and good provider. We were very close when he died. I mourned him, but death is as much a part of life as birth and thunderstorms, love and mountains. It's just the way it is," answered Jameson serenely.

"I don't know what it is like to lose someone you love. I am as yet a stranger to death. I can acknowledge its inevitability and its ubiquitous presence, but I have no personal experience to append to its existence," pondered Aaron in response. They walked the rest of the trek in the silence of their own thoughts.

"Up there are the foundations of the basilica of the Sacred Heart," Harry announced as they neared even steeper streets. He looked back to Aaron, "Be careful what you wish for... it's just a pleasant walk..." and smiling he shifted Hannah to his other arm. He realized she needed a change of nappies and stopped. He laid his coat on a bench and placed Hannah on top of it as he rifled through the bag on his shoulder for a fresh change. The others of the party took advantage of the halt to look about the little square into which they had wandered. Harold and Chloe approached a brasserie, and soon they all were seated around the little tables sipping beer or lemonade. Mandy watched closely as Harry attended to Hannah's changing, and remarked to Hipolyta that her brother was very unusual, "Men are not generally so attentive to children... let alone infants."

"Harry is rare, to be sure," answered his sister objectively.

"This is a side of him I've never seen," insisted Mandy after the curt response.

"But you never looked at him through eyes other than your own have you." It was a statement not a question.

For her part Becky was touched deeply by the sight of the powerful man she knew Harry to be from their mutual endeavors, being so incredibly tender and gentle with the baby girl in his care. "I'd have never suspected him of this degree of parental nurturing," she remarked to Titania.

"Harry took care of Hipolyta and me from the time we were

52

born. I've never *suspected* anything less of him," answered his other sister.

Harold was seated in a position to overhear both interactions and said loud enough for both ladies to hear, "I am familiar with Master Henry Livingson from a vantage few others have witnessed, and I can say without fear of contradiction: *Nothing* about *that* man can surprise me in the least." Chloe grinned, and Kaitlyn flushed. "He is what all men aspire to become, whether they know it or not."

Harry finished his little chore and rejoined the company as they finished their refreshments. He said, "We're almost up there." He gazed up the last steep lane leading to the summit, "I suppose by the time we make it back down here we might decide then whether to return on foot or find a ride of some sort." He held Hannah up in front of his face, "You don't get a vote; so you'll have to let the others decide!" To this she burped loudly and a bit of regurgitated milk dappled her chin. Harry dabbed at it, "That's what I'm talking about, always trying to have the last word..." He turned back to the group, "Shall we?" and he began the ascent with Kaitlyn at his free arm.

"Is Uncle Harry embarrassing you in front of all your admirers sweetheart? You just say the word and I'll have him on his knees begging for your mercy and forgiveness," cooed Kaitlyn to her precious niece.

"Listen to your MamaKat, Hannah, she's the one in charge here," reassured Harry, and they saved their breath for the climb.

Aaron was gasping for breath as he brought up the rear with Jameson, next to whom he slumped in stark contrast. Jameson walked slowly at whatever pace suited his new friend---It was a *very* slow pace. So he was not only *not* winded, but suggested they circle the massive foundation of the fledgling construction. Only Titania and Hipolyta took him up on that, and they were off to discover the path around and any stairway up. Mandy and Becky sat on the broad steps in front of the construction and looked out over the city. The others who were not on an expedition to higher ground settled next to them. The city lay before them. The dull sounds of the traffic wafted up to them as the late afternoon sun just peeked out from behind a scuttling formation of clouds. Their position also commanded a view of the dim fringes of green from the distant forests, and the winding turns of the Seine as she flowed along her ancient banks into the mass of buildings and monuments and out again.

"We shall not be walking back." Harold said on behalf of them all. When they were all assembled together once again, they returned down the hill in search of transportation---in the reverse order of their arrival. So Harry and Kaitlyn followed the rest of the group.

Jameson and Aaron were in the lead. They were followed by the four single ladies in a group. They processed past the last of the steeper streets and entered the Pigalle neighborhoods as the dusk descended. There had still been no sign of a taxi so the little troop carried onward. As Jameson turned to look back at those following, Aaron made a turn at a street corner and walked a little ways before he realized no one was with him. He returned to the corner and just saw Harold and Chloe with Harry and Kaitlyn in front of him. He hurried his pace and caught up to them. He was more than a little disturbed at his own missing sense of direction.

Ahead, Jameson slowed to join the ladies, and looked back again to be sure Aaron had rejoined the group behind. Satisfied, he put his attention on the sidewalk ahead of him---none too late. A knot of men were gawking in the doorway of a very tawdry cafe. He moved to the inside closer to the buildings between the ladies and the little crowd of now ill-smelling people. Once past those men, they were facing similar scenes all up the avenue. He checked the other side of the street. It seemed less inhabited so he made mention that they should cross over.

Harry witnessed Jameson's actions and imitated his decision. Soon all the company was across the street. They might have been safer on the side with all the cabarets. As the lead group reached an alleyway, three unsavory characters stepped onto the sidewalk and barred their passage. Jameson summoned what little of the language he had acquired and asked to pass. At least he hoped that's what he asked. Two larger men emerged behind them. Harold, Chloe, and Kaitlyn quickened their pace to join their impeded companions. Harry was still holding Hannah and walked slowly forward after them---with Aaron still just a little behind him. The now five men were looking hungrily at the ladies, but it wasn't until one made the mistake of pawing Hipolyta that anything amiss began.

She clamped his hand where he had grabbed at her shoulder, ducked and spun as a loud snap could be heard along with the man's scream of anguish. That prompted the man beside him to try and grab her as she let go of the wounded man. She crouched and spun; his legs went out from under him, and with a thud he landed on his back on the sidewalk in front of Chloe and Kaitlyn. Two of the three men nearest Jameson made a failed attempt to bludgeon him in the head; they each clubbed one another leaving just the one remaining miscreant reaching for Titania. This might have been dealt with more gently, but he produced a straight razor in his other hand supposing to regain control of the already failed attack. She leapt straight up from the sidewalk, spun in the air and as she landed the thug's head was captured in the bend of her right knee. She pivoted and a nasty crackling noise came from his shoulders; he dropped to the rest of the way to the ground unencumbered, with his arm holding the razor outstretched above him. Titania removed it from his now pliant fingers, closed it, and put it into her little hand bag. "This will need a good scrubbing no doubt," and she walked on a little way passed the fracas.

Harry had just walked up to the rest of his companions They parted at his approach, "Do please watch where you are going; we have a baby with us this evening..."

Kaitlyn joined him as he passed the moaning and crumpled. Harold and Chloe waited for Aaron, Becky, and Mandy to get up closer to Harry and Kaitlyn before passing Jameson and the twins--- allowing them to bring up the rear. Before they had gone two more blocks they were *again* impeded. This time it was by only two poorly dressed men in broken top hats with broken teeth decorating their leering faces. Kaitlyn stepped in front of Harry toward the broken smiles of the two thugs in front of her. She kept up her pace as if intending to walk between them; they didn't part to let her pass. Without breaking stride, she leapt into a forward somersault, knocked their hats off, landed in a crouch behind them, and swept their legs from beneath them with such force they landed hard enough to knock their uncovered heads on the concrete. She rose and didn't even glance back at their fallen and whimpering bodies. Harry stepped between them and gained Kaitlyn's side once more. Their companions did the same. At last they reached a broad thoroughfare: the Boulevard de Clichy. The sidewalks were wider and allowed the travelers to walk nearly abreast as they strolled on towards the Arc de Triomphe and the Etoile.

Harry halted them at the gates of Le Parc Monceau, where they gathered around the several benches between the closed entry gates. "Kaitlyn my love," and he passed Hannah to MamaKat. "Are we all still in one piece? It's a shame we didn't find a taxi."

"All fine here Harry," Jameson said standing beside the twins and Mandy.

"Good here sir." Harold answered with Becky and Chloe on either of his sides. Aaron was just walking up beside them.

"Lovely. Well perhaps Jameson might find us a good restaurant? Something not too far away?" Titania and Hipolyta dragged him along, pointing to a brightly lit series of somethings across the narrowed boulevard.

Mandy moved closer to Kaitlyn who was quite inconspicuously nursing. "Did I see what I thought I saw back there?" began Mandy. Becky also moved to within their little circle with Chloe and Harold standing nearer Harry and Aaron.

"That depends I suppose. What is it that you think you saw?" replied Kaitlyn evenly.

"Those two cute little twins that I have known from birth destroyed several large, ugly men on that street back there. Then you walked through two even larger men as if they were sheets on a clothes line?" she recounted accurately.

Becky added, "Is this what you meant last night when you talked about 'the wall,' and 'the thief,' and 'the tiger'? I thought you were speaking, you know, metaphorically or at least poetically."

Kaitlyn answered impassively, "There is nothing poetic or metaphorical about the dangers lying in wait around the next corner---no matter where you go: be it city, village, forest, or farm. Higher consciousness only does *you* any good or any good for *anyone* else if you are alive. What happens after that... well, we'll see. *But not tonight.*"

Aaron had remained uncharacteristically silent since his missed directions in the Pigalle neighborhood. He at last turned to Harry and asked a short question, "So what Mrs. Leonowens told Becky and me... that *was* true?"

"In some sense, yes. From her description of the man from southern China which you related to me---that was very likely my Great-uncle Lin Fong. He was honest in admitting he chose not to follow his father's path, and because of that he couldn't offer anything but a *sketch* of what he *imagined* was a part of The Way. *Very incomplete*," replied Harry with a touch of sadness for his relation.

"Which means that everything I practiced and attempted to attain growing up..." he faltered as tears rose to choke his voice. "Harry I have been a smug, self-indulgent, self-centered boor I have been convinced of my own importance and accomplishments--- though they were mere hollow echoes of what is really available to a man." Becky put her arm around her brother, and he cried unheeding of who heard him. Straightening a little he looked into the compassionate face of his friend for the first time seeing him for who he was. He knelt. "If you can bear the sight of me, would you consider me as a candidate for training?"

"Aaron stand up," insisted Harry. "You're no uglier than you were five months ago when we stuffed 'Guy' together..."

Aaron stood up again but with his head still bowed in mortification, "But you hardly knew me then," he muttered.

"Didn't I?" answered his friend kindly. "Come let's eat something. Jameson has found us all a great place to dine." And Harry dusted off the knee of Aaron's pant leg and the shoulders of his coat as if tidying him up for an important engagement. "I've just been waiting for *you* to see things a bit clearer for *yourself.*"

Aaron looked up then and managed a feeble smile, "You might have been waiting a very long time. How shall I atone for my already considerable tardiness?"

"Dinner's on you tonight!" smiled Harry, and he turned to receive Hannah back into his charge. Becky continued to hold her brother's hand as they all proceeded to the restaurant in front of which Jameson and the twins were waiting. Kaitlyn took her husband's arm, and Mandy walked behind with Chloe and Harold.

Harold whispered an aside to the ladies next to him, "Took him bloody long enough; I like him already."

Chloe responded in kind, "That's only because you took only two months to break down, and you already had the excuse of being in love. Honestly dear, you didn't truly even begin in earnest until after visiting the Clive House undercroft. Be nice!"

Harold felt his neck and cheeks warm and answered simply, "Yes my love."

It was another very good meal, perhaps due to the appetite acquired from the exertions of the day. At any rate they ate well and lingered around the large table well after the meal. Glasses and brandy were delivered, and bowls of almonds and of cherries were placed in the center of the table. Harry was still holding Hannah and merely asked, "Would someone please *just* pass the nuts?"

The table erupted into uncontrolled hilarity. Kaitlyn blushed from toe to head, and whispered her confession to Harry about her role in that last evening at Chelsea House. Between spouts and gasps of laughter Harold recounted to Becky and Aaron the cause of the sudden breakdown in their friends otherwise sedate demeanor. Mandy was at last laughing with the rest of them, and truly enjoyed Harry's expression of bewilderment---which had been hers at the last utterance of those very words. It was very late indeed when they at last returned to the Splendid and regained their rooms."

"You've no doubt studied the chart you constructed. Have you noticed anything about which you would like a more in-depth explanation?" asked the guest.

"I have been trying to remember every vibration of the map to see from which part of me some of my more ridiculous... uh..." he faltered.

She interjected in assistance, "Manifestations?"

"...Yeah. Ridiculous manifestations---Where are they coming from. It's a lot to keep in my head. Is there another way I can approach 'digging out the roots' once I've made an observation of something in me that I don't like?" asked the young man.

His elegantly poised guest relaxed a little into her chair, and with a pleasant smile twinkling at the corners of her eyes attempted to respond. "You have hit upon a most essential need for which there are a number of tools available that you may employ. That you are making the effort to 'do' is a wonderful indication that you could make use of them."

He wanted to pat himself on the back for her praise, but he also needed to hear what she might tell him; so he postponed the self-inflicted ovation. She continued, "Perhaps it will be instructive if first you are made aware of the nature and properties of that singular asset which is: our attention. I must in this endeavor defer to that same venerated seeker of the truth from Alexandropol in the Caucasuses. The son of a storyteller, Georges I. Gurdjieff spent his life trying to answer the, for him, central question of existence:

'What is the sense and significance of life in general, and particularly, the aim and purpose of the life of man?' From his search there is something which will assist us here." She gathered her focus and proceeded, "For the definition of this property in man, which is called 'attention,' there is, by the way, found also in ancient science the following verbal formulation: *The degree of blending of that which is the same in the impulses of observation and constatation in one totalities processes with that occurring in other totalities.* He used this definition as a starting point for explaining to himself the curious nature of that peculiar sensation, common to all of us, which is: that it seems as though there are, at any given moment, several beings living inside of each of us. Now, you have a map of man's inner world as a guiding reference, but let's examine the topography of that map. Early on you were told that we are made up of three dualities, each with a 'given' side, and an 'acquired' side. Those three dualities, the three 'stories' of our bodily house, if you will, are the 'totalities' mentioned in that definition.

So, if I rephrase it slightly, perhaps the essence of it will become more accessible for your future understanding. Each totality exercises an attention unique to itself, with its own flavor you might say. The impulses of observation and constatation are simply another way of saying: what strikes its fancy at any given moment and which it then continues to dwell upon. Let's take a simple example and see what might be happening. The first story, or totality, notices and appreciates the warmth and glow of a fire in the hearth on a chilly morning---how it smells and the sounds of the crackling and popping fuel. The second story, or totality, experiences the recollection of the satisfied, or dissatisfied, feelings from all the previous times we sat before the hearth, and depending upon those recollections, evokes in us a certain mood or background emotion. The third story, or totality, generally fainter in strength for most people, may ponder the significance of simply *having* a fireplace to warm oneself beside, or the fascination with the origins of fire, or perhaps the objective gratitude one must ultimately acknowledge when one finally realizes what we generally take for granted in the world around us: that it did not spring into existence when we were born. Everything has its own origins and history that predates our encounter with it.

Those three separate and unique processes of observation and thought, blend. So that as an individual, each person senses the echoes of several voices regarding the incoming impressions. The resultant of that blending is the human property of attention. So whichever totality, or even constituent center, shouts with the loudest voice, if you will, at any given time is the center of gravity of an individual's overall attention." She looked into her host's face for an indication that her explanation was in some way illuminating.

"Okay, I think I can see what your driving at," he tried to say aloud what he thought he heard. "Every center perceives the world in its own way, and when the centers are paired off, each of their unique perceptions are mixed together, and that mixed something represents the strength, or weakness, of my attention at any given moment. Not only that, but like in your example, if my mind wanders off to when I sat by the fire with my girlfriend for the whole winter's evening, and I don't pay much heed to how close I am getting to the fire, and scorch myself; then the center of gravity of my attention was more in my second story, and muted the screams of my first story sensing the extreme heat. And who knows what my third story might have contributed..."

She smiled encouragingly, "That's as good an extrapolation as we can approach just now. It seems you're getting the gist of it, anyway. Good." Now he allowed himself a moment of self-satisfaction and almost missed what she began to say next.

"So, to respond to your initial request, 'to know from which part of me some of my more ridiculous manifestations are coming, and digging out their roots,' let me suggest that while your map is indispensable to the task at hand, there is yet the topography to further resolve." And here, she settled herself into a posture which would allow her to both deliver the needed information, and keep an eye on his reactions and responses. For she had need of his participation in the following explanations, "Turn your notes back to your copy of the map, and fetch a deck of playing cards..."

2

An Awakening

"Without change, something sleeps inside us, and seldom awakens. The sleeper must awaken."
--Frank Herbert

When he returned from inside the house, she picked up the conversation as if he'd never left. "You notice that the vibrations which belong to Scale Two alone are all the RE through TIs of those nine octaves?"

"Yes, I see that. They are the vibrations created in that scale between the DOs which came from the scale before... I remember this," answered the host.

"Alright; there are how many vibrations created?" she posed.

"Fifty-four."

"Good. And how many vibrations were created in Scale One?' she continued.

"Eighteen."

"In the Scale Zero octave, there are six notes which come into existence between the two DOs, and those two DOs, one could postulate, came from some grand unknown octave and so forth. Do you see that?" and she paused to allow him the opportunity to digest it. He nodded.

"This series: fifty-four, to eighteen, to six, to two, whether through intention or by serendipity, is 'played out' in that deck of cards there." He groaned slightly at the pun. "Fifty-two playing cards, and two extras: an extra Joker and a Joker. There are fifty-four cards, all told. If we remove the numbered cards, leaving only the cards with letters representing their identity, we have how many?"

His eyes began to widen, as he recounted, "Eighteen. The face cards, the aces, and the jokers."

"Just so; six are left when we remove the face cards, so that only two remain after eliminating all the cards generally used for common games: the two jokers. Fifty-four, eighteen, six, and two; again." His expression was becoming less of curiosity and more of wonderment. "If we arrange your map of vibrations composing man's inner world into the three stories to which we often refer, what do we find?"

It was a challenge; he sat down on the floor with his map in front of him and readied himself to lay out the pattern in cards. Then looking up to her he asked plaintively, "Which suit represents which center?"

"Because we are moving from a mathematical construct into an even more symbolic one, let's allow the symbols on the cards themselves to dictate their representation. There are diamonds, clubs, hearts and spades. Diamonds have four sides, clubs are a trefoil—three lobes, hearts are dual-lobed, and a spade points always in only one direction---like a spear head. Four, three, two, one. The numbered cards have the numeric value and an accompanying number of pips, face cards have letters which refer to the image in the dual pictures of the faces, but no pips. Aces are curious, they have a single pip as a numbered card, but are represented by a letter like a face card is. Then the jokers are often represented as having some element of each suit represented in his image---sometimes on his hat, or somewhere about his person.

It is this way, numbered cards may be used in one scale only, Scale Two. Face cards are interesting in that the image portrayed is a double image, perhaps meaning they exist in two scales. The aces, which are either valued one, or eleven, have a place at both ends of the series. They are like the numbered cards, because they have a pip, and they are like the face cards because they are represented by a letter; three aspects---perhaps to indicate they are used in three scales. Jokers, then, are the most versatile. They represent all four

64

suits, suggesting they are used in four scales..."

The young host looked at his guest with his brow puckered in confusion, "But there are only three scales in this map..."

"Yes. But remember, the two DOs of Scale Zero came from an unknown, grander scale... so, four scales. Let's start by laying out the diamonds, begin with the bottom-most RE of Scale Two and continue laying out the numbered diamonds on the RE-TIs above it." The host did as he was bid. "Now, lay out the numbered clubs from where you left off, over the rest of the RE through the TIs up to the DO of Scale One that came from the MI of Scale Zero. Then do the same with the hearts and finally the spades on the RE-TIs of Scale Two between the next DO to DO of Scale One---MI to SOL of Scale Zero, and we shall have all the 'parts of parts' for the four centers up to the SOL of Scale Zero. But each center has three parts, which are the major divisions of that center, under which we find those 'parts of parts' already laid out. Let's lay out the corresponding face cards for each suit on the Scale One vibrations created, beginning with the bottom RE of the bottom octave of *that* scale. The Jack of Diamonds, representing the mechanical part of the instinctive center, goes there. Then the Queen of Diamonds is the MI, the emotional part of the instinctive center, and the King of Diamonds is the FA, the intellectual part of that center. Next the Jack, Queen, and King of Clubs, on the SOL, LA, and TI---the mechanical, emotional, and intellectual parts of the moving center."

The young man was delighted, indeed, and began laying out the Hearts and Spades in the same manner: between the Scale Zero MI and SOL---Scale One's middle octave from the DO to DO---upon the RE through TI to represent the vibrations created in that scale. "What about the Aces?"

"You may lay the four Aces on the first four notes created in Scale Zero itself, RE, MI, FA, and SOL," she answered, and he looked at the assembly and smiled in a brief moment of satisfaction. Then his smile faded and his eyebrows drooped as he noticed of the complete lack of cards in the top story, SOL to DO of Scale Zero.

Before he could begin to put voice to his dilemma, the guest said, "The Ace of Diamonds can now be seen to represent the whole Instinctive Center, as the Ace of Clubs stands for the whole Moving Center, the Ace of Hearts for the Emotional Center, and the Ace of Spades for the entire Intellectual Center. Each with their three parts, the Jacks, Queens, and Kings, and each of those parts with their own 'parts of parts,' the Twos, Threes, and Fours supporting the Jacks, the Fives, Sixes, and Sevens supporting the Queens, and the Eights, Nines, and Tens supporting the Kings of each suit." He listened, but still the top octave remained vacant of cards.

"What about up here, where the two highest centers reside, the Higher Emotional and Higher Mental Centers? There are no cards left except the two jokers."

She answered with such compassion that any listener would have been convinced a mother was consoling her child after he or she found out there was no tooth fairy. "But that is the state of things in our inner world isn't it?" she responded. "Most all of our manifestations arise from one of the centers already laid out in front of you?" Then without letting him get too maudlin over that realization, "In every heroic saga, in every tale of a seeker on a quest, there nearly always occurs a moment when the protagonist reaches the end of his or her strength, and surrenders to the forces too powerful to overcome, or the task too great for them. It is that moment that they inevitably cry out for assistance. A death of sorts, the realization that the way they were wont to succeed has been obviated." The young man looked up at her, grasping at the hope she dangled before him.

"The reason our Conscience is 'buried,' the cause of our inability to remain always in a state of higher consciousness, is simply due to what you see before you. But, let's accept this analogy and see what it means to regain our Conscience. Remember I stipulated that the face cards were used in two scales? Alright, populate the Scale Two 'parts of parts' of the Higher Emotional

Center, beginning from the bottom with the face cards of the Diamonds, Clubs, and Hearts." He did so, removing them from their stations as the representatives of the mechanical, emotional and intellectual parts of their lower centers, and placing them in the subordinate positions of 'parts of parts' of the three parts of the Higher Emotional Center.

"Good, now the Aces---which will be used in *three* scales—-move them also to the subordinate positions as the representatives of the mechanical, emotional, and intellectual parts of that higher center. It is a real 'stepping down' for those cards, those representatives of entire centers, to now be in the place of mere parts of a greater whole." He did so, and then recognized there was no card to represent the whole of that higher center, and said so. "But there is," she responded, "lay the Extra Joker in the place of the LA of Scale Zero. That is the precise model of our buried conscience; we do not have a specific physiological seat for this center. It is comprised of the lower centers working in symphony, a harmony if you will of once separate entities united into a coherent new organization---our Conscience, whose properties are new in the machine of man: objective self-consciousness, the seat of real compassion, the permanent observer of our manifestations."

Once again, the host's spirits began to rise with his dawning comprehension of the realities his guests had been elaborating upon when speaking of the inability of average, common people to act properly... How could they? How could he? "And the Higher Mental Center?" he whispered.

"The second death, so often referred to in ancient philosophies and sacred texts. There is a second surrender, another subordination to a higher purpose. The mechanical part of the Higher Mental Center, the seat of Objective Reason, is the Ace of Spades, move that representative of the entire Intellectual Center into its subordinate position there, as the SOL of the top octave of Scale One. The Jack, Queen and King of Spades are its 'part of parts.' Now, the Extra Joker steps down and becomes *not* the representative of the entire Higher Emotional Center, but merely the emotional part of the next higher center. Finally the Joker himself takes the position of the intellectual part of his own center. Move the three Aces representing the three parts of the Higher Emotional Center to the subordinate position of 'parts of parts' of the Emotional part of the highest center, and we are nearly complete."

He did so, and looked at the empty spaces of the intellectual parts, and its 'parts of parts' in the highest center. "Again?" he almost couldn't believe the construction.

"Yes, remember we said the Jokers were in four scales. They are the DOs at the bottom and top of Scale Zero, they are the representatives of the Higher Emotional and Higher Mental Centers, they are the emotional and intellectual parts of the highest center, and their final surrender is to become 'parts of parts.' So in the Higher Mental Center under the Jack of Spades—the mechanical part of the mechanical part of that center, gather up the Two, Three, and Four of Spades and place them under that Jack. Under the Queen of Spades tuck the Five, Six, and Seven, and under the King —the Eight, Nine, and Ten; the Ace of Spades represents the *entire* Mechanical part. Under the Ace of Diamonds we must assemble the entire suit—the Jack with the Two, Three, and Four, under the Queen with the Five, Six, and Seven, and under the King with the Eight Nine and Ten---all of them beneath that Ace. The same collection under the Ace of Clubs, with its whole suit, and the Ace of Hearts sitting atop its whole suit. Next, the Ace of Spades must perform the same action its colleagues have had to perform, it takes a lower position as the mechanical part of the intellectual part of the highest center with the entire suit of Spades beneath it. The Extra Joker *was* the sole representative of the Higher Emotional Center and now it must at last fulfill its destiny as the emotional part of the intellectual part of the Higher Mental Center, all the three remaining suits are now underneath that one card." And the guest condensed the three suits into one place under that card.

"Which finally leaves the Joker himself as his own third part---

the highest 'part of part.' By the way, the whole deck of the other fifty-three cards would be assembled beneath that one card when it takes its place as the sole representative of that center." She finished the object lesson and waited for her protege to recover himself. After a long pause of silent awe over the entire machine being condensed as it was now... she almost whispered:

"From many, the One---or in latin: E Pluribus Unum. The mighty oak tree waiting inside the acorn, the first union of sperm and egg---the primordial force behind our arising---from which we are born and back to which we strive to rejoin... Beautiful, isn't it?"

After refilling her coffee cup, she returned to the tale...

"The next morning, as arranged, Harold and Jameson met Harry in the hotel's patisserie for a conference. The developments of the last couple days forced Harry to reconsider the circumstances of their tour. "We need to make a small adjustment to our itinerary: Venice should precede Vienna. Jameson would you be so kind as to find time today to purchase our train passage for the day after tomorrow?" Then turning to Harold, he opened a different line of questions.

"Harold, I genuinely do not know what contacts you have acquired in Europe through your business..." he opened; to which Harold responded quickly.

"Some few, if I am to speak modestly; a great number, if you need something done."

"Well, yes, the latter I'm afraid. Would you make inquiries for real estate on offer in Venice? A good sized penzione at a reasonable cost would do nicely," answered Harry cryptically.

"A boarding house? How about a villa or a hotel, or better yet, the Doge's Palace? It may be available, the economy being what it is," countered Harold, trying to grasp the weight of the request and resorting to his natural penchant for understatement.

"If it is available at no more than this amount..." and Harry passed a bank draft to Harold. He looked at it, folded it and slid it into his inside coat pocket with his wallet. "Okay, not the palace. May I ask what 'we' are planning?" he returned.

Jameson had followed the brief interaction and was considering the ramifications himself, "If I may," he responded before Harry could answer, "We now have the charge of three students---fate, destiny, cause and effect, call it what you will; the situation remains. Harry needs a school house." He sat back and continued his private deliberations.

Harold looked between the two men and rolled his eyes, "Alright Harry, I'll find a Penzione."

Harry put his hand on Harold's, "In two days, and preferably in very poor repair, but with a decent water supply and electrics."

The company assembled for the continental breakfast which they were becoming used to expecting in Europe. The Galleries and the Museums were at the top of the list for the day, according to the ladies. Kaitlyn had already prepared her two charges; she gave them very particular instructions for how they should exercise their attention on the sightseeing excursion. Harry offered Aaron the task of: not viewing anything in his habitual manner, but rather to attempt perceiving whatever was in front of him as if he'd no idea of its history, background, purpose, or actual meaning. "I realize this may cause you some disquiet at first; you are a most well-informed individual. However, appearances can be deceiving," and he left off the instructions on that curious note.

"As you wish, sir. I shall make the efforts required," accepted Aaron simply and resignedly.

Harold begged their indulgence, saying he was compelled to ferret out some business for his company and would join them perhaps in the late afternoon. Chloe kissed him tenderly and winked before he had the chance to explain his ulterior motives. Slightly undone by his wife's seeming foreknowledge of events, he kissed Hannah and departed. "This should be interesting," he muttered to himself as he went out onto the street and headed for the business of a reliable contact.

Aaron, Becky and Mandy, each on their own personal instructions for the use of their attention during the outing, were in a word, somber. The intentional management of their otherwise habitual perceptions made not only for a novel day, but also yielded some rather interesting revelations to each of them. Chief among those, commonly, was the distinct recognition that observation, when intentionally directed, is a lot more effort than merely looking at 'stuff.' Next, in order of degree, they each also noticed sounds and smells that hitherto had gone unnoticed. Each building had its own distinct aroma, every street and lane offered a panoply of noise, music---a cacophony unique to itself. In the visual field: subtleties of color and texture came to the foreground of their vision out of the plainness they each once merely ignored. By the time Harold rejoined the group in the Tuileries, one of their predetermined rendezvous locations, 'somberness' had been replaced by humility. A nuance of demeanor, to be sure, yet palpable to the observations of their mentors and profound for themselves.

The company returned to the haven of the Splendid, and enjoyed bathing and redressing for the evening's anticipated entertainments. Jameson made a detour in his return to the hotel to arrange the rail transportation for the afternoon two days hence. After a sponge bath, he arrived downstairs in fresh clothes. Harold passed the address and receipt of the morning's request to Harry, just as Jameson delivered their train documents. The gentlemen handed the ladies into carriages which were hired for the entire evening. "Hors du Cabaret Chat Noir," directed Jameson to the drivers.

"I thought it might be better this evening to take our transportation with us..." Harry intimated to Kat once they settled in the coach as she happily arranged the corsage he'd given her as an accessory to her elegant dress.

"Yes, dearest, very thoughtful," she replied. Then to Hannah she cooed, "Doesn't MamaKat look scrumptious tonight, Hannahbelle? Uncle Harry is trying to make up for her having to keep her kittens safe last night. Isn't Uncle Harry the most contrite of men?"

Chloe and Harold simply had to laugh out loud at that, "Well I think you've done splendidly, all things considered, for a gentleman on his honeymoon that is..." inserted Harold.

Chloe winked to Kaitlyn, knowing full well her sister's absolute ecstasy at having her treasured husband dote upon her so. Mandy was still practicing the directed exercises of the day and became positively mesmerized by the aroma of the corsage mixed with the freshness of her companions' clothing, the scents of the wet cobbled street, the lighted attractions and traffic of Paris after sunset... The world was quickly becoming far vaster than ever she had experienced it before, and she was at last rising to its voice of introduction.

The shadow theater, the music of the little quartet, the local cuisine, and of course the exquisite company made for a quite memorable early evening. They next went to the performances at the Folies Bergère, on Rue de Richer, not so very far from Boulevard Rouchechouart and the 'black cat' from whence they'd come---it *was* on the way to the hotel, after a fashion. Hannah had gazed in seeming enchantment at the images in the shadow theater, to the delight of her elder companions, but she slept through the later entertainments of the second venue once she'd been fed and changed. It had been a most full day and evening and the travelers were almost as pleased to reach the Splendid this night as they had been the night before, but for different reasons. All slept well.

The last day in Paris was devoted to gathering the souvenirs, books, pictures and paraphernalia the company wished to keep as treasures. They were very discriminating. Kaitlyn pressed her corsage between two books with the handbills from the cabarets. Jameson made a last attempt to note the secrets of the bakers' methods for making croissants so light and airy. Harold confirmed two more additions to his company's network. Chloe found a new supply of diapers and a new tote bag for keeping the supplies together, fashionably. Aaron, Mandy and Becky took individual walks along the Seine and its bridges on a final task before boarding the all-night train for Venice. Harry made inquiries of an odd assortment of businesses, leaving tentative orders and arranging terms of credit. Titania and Hipolyta browsed book stores and a few clothing stores, in search of what, only they knew, and did not share.

The company wasn't at all discomfited at the change of destinations from Vienna to Venice. Truth be told, one European city beginning with 'V' was as good as another to those from the States at least. The porters at Gare de l'Est station followed Harry's lading instructions and were tipped nicely. The company boarded and went to their arranged cabins in the two coaches; for convenience sake they carried aboard only what they would need for the evening, night and morning. Once the train was underway, Harry and Harold wandered back to where the coach conductors gathered at the end of the last coach. They were Italian, predominately; so armed with their college Latin, the two men engaged the trainmen in conversations. They talked about everything from football to Tuscan politics. By late that night the two men were confident of their ability to converse rather fluently with the hosts and merchants of Venice and Florence whom they would encounter over the next several weeks.

As they made their way to Harry's cabin where Chloe and Kaitlyn waited, they maintained conversant Italian, as they opened the cabin door they shifted back to English instantly. "...Then after getting you six situated, we are to head on to Tuscany," finished Harold.

"What's this?" asked Chloe. She looked at Harry and held up a little oblong wooden dish-shaped object.

"That is what I wished I had available for the next several weeks. I've asked around at ship-building businesses, and others I thought might have an insight as to what I should expect in the canals of Venice."

73

"It's a little small isn't it?" replied Chloe with a straight face.

"But *everything* is smaller over here in Europe compared with home. I didn't want to frighten anyone with the full-scale version," answered Harry in an equally casual tone. "At any rate, I shall have to improvise."

Kaitlyn then brought Harry up to speed on the topic of Harold and Chloe, Jameson, Titania, and Hipolyta's separate excursion to Florence. Hannah's first teeth would be coming in before long; she was already becoming a bit sensitive to the constant changes demanded by travel. It seemed Hipolyta was putting her foot down about staying in Venice... and the four ladies had come to a novel solution which would accommodate Hannah's needs. Instead of Hipolyta going to Florence to help with the baby's care, she would be helpful to Kaitlyn caring for the angel in Venice in Chloe's absence.

Harry simply nodded; 'forces beyond one's power to overcome.'

Hipolyta's motives weren't entirely attached to her niece. Since first meeting Aaron, and his recognizing the distinction betwixt herself and her sister as Jameson had so many years ago, she was willing to give him the benefit of a doubt. Although he was very intelligent, witty, and humorous, his tendency toward arrogant self-absorption was an unpleasant undercurrent. If his initial encouraging steps toward transformation were a legitimate foretaste, she decided she wouldn't rush to judgement. White Feathers would be proud.

Once the train passed onto Italian soil and entered the first few towns in the wee hours of the morning, the atmosphere of the train gradually changed. It seemed the latin cultural disregard for the strictures and precision of schedules had most fortunately not affected the service in the dining car. The company assembled for breakfast as usual. The city of Verona sped by outside and they were beginning to anticipate their arrival at the Santa Lucia station. A couple hours later they were at that station looking for porters to assist with the baggage. After a brief dialog with the assistant station manager, Harold informed Harry, Jameson and Aaron they were on their own to remove the luggage. "The porters are not exactly content with their wages and have decided to adjust their hours to the wages paid. They won't be here until the afternoon train."

They located a few trolleys, and after haggling over their rent, they left the station. At once they were greeted by the morning sights of the enchanting island that was Venice. Other passengers were blinking at the bright day all around them and studying their guidebooks and translation dictionaries for phrases to answer the cloud of hawkers swarming about them. Harry, with map in hand, led the company through the broad walkways until they arrived at Calle Zancana and the former Penzione Tigre d'l Mare. Harold stopped the trolley he was pushing, looked up at the obviously ancient facade and entry, broken balconies and stained walls, "Who were the last tenants? The Crusaders?" then louder to Harry, "Well, you said: 'in need of repair'..."

Titania and Jameson, closest to hear his first comment though he tried to keep his voice low, giggled and chuckled. The others came up from behind,

"Why stop here?" Hipolyta asked, glancing up at the decrepit edifice. Harry walked up to the door, opened it and pulled in the trolley he had pushed from the station. She gaped in surprise as her brother entered, "Oh my..."

To say it was dusty, would be to say the sea was damp. He waited until all the party entered then he went to open the few windows in the ample entry hall and sitting room. "Perhaps we should explore in pairs," he suggested.

He took Kaitlyn's hand and started through the hallway leading off one side. The others looked at each other, perhaps a little traumatized, and imitated the elder Livingson's example. Just as a precaution, they left the trolleys loaded. In pairs they tentatively walked forward and explored. Jameson and Titania unstuck the louvered double doors at the back of the extensive front room and the light of the morning glared into the room. They walked through into a most neglected courtyard. Weeds and vines crept up through the cracks in the tiles, the basin of the central fountain looked more like a large planter. The weather had done its job on the walls and window frames; the generations of paint that once protected them was peeling off in large flakes. Three other sets of double doors led through the other walls around the ground floor; they picked one set at random and spent a while trying to open them. When at last the doors yielded to their efforts, the blank and staring faces of Mandy and Becky looked back at them from beneath a window on the far wall of the room they entered. The lack of anything but an ancient-looking metal oven gave the impression Harold's initial comment might be accurate after all.

Aaron and Hipolyta met with a bit more satisfaction. They dared a stairway they found behind a door near where Harry and Kat had disappeared. On the second level, they picked one of two doors and went through. They walked the circuit of the open balcony hallway that encompassed the courtyard expanse. They looked into room after room, none of which boasted any furniture save the errant chair or two. When they had made the full circle, they looked through the last door which was already standing open. Inside were Harold and Chloe. "This seems to be the main residence's rooms, the owner's, or host's I suppose. They stretch the length of the front of the building," Chloe announced. "Has anyone checked the floor above?" and she pointed up at the ring of windows around the courtyard higher than where they stood.

At that moment, Kaitlyn called down from the roof directly above them. "Hello... come out, come out wherever you are." Jameson, Titania with Becky and Mandy, appeared in the 'kitchen' doorway at the lower level, and Harold, Chloe with Hipolyta and Aaron walked out into the open corridor on the second level. "If you take any stairway leading up, you'll eventually reach this upper level. There is a lovely view from the front terrace. Come on up!" she called.

The company disappeared back into the building to find those stairways. When they reassembled on the terrace, Harry was pacing back and forth from one end of the low wall overlooking the street to the other, cooing and whispering to Hannah. They all took in the view of the canals on either side, the little square across the way, the buildings and rooftops surrounding them. Harry's voice sounded an official tone, "Welcome to the 'Tiger of the Sea' Inn. I'll be your assistant host during your stay here. I'd like you to meet my boss, Hannah."

Hannah's little hand emerged from under the baby blanket and waved. That was greeted by chuckles, as no one could see how Harry managed to get her to perform the well-timed feat.

"Our first order of business will be to return the trolleys before the porters at the station require them for the afternoon train. Therefore, we have them for..." he took out his pocket watch, smiled at the inscription and said, "...Four and a half hours. We have then that amount of time to employ them for our own requirements..."

He ticked off on his fingers, "One: brooms, mops, cleaning supplies and other tools. Two: Kitchen supplies, an ice box, utensils, cookware, groceries, and a fair amount of elbow grease..."

He paused and turned his ear down closer to Hannah's upturned face. "Oh, you're right of course, boss..."

Turning back to the rest, he announced, "Scratch the elbow grease; we already have that in stock. Three: mattresses, cushions, chairs, tables... in short: furniture. Four: Illumination, candles until we have the electrics on, lamps and bulbs, linens, towels and pillows." He looked at the amused but staring faces.

"Volunteers?" and he produced envelopes from beneath Hannah's blanket, "Thank you boss," he said and waited.

Jameson said he'd make the kitchen oven and stove operational, and Mandy and Titania would find the needed inventory for the rest of that room. Harold and Chloe said they would arrange the furnishings, but would likely need a trolley for some of the smaller pieces. Becky, Aaron, and Hipolyta claimed a trolley for gathering tools and cleaning things, which left Kaitlyn to arrange illumination, and Harry to explore the plumbing and electrics.

"May I have an inventory of the existing fixtures?" asked Harry.

Aaron said he'd investigate before helping with the tools detail. Each group was handed an envelope containing their task-apportioned funds before they returned downstairs, unloaded the trolleys and stacked their trunks near the doorway. The gentlemen removed their coats and rolled up their sleeves as they had noticed was the local custom.

The ladies also rolled up their sleeves and placed orders for aprons, "And if you find a shop with secondhand clothing, do note its location..." Mandy called to the others beginning to disperse onto the streets.

Harry and his 'boss' went around the building looking at the general structure and for where the utilities might possibly have been designed to enter. He came through the rear door from the alley, looked up at the electric lines and where they seemed to disappear on the top floor. Taking the time to open every window he came across in his inspection, he reached the junction box. Perhaps the last act of the previous tenant was to have the electrics brought up to code---whatever codes to which the Venetians deigned to adhere. He threw the main switch. Nothing happened, and he was extraordinarily grateful. He tested one breaker after another; none of them popped. So, continuing the bold experiment to it's next phase, he went to the one room he remembered seeing a light fixture with a bulb---the kitchen pantry. He descended the back stairs and stepped into the bare room. He went over to the pantry and reached for the little cord dangling from the socket. "Okay Hannah, cross your fingers." He pulled the string. Light! "We'll have to make your father something very special for Christmas this year, angel. Daddy's been a very good boy, indeed. Okay, now the plumbing."

He had found an iron crow in the alleyway, probably left by a workman as it was just visible beneath a pile of rubbish against a neighboring building, and deposited it inside the back door. He returned to the rear wall outside the kitchen and poked along the cobblestones where the wall met them. Tapping and tapping until he heard what he was hoping to hear. Noting the distance from the door and the corner to his position, he reentered the building and paced off the same distance. "Well, sweetheart, there was no valve outside; it must be inside, somewhere."

Hannah looked back and forth as if searching the floor; Harry smiled and began searching for evidence of a covered access, always working back towards the fountain in the courtyard. There didn't appear to be what he sought in the flooring between the point of entry he'd located and the double doors of the inside wall, so he picked up the crow bar again and entered the courtyard. He tapped back and forth from the courtyard wall in line with the predetermined ingress of the water line. He got to the fountain itself and at last tapped a thick tile which tilted at his probing. He took off his vest, laid it on the weathered ground and set Hannah upon it. "Watch closely dearest, Uncle Harry is going treasure hunting."

He pried up the tile and below it, silted nearly as much as the fountain itself, was a valve barely visible above the soils. "Hmm, Precious we need a spade and a pail. But as we do not have a spade and a pail, we shall make do. Your Auntie Tania and Poly would laugh out loud if they saw Uncle Harry digging a hole with his fingers..." and he began the task of excavation.

Fifteen minutes or so later, the valve was exposed. "This is the tricky part dearest," he ticked off their options on his fingers an she sat rapt in fascination, "If we turn the valve and it breaks, we have a leak. If we twist the valve and it doesn't break, the pipes throughout this old Inn are going to fill and push out all the air that's in them, they could go 'POP,' and leak. If we go and open every tap and valve that we can find in the house, we might stand a chance of catching a leak before it gets too terrible." He held the three fingers in front of her, "What do you think we should do?" She grabbed at one of his fingers. "You are just like your mother and father, daring but prepared. Okay, let's go open valves and taps."

They spent the next half an hour making sure they had found all

79

the places in the building where water was *supposed* to come out. "Uncle Aaron made a good inventory; didn't he."

They went back to the main valve. Harry looked at the fountain basin again. "We really should remove the soil from in here; it may be that it will just start spouting when the water is on... Thank you for reminding me Hannah, you're right, we don't know if the fountain has its own shut-off or not, and if it does, is it a secondary shut-off for the rest of the place?"

He began tapping around the basin. On the opposite side he found a similar valve to the first, though less silted. Cleaning out the impediments, he sat back and reviewed all that *he would have done* to plumb the building if were *his* project. He went to the main entry and returned with a sheet that had covered the only abandoned furniture in the room, a very ornately carved bench. He spread the sheet next to the fountain and began to scoop out the accumulation of dust and soils. Three-quarters of an hour after that, there was a mound of dirt on the sheet and very little in the basin. "Okay, Hannah, turn on the valve."

His niece looked back up him, blinking her eyes in the early afternoon light. "Must I do everything? Well at least watch so you can take care of it when you have to..." He put his hands to the dish-sized wheel and exerted a slow and increasing pressure counter-clockwise. He didn't wish to destroy their chance of keeping the valve workable by any sudden yanking. Sweat began to bead at his temples and roll onto his cheeks and chin; still he kept up the constant tension. His arms and hands screamed in torment at the prolonged and unrelenting exertion. After the minutes had begun to seem interminable, there was a faint, slow, barely perceptible movement in the wheel. A moment later and even Hannah might have been able to detect its turning, but it wasn't yielding easily. Still he maintained the pressure, and at last: sinew and will overcame the frozen valve. The sound of flowing water met their ears and he turned the valve as far as he dared. Through the open doors into the kitchen he heard water splashing into the wash sink. He walked around to the other side of the fountain basin and reenacted his first exercise of determination. This valve surrendered much more quickly and dribbles of water began bubbling from the fountain spout above the basin, he opened her up as far as he dared and the dribbles became a gush, which became a steady eruption. He removed the cover over the little grate for the fountain drain and pushed the end of the crow bar directly down until there was no resistance. The gathering water flowed out slowly. Satisfied that the fail-safe worked, he closed the cover to the drain. The wider channels in the tiled ground of the courtyard began to moisten, and it dawned on Harry that the fountain wasn't the *only* water feature. He grabbed the iron crow and began scraping along the broader still silted channels. Streams of water flowed in the wake of the gouges he made. Again satisfied, he went back and closed the valve to the fountain.

"We really should have gone to check the rest of the fixtures before Uncle Harry tried to make mud pies..." He gathered up Hannah and began the inspection tour just as Kaitlyn returned with boxes of candles, light bulbs, and packages of linens, with bags and bags of pillows.

She held up a box of the tapers, "We may stick with candles; they are cheaper by the hundred than the light bulbs." She took Hannah into her own arms. "Harry, what's that noise? It sounds like a waterfall?"

Harry dashed up to the first floor bathrooms. The water was filling the tubs, but none had run over; at least the drains weren't clogged. He turned them off one by one---the sinks, the same. He hurried to the second floor and repeated the inspection and procedure---still good. Now for the next daring test: the toilets. He looked in each tank and basin that he flushed. Some of the soft parts would need replacing, and a few of the valves were a bit corroded, but for an abandoned penzione after what had likely been years, it was in pretty good shape. Harold was definitely going to get something special in his stocking this Yuletide.

Jameson returned at the same time as Kaitlyn. He pulled his trolley around to the back door. It was laden with some wire brushes for scrubbing and a variety of spanners, but what occupied the most space was an inverted prep table. He left it on the cart until someone was there to help him move it into the room. He looked at the open 'lighted' pantry and smiled, "Harry, stop playing with Hannah and do something useful..." Then he went to the iron monster near the wall to determine its state of neglect. After a prolonged inspection he began scrubbing the fire box, the dampers for the flue, the oven chamber and stove top. Sweaty, sooty, and content he went to the sink and without a second thought, turned on the tap. He washed off the grime he'd proudly collected and turning off the water; he looked around for a towel. That's when it occurred to him that: there was water in the house! He rushed out into the courtyard and hollered, "Harry, if your going to mess with the plumbing, at least set out soaps and hand towels!"

He heard the echoes of laughter from one of the first floor rooms and Kaitlyn called, "Soap is on its way; perhaps you should go find enough towels in the boxes by the door for six bathrooms and the kitchen." Hannah made a squawk as emphasis that that was a very good direction. Jameson did just that, then asked Harry for assistance with the large kitchen table before he left on his next mission.

As Jameson returned the trolley to the front door, and Harry came out of the kitchen through the courtyard, Mandy and Titania arrived laden with provisions and cookware. Right behind them were Aaron and Hipolyta with a trolley of cleaning materials and tools. Both trolleys were taken around to the kitchen door and unloaded. Harold and Chloe came in the front door while the others were in the back. The trolley Harold pulled was stacked with chairs which he set around the room. He looked at his watch and called, "Anybody home? We need to return the trolleys."

The company reassembled in the main room downstairs and Titania, Hipolyta and Becky took a trolley apiece. "We'll be back before you know it," they said. Chloe mentioned to Hipolyta that there was a shop along the way with some very attractive second-hand offerings should they decide to stop in and gather a few items for the others. "...Aprons, smocks, that sort of thing..."

The rest of the party toured the latest improvements, lights in fixtures in all the rooms, running water in all the bathrooms and the curious courtyard fountain installation. Harold had just pulled out his watch again to check the time, when Kaitlyn and Chloe announced that it would be a good idea to eat something before tackling the afternoon. Harry noticed Harold's preoccupation with the time and had to ask, "Is there something else time sensitive about our afternoon?"

Harold kept his voice low as he answered, "There will be a delivery. Maybe sooner, maybe tomorrow... Italian time is different than my accustomed perception of time. But I was made to understand from the merchant that the furniture would arrive 'soon'."

"Have a bite to eat and we'll get to cleaning this room first as a staging area. Relax, you deserve it. This Inn was a most fortunate find." Harry tried to reassure his friend.

Harold looked around, sighed then laughed. "You are an optimist to the core!"

Mandy set up the prep table as a buffet and directed Jameson to uncrate some dishes. "Finger food, so no need for flatware at this meal..." Breads and cheeses, sliced meats, and fruit decorated the table, and a few bottles of wine were opened just as the trolley crew returned and joined in the feast. They carried the chairs out to the courtyard and sat amidst the shards of broken planters and weeds. It was a very satisfying and happy gathering. Harry explained what Hannah had discovered about the utilities, and Kaitlyn mentioned the candles and lights. Mandy and Titania extolled the outdoor markets and supply shops. Aaron and Hipolyta listed all the stores in which they had searched for mops, brooms, and the other necessities of keeping a house in right order.

Becky was fascinated by the temperature of the courtyard, "...And at mid-day when it should be getting the warmest. This building design is ideal for not only the temperate climate here but I dare say it would do well in a chillier climate as well."

The wine was exhausted and the remnants of the meal were wrapped up for the evening snacks, when someone at the entry called aloud. "Blast..." Harold muttered under his breath, "Who knew I'd deal with the only Italian for whom 'soon' really meant *soon!*"

Six large heavily laden carts stood at the doors and a smiling merchant in waistcoat and hat waited beside them. Harry introduced himself and pointed to Mandy, then began a lively conversation in rapid Italian. Harold quickly got the others to begin sweeping and mopping the great room floor. By the time the Merchant and Harry had begun to shake hands, the delivery men were more than anxious to unload the furniture and go home. Harry passed Harold and whispered, "Did I stall for long enough?"

Harold smiled and waved in the first bundles and pieces of furniture. "Yes, thank you. What were you talking about so long? All I caught of it was something about 'very particular tastes and discretion'?"

"It's an interesting story; I'll tell you about it...later," answered Harry, and directed the others to begin cleaning the other rooms and then the upper floors. "Sweep the floors once, follow with a good mopping, use the bathtubs for rinsing and such, then move to the next rooms and floors."

Harold had the great room furniture set in a corner of its own while he kept them from unloading the knocked down bed frames, mattresses and bedroom furnishings too soon. He directed the movers to the sitting room with the furnishings to be settled there, and just as a cleaning crew vacated another room, he directed the deposits of its furnishings. The entire unloading of the six carts took nearly three and a half hours. When the last mattress was carried up two flights of stairs and installed in the last suite on the top floor,

Harry and Mandy brought out a case of wine with glasses and began serving the workmen. More bread and cheese was supplied until it resembled more of a festivity than the chore it had seemed throughout the afternoon. While the wine flowed and spirits were high, one or two of the women at a time would try to rearrange some odd bit of furniture, or assemble a bed frame, to which the workmen responded instantly with bravado, taking over the sundry tasks. They smiled and joked at the women's notions of moving and assembling it all by themselves.

As evening approached, the company waved farewell to their deliverers and retired to seats in the great room, thoroughly exhausted. Harry stood up with Hannah again in his arms, "Welcome to the La Tigre d'l Mare Penzione, I apologize for not having everything ready when you arrived, but you have been most patient and gracious guests." Since there were no lamps yet in the great room, candles burned in holders and the floor reflected the light. The freshening evening air replaced the musty smell of the place from their first arrival. He continued, "Unfortunately, our hostess has not taken the time to prepare each of your rooms," and he looked at Hannah sympathetically, "but I feel certain you all will be able make do with the supplies provided."

Each member of the traveling party looked around them. They knew that they had been involved in the minor miracle of the Inn's one day transformation, yet still they marveled. Applause and a standing ovation greeted the end of his little speech. He held Hannah in just such a posture so that it truly appeared that *she* was taking the bows in acknowledgement of their ovation. He continued, "Tomorrow: the courtyard, and the next day: maybe we should see some of the sights of Venice?" which received more applause and laughter.

Kaitlyn, with Harry carrying Hannah, climbed the stairway to one of the upper suites. Harold and Chloe took the one opposite. On the first floor all the rooms were claimed one by one and everyone set about making beds, hanging towels, putting out soaps, and opening their trunks in lieu of dressers. Harold, Chloe and Kaitlyn with Harry and Hannah stood on the same terrace they stood upon only eleven hours before. Now it was mopped and the marble shown in the rising moonlight. Folding chairs had been brought up and they sat silent and content, listening to the laughter and conversations on the floor below them across the open courtyard. Harold yawned, "Harry, next time, perhaps maybe not so *much* 'need of repair'..."

Harry arose very early; the sun had not yet brightened the sky more than a mere glimmer of hope of the coming dawn. He left a note for Kaitlyn with some very detailed instructions for the day; he looked over his shoulder at Hannah and her MamaKat sleeping like angels on the bed as he closed the door and went on an errand. He walked the broad walkways of the sleeping island back to the train depot. He 'borrowed' a jacket laying on a bench near the coal piles for the trains. He grabbed a trolley, which looked as much like the coal carts as anything else, draped a tarp, again borrowed, from a near at hand pile of parts and began to load up a modest supply of coal. He tied the tarp closed and, leaving the jacket behind as he passed the bench on which he found it, wheeled the trolley back to the kitchen door of the penzione. Once the supply was deposited in the bin, and some put into the kitchen pail, he set off for the depot once again to return the trolley.

As the sun began to streak the sky in pinks and orange, Harry stepped out onto the Vaporetto. He chatted with a boatman who was getting his boat ready for the morning train's passengers to arrive and seek his services. After a few minutes, the boatman agreed to ferry him up the canal a little way to where the fishermen were just setting off for the morning. With a mutually friendly farewell, Harry wandered among the docked boats in search of that one particular boat he needed. As the fishermen rowed off by ones and twos, the object of his search was left next to the last fisherman on the wharf. Harry haggled a little over the vessel, barely still afloat. His purchase was a foregone conclusion; it was clear that the fisherman hadn't any lingering attachment to it. With a handshake and a promise of delivery, Harry started back to the Inn.

When he came down, out of routine, to the kitchen in the morning, Jameson naturally marveled at the coal awaiting him next to the oven. He rummaged through the supplies which Mardy had procured the day before. Finding the coffee *and* a grinder, he stoked the oven and readied the kitchen for the breakfast preparations. When Harry came through the kitchen door he was greeted with the enticing aroma of morning coffee and toast with sausages. "You are a miracle worker," he announced as he closed the door.

Jameson looked from over his first cup of coffee at him and smiled appreciatively. "That from Mr. Livingson is flattery indeed. Making breakfast is hardly a miracle; have some coffee. I heard footsteps upstairs; the rest of them should be drifting down soon."

"That's *not* what I was referring to..." Harry recounted how and when what he perceived to have been the 'miracle' to which he referred was to have taken place. Jameson acknowledged both the circumstances and details. The footsteps did indeed grow louder. "This courtyard is an interesting version of dad's holding pond and drainage channel..." He explained the job which would likely occupy most of the efforts of all the company during the day.

Titania came in and went to the oven; she poured coffee. "We'll need to do what with the pottery shards?"

"Your husband will fill you in; I have to make a few more preparations before your trip to Florence." He kissed her cheek while her countenance remained in the frozen gaping expression which formed on her face at hearing the words: 'your husband.'

Jameson waved a hand in front of her face to get her attention. She acquired her focus again and looked inquiringly at him. "He knows." Jameson said to her clearly.

"But..." she attempted.

"Drink your coffee; I'll try and explain how I *think* he found out," her beloved soothed. Then Harold, Kaitlyn and Chloe came in and joined them.

Harold grinned, "Well if it isn't the happy couple who still sleep in different rooms..."

"Does *everyone* know!? I should have sent out announcements!" cried Titania, and she wilted in her chair while Jameson poured coffee for the new arrivals.

Harold looked suddenly confused, "What did I say?" He'd thought he'd made just a light-hearted comment about their being so long in each other's company etc.

Kaitlyn pulled a chair to next to Titania. "My dearest sister," she began in a whisper, "Not everyone knows, but your brother has an uncanny ability to see quite through anything---Your trip to Tomberlaine, and your glowing face when you joined us for dinner that evening---that was enough to convince him that you had finally overcome any impediments to you happiness. The rest of your family and friends passed it off to just the thrill of the journey. Harry has only told me the cause of your apparent bliss."

Titania whispered back, "And then you told to the rest of them?!" she sighed. "No," she acknowledged, "you wouldn't have done that; I'm sorry. I tried so hard to pick just the right occasion, unnoticed. You understand why...remember?" Titania moaned.

"Your correct, I did not. And yes, I remember, but I also told you to follow your heart. He made sure that I moved our things out of the suite we were in; it is for you and your husband. And as for the 'rest of *them*,' even your twin sister hasn't said a word. So you can take *that* as a measure of accomplishment."

"She's preoccupied with Aaron. I've had to repeat almost everything to her lately," Titania retorted, "S*he could have been there and forgotten the event.*"

Kaitlyn looked up to accept her coffee from Jameson with a look of helplessness. He yielded, "Don't ask me! It was all I could do to stay in another room these last seven nights."

Titania exclaimed vehemently, "Well! You won't have to *struggle* from now on, except to *keep up!*" She grabbed Jameson's wrist and hauled him toward the door. "We'll be *indisposed* for the rest of the morning!" she announced with an air of finality, and they disappeared upstairs. The last that the trio in the kitchen saw of them that morning was as they closed the door to Kaitlyn and Harry's suite on the top floor.

Harold looked at Chloe and Chloe looked at Kaitlyn who was standing there in her robe. "You can borrow some of my clothes..." Chloe muttered, and looked back up at the closed door.

Kaitlyn began to explain that she needn't bother, when Hipolyta came in followed by Becky. "Good morning, did I miss anything yet?"

The gaping trio broke into peals of laughter. Harold controlled himself just long enough to say, "There's fuel for the stove, food in the skillet and the coffee's still hot."

"Oh good, another wonderful day begins!" Hipolyta purred as she poured cups for herself and Becky. Becky accepted her mug and asked what the three of them were staring at.

Kaitlyn pulled herself together and began to explain what Harry told them last night about the courtyard and its fountain. "There should be a return drain to the fountain basin, so that with the water in all the channels---between providing nourishment for plants and evaporation, the fountain spout can be regulated so that there is a constant water level. Our task is to clean the floor tiles and all the channels, then decide upon the right plants to keep for our necessities."

"Like maybe herbs for the kitchen..." asked Mandy as she entered and poured coffee.

"Exactly, and aloe vera perhaps a lemon tree..." added Hipolyta.

Kaitlyn was nodding at their suggestions, "First we need to see how the channels are actually arranged and modify or simply use them as is."

Chloe interrupted, "Kaitlyn, there is a shop I came across while we were shopping, where the twins found the aprons and smocks...a resale shop of sorts. Shall we go and fetch some 'work clothes'?"

"Yes, thank you; just let me change and we can get started on the courtyard as soon as we return." They went up to change and were soon out the front door headed for the shop.

Harry took receipt of the derelict boat below the bridge on the canal next to the penzione. He tied it up, took measurements, and went in search of the craftsman recommended to him for fitting a forcola to the center stern. The old artisan was carving as Harry entered. Harry sat on a stool and quietly watched without being noticed. After nearly half an hour, the old carver stood up to have a thick cup of coffee when he noticed Harry sitting there. Unruffled, and a man of routine, he made a second cup for Harry and they chatted about the weather, the tides, oars, and rowing styles. Harry showed him the model he'd made for his search---before he'd settled for the used boat. The old man said he knew that boat; it was a 'sempian.' His father built one after spending years in the South China Sea on a Venetian merchant ship. It was a solid design, nearly unsinkable and easy to maneuver. Harry smiled, told him of his own father's two boats and then explained what he needed.

Without hesitating, the old man stood up and walked to the back of the shop, then remembered he had not invited his guest to follow him. He waved him back in a toothless grin. Harry hopped down and followed. Through a little door which led to a boat house over the canal proper, hung on the far wall was the old man's father's sempian. It was in good condition and the old man merely said, "I am old, my sons will not row. Take it, use it, it will be glad to be in the sea again."

Harry helped him lower it from the wall and into the canal, an oar was passed to him and the old man simply waved over his shoulder as he went back to his carving bench. Harry blinked at what had just occurred, but put the oar to the oarlock and like a fish in water, made good time back through the canals. He re-evaluated the derelict boat. An idea struck him and he looked for someone to direct him to a sailmaker. Before long he found what he was looking for; he described with precision the dimensions and particulars of his needs, arranged for a delivery date and headed back toward the Inn and the open air market. He tied off the newest boat, pulled the other out of the water and left it upturned beside the canal. He'd have to wait until Jameson could give him a hand carrying it to the back of the Inn where he could make the necessary repairs and modifications. As he came to the courtyard, he saw Mandy, Becky, Tania, Hipolyta, Aaron, and Kaitlyn scooting around the tiled ground frog-walking and cleaning the tiles and channels. The work was expedited with all their attentions on the task and the builder's original design was being revealed, at last. Jameson waved him to the kitchen. There was a man at the table sipping coffee with his hat in his hand; he stood when Harry entered.

"Harry this is Giovianni," introduced Jameson; the man smiled and nodded. "But I don't know exactly why he is here. I think it has something to do with the coffee?"

Harry introduced himself and asked the man's trade. They chatted for a while, sometimes serious, sometimes laughing. At last Harry invited him to sit down again and he explained to Jameson, "Gio is an inventor, and you were right, it does have to do with coffee. He has been looking for a commercial installation to use his machine. He doesn't have a shop of his own, and he has spent all his money developing it..." Aside to Jameson, Harry intimated that he lived at home taking care of his aging parents. "He saw us open the penzione and thought we would consider allowing him to setup his invention as an additional amenity. The other proprietors in town simply laugh at him."

Jameson was already warming to the gentle man. "Ask him what kind of space he would need, because you know Harry, that whole front room area... the entry and great room... we could arrange a counter area near the dining room doors." He stopped, "what does his invention do?"

Harry smiled, "It makes coffee using steam forced through

finely ground coffee beans, very fast."

"Rapida!" Giovianni said aloud, grinning.

Harry asked a few more questions, and Gio began gesticulating, mildly at first, then he grew quite emphatic. Harry repeated the key points and Gio nodded vigorously. Harry and Gio shook hands; Gio kept nodding and bowing as he left through the kitchen door. "Show me what you have in mind and put together everything you can think of that will make this happen---including a possible menu. I thought perhaps a sidewalk morning cafe might be nice. It would be a good start, but everything we do here will have to be self-sustaining, you understand?"

"I think I see where your going with this; I'll do my part Harry," confirmed Jameson, delighted that he had something to occupy him that would help improve the Inn over the next couple days. He began to sort out those tasks against the ever-present attentions which must be paid to his bride.

Harry looked into the courtyard to see their progress. To his surprise the tile was marble and very white at that. Aaron had just begun mopping the channels after already making the walking surfaces shine. Chloe and Hannah came in the front door followed by delivery men with carts. Large pots filled with rich loam were brought in and placed in the recesses all along the perimeter of the space. Four of the pots were already planted with short trees. Following the planters the delivery men brought in rod iron tables and chairs to be placed around the now immaculate courtyard. She left the directing of their placements to Kaitlyn, and took the seeds to Jameson that he had requested. "Here you are love, they didn't know what 'sage' was; it appears that here it is called salvia."

"Thank you, thank you, you wonderful woman. There is a carrot cake with your name on it in the kitchen." Chloe quivered with the anticipated delight she knew would be hers this evening. Harry casually questioned each of the students as they put away their tools, and gave Kaitlyn an embrace that caught her breath away.

Jameson then followed him to the canal and helped him bring

the upturned boat to the back of the Inn. "So, you've been here all of two days and you have as many boats... and you plan to be here several *weeks*?" Jameson rolled his eyes, "Shall we expect a fleet moored out there upon our return?"

Harry smiled, a little chagrined, "This one will be a fine sail boat when I'm done with it, and you know what that one's for..."

Jameson looked at the sampan and became nostalgic, "Yes indeed, those were the best days of our youth."

"Now brother, we have a wedding feast to prepare, do we not?" Harry added, "...although it's just a wee bit tardy."

"Yes sir, I've begun the meat, and if you don't mind, I'll leave the rest in your capable hands. Titania made it quite clear that when she finished helping with the students in the courtyard, she would insist upon a most thorough bathe," replied Jameson shrugging his shoulders, "and she's already heading up the stairs... if you will excuse me..."

Hipolyta barred his access to the stairs, "Jameson, I believe you have an obligation to fulfill before you go upstairs to see my sister." Her hands were on her hips and she looked stern.

"What is that?" asked Jameson, uncertain of her tone and meaning.

"Receive a kiss and a blessing from your sister!" She threw her arms around his neck and whispered, "I knew it would happen some day, but this is just wonderful! I am so happy for you and Titania; I could cry..." In fact tears streamed down her cheeks at that moment.

"Thank you Poly, it means the world to us, coming from you," he kissed her and sped up the stairs after his bride.

Harry announced, "We have quite a meal to finish preparing. Mandy would you do the honors of directing our activity?"

"Direct? I'll handle the whole thing! This has been quite a day already I must say," answered Mandy tying on an apron. She shooed everyone out of the kitchen but Hipolyta---whom she knew would *insist* upon helping with her sister and brother's wedding meal

Harry went into the courtyard and turned the valve for the fountain. It rose in a nice symmetrical sprinkle and began filling the basin. The others of the company looked on from doors and balconies. Once the basin filled, it overflowed into the channels and was carried to each of the planters; the water level over the whole watercourse and reservoir gained equilibrium. It was beautiful and sounded refreshing. The heart of the Tigre came to life once more. There were cheers and laughter at the spectacular transformation of the Inn over such an incredibly short span of time. They didn't have to be reminded by the inscription on Harry's pocket watch about the uniquely subjective character and nature of time; it was a part of their experience now---they understood.

At the wedding feast they dined around tables in the courtyard, with all the double doors opened leading into the rest of the ground floor. Visible through the Dining Room doors, upon the dining table was a three-tiered wedding cake. Candles on low tables throughout the ground floor, as seen through the other doors, gave the impression of a vast space dotted with stars. The atmosphere was magical and the enchantment wasn't just in their surroundings. The hearts of the company were so opened to each other's joyous state and condition of increased being that it was more the celebration of a single individual with separate avatars of manifestation than a collection of discreet persons. Harry united them further by reciting their common journey's first story, mostly for the benefit of Aaron who had not yet heard the fabled beginning of his journey,

"Once upon a time there was no donkey in the Guang. So someone from the Heavenly Court sent one there, but the farmers and peasants finding no use for it, set it loose at the foot of the mountain.

A tiger ran out from the mountains. When he saw this big tall thing, he thought it must be divine. He quickly hid himself in the forest and surveyed it from under cover. Sometimes the tiger ventured a little nearer, but still kept a respectful distance.

One day the tiger came out again. Just then the donkey gave a loud bray. Thinking the donkey was going to eat him, the tiger hurriedly ran away. After a

while he sneaked back and watched the donkey carefully. He found that though it had a huge body it seemed to have no special ability.

After a few days the tiger gradually became accustomed to its braying and was no longer so afraid. Later the tiger became bolder. Once he walked in front of the donkey and purposely bumped it. This made the donkey so angry that it struck out his hind legs and kicked wildly.

Seeing this the tiger was very gleeful, 'Such a big thing as you can do so little!' With a roar he pounced on the donkey and ate it up."

"We master the art because: in order to be able to unite the machine of man, all his lower centers must be active, strong and willing to surrender to the higher center's will. This must be trained in a man, it can not be left to chance. Otherwise he will be like the discarded Guang donkey, helpless before the forces of nature, and never recognized as the helpmate to mankind he was meant to be.

We are the faithful, and humble bearers of truth. The wall around the house isn't only for the thief or the tiger, but to keep honest men from the temptations of riches they can not bear unassisted."

When he finished, silence pervaded the Inn as if they were, in some intangible way, joined by the generations of their ancestors adding their unheard blessings to the company on behalf of their most honored membership. Harry spoke first after the silence had been absorbed like another course of the meal. "We are the bearers of the new traditions of that ancient lineage. All here are the beneficiaries of, and live as testament to, the foresight and resolution of two remarkable humans," he raised his glass and the others followed suit, "To Belle Livingson."

"To Belle Livingson!" They repeated with reverence and pride, and drank the toast. Tears of inexpressible joy filled Harry's eyes as he looked from face to face, "and to the man she loves and serves, whose unparalleled wisdom and humility first ignited our conscience---to George Livingson." The others again drank to their benefactor. "To the *first* of the lineage---whose name is lost in the dimness of human time---for his determination to create a repeatable, practicable avenue to awake the submerged Conscience of man." All the company consecrated a profound moment of silence in genuine reverence in honor of that most worthy initiate.

Kaitlyn was overwhelmed by the power of the spoken dedication. She began a song which Belle had sung to her often when they worked together; the same song which had captured George's heart so long ago. It was a song of joy that gently mingled with the voice of the breezes and recalled the rustling leaves of a forest. A lilting and haunting melody borne by a voice both sweet and strong; it rose as a invocation to the union of sky and earth, and tumbled from her voice as the water of a gentle rain or splashing stream. As she allowed the song to trail off, until it became indistinguishable from night air itself, the company sighed as one voice. Harry took his plate to the cake and sliced off a serving, then delivered it to Titania who repeated the act and delivered it to another, and on the little ceremony continued until Jameson delivered the last slice to Harry.

The next morning, having leftover cake and fresh coffee, Harry announced that he and Aaron would be going out in the boat. He made sure the three students realized that henceforth they should be up very early, wash their heads, arms and legs in cold water and be waiting at their posts for each day's tasks. Jameson packed a basket of bread and cheese for them and they were off. Kaitlyn gathered Becky and Mandy in the front of the penzione and explained what they were going to do with the walking sticks she handed them. Arranging their hands 'just so,' and demonstrating how to walk with them, she led them on an early morning jaunt through the maze of Cannaregio's more obscure lanes and alleyways.

Harry stood at the stern with oar in hand and set off through the canals, explaining to Aaron the state of man's being and the structure of man's machine, that it is a microcosm of the great world and how it is supposed to function. Then he detailed the necessary steps which enabled it to perform as intended. At length, he sat quietly as his friend absorbed the information.

"When may I start?" asked Aaron at last.

"You have begun to build the lasting foundations of your

96

internal training; you may begin external training when you wish."
Harry added, "But it is not an everyday wish like, 'wishing for more
pie,' it is a wish that must command your whole attention. When you
begin, there is no turning back. They had reached the end of the
Grand Canal and now bobbed on the waves before the open straight
between the big island and the barrier islands of San Giorgio and La
Guidecca. Aaron took some time shedding his preconceptions of
the methods and fruitless hours he had spent pursuing his
misconceptions.

"Harry, I am ready. I shall follow where you lead. May I start
now?"

Harry smiled and said, "O.K., row us back." They traded places
and he instructed, "Hold the oar like this." Harry leaned to him and
adjusted his hands. "Good," he said. "Now stand with your feet
here." Harry set each foot into position. Aaron dipped the blade in
the water and pushed the handle out, then pulled the handle back.
"Wait." Harry stopped him again. He got up near Aaron; he reached
around him, placed his hands near his friend's, then went through
the movement once more. This time Aaron could feel the boat
propelled through each push and pull of the oar's motion. Harry sat
back down and let Aaron continue unassisted.

He pushed with all his strength, keeping his hands and feet 'just
so.' Then he pulled back with all his strength, watching that his body
remained in its posture and position. And so he kept at it, until his
leg and back muscles ached and his arms and hands were sore. Every
so often his teacher would direct him to repeat a push stroke, or
repeat a pull stroke to keep their progress on course and avoid
collision with this or that obstruction in the canals. Then after hours,
ahead of the prow, he could see the entrance to the penzione's canal
from across the Grand Canal. He pushed himself to greater efforts
and got them back to the Inn at long last. As Aaron settled the boat
next to the docking post, Harry commended his strength and his
spirit before they tied up the craft and went into the Inn.

When Kaitlyn and her two charges returned after several hours of winding through Venice, she explained what they were going do about the broken and peeling facade. Harry had contrived sanding blocks, the use of which she demonstrated. As they began sanding, she mixed plaster and set about filling in the cracked and missing sections. Jameson had constructed a scaffolding for them in their absence and left them meager morsels for a light lunch in the kitchen. He and Harold set off to gather and prepare the counters and work space for the cafe project. When Aaron had devoured his own 'lunch,' he joined the ladies and Kaitlyn repeated her instructions for the use of the blocks. A wide clockwise circular motion for the right hand and an equally large circular, counter and syncopated motion with his left. The three worked diligently and silently for the rest of the afternoon, until the long shadows of evening and a completely sanded facade brought them release from their labors. Plates of food were set out for them at the table and they began a meal they couldn't finish. Three weary heads drooped toward unfinished plates; the other members of the company helped them to bed. They slept very well that night.

Harold and Chloe with Jameson and Titania left on the morning train for Florence in anticipation of a most rewarding honeymoon in Tuscany's verdant hills and valleys. They were to be absent from the Inn for only a week or so... but no certain date was set for their return. Hipolyta kissed them all farewell at the Santa Lucia station and waved Hannah's little hand to them as the train pulled away. Baby bottles were introduced to the baby as a stop-gap measure for when Kaitlyn wasn't back in time to satisfy Hannah's idea of a schedule. At those times Hipolyta was most happy to stand in as a surrogate. She prepared all the meals and generally kept the Inn functioning nearly single-handedly.

The next morning and the next, Harry and Kaitlyn were waiting for the rower and walkers as they emerged from the Inn, their hair still wet from the cold water. Aaron and Harry set off for another destination with Aaron at the oar and Harry in the bow feigning a nap. Kaitlyn led the women off on another expedition through a different maze of lanes. When they reassembled at the Inn, another wall was prepared as the first and so the days continued. Rowing for Aaron, long walks for Becky and Mandy and afternoons of sanding, until one morning their students were waiting for *them* at the starting places of the morning's tasks. Kaitlyn left with the women as usual.

"Ladies, your walking stick is your friend and these lanes have done you no harm. Please do not poke at them as you walk." The clatter they had been making ceased. She walked on with them in this manner for a while longer then, when she was certain they were comfortable with the motions, she said, "Switch hands." They each took their staff into the other hand and, after adjusting their grip, continued on. "Stop." Kaitlyn called, and went ahead of them to demonstrate how she wished them to exchange the staff from one hand to the other. They watched closely: when her staff hand was behind and the opposite foot was forward, she pivoted the staff up across behind her and caught hold of it with her free hand, and after setting her grip 'just so,' continued her stride smoothly and without disruption; the staff now swinging in the new hand. "Now, you'll do it."

They continued a few paces and Kaitlyn again said, ' Switch hands." This time in a much more fluid display, each woman passed the staff to her free hand without breaking stride and with a 'proper' grip on the staff. "Better," Kaitlyn said aloud. That continued for the duration of their walk over the next almost three hours. Every so often at odd moments she would call, "Switch hands," and they would execute the exchange better and more smoothly each time.

Aaron launched them as usual, but before they had gotten too far and without waiting for a place where the boat could be steadied, Harry told Aaron to shift sides of the oar. With a bit of fumbling, Aaron switched to the other side of the oar. "Wait," Harry said aloud. "Shift like this." He traded places with his friend and demonstrated the movement. It was a fluid transition in which: during his pull stroke he lowered his body, back straight, swiveled on the balls of his feet and rose up on the other side of the oar without a splash or bobble, nor the blade losing its powerful stroke through the water. "Here," he said simply and they traded places once more.

Aaron took up his position, made a couple usual strokes, then at his mentor's command he shifted sides nearly as he was shown. "Almost," said Harry. Set your feet first, then be sure the oar doesn't notice you've moved. Try again." This time Aaron complied smoothly and was on the other side of the oar with very little wobble. "Better," Harry commended. "Watch where you're going," he added as they almost collided with a mooring pylon. Aaron had no sooner brought them back on course, when Harry called out, "Shift." Aaron made the maneuver as smoothly as before and resumed from the new side. Harry settled into his usual posture in the bow and every odd moment or so would call 'Shift,' to which his protege would readily comply.

The routine of their days continued unabated, only the afternoon tasks changed after they sanded the entire outside of the Inn. Painting came next and Kaitlyn instructed them in the motions expected. With the brush held 'just so,' they were to make an upstroke, hold, then a downstroke with another momentary hold. "Switch hands every twelve strokes or so..." she called, and left them to their chore. As one whole wall was completed after a couple days, they moved to the next, and to the next. Every wall they began, their strokes were shifted from vertical to horizontal; their hands on the brushes didn't change, just the orientation of their strokes.

On the ladies walks, when they came to one of the many bridges, Kaitlyn began to have them climb or leap up onto the low walls at either side. With their staffs held above and in front of them in their extended arms, they made squatting side lunge movements with their legs. With a pivot to alternate the step of their advance, they were to make the length of the bridge's walls and resume their usual walk on the opposite side of the canal.

The exterior of the Inn was renewed after a week and a half and they started on the courtyard walls. Before the end of each day's chores, they squatted on the tiled ground of the space and with rags or towels in both hands extended before them and cleaned up the debris of the afternoon's scouring. They looked like three large inch worms cleaning a very large table top. Harry used the afternoons to complete his modifications to the 'sailboat.' Since the beginning of the busy mornings, he had gradually turned the worn out fishing boat into a sleek sailing vessel. When he and Jameson returned it to the water and rigged it so that the mast could be raised once it reached the Grand Canal, Titania and Hipolyta took Jameson for an inaugural voyage around the islands of San Giorgio and La Guidecca, then out to Murano and back.

Harry forewarned Kaitlyn that any morning now they might encounter an awakening in their charges which would signal the beginning of the end of this phase of their training. As predicted, at the beginning of the last week of May, well after the honeymooners had returned from their Tuscan retreat and the maiden voyage of the *Little Tigre*, it happened. The rest of the company had also been apprised of the impending development. One morning the ladies met Kaitlyn outside the attractive facade and entry of the Inn without their walking staffs; meanwhile over by the canal, Aaron refused to untie the boat and resume his position in the stern. In so many words each of the students explained how they had seen the utility of the work performed upon the Inn, however oddly they were required to perform those functions, but the purpose behind the tedium of the morning activities escaped them. They were each told to 'hold that thought' and to meet their respective teachers on the terrace. As the three mounted the open roof patio, Becky and Mandy were as surprised to see Aaron, just as he was at finding them. They compared their various morning tasks and all agreed they could not establish a rational purpose for those exercises. When Harry and Kaitlyn joined them, moments after their own arrival, the students announced their common complaint. Mandy and Becky pleaded for some justification of the activity, while Aaron simply stated their mutual plaint, "What was the point?"

Kaitlyn went to a seat near one corner as others of the

company, who had taken similar positions unnoticed, watched Harry go to a near wall and grasp a staff, leaned there for the purpose. He returned to the standing students and as he came to just within whispering distance of them, he jabbed each of them in turn in their own solar plexus so quickly and without forewarning so that one after the other winced serially and repeated their own version of 'ouch!'

"Let's try that again. Ladies pick up your staffs," Harry offered.

Kaitlyn called out, "Shift," upon the mere mention of the command, they instantly each performed their versions of the fluid movement. Harry swung a blow at Aaron as Jameson called out "Aaron, 'Shift'," the blow was deflected easily as Aaron went through the instilled motion.

Harry didn't let the staff linger unmoving for an instant; he aimed it across at Mandy, intended for her ribs. Hipolyta called, "Mandy, 'Shift'," and again the fluid motion blocked the cross blow with a loud "clack." The staff in Harry's hands sang out again, this time aimed at Becky's head. Chloe called, "Becky, 'walk the bridge'," again the 'crash' of the staffs was heard as Becky reenacted the routine motion. Harry picked up his tempo and with fore-shouts from the gallery to each of the victims, the three students were soon blocking, dodging, deflecting and avoiding the menacing arcs of his staff. Harry's hands became a blur, and the pole in his hands nearly invisible as swipes, arcs, jabs and blows were administered to each dancing pupil---as if they were the only one receiving the deadly barrage of strikes. After several minutes the loud directions from the gallery ceased and Mandy, Becky and Aaron began to move intuitively to protect themselves from the rain of Harry's attacks. They ranged across the terrace, hopping, lungeing, rolling, and making impromptu somersaults when necessary. Although they distanced themselves one from the other, Harry's lethal onslaught continued unabated and with increased frequency against each of their defenses. He was becoming almost invisible himself.

Probably from an instinctive need for unity against their mutual adversary, the combatants at last tried to gather at one side of the whirling menace. When they were almost assembled into a single front of deflection, Harry espied the opportunity for which he'd patiently awaited: to make a final coup d'grace in one motion to end all their struggles in one massive strike. As the staff sped at them, quivering in the fully invested power of the stroke, two things happened simultaneously: Mandy and Becky dropped their walking sticks and reached for the staff as Aaron crouched and made a ferocious sweep at Harry's legs, which could have caused immense damage to his knees---if Harry were still there when Aaron's arcing leg reached him. Harry sprang up and over the staff, now securely gripped by the ladies as they crouched in a mutual expression of the 'walk the bridge' position. He vaulted in a double somersault through the air and landed upon one foot precariously balanced on the front wall of the terrace overlooking the street nearly thirty feet below.

He remained as motionless as the three students in their variations of frozen crouching lunges, each gasping at the air to fill their screaming lungs. Harry leapt down toward them, motioned for them to stand, retrieved the staff from the ladies willing hands and bowed to each of them in turn.

He said simply, "There are few ways that a person will willingly yield their will to someone else. That each of your exercises were designed for a purpose about which you knew nothing, yet you persisted in obeisance to the will of the teacher---That was the point. Learn from that lesson." Their blank expressions followed him hypnotically as he leaned the staff back against the wall. "Today, you each have purchased at great price the rest of your lives." The gallery stood and bowed, one by one to the three still standing where they last stood. As the last of the company exited the terrace, Harry made a final bow to them saying, "Your journeys begin *Now*," then he left the terrace.

Aaron blinked as he reviewed the sequence of events in which he himself had been an actively involved participant. He made his way down to the docked boat on the canal, cast off and rowed away toward a destination of his own choosing, every now and again 'shifting' upon his own whim. Mandy and Becky came to similar realizations and gathered up their walking sticks. They were last seen turning the far corner in the lane, 'shifting sides' with a new confidence of purpose and with a timing determined by their own individual inclinations.

When Harry reached the ground level, the other members of the company were assembled in the courtyard. As he emerged into the open air, they all as a single entity bowed deeply to him and held that posture of deference until he was genuinely abashed at the show of respect. When they raised up to proudly erect postures once more, Jameson stepped forward and said on their behalf, "Master, we are honored by your allowing us to be present at the impeccable demonstration of what is possible for the human machine. We shall strive to emulate your unswerving discipline," and they solemnly bowed in a tacit oath of their pledge. Harry made a deep bow to each of them in turn and answered, "It is our common human birthright to do so."

In twos and threes they left the Inn to stroll through the lanes and piazzas of Venice. Each person wore an expression of contentment and determination. All of the companions rejoined in front of the Inn much later. They walked to a nearby ristorante for a welcomed repast. Everyone present noticed that Aaron took Poly's hand every now and then as they sat in conversation. After supper the rest of the evening was spent in the folding chairs on the terrace looking up at the star dappled spring night sky.

Aaron had to leave for Manchester to take up his new position at University. He was cutting it close, but he would have a day and a half to spare if all went well. Hipolyta took a stroll with Harry and broached the topic of returning with Aaron to register for her own admission to coursework at the University. She admitted that before they left England she had wired Sarah Bunker to send her transcripts and Letter of Recommendation to Greengate, and that they should be waiting for her when they returned. Harry outlined the path she was considering, and once he was satisfied that she fully appreciated the implications and ramifications of her decision, she went to her room and packed in order to leave at the same time Aaron was scheduled to depart. She would reside at Greengate with Harry and Kaitlyn for the duration of her College career. Aaron was more than pleased when he was made aware of her resolve to enter Victoria University.

The next day the gentlemen finished the cafe service area in the great room and installed retractable awnings on the front of the Inn. Giovianni arrived on schedule for Harry to install and electrically connect the invention. The tables from the courtyard were moved out under the awnings and a trial run of the Rapida coffee-maker was undertaken. Gio, that gentle man, worked the counter-mounted contraption and delivered demi-tasses of the strong coffee to the waiting party. Mandy rose and assisted him, peppering him with questions which Harold or Harry translated for Gio, as well as his own responses and counter questions. Mandy was picking up a little Italian and Gio employed the smattering of English he'd acquired after a lifetime of living in Venice and interacting with its British seasonal guests.

It turned out that Gio was a few years older than the rest of them. He had served in the Third Italian Independence War and had been conscripted to the Austrian merchant ship, Stadion. He and other conscripts had been able to sabotage the mission of the scout ship, and their 'service' was remitted a week or so later when the Prussians signed an armistice. That was followed not long after by Austria ceding Venitia to the Italian Kingdoms. Since then, Gio led a life of a very competent jack of all trades capable of turning his hand to nearly any task with skill and deftness. As Mandy and Gio maintained their translated conversation they absorbed the subtlety of expression and inflection which oft-times communicates more than words. Mandy respected the man who found work doing anything to support his aged parents, and Gio was quite taken with Mandy's deft handling of her career as a restauranteur.

By the middle of the first week in June, Mandy was catering to the early morning vendors and tourists at the morning cafe as if she were in Tahoe running the 'Concession.' Her own accelerated training seemed to have transformed the frenetic drive she was wont to employ in that capacity. She maintained an easygoing very naturally amiable attendance upon the early patrons of the little cafe. Gio seemed to read her mind as they served their very appreciative clientele. Harry helped them clean up after one morning's spate of customers and opened a dialog with both of them.

"We are preparing to leave Venice for Basel, Switzerland in the next couple days," he began. Mandy and Gio both stopped what they were doing and became instantly attentive. "I acquired this Inn for the simple purpose of using it as a base of operations for training." Gio asked what he meant and Mandy made an explanation of 'training' to be an inner version of the outward renovation of the Inn. Gio accepted that easily. Harry continued in English, "I had planned on simply putting the Tigre back on the market and using the sale to recoup my expenses," which he then enumerated omitting nothing. "I am open to suggestions for how I should word the advertisement."

Mandy Hill was a different person than the woman who had greeted her 'vacation' as a frightening uncertainty---what seemed like ages ago. She looked into her heart and came to the startling realization that she owned her own thoughts and destiny. She was no longer bound by the tethers of her youth to the ebb and flow of Tahoe City's fortunes.

"Harry, perhaps you would consider another disposition of the Inn?" She took a deep breath then asked Gio if he would be willing to make his participation in the Inn permanent.

With his vehement affirmative of: "Whatever you decide, I shall stand with you," in broken English; she outlined her thoughts of an alternative.

The Inn was fully functional, the cafe had proven itself, the groundwork was already laid for the development of a full blown ristorante as an additional source of revenue. "Allow Gio and me to get it up and running as a genuine Inn for the rest of the summer tourist season. If it is successful, your investment may make a greater return." Gio nodded enthusiastically, not wishing to return to the obscurity he'd languished in before the penzione opened.

Harry quietly reviewed her 'alternative,' and said at last very seriously, "Alright, until the autumn tourist season then, but no longer. We shall revisit the sale of the Inn in September." As if as an afterthought, he asked, "While we are talking about it, what would you call this new venture? We haven't repainted the marquis yet."

Mandy pointed up to the vacant wall above the awnings and Gio caught the meaning of her puzzled expression. He whispered to her, and she brightened instantly. "How about, *Accommodations of The Final Concession?*"

Harry positively beamed at the suggestion. "We'll paint it at once. I'll ask Harold to make the appropriate announcements in a few papers in England and the continent; perhaps you two should sit down with Jameson and create menus you are sure to be able to replicate. Titania is well versed in the running of the Lodges so she can provide insights on that front."

Those activities were commenced, as well as hanging the sampan in a prominent position on a wall in the great room. Mandy insisted upon it being there as a constant reminder of the ongoing efforts required to maintain her inner balance. The *Little Tiger* was moored securely and would serve as their primary means of transportation. Gio was a very adept sailor and promised to teach Mandy at their first opportunity.

At supper that evening, Kaitlyn with Harold and Chloe talked about all their efforts since their own journeys began to Becky and Mandy. Jameson served and added a comment now and then as Harry and Titania listened with admiration. Kaitlyn prefaced their comments by explaining to Becky and Mandy what they had accomplished over the last few weeks and the purpose behind every task. She elaborated upon how they had done it and why each effort brought them nearer to their aim. She reminded them that only humility and confidence of presence would allow them to progress along their journey. "You will always have an opportunity to do what is right, others may not understand your actions---but *you* must." Her words reinforced their own new sense of their abilities and strengths. "Unlike the discarded Guang donkey, helpless before the forces of nature and never to be recognized as the helpmate to mankind he was meant to be, you are no longer helpless."

Chloe told of her struggles to shed her emotional dependences, Harold explained how every step toward a greater awareness of himself yielded a greater humility and effectiveness in all of his endeavors. And finally Kaitlyn reminded them of the long line of those who came before them to enable their new possession of themselves. "It is upon the shoulders of every generation and the sacrifices of many that allow this conversation to even take place." Each of them made a solemn promise to themselves alone to make the efforts required of a real human being in pursuit of fully claiming their part of the birthright of every man.

As they packed that night Harry told his wife again how absolutely fortunate he was to be her chosen beloved. She blushed at his attentions and offered the only response that could truly express her own feelings. The other couples, in the privacy of their rooms and suites, were at the same time engaged in similar attempts of expression. In the morning Jameson, Titania and Becky went to rent trolleys from the Santa Lucia Station Manager. When they returned the company's trunks were loaded. Gio and Mandy sat down with them all to enjoy their last coffee at the cafe. Finally, with embraces all around, the travelers bid farewell to the *Accommodations of The Last Concession*.

The conductor finished his debate with the Station Master over whether Milan should begin their own football Union as was established in England. It was a little unclear which side of the argument either man espoused, as they kept forwarding alternating views on the subject. An hour after the time for the scheduled departure, the train left the station practically on time by Venetian standards. Harold outlined the cities and towns he wished to scout in Bavaria as the gentlemen looked over the KD Steamer brochure. The ladies discussed how Mandy, with her renewed perspective on the world around her, might deal with any of the crises that were inevitable in the hotelier/restauranteur business. Hannah listened intently but didn't contribute to their conversation. When the train passed Milan and headed north, the views of the Italian Alps from the train gradually drew their attention away from speculations.

They arrived in Basel rather late in the evening, but since they had reservations at an Inn near the station it was not the debacle it might otherwise have been. In the morning they boarded the KD Steamer and found their cabins. The accommodations were comfortable and charming though not as ample as those provided on the *Britainic*. Another facet of the river cruise which contrasted with the trans-Atlantic passage was the relative lack of constant roll and pitch.

Strasbourg offered Harold his first opportunity to scout while the rest of the company simply went sight-seeing. The Strasbourg Cathedral dominated the picturesque view of the city from their boat at dock on the Rhine. The series of the city's walled fortifications and the University had an architectural appeal that was captivating to Harry and Becky.

A day later they arrived at the confluence of the Neckar River and as planned Harold departed the ship's company. He wished to not only to see Heidelberg, but travel back down to München and then up through Nuremberg, Frankfort, Cologne and Dusseldorf to meet with them in Amsterdam five days hence. His absence allowed Chloe a great deal of time for continued encouragement and advice for Becky and her anticipated return to work-a-day life.

They arrived in Amsterdam and fell in love with the cleanliness of the concentric streets and canals spreading out from the port. The newly opened Rijksmuseum kept them wholly entertained until Harold rejoined them after a successful side trip. They embarked from Holland for Liverpool on a merchant ship whose captain happened to be an acquaintance of Captain Perry of the White Star Lines ship *Britainic*. The passage through the North Sea, the Channel and around to Liverpool was relatively brief and comfortable. Harold and Chloe arranged cabins on a returning White Star Line ship to New York for themselves and the Connors before the short train ride to Salford and Greengate."

"Now you have more tools in your toolbox of work. It will probably be a good time to give you some indication of how to use those tools. The greatest tools in the world will sit in the rain and rust if left unused and neglected. So with that in mind, let's return to our original symbol of the enneagram, that ancient symbol of Reason. You were able to decipher a bit of it and out came the Law of Three Forces and the Law of Octaves, the diatonic structure of any whole phenomenon, inner octaves and a symbolic map of the inner world of man. I think we can still get a bit more from this image; shall we investigate?"

The young man put aside his journal for the tales and opened to a new page of his 'dialogs' notebook. "Okay..."

She crossed her legs under her and began, "The process of thought is analogous to any other complete event. Let's take the activity of feeding the community first and work our way back to the proper pattern of mentation for a man. First let's adjust the diagram to reflect the world's actual state of existence---all existence as we know it is diatonic and not in even sevenths. Therefore draw out another circle which shall represent the line of time. Divide its circumference into an eighth, a quarter, a third, a half, two-thirds, seven-eighths, with the whole---DO at the top of the circle." The host did as directed.

"Now, re-insert the line representing the law of seven: 1-4-2-8-5-7, and back to 1. It's squished a bit on one side but it is more reflective of how the world we live in functions. The triangle is still there in the background: the top point we'll label the *Function*, the next, clock-wise, we'll recognize as the *Being*, and the last is *Will*. That which emanates from LA is the Will behind the event. FA stands in the place of what must be transformed: the Being. The DO is the cyclical 'workshop,' if you will; the Function which will be utilized to transform the Being to the desire of the Will. Clear enough?" she asked. He made the notations and nodded.

"Okay. Let's feed the community. What is required to successfully feed a community of people?"

"Uh... food," the young man answered not looking up from his notes.

"Good start. What kind of food? Is this for a meeting of vegetarians? A Jewish family reunion? A Cattlemen's convention? A backyard picnic?"

"Okay, okay... It depends on who is eating." he corrected.

"Good, so we look to the Will of the customer---the people who are hungry. Perhaps we only have a certain selection of foods and they are simply hungry enough to eat anything. As you have no doubt noticed, the food is determined by the desire, or Will of the hungry. Where shall this 'food' be prepared? What functional place or situation is ideally suited to effect a transformation of raw food into edible meals?"

"A kitchen," he answered again.

"Yes, the place where there are appliances for cooking, tables for preparation, utensils and tools for the tasks of food transformation. It is cyclical in that all the pots and pans, the spatulas and measuring cups, the spices and staples are all in their cupboards or drawers or on shelves and hooks before preparation is begun. After it is completed, the kitchen is returned to the same state---cycle after cycle. That is our Function for feeding the community, our DO. Next around the line of time are: the 'workers' at RE. Somebody has to actually lay their hands on the food and manipulate it, whether it's the kitchen staff or you in your kitchen making a ham and cheese sandwich. Next along the circle are: the 'tools' at MI. Even if your only tools are a sharp knife, a pointed stick and a fire pit, your kitchen must have tools. Fortunately most kitchens are a little better appointed than that. Often there is a selection of sharp knives, each one designed for a specific use: corers, choppers, cleavers... on and on. You'll see as we go through one event that we bring the experience forward to the next event. So our workers gain experience, our tools are improved or new ones are invented; everything about the kitchen can lead to greater efficiency and productivity through the cycle of experience.

Next on the circuit of the symbol, as we have already indicated, is FA---the Being---in our example: the food. The food must be transformed, and here is another point at which experience becomes useful. Will it do any good to anyone to make sandwiches of moldy bread? How about trying to cook meat that has already passed into decay? Or, vegetables which have begun to rot? Certain transformations are going to occur to the Being as the result of entropy: the natural tendency for all things, with rare exceptions, to decay and pass beyond the point of no return, if you will.

At SOL the chef enters the event and the cooking commences. Between SOL and LA is the period of transformation. This is the only point in the cyclical event where the chef and the line of time coincide and move together. This interval is also known as the point of most tension, the place wherein the Being, or food, is *irrevocably* transformed. In ancient knowledge it is called the *Harnel Aout*. The fruits, vegetables, meat or juices change from raw to cooked. Not surprisingly, the change is so dramatic that the cooked food will outlast its uncooked cousins in many cases. It has been irrevocably transformed, and in the vast majority of instances, longevity is one of the properties derived from the process.

At LA the meal is presented to the customer. All the preparation, the cooking, the timing, the presentation of the intended dish is complete and it is now up to the customer---the community, the Will behind the event---to choose to eat or not eat.

From LA up to TI the results of all previous labors are assessed for their success. Did we use the ingredients which were appealing to the customer's tastes? Was anything cooked for too long or for too short a time? Was everything presented at once to the diner, or were the vegetables done long before the meat, losing their 'freshly cooked' appeal. Did the hot rolls dry out while waiting to be served? And so on. Will the customer be satisfied?

At TI the kitchen is put back into order. Everything is scrubbed and cleaned and put away for the next event. It is at this point that we now know whether it was a successful adventure or not: whether people praised the chef or got sick over it? Did they eat or leave hungry? The resultant data will instruct any similar future event: the workers may learn new techniques, new tools may be added to the kitchen's arsenal, recipes may need to be tweaked or new recipes developed.

What we have just viewed was the linear process of the event seen in the sequence of time. However the *inner line* which runs from 1-4-2-8-5-7 and back to 1 is called the *line of supervision*. In our example of feeding the community it is the process which the head chef must follow.

The process begins at LA, the Will of the customer---the hunger of the guest. An order is given to the kitchen: the line from 7 to 1; here the chef must determine who is the best worker for the tasks of food preparation and assisting with the cooking. He probably won't put the pastry cook in the position of preparing and grilling the meat, or vice versa. He must decide who is best fit for the job dictated by the order.

The line from 1 to 4 indicates that he must look to the food itself which is to be prepared. What are the best choices of bread, the best cut of meat, the freshest vegetables, etc? What will be the methods he'll need to think about for dealing with those 'foods?'

The line from 4 to 2 is an assessment of sorts, an evaluation that will determine which tools will be required. Can we chop the garlic, or use the garlic press? If we must sift the flour---we will need different tools than scooping it straight from the sack. Should the vegetables be peeled? The evaluation must be thorough. And here is where the chef must have a view of the larger picture.

The line from 2 to 8 is a peek into the future, a look at the desired result. Here the chef envisions that result and reassesses everything from the ingredients to his past experience with the recipe to assure himself the desired result will be achieved. If he begins the cooking process, will it result in the anticipated success. Perhaps he will need toothpicks to spear an olive on top of the sandwich, a sprig of parsley atop a sliced tomato, or a swirl of syrup to decorate the crepe---all those finishing touches which will make the dish as appealing as possible and stack the odds in favor of the meal's success. Has he estimated the correct proportions? Is the kitchen and staff prepared to begin the cooking---knowing how it *should* turn out?

The line from 8 to 5 represents his confidence in this careful assessment; only after the chef is completely convinced that all is prepared will he enter the event and perform the action of cooking.

The action line from 5 to 7 requires precise timing and judgement. He must time some things to begin first, second and last so that all will emerge ready at the same time. He must pay attention to quantities and to the quality of the process: How hot are the ovens or stove? At what point is the food transformed but no further to avoid burning or over-cooking? The many facets of the transformation itself must be accomplished in a timely fashion.

At LA the meal is presented to the customer---the community. Even if the chef has accomplished *all* he evaluated, prepared, envisioned and intended to perform... it is now out of his hands and up to the Will behind the event. Was the order filled to the satisfaction of the diner?

This process can only bring the event up to LA. In this example it can only serve the food. If we studied the function as the legal system, the attorneys can only present their evidence and arguments and then they must rest their case at LA and wait for a verdict at TI.

114

If an event is to be repeatable, it must conform to this process. An accidentally or haphazardly successful event is not repeatable and therefore does not conform to this pattern.

This is the paradigm of intentionally repeatable manipulation of circumstances toward ever more successful outcomes. Even with all of this---nothing is guaranteed. For instance: You are hungry. You are the cook. You have the proper tools for the sandwich you want. You have the ingredients you want. You know how it should look when you're done. You toast the bread just right. You arrange the ingredients in a way which pleases yourself. You even add an olive on a toothpick on the top. It is a supremely attractive, and precisely the sandwich you wanted. You put it on a plate, but then decide you aren't hungry anymore! There are no guarantees. However, you can stack the odds of success in your favor through following this most ancient and proven process.

We used the example of feeding the community. Yet the enneagramatic process may be applied to a vast number of things which must be irrevocably transformed: building a house, constructing a new device, hunting, fishing, our own attitudes, wrong-thinking, our very personality can be addressed through this pattern of right-thinking; the list goes on.

Now we have reached the LA of this explanation. You think of more questions; I'll return tomorrow and we shall continue." She rose to leave.

The young man was still jotting down notes and making his own lists of subjects for transforming, after his statuesque guest had disappeared around the bend in the road.

J. L. LAWSON

3
Awareness and Struggle

"Listen to the cry of a woman in labor at the hour of giving birth - look at the dying man's struggle at his last extremity, and then tell me whether something that begins and ends thus could be intended for enjoyment."
--Soren Kierkegaard

The next morning they were settled again in their usual seats, and sipping the first hot coffee of the day. The chilly breezes, which always accompanies the rising sun, were just dying down and the air was as crisp as after a sudden rain. The falling willow leaves gathered into colonies at the pond's extremities and every now and then a bass, or crappie, would slurp at a bug that had stayed too long on the roof of their underwater blind.

Mocha napped peacefully on the woman's lap, as she asked her host if he had clarified any questions about anything discussed thus far.

"A while back I asked you how I could best remove certain undesirable manifestations which I had noticed in myself. That question, apparently, solicited all the schema of the 'cards' as well as a further investigation of that ancient symbol in the direction of, as you put it, 'right-thinking'." He didn't know how to approach what he wanted to ask so he just plowed into it. "If I want to stop this unending chatter in my mind, what should I do? How do I think 'rightly' about that problem?"

She raised an eyebrow and nodded in understanding. "That is one of the most pervasive dilemmas plaguing any normal person. How to overcome our own inner dialog?" Her host nodded also with a mingled expression of ignorance, confusion and most importantly of surrender.

"Can you help me?" he asked simply. "You mentioned at the end of your last description how attitudes and even my personality can be changed through 'right-thinking.' Would you elaborate on the application of the process of the enneagram to those things? Those are the urgent changes I need."

"To begin with, let me explain precisely, according to our structural maps, the way *wrong* attitudes and *mis*-beliefs get embedded in the human machine. You can make a little diagram to follow along---three rectangles stacked upon one another and each divided into two equal sides will do nicely. Put a diamond for the Instinctive center in the bottom left box, in the box right of that a club symbol. Above the the diamond's box, a heart and to the right of that the spade's symbol. The top left box, of the Higher Emotional center, we know contains diamonds, clubs and hearts, and the highest center to the right of that contains all of the 'suits'."

He held up the sketch, she nodded and continued. "Impressions reach us through the Instinctive center and are recorded there. Whatever we perceive through our senses enters through that gateway. The Moving center functions are a response to those impressions. Sometimes impressions come in with such force that they are also registered in the Emotional center. For example: a beautiful sunset, the smile of a baby, sights, sounds, sensate experiences of such magnitude we attach meanings to them. Subsequent impacts of impressions upon the Emotional center, which are similar to previously perceived impressions, are written into the Intellectual center as memory. Those meanings become codified if you will. Now, if a man unites his lower centers and revivifies his conscience, those impressions which came into the machine under such a force they were registered the Emotional center also begin to resonate in the Higher Emotional center." She let him finish his arrows and notes before continuing.

"Now, if those last mentioned resonant impressions were perceived rightly, meaning that they are consonant with reality and actual experience, the Higher Mental center will begin to function, giving birth to objective reason and impartiality. The function of the Higher Mental center can impart that objective reason to the Intellectual center. This connection, in its most fundamental form, allows the Intellectual center to be able to constate, that is to be actively cognizant of, various realities without having to experience them through sensation. Thus the creation of an intellectual construct based upon the perceptions of objective reason will create the requisite supporting belief structure in the Emotional center, which it must do to underpin the given intellectual model." The host was nodding and finished the flow diagram.

"Okay, that all makes good sense. Where's the problem?" he mused.

"Ah, but herein lies the grand dilemma. We are subject to a wide world of influences which have nothing whatsoever to do with reason." She then listed---

"We are influenced by the form of the things around us, whether shocking or beautiful; we label them and forget them. We are unsettled when they are absent and conversely oblivious when they are present.

We are suggestible, hence our closely held notions derived from old wives' tales and urban legends---hearsay for the most part.

We are moved by relationship; our friends think thus and such, we think thus and such. Those 'others' think a certain way, we avoid thinking like that... however similar and logical.

We succumb to the superiority of others. No wonder advertising employs so-called authorities and celebrities, it works.

And all of this, while inside of us the turbid insurrection of 'I's persists unabated---our background attitudes and moods lead us to become either immune to, or susceptible to whatever is coming in through our senses, irrespective of our needs. And our own inept and uncontrolled gestures and postures, in their turn, elicit a response from the world we encounter diametric to our own wishes and desires." She paused to allow him to complete his lists.

"These problems and dilemmas arise when a man has *not* awakened conscience. So there is no impartation of reason from its objective seat of influence to the Intellectual center, and he becomes merely a slave of all that surrounds him; influenced instead by half-truths, misinformation, hearsay and the rest. This erroneous data so conditions him, that he maintains a truly false intellectual model of the world and reality. And just as before, the Emotional center inevitably creates belief structures to support those inaccurate, false and even deleterious constructs. *That* is the relationship between those centers whether for good or ill. *That* is how wrong-thinking, inappropriate attitudes, a false personality is formed. Unfortunately it doesn't stop there; these false structures of intellectual models and emotional underpinnings will condition a man's sensations and movements. This is readily seen when someone has been told repeatedly that, for example, 'snakes are slimy.' Functioning from an emotional belief structure and intellectual construct devoid of reality, *even* if that man were to touch an actual snake he will believe it is slimy, although it is certainly not."

The young man sat silently, a scowl was forming upon his features. "Uh oh... I just began a quick look at how many things I have heard and repeated *myself* to others about things I have actually no direct experience nor even direct knowledge. Somethings may have been innocuous enough in themselves, but this pattern of behavior is ubiquitous..." He began staring out at the pond without any focus in his eyes.

His gracious guest acknowledged his observations and consoled him, "Fortunately, the first step toward uprooting long held attitudes and the errata, of which we are so often unaware is even in our machine to begin with, is to see it for what it is."

She sympathized, "'...better to light a candle, than to curse the darkness...' is a message of hope to someone who at last glimpses the depths of his own darkness. Remember: Believe nothing! Verify everything."

He finally got up from his chair and went to rinse his swollen eyes and wash his face. When he returned from inside the house, she picked up the story as if he'd never left.

Hipolyta greeted them at the Salford station with embraces and so many questions, one might have thought she had not seen them for years, not the mere two and half weeks it had been. She would not release Titania's hand. Harry did mention to her before her departure from Venice that she would experience some unfamiliar emotions due to the separation, but she didn't realize that actually being physically parted from her sister would make such an impact on her psyche. It is easy to *imagine* being away from a loved one, while they are near, but when physical distance actually intervenes, only then can one finally recognize the inadequacy of mere intellectual imagination. "I can offer you several exercises which will lessen your emotional anxiety, but you will be here with Kaitlyn and me," offered Harry, then asked, "When does Aaron return for the day from classes?"

Hipolyta blushed, "Aaron gets home about four everyday."

"*Home*. Where the heart is..?" interjected Kaitlyn, smiling. Hipolyta became positively crimson. Titania squeezed her hand and asked about the courses she was going to take in the autumn. They nearly raced off up the stairs, and Harry watched after them recalling them as little girls in the hardware store.

Kaitlyn walked after them, "I'm curious about her choices also."

Harold and Chloe with Hannah went with Becky to meet her parents and to get her settled. They were invited for dinner and accepted readily. Becky was composed during the meal, that pleasant little smile playing at the corners of her eyes. Her mother noted the change in her daughter; she constructed her queries to elicit more about Becky's new perspective than simply the sights she had seen.

Harold tended to Hannah throughout the evening and Mr. Backhouse reminisced about when Aaron and Becky were Hannah's size. He mused nostalgically, "The long nights, the walks in the park. It was one of the pleasures of fathering twins that I always had one of them in my arms. Glorious days."

Harold nodded and related some of Hannah's best moments over the course of the tour. When it was time to say goodnight, there were hugs and kisses all around, and the Bessamers took a carriage home to Greengate.

An early summer shower greeted Greengate for breakfast. Aaron excitedly told of his novel approach to teaching his classes. He relied more upon questioning his students, challenging them to discover answers and solutions on their own rather than relying upon him for simply pouring information into their notes. The atmosphere in the lecture hall became far more conducive to discussion rather than lecture. His mentoring professor sat in on the last class and, although he was surprised by the format, he was genuinely impressed with the students' retention and understanding of the material. Hipolyta merely sat grinning with pride as Aaron explained his 'discoveries.'

Titania wondered how long it would be before her sister joined her as a thoroughly blissful married woman. She needn't have wondered. Aaron asked that he be allowed to take them all to an early dinner, which was greeted with approbation. As he left for the University he told Harry where to meet him after his classes. The venue led to but one conclusion, and Harry grinned. He knew what was coming, but then it didn't require the immense deductive powers of the now famous Sherlock Holmes to make this short leap to the obvious.

The pub near the Natural History Museum did have a reasonably priced evening menu, although it was not the cook's forté. The Livingsons, Connors, and Bessamers weren't discouraged by the fare. That Aaron had brought them back to the place where he and Hipolyta first met was worth having a meal which was below Jameson's standard of excellence; they weren't there for the cuisine. As before, Kaitlyn made the seating arrangements, Becky arrived and sat where Mandy had sat the first time. Hipolyta remained far more calm than she had all the last couple months when usually sitting next to Aaron caused her to smile uncontrollably.

After everyone had been served drinks, and the pleasantries had dwindled, Aaron waited for the first pause and began. "Harry, I am at a disadvantage in this endeavor yet I am compelled to follow my instructions to the letter," he began enigmatically. Harry's interest was piqued at this introduction, as was everyone's, save Hipolyta.

"When I was still a foolish and admittedly arrogant fellow, I was fortunate enough to make your acquaintance under circumstances for which my sister was wholly responsible," he inclined his head in sincere gratitude to Becky. "I have valued your friendship and I am entirely beholden to you for guiding me to the path which I now boldly follow with my eyes wide open." Aaron glanced at Hipolyta, and she offered him the confidence of her presence. "The inheritance I was to receive upon coming of age, I have arranged to have put back into the Trust---and not without a few raised eyebrows to be sure. My intentions, therefore, are above reproach when I ask what I am soon to ask." The company's eyes widened, yet they remained silent. At the same time they turned to Harry, who sat impassively also silent.

"I have known Hipolyta less than two months, yet I understand the truth of the inscription on the inside cover of your pocket watch." He again looked to Hipolyta, and she still steadfastly offered him her confidence in her clear and unmistakable expression. "Would you please read that inscription aloud to me, I do not know what is written there that I am to have already understood," admitted Aaron.

A growing smile of comprehension began to illuminate Harry's features as he pulled his pocket watch from his vest, opened it towards Aaron for his own eyes to read as he recited from long memory, "Time is the uniquely subjective phenomenon."

Aaron simply beamed. "Yes! I do indeed understand the truth of that, most intimately!" he crooned. "Harry, I ask for your blessing on us for my marriage to your sister Hipolyta. She is truly the wisest and most remarkable woman I have ever known and I love her entirely."

At last Hipolyta, who had remained so reserved throughout Aaron's ordeal, grabbed his arm and pressed her head to his shoulder and said, "Harry, I am very proud of the man I love; I also ask for your blessings and those of all our family and of our dear friends assembled here."

Becky rose instantly and went to hug them at the same time, "I am so happy for you," and she kissed Hipolyta, "and proud of you," and she kissed her brother.

Harry and Kaitlyn rose and embraced Aaron and Hipolyta. "On behalf of our father and mother, I offer you the blessings of our family. May all that is good and noble be yours as a son of this family." A bell tolled the hour at that instant and Titania squealed with the joy she'd long hoped for, for her beloved sister. Both were in tears, but all the handkerchiefs at the table were already moist.

Jameson hugged Aaron and offered his heartfelt congratulations for already learning to listen to his wife, especially when he had no idea why she did what she did, "A very good beginning, very good!"

"Well, kiss the bride. Sister, kiss your husband." Harry encouraged.

Hipolyta raised her face to his, and with the tenderness of deepest affection, he kissed her lips. The table erupted in an ovation which lasted nearly as long as the kiss itself. It was infectious; Harold kissed Chloe, Jameson kissed Titania, Harry kissed Kaitlyn, and Becky was beside herself in unparalleled joy---which is what a kiss is, essentially.

When they finally sat back down, the waiter approached and asked, "May I take your orders?"

Aaron answered for all, "A wedding cake please, and champagne."

The waiter smiled and answered, "Yes sir."

Hipolyta looked at her husband quizzically, and he nodded in the direction of the retreating waiter. She looked in the direction of his gaze and her mouth opened in silent shock. The kitchen staff were wheeling out a three tiered wedding cake and carrying several bottles of champagne with glasses for all. It was Hipolyta's turn to enjoy a surprise.

"Well done, well done indeed," said Harold, who truly enjoyed a well planned surprise perhaps more than anyone at the table. 'By the way Aaron, what will become of the Trust funds you've declined?"

Hipolyta answered for him, "Oh, there will be more little Backhouses before too many years. The Trustees will still get to make disbursements; *all will be shown for its true worth in time.*"

Harry raised a glass, "To love and to the people who bear it."

They all answered, "To Love and to those who bear it;" all drank the toast and celebrated their newfound joys.

Jameson and Titania arranged for a short trip to Edinburgh to visit his relatives, introduce his lovely bride, and mourn his mother and father's passing with his closest relatives there. Meantime, Harold and Chloe took Hannah for a last visit with her grandparents in Redditch, leaving Greengate to the daily routines of the Livingsons and soon to be Backhouses. When they returned from their jaunts, the Bessamers and Connors repacked their trunks once more in preparation for their leave-taking. Harold wired ahead to the Chelsea House in New York City, then to the Rail Companies for amended ticket reservations.

The next item on the future Mr. and Mrs. Backhouse's agenda was to visit his parents, and formally present Hipolyta whom they had never met. Aaron arranged to dine with them and gave his father a brief but pointed description of his intentions. Aaron offered her a few words of advice about the Backhouse matriarch. Hipolyta wasn't at all anxious over the upcoming meeting. After all, she was Harry's sister, Aaron was there trusted and beloved son... what should she have to worry about?

That Friday evening they arrived for the engagement a little late, as their earlier appointment overran its estimated duration. They were admitted by the house steward. They were seated in the parlor as if they were friends, but friends held at arms length. That should have been her first clue. But being with Aaron in his boyhood home and upon the errand they were, she didn't pay heed to the lack of welcome. Mr. Backhouse entered the parlor smiling. Aaron took his hand and introduced Hipolyta.

His father's eyebrows rose as he greeted her, "Harry's sister? My what a welcome treat. We do enjoy your brother's company whether here or at Greengate." This should have been her second clue, that his father, and perhaps his mother, weren't informed it seemed of just *whom* Aaron was bringing with him for dinner. A glimmer of a suspicion rose in the shadows of her mind and was dismissed. Aaron and his father discussed Aaron's University activities and such, then Mrs. Backhouse entered the parlor.

To say she was taciturn would be misleading, for she was very pleasant to her son indeed; that countenance, however, was not extended to Hipolyta.

"Mother," began Aaron, "May I introduce Hipolyta, formerly of Tahoe City, California, USA, and now of Victoria University, Manchester."

He turned to Hipolyta, "Hipolyta, this is my mother Eugenia Backhouse."

The ladies touched hands in a weak handshake and Hipolyta's suspicions came marching to the foreground. She remained impassive to the rising perturbations in her mind and heart, and simply continued to behave quite genially. She opened with, "Mrs. Backhouse, Aaron has told me so much about his boyhood and of his parents' great influence upon his development; I am very much looking forward to deepening our acquaintance," and she curtsied.

"My son often exaggerates, although it appears his description of you, some months ago, did not do you near justice. You are quite a beautiful *young* woman. Aaron you didn't mention how darling she is..." Hipolyta wasn't blushing, the growing rosiness in her cheeks was from another emotion entirely.

She responded as if truly complimented and they were led on a tour of the estate before adjourning to the Dining Hall. Mrs.

126

Backhouse took her arm as they walked, "You are Harry's *little* sister then, and a twin if I remember correctly?"

"Yes ma'am, I am both. My sister arrived with our party but is soon to return home, and I shall then be missing a dear friend and confidant." Hipolyta answered formally, wishing at all costs to be remain amiable.

"That will be a struggle I am sure. I know when Aaron and Rebecca were a little younger than yourself, they were nigh inseparable. You *have* met my daughter, haven't you? A very successful woman in her own right you know, succeeding in a sphere of industry which has historically been dominated by men. She is a very capable woman indeed. We are very proud of *her*." And in a flash of insight Hipolyta saw the woman before her plainly as if she had known her all her life. Hipolyta felt a measure of compassion mixed with a sprinkling of pity for this proud woman.

"I am very close to Becky actually. She is becoming more remarkable every day, I assure you," replied Hipolyta. "But tell me, please, what was she like as a girl that she should have become so powerful, so young."

The ladies continued there banter, Eugenia Backhouse made every effort to exert her superiority and dominance throughout the discussion. Those were the very traits which Becky had acquired in youth, and used with success in her chosen field. All the while, Hipolyta, through an extraordinary discipline, took the subordinate and submissive role which the elder woman tacitly dictated she assume. The tour of the estate was no doubt intended to cow her into a sense of awe and unworthiness, for whatever Aaron's parents professed as to being unaware of the purpose of the visit. they knew full well why Aaron and Hipolyta requested an engagement for dinner---and Eugenia was having none of it.

They at last arrived to the dining room. The table was set with the Backhouse's best silver, gold chargers and candelabras, the china was decorated with the family crest as were the crystal stemware for water and wine. There could be no mistake that the cabinets were emptied for this occasion.

Hipolyta made sure she made the proper gasps and that her expression of great impression was as sincere as she could manage. Even the Royal Shakespeare Company's Artistic Director would have found no fault with her performance. Her response had the desired effect upon Mrs. Backhouse, who was certain now that this pretty even admittedly beautiful backwoods girl, who was so obviously after the Backhouse wealth, must realize she was completely out of her own league.

Aaron held out a seat for his beloved directly across from his own seat, and held her shoulders in an affectionate squeeze before rounding the table. It took Eugenia Backhouse no time at all once she finally established for herself that she did have the clear advantage, to open the dialog of the most questionable timing of her son's unfortunate possible engagement. It seems Mr. Backhouse had not informed his wife of Aaron having declined his own inheritance; deferring it, instead, to the benefit his own future progeny. Perhaps it just slipped his mind...

Eugenia began, "I was most startled to receive news of Aaron's wish for this conference, however vague his intentions for the agenda," she maintained an almost overly formal air as she continued, "I can only surmise that you, my dear, are in some way connected with his decision to grace his family home after such a long absence." She almost glared through her faint smile towards her son.

"This meeting wouldn't have anything to do with the conditions of his Trust Fund I hope, for even the finest and well-bred of young men will make rash and impetuous decisions when faced with the loss or gain of considerable property." She let the suggestion linger there before the assembled, yet no one accepted the duty of confirming nor denying it, so she pressed forward. "For example, take my Aaron here, he is come of age and has now a foretaste of the great expectations which await him upon the occasion of his entering a suitably beneficial and acceptable marriage to someone of family and fortune. To allow himself to enter into any arrangement less than this would of necessity arouse suspicion of unspoken intentions. His future bride shall and must have her own resources, naturally, to avoid any unpleasantness over estates and such."

Mr. Backhouse did not once make any movement to caution his wife to bridle her overt elitism in front of their guest, nor could he. Aaron had made his wishes regarding this evening quite clear to his father and made him promise to allow his wife full rein of her prejudices and snobbery. Neither was there a response from Hipolyta, who had also been simply cautioned to allow Aaron to 'do the talking.' Aaron himself was not speaking as yet. So they ate in silence for a moment or two more, then Eugenia began again on a different tack.

"Hipolyta, dearest *girl*, it may seem to you at present that my son is enamored of you, no doubt on account of your native beauty, which appears to have some Asian influence, but which of course is of no consequence. Yet in time, perhaps very little time, beauty fades and the attraction is lost only to be offered to another. So you do understand how any petition that might be forwarded which involves a union of such incompatibility must be dismissed out of hand," and she waved her hand in the air as if declining a dessert. At last there was a response.

Aaron began to chuckle and that rose to a hearty laugh, which he soon brought under control. "You remind me of a tale from Chaucer, mother. Although it seems to be in counterpoint to the tale told by the Wife of Bath," he began. "With insufficient knowledge, and without any prompting, you have suggested and overtly stated that Hipolyta is low born, poor and although beauteous now, is doomed to eventual ugliness. I won't even honor with a comment your aspersions upon her native heritage."

It became clear that no one in the Backhouse family had ever risen to affront Eugenia before; her mouth wasn't gaping per se, although white-lipped in anger would also be inaccurate though closer to the expression she now wore.

Aaron recited from Chaucer to make his points,
"But when you talk about gentility
Like old wealth handed down a family tree,
That this is what makes of you gentlemen,
Such arrogance I judge not worth a hen.
Take him who's always virtuous in his acts
In public and in private, who exacts
Of himself all the noble deeds he can,
And there you'll find the greatest gentleman.
Christ wills we claim nobility from him,
Not from our elders or the wealth of them;
For though they give us all their heritage
And we claim noble birth by parentage,
They can't bequeath--all else theirs for the giving--
To one of us the virtuous way of living
That made the nobles they were known to be,
The way they bade us live in like degree..."

"For poverty you scold me. By your leave,
The God on high, in whom we both believe,
Chose willfully to live a poor man's life;
And surely every man, maiden, or wife
Can understand that Jesus, heaven's King,
Would not choose sinful living. It's a thing
Of honor to be poor without despair,
As Seneca and other clerks declare.
To be poor yet contented, I assert,
Is to be rich, though having not a shirt.
The one who covets is the poorer man,

For he would have that which he never can;
But he who doesn't have and doesn't crave
Is rich, though you may hold him but a knave.
It is a hateful good and, as I guess,
A great promoter of industriousness.
A source of greater wisdom it can be
For one who learns to bear it patiently."

"If I (grow) old and ugly, as you've said,
Of cuckoldry you needn't have a dread;
For filthiness and age, as I may thrive,
Are guards that keep one's chastity alive.
But nonetheless, since I know your delight,
I shall fulfill your worldly appetite..."

He enjoyed the recitation more than his mother, to be sure. Mrs. Backhouse was nearly fuming. "*You* have the audacity to chasten *me* for my legitimate concerns as a mother, who has only the welfare of her son at heart?" She stood as if to emphasize her rightful position.

Her husband said calmly, "Aaron, I know you asked me to remain silent, but---*Eugenia sit down!*" Although she shuddered at her husband's voice of command, as he had not once ever used it towards her, she did in fact finally gape in surprise. Then with a somewhat embarrassed expression on her face... she sat.

Aaron was careful not to smile, "Mother, I have declined my rights to the Trust. For my part, money is not a viable issue in this matter, but since you broached this subject with such vehemence I will say that Hipolyta is quite everything you have enumerated as necessary for my proper match. She is the beneficiary of an estate which makes the failing Backhouse resources pale by comparison. Her family is one of the noblest and wisest collection of remarkable individuals beside whom one could never hope to find a peer. And as to her 'fading beauty,' more light shines through her eyes than illumines the vast heavens---her beauty is ageless, timeless beyond compare." He paused merely to offer Hipolyta the confidence of his presence as she had, so many times done for him, "And finally, we did not make this appointment to petition for your approbation, although your blessing might have been a nice concession. However, I know how you are and have always been, and did not *expect* anything so courteous or generous. I failed to make proper introductions upon our arrival," he stood and walked around to Hipolyta's seat, "please allow me to rectify that oversight. Hipolyta dearest, may I introduce Winston and Eugenia Backhouse, my parents. Father, Mother, may I introduce my bride, Mrs. Hipolyta Backhouse."

Eugenia swooned; Winston rushed around the table passed his wilted wife and embraced his son and new daughter-in-law, "This is the most wonderful news. I can not express how utterly happy you two have made me." He glanced at his rousing wife, "Well done, indeed!"

The elder Mrs. Backhouse roused herself and blinked. Winston directed, "Eugenia, apologize this instant to your daughter-in-law and your son!" and his eyes showed there would be no quarter offered for ineptitude.

She gathered what little was left of her dignity and made the required attempt, "Hipolyta, I deeply regret my behavior and the callous words I have used against you this evening."

Then to her utter astonishment, Hipolyta reached for her and slipped her arms around her neck, whispering, "Aaron was perhaps too rough. You and I shall become much better acquainted and we shall speak no more of this evening."

Tears welled up into Eugenia's eyes and she offered a most sincere return of her daughter-in-law's embrace. Winston looked on, much more satisfied with his wife than he'd been in a long while. "Aaron, again, congratulations. I am not sure but that *you* may be the more fortunate one of this union!" Hipolyta turned instantly to Winston upon hearing those words.

"That is wholly unfounded! My husband is one of the most gentle, resourceful, loving, intelligent, noble and humble men of true integrity I have ever met. I am the most fortunate one in this marriage," she crowed.

Aaron smiled, "Obviously she's enchanted... but I do hope the spell holds. I am grateful it lasted at least through the ceremony, so that when she comes to her senses I have a contract to which to hold her." Even Eugenia chuckled with them at that.

"We have a very busy day tomorrow, so we will bid you good evening," announced Aaron. They had indeed, as there were many possessions he still had to have moved into Greengate, where Harry and Kaitlyn insisted the newlyweds reside; 'Until we're ill at the sight of you...' Harry had said.

The elder Mr. and Mrs. Backhouse saw them to the door and waved to them until their carriage was out of sight. "You were splendid after waking from your faint, Genie." Winston said.

"Yes it quite revived my wits. She *is* a most beautiful and caring woman, isn't she dear?" Eugenia cooed.

"Aaron has done very well indeed. They will make some very capable, handsome and pretty little Backhouses to be sure!"

Harry returned to the Waterhouse offices with Kaitlyn on his arm to make good her promise of meeting Mr. Waterhouse, which went swimmingly. Hipolyta purchased the texts for her autumn coursework in Interior Architecture and Decoration and began to study them with singular dedication. Kaitlyn spent a great deal of time in the reading room of Greengate with Hipolyta, reading and discussing the subjects presented in the books, until she had quite convinced herself that she would enjoy auditing the initial courses her sister had chosen.

When they next visited Becky, they had a proposition for her. Becky greeted Hipolyta with such effusive delight, one might have thought they had not seen each other in years. "I spoke with mother just this morning and she positively sings your praises! I can not for the life of me imagine how you managed that minor miracle, for she will say not a word about it. How did you do it?"

"Honestly, I didn't say more than a few dozen words all evening... I am at a loss to know how I might have made any impression at all. However, your *brother* certainly must have left a new mark upon the once conventional state of conversations at the Backhouse dinner table," answered Hipolyta.

Becky evinced her surprise at that, "Aaron? Aaron broke down the boundaries of convention at *mother's* table? He was always the one who policed those boundaries, and I have often been the one arrested, mid-dialog. Well, that *is* quite a development. I might look forward to more pleasant evenings with her henceforth. Now to what do I owe this visit?"

Becky listened to the outline and conditions of their proposal, posed well-considered questions about the timelines and business plan of the endeavor. She then assured her friends she would give the matter her most careful attention. When Harry and Aaron were informed of their aspirations, they applauded their foresight and industry. "After graduation, in two years you say?" repeated Harry, more to himself than aloud. Aaron said that the duration of the coursework could be reduced, if she resolved to attend four consecutive semesters, saving half a year's wait for the launching of their enterprise. The ladies were most amenable to the suggestion and apprised Becky of the accelerated plans. In the interim, Becky had made inquiries and conducted interviews with a few of her key contacts, all of whom she was sure would offer a most critical assessment of the possibilities and processes for pursuing the endeavor.

"I have good news and bad news..." announced Becky when she visited the next Saturday morning in mid-August.

Hipolyta was unsure which item of news she wished to receive first. Kaitlyn simply answered, "The good news?"

Becky ticked off on her fingers, "One. There is a dearth of truly capable designers in northern England employing the philosophy which this company is to espouse. Two. Although many established Construction and Architectural firms are reticent to award contracts to unproven design companies, let alone one owned and operated by women, there are innumerable opportunities to apply directly to businesses and individuals for their redesigning needs. Three. I have found very reasonably priced office spaces in a few respectable areas of Manchester. Four. The reputable suppliers in this field respect pounds not personalities, so the enterprise should have no concerns for meeting any deadlines to which it is committed," she held aloft her four fingers as a triumphant symbol of her investigations. Hipolyta and Kaitlyn graciously accepted that news with careful poise, then...

"And the bad news?" Hipolyta asked reticently.

Becky took one of each woman's hands into hers. She took a deep breath and began, "I have placed a deposit upon the best of the office spaces that I found. I have resigned my position with Brown & Backhouse and am committing myself to the formation of this company... if you will have me as a partner."

The ladies leapt to their feet and embraced Becky instantly, "Of course. Oh yes! this is better than we could have hoped! We did not think to presume that you would be interested in our idea, else we would have asked straight away!" Both women were speaking at the same time, and so rapidly, Becky could just make out that they did not consider this as 'Bad News.'

They next applied themselves to determining a name for their business venture; a company name that would not only describe both their capabilities and design philosophy, but at the same time represent themselves for who they were and make a professional impression in the estimations of potential clients. It was taking longer to accomplish this little task than it did to put together the business plan.

Becky had indeed come to the meeting with a full commitment to the venture; she moved her already packed and boxed possessions from her parents home to Greengate that afternoon. At a late dinner, the dilemma of the company naming arose as the focal discussion of the meal and carried on through the rest of the evening. Harry and Aaron offered idea after idea, and Hipolyta kept a list of every workable identity. They resorted to taking slips of paper, writing single word descriptors of each and every facet of their deliberations upon each slip, and selected them by random from a hat in groups of twos, threes and fours. This created quite an atmosphere of hilarity as the random words were assembled in various combinations. It became something of a Parlor Game. In the wee hours of the morning they happened upon a combination that, at that hour, seemed to answer their desires.

"Crafted Native Eurasian Design." After the rest had retired for the night, exhausted, Harry lettered the company name in large print on a banner. He added the word 'All' so that it yielded the acronym 'CANED, Ltd.' and he tacked it up on the parlor wall above his other sketches and drawings.

In the morning, even before getting coffee, each of the ladies visited the parlor to view the result of last night's efforts. Each of them smiled at Harry's small contribution as it both allowed for an acronym that symbolically reflected an element of the design movement, but also offered an abbreviated reference for clients. They set about divvying up the specific job responsibilities for each partner. There was a lot of overlap, but that was essential to their guiding principle that each partner should be the company itself when in intercourse with their clients and potential clients. Becky and Kaitlyn would of necessity shoulder the bulk of their early business, while Hipolyta attended to her coursework. Harry and Aaron watched their progress with great pride and offered encouragement at every opportunity. They also took over the lion's share of the household chores. It never occurred to anyone in the house to hire a maid.

Harry sent off a missive to Mandy and Gio in Venice at the end of the month. It wasn't intended to provoke a prompt response; he simply told them of the Bessamers and Connors' departure, offered a recounting of Aaron and Hipolyta's engagement and marriage, related the development of the CANED Ltd. enterprise, and asked after the growth of penzione business. None of this should have brought such a quick and informative return post from Mandy, but it did.

August 30, 1888

Most honored Harry & Kaitlyn,

I hope this finds you each in great health and prosperity. The Last Concession has taken off very well indeed; our rooms are full, the restaurant does more than adequate business, and the morning caffe still retains a devoted clientele. It is partially about the penzione, in fact, that I respond to your letter so quickly. I should very much like to take ownership of this venture. I am prepared at this moment to contact my banker and arrange for the remittance of the amounts you specified before your departure from Venice. Additionally, I would like to include a twenty percent return upon your initial investments. I have already spoken with that banker and have transferred the Grand Concession in Tahoe City into Jameson's capable hands. I am therefore most anxious for your response to this request.

Your devoted friend and student,

Mandy Hill

Harry read the letter aloud to everyone at dinner on the day of its arrival. He had made it clear to them shortly after returning to England, his intention that Mandy should have the *Last Concession* once she decided for herself that was what she wanted. Each of the household offered their own approbation to the arrangement.

"It will be grand to have a destination in Italy, should we ever again have the opportunity to enjoy a holiday..." remarked Hipolyta.

Jameson and Titania were greeted as returning heroes by their family and friends, partially because it relieved George, Belle, Lawrence and White Feathers from their *Concessions* tour of duty. They were formally met by their new titles, Mr. & Mrs Connor, which caused them both to grin proudly. Lawrence wanted to hear everything they could tell him about Kaitlyn and Harry, even though he had regular correspondence with both already. Everyone seemed fascinated by Mandy Hill's decision to remain in Venice and run a newly opened penzione. That Hipolyta was to stay for her University education was not so surprising as her marriage and the formation of a design company with her new sister-in-laws.

"You all were very, very busy over the last few months. We evidently had it far easier here than we thought"' remarked Lawrence.

Neither George and Belle, nor White Feathers voiced any surprise at the overseas developments of the last several months. They had been apprised and commended whole-heartedly by their own counsellors as each rite of passage was triumphantly passed. "I suppose we can get back out on the lake this weekend; what say you gentlemen?" announced George to White Feathers and Lawrence.

White Feathers replied with a sigh of relief, "That is the best suggestion I have heard all week!" Lawrence seconded that emotion.

Mr. Connor made an inspection of his kitchens and to his great satisfaction all was as it was intended to be. He held a meeting with the staff who had served so admirably under Belle's management and outlined the additions to the restaurant's menus which he was soon to incorporate. Each of the servers and kitchen helpers were former graduates of the Tahoe City School and already held their boss in the highest esteem, as he had been one of the three first gradates of their alma mater. The Concession transitioned into full operation for the end of the theater season and summer tourist trade without a hitch.

Titania had a long talk with her mother over tea. They decided that the Connors would have Bungalow Two as their own, unless at some point in time they wished to build a home of their own. They didn't have need of a kitchen in their residence since across either street there were kitchens they could use anytime; the ice box and franklin stove in the bungalow were more than sufficient for their meager needs. Titania also made a commitment to running the Lodges, which made Belle the proudest of mothers. "I had truly hoped you would wish to one day take the reins of that business. I can perhaps actually begin weaving again after such a long time away from my loom."

Once their things were moved into the new residence, the Connors hosted a dinner party at the *Concession* for all the family. Titania set places for their absent brothers and sisters as she knew *they* did at each meal on her and Jameson's behalf. Lawrence cried when, to begin the dinner, Jameson reiterated the toast Harry had offered at Aaron and Hipolyta's engagement party, "To love and to the people who bear it." The whole family swelled with the pride they all felt for Harry and his Kat.

The Bessamers resumed their life in Pacific Heights. One of the first things Harold had to decide on after his return to the office was the disposition of a fifty foot gaff rigged schooner, originally acquired by a now deceased partner of the company. With no wife or children, his will left everything of value to the other partners of the firm and Harold was the lucky recipient of the sailboat. It was presently docked at the Pacific Coast Steamship Company's Marina on Monterey Bay, so a trip south was arranged. Hannah was nearing her first birthday and Chloe planned a trip to Tahoe for the occasion. Before September arrived, Harold took his little family to Monterey for a long weekend and then a week to sail back the schooner. He had been to the southern end of the bay several times on business and marveled at its natural beauty as well as the thriving resort, Hotel Del Monte, which is where they lodged for the weekend.

Chloe was delighted by the resort's Victorian elegance and setting; it was so much like an overgrown version of Clive House that she was nearly homesick. They most thoroughly enjoyed the excursion along the seventeen-mile drive, the forested hills, the oceanscape and interestingly enough the Hotel's coffee service. Harold was also quite taken by the brew, as they had not had as good since Venice and Gio's Rapida coffee---very strong, very flavorful. He made a mental note to discover its source; always 'at work' Harold rarely let a good thing get by him.

"I do wish Gio had let me bring the plans back to the States; I was more than willing to obtain patents for him. What I wouldn't give to have his coffee every morning, let alone the manufacturing and distribution of his machine world-wide..." mused Harold over breakfast.

Chloe reined in her husband's imagination, "Sweetheart, Gio has led a life of nothing but hardship. It's small wonder he keeps his own inventions so closely held under his own control. It may be that after some time, and Mandy's influence, he may become more amenable to the idea. My, but that *was* good coffee."

She readjusted her little girl in her lap, "Hannah, my cherub, would you like to watch mummy trounce daddy on the tennis courts today? Daddy has challenged mummy to a match and your dear mother would sorely enjoy not doing dishes for a week." Hannah looked between her mother and father as if gauging the best candidate for her support.

Harold couldn't let that barb go unanswered, "Angel, don't be too hasty... neither of us have stepped onto a court since leaving Redditch. I'll be very much surprised if it weren't an absolute draw."

"A draw!?" Chloe raised an eyebrow. "If I don't hand you your hat in straight sets, then I shall suspect you have been practicing secretly or something else is terribly amiss," dared his wife. There was nothing amiss. Harold would be doing a lot of dishes the next week, beginning in Tahoe.

On Monday, after leaving the Del Monte, they took possession of the *Victoria*. Her underside had been repainted and new sails fitted before the change of ownership. Her prow presented a long bow sprit which made her overall length well over fifty feet, she could sleep ten adults comfortably and she was sleek and fast. Harold had not owned a sailing vessel before, although he had logged quite a bit of time at the helm of smaller ships in Bristol during summers breaks in his University years. They loaded their baggage, and after Chloe had secured Hannah in the saloon below deck, they headed up the coast to the Golden Gate and a new slip for *Victoria* at the San Francisco Yacht Club's marina at Mission Rock.

Before they wound up their visit on the Monterey Bay, Harold was able to obtain the name and location of the coffee supplier. It turned out to be a rather local company which had begun operations in Oakland, just a short ferry ride from San Francisco, very convenient. The Bessamers made that ferry trip as they set off for Tahoe and they made the short side trip to the food and coffee supplier's facilities. Harold was at once impressed that there were the seeds of a viable future in the little operation, so the "Del Monte" coffee supply company dominated their conversation for the rest of the journey 'home' to Tahoe.

Chloe pointed out that a reliable canned food supplier who maintained the highest thresholds of quality would be a real boon to not only California but to the rest of the country as well; the technology behind it was already well established back home in England. "I can't remember when the Clive House pantry wasn't simply laden with tins of all sorts of staples, mostly meats and candied things, along with many pickled items. In the second place, the first striving of any person is to fulfill the requirements of everything necessary for their body. No one will think of higher ideas if they are starving."

"Agreed. I'm sure there is no doubt that the 'business of food' is not destined for obsolescence in the foreseeable future. Yet your suggestion intrigues me, darling, are you hinting that *we* might take a more vested interest in this business?" asked Harold. This conversation was arousing his entrepreneurial spirit, never far below the surface of his thoughts.

"I am indeed," she corroborated. "Instead of your spending so much time away from Hannah and me on business which is more for the sake of just business itself, I could actually manage to support your absences were they for something as utile as food distribution. California will be, if it isn't already, the world capital of fruits and vegetables. And what with the extensive rail system established in the

States and refrigerated train cars, quality foodstuffs could be quite the attractive industry." Chloe was the true daughter of her father, far-sightedness practically applied to any endeavor, and she expected results no less than did her very successful father.

Harold was already way ahead of her but as with so many things between married couples, one of them must act as the regulator for their grander plans. "My love, may I be allowed a brief period in which to ascertain the market and viability of all these issues before you present the coffee house an offer for their operations?"

Chloe blushed a little; she had begun to get a little carried away with the proposition, "Perhaps between Lawrence and yourself that brief period could be reduced in length even further. Would you broach the topic with him? As I am more of a behind the scenes sort these days," and she glanced at Hannah snoozing peacefully in her father's lap, "I think Lawrence would be a most suitable partner for you in this adventure."

"Just so, just so, my love, a very good suggestion indeed. I shall speak to him upon our arrival," and the matter, for the present, was settled.

Lawrence listened to Harold well into the late evening, Chloe offered a thought every so often but by the end of the brainstorming session, Mr. Spelman was as enthusiastic about forming the enterprise as Chloe herself. "You are right of course, Chloe, an endeavor which might assist in a more direct way the progress of a sound society, even a civilization, is a far more satisfying vocation than that which either Harold or I have been involved throughout our previous careers."

In the morning all three persuaded White Feathers, George and Belle with Jameson and Titania to sit down for a while at the Concession and act as sounding boards for their ideas. They hoped in that way to perhaps gain a more objective perspective of what was quickly becoming a firmer opportunity in their minds. George and Belle listened also to the commentary offered by Fong Li in the form of a cautionary tale. "*The sandpiper is a type of bird that lives by the water.*

142

THE THIEF

He loves eating small fish and insects. One day a sandpiper was next to the water searching for his next meal, when he spied a river clam spread open sunning himself. The sandpiper looked hungrily at the clam's soft white flesh, and suddenly pounced on the clam poking his beak in. Immediately the clam clamped shut, hard on the sandpiper's beak and trapped him. The sandpiper struggled, still wanting to eat that soft juicy clam but unable to move. Then to the clam he mumbled, "If you always clamp me like this what good is done ? If it doesn't rain today, tomorrow or the next day, will you be able to survive?" The clam in reply said, "If I don't let you go today tomorrow or the next day what are the chances of finding a live sandpiper?" So both sides remained in this way. Later a fisherman happened to come along, without the slightest effort he grabbed them both and left. In the end both the sandpiper and the clam found their way onto his dining table."

Grandmama Lizette continued, *"In a venture of such competition, to watch for those moments of opportunity, and act swiftly, yields great benefit. When all strive toward the same goal, the journey becomes easier, and the aim is achieved."*

After hearing them out, White Feathers asked simply, "Are they interested in selling their business, then?" That was a poser which brought only silence for a moment or two, followed promptly by self-deprecating laughter on the part of the three presenters.

"Good point; well taken." Harold began, "Note to self: See if they are interested in selling their operation. Excellent. Next question?"

Belle suggested that "...if they held to their wish to unite the efforts of California farmers and canneries toward the singular purpose of making 'California-grown' fruits and vegetables synonymous with quality and reliability, they would do well to win the respect and support of the growers first and the canners would ultimately yield to their voices." George nodded.

Jameson, it turned out, was far more of a skeptic than any of the others. After all, it was Jameson who had been on the receiving end of food suppliers for the last many years and he had some very insightful suggestions for their consideration, all of which were

143

intended to get them to consider the consumer as the first priority after the quality of their products. "Even the best peaches in the world are useless if they're shipped improperly, too late or to the wrong place... Local representation of your organization is not a trivial matter either, I can't tell you how frustrating it has been to have only a relationship of correspondence with a vital supplier. Now if that can only be a regional rep, fine, but someone who is the face of the company and speaks with the authoritative voice of the company is invaluable to maintaining accounts for the long haul." Harold was taking notes and sketching out a workable company hierarchy, which was looking more horizontal than vertical.

Belle and George had only to add, "It would be nice to have out of season fruits and vegetables, that weren't dried that is," "...and if there were a grand variety, I can see really promising markets in both cities and rural communities..."

Chloe had to point out that tins of goods in England had certainly changed the daily shopping patterns of households great and small. "Although, there *has* been the constant challenge of proper packaging... the canning itself, I mean, and the materials."

The discussions and side conversations continued, Jameson and Titania went to the restaurant kitchen and put together a dinner for their guests who were still talking when they returned carrying trays of food. Jameson offered a few more encouraging words, "Canned items like meats, pickled things and condiments have found ready markets, canned fresh fruits and vegetables would be a most welcome asset not just to households but to commercial enterprises as well. While fresh fruits and vegetables are the first choice, naturally, to have canned supplies as back ups or even for use in routine dishes would be a very attractive alternative to depending upon the vagaries of local resources."

The next morning Harold and Chloe were again in the Connors' restaurant for pastries. It was when Jameson brought them coffee that their eyes lit up. "This is as good as Gio's! How did you do it? Chloe we must have this at home." Harold was exhilarated.

Jameson grinned, "Thank George. We sat down when I got back and I explained every thing about Gio's invention that I could remember. He asked a few questions, went to his workshop for a couple days and voila! Come see."

He led them toward the kitchen, adding "Of course, Gio's machine keeps a large quantity of water near steaming, so he can make more faster, but this does the job nicely. I've asked George to make a dozen of them at twenty dollars a piece. Right this way." There on a stove top were two sort of normal looking coffee pots. "The secret is obviously inside..." and he began to disassemble the empty one of the two. "You see the bottom is a sealed chamber, like a pressure cooker where the water is turned to steam which goes up through this screened chamber where finely ground coffee is placed, then on it goes up into the holding vessel in the top section. Pure simplicity."

Chloe had to know how he could grind the beans fine enough, as she looked at the large coffee grinder across the work space on another table. Jameson followed her gaze, "Oh, I can't use that for this. I have to use the burr grinder I use for spices---kind of a larger version of a pepper mill." He made a gift of the empty one to them and Harold was ecstatic. One might have thought, by his expression, that he had just discovered the cure to the common cold.

Hannah's birthday party was quite the gala; everyone sat on the floor with her as she attempted to destroy each wrapped gift handed to her. Most of the 'gifts' were boxes of cloth scraps and simple items, wrapped so that the little girl had something to tear apart. Belle and George were vividly reminded of their twins' first birthday as Hannah tossed the wrapping scraps into the air.

Lawrence Spelman accompanied the Bessamers back to San Francisco and they all stopped in at the cannery in Oakland on Monday afternoon. "No, the owners hadn't mentioned that they were considering selling their company at present." The floor manager answered Harold's initial inquiry. When they later were ushered into an appointment with a partner of the business, he asked, "What kind of offer did you have in mind? If it wouldn't be too much to ask, just on the off-chance Fred is ready to give up on the business."

Harold passed a reasonable figure, written on a business card, to the curious partner. His eyes rose noticeably and he whistled, "How did you arrive at this number? Are you psychic or something? This is nearly precisely our inventory, overhead, and labor costs plus one year's projected profits!"

Harold, Chloe and Lawrence looked at one another then back to the partner, "Mr. Chambers, I must admit it has been my occupation for the last several years to make this sort of analysis on behalf of my firm; I'd be surprised if that figure was off even by two percent," replied Harold without emotion.

"Fred, Mr. Tillman, that is, will be in this afternoon. I shall be glad to make him aware of your offer. Neither of us are getting any younger, and... well, I personally would like to spend a bit more time fishing and playing with my grandchildren..." Mr. Chambers smiled as he bid them good day and promised to send word of their decision as soon as possible.

Lawrence and the Bessamers went on to Pacific Heights and put away their baggage. Chloe was willing to allow Harold the night off from washing dishes, "Lawrence, how would you like to dine in the oldest restaurant in California?"

"So long as the food is fresher than the tables, I'm game," he answered. "Just let me freshen up a bit and I'll be rarin' to go."

Harold dressed Hannah in an outfit which matched her mother's dress down to the ribbon in her hair, and they set off for the New World Coffee Saloon straight down California Street from their neighborhood. The menu was savory and the food was too. When they got back home, they sat down with Hannah and played with her building blocks, and other toys until it was bedtime. With a bit of coaxing, she constructed a factory, had little trucks hauling canned goods and, to round matters out, insisted that she needed trains nearby.

Mr. Fredrick Tillman was indeed interested in their offer, but not so much in the way they anticipated. When Harold and Lawrence went to their appointment with him, they were mildly surprised at his counter-offer. "After you spoke with Claude the other day, he made me aware for the first time of his own desires for leaving the company. What I would be interested in, is not so much to turn over this cannery to new ownership, as I am to take on partners who would make possible the expansion of our line of products and extend our markets."

Harold gave the suggestion a moment's thought, "Mr. Tillman, here's what we had in mind..." and he elaborated the quality controls, the horizontal marketing and hierarchy, as well as his own and Lawrence's contacts in transportation and associated distribution networks. He included their own long-range goals for the enterprise and finally the essential need for a contractual enlistment of key California growers as the necessary resource upon which all else depended.

Fred listened carefully to Harold's plans and once completed, he beamed in consonance with the outline. "That's precisely what I have been hoping for. The offer you left us would go a long way toward accomplishing the fundamentals of that plan. So instead of using that capital for a changing of the guard, so to speak, what would you say to a partnership---which should provide you a very handsome return in the short-term, and present longer-term benefits as we gather more growers and canneries into the fold and propel our way into new markets."

It was Lawrence's turn to reply, "We had not considered the prospect of underwriting this endeavor only, but expected to have a managing say in it's expansion, shall we negotiate control issues and such, disbursements of profits and with whom final decisions shall rest?"

The meeting lasted well into the late afternoon so Harold invited Mr. Tillman to dine at his home that evening that they may keep the discussion alive and vital through to its conclusion. That was met with glad acceptance and they all left the Oakland office and headed for Pacific Heights. Chloe was unruffled at the arrival of another mouth to feed for dinner, there was plenty and she made Mr. Tillman feel right at home. The only real stumbling block during the negotiations was the question of *how* to implement a fully functional research and development arm of the company. The cannery was already near capacity and nearby real estate was priced prohibitively.

Chloe forwarded a simple question, "If the goal is promoting and distributing California-grown produce, why can't we contract another company as our own development arm? Isn't there a Cutting Fruit Packing Company near the New World restaurant? I am almost certain that I noticed it the other night."

"Frank Cutting is a good businessman," remarked Fred. "While he is a competitor, of sorts, he's also a visionary when it comes to opening markets. It's possible he'd be interested in such a contractual arrangement." Harold and Lawrence agreed with Fred that an appointment with Mr. Cutting was the vital last step in their planning.

Mr. Tillman returned to his Oakland home and would meet them at the Sacamento Street Cannery for the appointment once it was arranged. Mr. Cutting allowed time for the interview soon enough and was amenable to the contract; his own proviso that both companies benefit from the results of the development was most agreeable to each party. It was an auspicious beginning. Harold resigned his position with his, now, former company and picked up the mantle of Vice- President for Marketing and Sales of the soon to be public Oakland Preserving Company. Chloe and Hannah still saw him as much as before the transition, but as Chloe had stated earlier---she didn't mind it so much since her husband's occupation was more directly contributing to real benefits for regular people. Lawrence remained a 'silent' partner of the Oakland Preserving Company. Although Harold was an active and key figure in the expansion of the canned fruits and vegetables markets for

California-grown produce, he was as heavily invested as his friend and so was also a 'silent' partner in that regard only.

Thousands of miles away in Manchester, three women were also making a direct impact on the lives of real people. CANED Ltd. had just received their first major commission: the lobby and admissions offices of soon to be constructed hospital facilities. A wealthy philanthropist left a generous will, and some of the discretionary funds were used to buy land to allow the movement of the central Manchester hospitals out of the crowded city center. The ladies' design company bid for the project and was awarded the planning opportunity. Their combined efforts at the design yielded a most inviting and appealing entrance hall for the institution.

Harry was becoming less and less enchanted with the Waterhouse firm's staid Gothic Revival buildings albeit to some degree eclectic; the plans he assembled for so many various projects were beginning to run together in his memory. His own sense of design was growing toward an imperative of functionality, but at the same time remaining aesthetically pleasing. He experimented with forms as he applied the use of different materials to accomplish the constructions of them, often the materials dictated aspects of the forms and shapes, sometimes the reverse. As his own investigations and modeled experiments progressed, his satisfaction with the results of the Waterhouse designs diminished. What he did enjoy was the pervasive esprit d'corps which had developed throughout the offices since his 'team' conceptual approach had spread to other departments. He had the respect and trust of the Waterhouse principles and the devotion of the other directors; what he lacked was an outlet for his own designs.

Harry received a curious letter from an aspiring architect residing currently in New York. It arrived through the Waterhouse post and was handed down to him through his Director to decide if their should be a response, or no. Harry took the letter home with him and decided to respond in his private capacity as a fellow architect rather than as a legate of Waterhouse. The central question of the letter revolved around the question of extensive ornamentation and the utility of a given design. Were they mutually exclusive? Harry responded in a tone of moderation, attempting to bridge the philosophical gap by providing his counsel in the form of examples from his own extensive experimentations. He informed his Director that the Waterhouse firm was in no way involved in his return missive, and the principals were duly informed, however unconcerned as they may well have been. Corwin, the young architect, responded rather quickly and wished to continue the exchange of ideas; Harry acquiesced, and a regular correspondence ensued through the autumn and into the early winter months.

Hipolyta maintained regular correspondence with her sister, and between them they decided upon a plan, which if successful, would bring the family as close geographically as they were in spirit. On Titania's end, once Hipolyta had sent along the required documents, she made appointments and submissions of interest to various institutions and individuals. Hipolyta's part was to prepare the Greengate society for a transition. Neither woman even once considered their plan far-fetched or unworkable. It began, as so many things do, with little things.

CANED Ltd. received requests for bid from three significant institutions in the States. This wasn't so surprising as one of their early clients had been an ex-patriot recently transplanted to Liverpool. The fulfillment of the commission was very well received, and he had said at the time that he would be telling his friends back home about the ladies' gifted design abilities. One request arose from a small town in up-state New York, a library renovation. Another was from the midwest city of Ames, Iowa, for a new bank installation. The last was forwarded to them from a long established San Franciscan company looking to reshape its corporate image in tune with the new design and social philosophies of the times.

Kaitlyn was drawn to the corporate venture, Becky to the bank and Hipolyta was content to imagine what a library could be if properly arranged and appointed. They brainstormed over a central thematic signature, so that should they win one or more of the bids, they would present a singular vision and image for future commissions.

The twins' covert plan was very nearly revealed in one fell swoop. Aaron, who was enjoying the end of the second term of his associate professorship with hearty commendations from his mentors, received a letter of request for application from the young University of California at Berkeley to fill out their Classical Languages and Culture faculty.

He read the request letter to the others at dinner that evening. "I am simply dumbfounded by their seeking me out from among so many worthy candidates... the Victoria University does have an esteemed reputation in this field... but why me?"

Kaitlyn cooed, "Probably, they got wind of the rumor that you were married to a most beautiful California native and they wish to keep their faculty in the family, as it were!"

Hipolyta blushed as Aaron accepted that reasoning without question, then with an approving smile at his wife, "Indeed, that must be it in a nutshell."

Hipolyta recovered by changing the subject, "Harry and I are familiar with the San Franciscan Bank that requested the bid for renovation. In fact, we are long-time investors with Sutro & Co. We can surely provide sketches of the present facilities and descriptions of the neighborhood. Do you suppose it will be in our favor to already be part of their financial family? 'Change from within,' and all?"

Becky was delighted at this and turned to Harry for more information on the current state of the institution. Kaitlyn remained quietly observant of her younger sister's expressions and gestures from that evening forward. There was something very curious indeed in the remarkable coincidences that all their household had been approached by State-side inquiries of interest. Then the next morning came the unforeseen capstone to Titania and Hipolyta's careful constructions.

Kaitlyn Livingson gave notice to everyone that dinner would be promptly at seven-thirty that evening and she prepared a most elaborate meal for the Greengate household. As they assembled in the dining room, well-dressed and expectant, Harry assisted in the service of the meal. When they had all finished the first course of soup, he rose to bring out the entree. "Just a moment dear..." Kaitlyn said and laid a hand gently on his arm as he began to rise from his chair. "I would like to make an announcement."

Aaron had waited for some clue to the cause for the formal meal, "Good, I was beginning to think you were inaugurating a new precedent for our evening repasts." The others chuckled as they each had wondered at Kaitlyn's request.

"Harry darling, your Kat is going to have a kitten, or kittens. I really can't say at this point, but the Livingson family is growing."

Harry was so quiet, so transfixed at the statement no one dared move or breathe. The pleasant smile, always at the corners of his eyes spread to his cheeks and then his mouth and in an instant he was so radiant with inexpressible joy the others were also filled with a most pervasive sense of glorious goodness.

"My love, we shall make arrangements to return to Tahoe as soon as can be." Kaitlyn's expression made it very clear that there could not be a more proudly fortunate woman on the face of the Earth at that very moment. "I am going to be papa Kat!" Harry repeated. Aaron, Hipolyta and Becky leapt to Kaitlyn and Harry's sides and showered them with their considerable happiness.

"I suppose I should respond to the Berkeley University as soon as possible!" Aaron announced.

"Ladies, let's focus on the Sutro & Co. Bank proposal; I've a notion we can wow them if we pour ourselves into it," declared Becky.

"We're going to have our own kittens..." Harry repeated again. Kaitlyn had for the second time in their long history, managed to knock his socks off. MamaBelle would be proud, she thought.

MamaBelle was indeed proud. George and she were instantly informed by their counsellors of the health and good situation of their new grandchildren. *"Yes, George, it's twin girls again, you most fortunate man,"* intoned Lizette. *"Harry is, even now, making all preparations for their return. While we can not see the future, what we do see of the way things actually are, it would be wise perhaps to locate land for their consideration..."*

Belle informed White Feathers and Lawrence at breakfast the next morning. White Feathers was elated, "That young woman will make a fine mother to their children; Harry is a most fortunate man. I've said so all along..."

Lawrence was beside himself, "Harry's *children* are the fortunate ones, mi amigo, that man is remarkable."

George introduced the question of finding land for the couple to review when they returned. Lawrence wouldn't hear of it. "Harry designed that house up there on the hill; they shall have it for their own. I'm down here at your home all the time anyway; allow me a bungalow and I'll be more than contented. In fact, I'll post Harry about its availability straight away.

Titania came into the great room and sat down with a cup of coffee, "You all look to be in high spirits this morning..." Her mother broke the news to her. "OH MY HEAVENS! We didn't see this coming."

Belle looked at her daughter with a puzzled expression, "Who is 'we,' dearest?"

"Oh. Well," Titania sidled nervously, "Hipolyta and I have kinda been active behind the scenes, nudging events along to get our family back to Tahoe..." She reviewed all that they had accomplished towards that aim and finished by stating that, "The other offers that went to CANED Ltd. weren't my doing, honestly, that was from their own successes."

Those at the table were genuinely impressed with Titania's story. "Well, it seems Harry and Kaitlyn's news is icing on the cake," remarked White Feathers, "Remind me to never underestimate women."

Belle cocked an eye at her Uncle, "Since when did you ever underestimate anyone?"

Before the end of February, Harry had accepted Lawrence's offer of the house and informed his superiors at Waterhouse of his imminent departure and its cause. While they were disappointed at losing his valuable contributions to the firm, they were also unanimous in supporting his decision to return his wife to their family. "You'll do well Mr. Livingson; the colonies always need a fresh talent to guide their efforts toward civilization." Mr. Strenhowell gave Harry a list of a few American firms with whom he was very confident Harry would receive a most hearty welcome, should he wish to interview them. Harry was very appreciative for his director's consideration, and said so. He made all possible final arrangements for a smooth transition of his team's leadership and the projects for which they were responsible and bid the Waterhouse firm a last farewell.

Mr. Waterhouse himself gave Harry a few words of advice, one architect to another. "It's the builders who make or break a firm such as ours. Once you've found them---the ones that see with the same vision as yourself---don't let loose of them at any cost. Always focus on your clients best interests, even if they are unclear as to what those are---you must know and act. Be fearless."

Harry returned to Greengate to complete the relocation plans. Above Aaron's expectations, Berkeley was anxious to have him take up his position as Professor of Classic Literatures as soon as the next Summer Term. "A full professorship, mind you, this is unparalleled," he repeated in constant surprise. CANED Ltd. was put on the short list in the bidding on the bank restoration. All the ladies could do now was to wait and respond promptly to any follow-up inquiries from the Selection Committee. Meanwhile, the house's contents were crated and packed, personal possessions were carefully stowed or shipped in advance, and travel arrangements were finalized for their journey. To Becky and Aaron it was an adventure of tantalizing grandeur; they were poised to take up residence in the great western frontier of the New World, which had so long captivated their imaginations.

Winston and Eugenia Backhouse were as supportive as they could be, under the circumstances. They were soon to be bereft of the constant communication with their only children, which they had expected to continue throughout their natural lives. "We shall come and visit you once you're settled," they promised as they began to realize fully the implications of the situation. Their children were no longer dependents and if they were to maintain any connection with them, it was up to them to initiate those contacts.

Kaitlyn didn't suffer morning sickness, for which she counted herself very fortunate. She had only her memories of her own mother's constant recollections of carrying her, and the painful bouts of all kinds of discomforts she'd endured. Thankfully, she was not her mother's daughter in this regard. Harry made a final walkthrough of Greengate. The larger items, like the piano, were to be picked up that day and laded upon the ship in advance of their own boarding. All they would need to be responsible for were their trunks, at least that was the plan. He reviewed all the arrangements once more, aloud, with the others just to be sure he had not overlooked any glaring discrepancy. All, but Harry it seemed, had utter confidence in the preparations made, and said so.

"Darling, this is most unusual for you... Of what are you so insecure?" Kaitlyn inquired after he finished the review.

"I suppose I am feeling the early pangs of fatherhood, Kat. I am starting to second-guess even simple choices. 'Is this the proper tie? Did I inform the delivery men of the correct address? Should I keep my pencils and pens with my trunk things in case I wish to sketch during the journey?' It's quite debilitating. I thought it was just women who suffered the drastic changes to their bodily chemistry during child-bearing..."

"My dearest Harry," Kaitlyn held him close, "No one is more

careful and capable than yourself; you'll adjust to 'the change,' I'm certain of it."

"Thank you my love, I don't know what I'd do without your support," he admitted freely.

Aaron stepped back in the front door, "Well if the expectant mother is ready, the coach is waiting to take us to the station... Come along MamaHarry." Both he and Kaitlyn, with Hipolyta and Becky all laughed at that, and they said a last farewell to Greengate.

Harry adjusted. The voyage to New York was a renewal of sorts for each of them. The invigorating spring weather in the northern hemisphere, the vastness of the sea, the freshness of the ocean air and the brightness of the night sky undimmed by the competition of terrestrial lights, all lent themselves to a vivification of their spirits, and a confirmation of the confidence they shared in their future. Before their departure Aaron had purchased the texts which would be required reading for his upcoming courses and he reviewed them most carefully during the crossing. Becky assured Hipolyta that she would not be deficient in the least as a contributing member of the company simply because her University education had been abruptly shortened.

Poly replied, "I *was* ahead of the lecturers, and our own labors have given me experience I could not have gleaned from any text. I will continue to advance my studies and I *will* be a vital contributor, I promise."

Becky took her arm in hers as they walked the promenade, "Sweetheart, I have no doubts at all regarding your participation, nor for that matter about our future successes. We shall each do whatever is demanded of us, of that I am sure."

Hipolyta brightened at her sister's encouragement. "Did you respond positively to Chloe's invitation to stay with them? It was very generous although perhaps she's hoping for a live-in nanny for Hannah in the bargain."

Becky chuckled, "That would be brilliant. She's a darling little girl and probably has grown quite a bit since we last saw her."

Kaitlyn was glad her husband chose to keep his drafting tools at hand during the journey. She further refined their submission to the Sutro Selection Committee, and consulted Harry regarding certain basic design principles with which she had gained an intuitive grasp already. "When in doubt, omit rather than add. So long as your foundational design is sound, the rest will evolve organically as it progresses," he reminded her. "If we start with the premise that nature has crafted our own perceptions of the world we inhabit, if we return again and again to the themes revealed through out direct contact with our world, nature itself will inspire and inform our decisions as we proceed along a given path."

He offered an example, "When I designed the Spelman House in Tahoe City..."

"Our house..." Kaitlyn interjected.

"Our house," Harry corrected, "I had to mentally inhabit that hillside for hours in order to recall its various attributes, so as to incorporate its 'personality' into the design with the appropriate appurtenances to be installed in the plan. The views, the terrain and the weather each had to have their say in the final product. Then all of those elements had to bend to the will of the designer, as I had bent to their demands---A harmony, or symphony, if you will of the designer and the designed. Does that make any sense to you?"

Kaitlyn nodded firmly, "It clarifies how wonderfully situated and how marvelously appointed the results of your efforts were executed. It is truly a masterpiece. Wait until you see it for yourself, it is only a shame that it is so removed from common viewing. It is the envy of those few who are invited to visit."

"That was one of the criteria your father insisted upon and I agreed with the stipulation whole-heartedly," replied her husband. "As for the materials, they gave their own unique life to the appearance. The mountain stone, the firs and cedars, the red clay tile, the hanging decks, all making an organic statement of... 'belonging'." They chatted for a while longer and decided to take a respite from the cabin to stroll on the deck before dinner.

A little over seven days from the Liverpool docks they were in New York City once again. It was a short cab ride to Chelsea House from the Chelsea piers and the small company was greeted by the Concierge and shown to *their* rooms. This visit, like the last for Kaitlyn, was so full of special memories neither Harry nor Kat were able to make their way to the suites upstairs without a few tears of sweetest remembrance. While Kaitlyn finished dressing for the evening's activities, Harry wandered downstairs and sat beneath two very large areca palms in one of the stuffed leather chairs in a little group around a low table. He looked over the room of little sitting areas and was soon joined by Kaitlyn.

"Mom and Dad will be down in a minute..." she offered and then silently made a show of surveying the room's appointments.

"This is my first visit to the theater," said Harry, remembering the first time they sat in those very chairs and how he tried to seem at ease. He remembered vividly the young Kaitlyn Spelman, that charming and beautiful young woman with whom he could not manage to be at his ease while her presence that first time. His former state was no longer an enigma to him, he knew know in hindsight just what that first impromptu conference held for his and her future.

"I've attended performances since I was a little girl," she continued the re-enactment, "and I have practiced voice for three years; I hope to be a soloist someday," She crooned in an exact imitation of that earlier evening, "but I think I still enjoy Shakespeare best, even though there aren't any musical numbers."

"I thoroughly enjoy Shakespeare's sonnets and plays," he rejoined enthusiastically. "I mean I've read them all, and performed many of them, the plays I mean, with my sisters..." he added.

That was what had done the trick last time, and Kaitlyn again glowed and looked at Harry with that same appreciation. "You've read them ALL? I've only read the one's everybody knows, *Romeo and Juliet*, *Hamlet*, *Julius Caesar*, *MacBeth*, you know, what they require at

158

school?"

"Uh, well no..." Harry muttered as he'd done before, "I don't know what they 'require at school,' I sorta studied on my own over the last ten years."

"On your own!" Kaitlyn's awe-struck 'wow' was a whisper of reverence which she felt all over again only now it was from the perspective of a grown woman very, very proud of her husband.

Instead of the concierge interrupting their tete-a-tete, Aaron and Poly with Becky came and sat with them. Kaitlyn and Harry just laughed to themselves at their private replay and the properly timed intrusion.

"What's so funny?" Becky asked, caught off guard by their good humor.

Kaitlyn reiterated for the three of them the first time she and her 'new best friend' sat in these very chairs, what they chatted about and how they felt at the time. Poly was most interested in the description and said with a sigh, "Oh... you two have had the most romantic life."

Harry interjected, "It didn't feel romantic at the time... my palms were sweating, my mouth was dry and this beautiful young woman was obviously more interested in the fireplace than my company."

"I stared at the fireplace because if I looked into your eyes long enough I was sure I'd faint dead away... you were so... so much larger than life." Kaitlyn tried to add perspective.

Becky's tummy growled and she said, "I think I must eat or else..."

They rose and went to the Hotel restaurant. They ate well and retired. After the long day's journey and a most satisfying walk down memory lane, that Harry and his Kat should at last be in their Chelsea House bed at the same time was a most fitting end to the crossing and a good 'welcome home' to America. Their pillow talk was about when the due date was expected, names for babies, and refitting a room for a nursery, which colors... and they drifted off to sleep.

The great American cities and country sides, the mountains, rivers and lakes, plains and forests were so eye-opening for Aaron and his sister, they spent nearly the entire six and a half days on the train staring out the windows and were a little disappointed each evening as the light became too dim to watch the land roll passed them. When at last they reached the Truckee station in the Sierra Mountains, they were sure they'd see mountain men and indians and miners. What they saw instead were *very* well-dressed men and women, and the welcoming smiles of the Livingsons, White Feathers, the Connors and Kaitlyn's dad, Lawrence. It took longer for every one to make the circuit of embraces than it took the porters to remove their trunks and stack them near the large crates and boxes being unladed from the cargo car down at the other end of the train. Aaron and Becky were positively timid upon meeting George and Bell and White Feathers, the very source and root of the lives they now pursued with such confidence.

White Feathers extended both arms to Aaron, "Welcome Professor, well come indeed," he hugged the near shaking young man and kept his arm around his shoulders when he hugged Becky as well. "You two are most honored here," he said. "Tania and Jameson have told me quite a lot about you two and I am glad to at last meet you in person." Hipolyta just beamed at her Great-uncle's warm reception of her beloved and new sister. Belle and Kaitlyn walked arm in arm and were still in rapt conversation when they boarded the carriages for home. Harry and his father oversaw the loading of the wagons and in a few hours they were on the River Road headed to Tahoe and home, following the others who were well ahead of them on the road.

George asked about his architecture career and about his plans, "It seems to me, there is nothing keeping you from setting up shop right here. There are more and more families moving into the area from the cities and they appear to have more money than sense. You could do well locally. I'm certain that if you were to have a hand in

---

Aaron and Poly's house in Berkeley, your reputation would surely spread..."

"Father, I had not thought of anything else. You're quite right, of course, an example of my work in the Bay area would be quite the advertisement for an aspiring architectural firm." As they came round the last bend, Harry's expression widened. "I had no idea that the village would be so grown after... wow, it's been five years almost to the day since I left."

George continued to iterate the previous subject, "And another opportunity may come through Harold and Chloe, they are the silent partners of a cannery in Oakland and the factory, from what I've been told, could stand a redesign---but without allowing for a cease in activity. Now *that* sounds like a real challenge," winked George and he sat back in the carriage seat beside his son. He began to work out how he'd pull off that task. Next to him Harry had taken up the little challenge as well. They were two peas in a pod.

The laded wagons rolled up the long entry road to the house on the hill and all hands were needed to relieve them of their burdens. It was getting late in the afternoon when the last emptied flatbed trundled down the hill and back to the livery. Jameson and Tania began a meal in the kitchen, Aaron and Poly helped when they were allowed. Poly had insisted they stay in her and Tania's old room with Belle and George for the several days before heading on to Berkeley. Becky stayed with Harry and Kaitlyn for the time being. All the party were gathered out on the hanging deck overlooking the little valley and the Tahoe in the near distance. Harry was quite satisfied that his plans, made in absentia, had been executed so very well and the views were precisely as he'd envisioned.

"I told you so!" reminded Kaitlyn as she took his arm and gazed with him at the long shadows of the Sierras reaching across the lake.

Lawrence made the transfer of title official and handed Harry and his daughter the deed. "Welcome home," he was just able to say in an emotion-choked voice. "I am so exceedingly happy, words fail me..." Kaitlyn hugged her father again and wiped his tears with her sleeve.

"Thank you Daddy, this was a most generous gift," she said simply.

"It is truly the least I can offer; my life since coming here has actually begun anew. Gone is the man I once was, and in his stead is a heart that is open and a mind that is clear." He looked to George and White Feathers, "Those two men there have been my guides from a dark land into the bright light of this new life." Both George and White Feathers inclined their heads in receipt of the praise.

"And he has still to learn how to make the perfect pastry!" White Feathers chided in fond memory of their long months in the *Concessions'* kitchens together.

The four from Kat's kitchen emerged with plates and trays of food and they all helped themselves, impelled by their great appetite from the afternoon's labors. Stories were retold, information was exchanged, some plans were made, but mostly there was the all pervasive experience of greatest joy which kept smiles upon the faces of George and Belle---their children were home, together at last, happy successful and healthy. And as if that weren't enough, grandchildren were on the way. Belle took Kaitlyn's arm and they went inside to have a very important chat, matriarch to wife and future mother, woman to woman, about certain unspoken aspects of what being a Livingson really means...

"Kaitlyn, my own daughter, I have a few things to tell you. Our family is far more blessed than anyone suspects and I have made preparations for your introduction into those blessings..."

Kaitlyn could not imagine what MamaBelle was leading to, "Introductions?"

Belle continued, "Lizette, this is Kaitlyn. Kaitlyn say hello to my Grandmama Lizette." Kaitlyn turned her head, looking around the room to see the person with whom she was being introduced. Then in a clear voice, *"Hello child, I have watched you for quite some time, and am very proud to at last make your acquaintance."*

Kaitlyn's eyes sprang wide, and in a faltering voice she answered, "I am pleased to meet you GrandMama Lizette..." Then in a tone of absolute wonder she asked Belle, "How is this possible!?"

Before Belle would answer, there were more introductions to make, "Great grandmama Poriva, this is Kaitlyn. Kaitlyn this my Great-grandmama Poriva." Again the warm reception by the strong voice of an extraordinary woman. The introductions went on for some time until all those ancestors who still offered there insights and counsel to George and Belle had made their greetings.

Lizette picked up the conversation, "*I didn't hear my grandmama or her sisters, nor did any of us, yet we have always spoken to each other when freed from the flesh and bones of Earth, and at last become the air and sky of the Great Spirit.*" Then her Great-great-grandmama responded, also, with the same story that was offered to Belle, so long ago:

"*Both the spider and the silk worm spin silk. One day the spider said, "I admit your silk is better than mine, your silk is both yellow and white, dazzling and bright. You use the silk that you spin yourself, to make a beautiful cocoon, then live inside-- thinking falsely you are kings.*

In your little cocoon you wait until the women come and put you in scalding hot water ,and peel your silk off strand by strand. Then your beautiful cocoons are all gone. What a shame, though you have the ability to create such beauty, you die because of it, is this not stupid?"

The silk worm thinking about what the spider said, answered "Our actions are actually like suicide, but we spin silk so that people can weave beautiful brocades, giving all the people the ability to look beautiful, can you say, then, that our labor is a waste? Look at you spiders, all that you weave for is to make a trap that will let you eat the cute little bugs that fly into it. You don't regret it either, but don't you think that that is a little cruel?" she finished. The story's last question hung like a caution in the quiet room. "*You see,*" she explained, "*like the silk worm...*"

Kaitlyn was seeing the larger picture at last and interjected. "You have left life behind, though your 'silk' need not be lost with your flesh and bones. Your wisdom can go on being useful. Not like the spider, whose achievements are for himself alone."

163

Lizette answered simply, "*Precisely. You are privy to our counsel a little sooner than expected because we are unwilling to leave the birth of your twin daughters to chance.*" She let that knowledge sink into Kaitlyn's understanding before saying any more.

"Twins?" Kaitlyn mouthed, "Daughters?" Her face radiated with the glow of angelic pleasure.

Lizette, then continued, "*Belle had our assistance with Titania and Hipolyta during the time she carried them, and Belle has assured us that this assistance should, most definitely, be extended to you. We concur. It is the tradition of this family that upon the birth of the first born our succor is delivered, yet we are of one mind upon this exception. Harry will not hear us until the appointed hour. Although, truth be told, he might not require nearly the input those before him certainly have needed. Your husband is a most rare individual. He has already gone further than most of us ever imagined a man could travel on this journey.*"

Kaitlyn was so overwhelmed by the gift of this boon and the honor with which these most venerated individuals held her husband, she was speechless. Her tears were rolling down her cheeks and Belle put her arm around her. "This is what being a Livingson really means. Welcome to the family."

Kaitlyn threw her arms around her mother's neck and sobbed. She had never been so totally overcome with such pure gratitude and love at the same time. Poriva added, "*By the way, dearest, your dispatch of that miscreant upon your arrival to England was a grand feat to behold, we were all most pleased you so thoroughly captured Harry's attention and married him before the moment evaporated. Most pleasing indeed.*"

Belle and Kaitlyn laughed through their tears at that. "Thank you, Great-grandmama. That means a lot to me." Kaitlyn humbly replied. Harry came through the living room with empty plates and trays.

"What are you two up to? Trading secrets?" he asked off-handedly.

"You have no idea, my love... You have no idea," replied Kat with a wink to Belle.

The next day was Saturday and the Great Tahoe Tournament was just a week away. Poly and Tania fetched their horses from Mr. Pierce at the livery and took Aaron and Becky on a tour of all their favorite places. Neither of the Backhouses had spent very much time directly upon the back of a horse before, and to be riding horseback around Tahoe, in the Sierras, was both a thrill and the fulfillment of life long dreams for each of them. They rode along the Lakeside Road, took trails into the mountains, and splashed through creeks on the grand tour. Becky was nearly convinced that she might just beg off her acceptance of Harold and Chloe's kind offer and stay right here in the mountains. The great Tahoe and its environs spoke to her soul in a voice she'd never heard. The very stones of the paths and trails called to her, the gentle breezes which set the leaves to dancing above her head and the grandeur of the mountains themselves all whispered their secrets to her ready ears. For his part, Aaron was like a boy again, joking, and singing snatches of folk songs he thought he'd long forgotten. Poly was the proud wife of a very happy man. "Poly, we must come here often, upon every occasion we can make an excuse!"

"Yes sir, my love. As you wish," replied Poly with a wink to her sister.

Harry moved furniture around until Kat was satisfied. Then they took a look at the room selected for the future nursery. Kaitlyn had to be careful not to spill the beans about their twins. So instead, she simply played the role of the unreasonable wife as she insisted upon the extravagances she knew would be needed, but were more than a single child would require. "And we'll need a couple rocking chairs, a changing table in here and in the bathroom. I think a nice robin's egg blue would be good for the walls, perhaps trimmed in a pale yellow and a wainscoat high band of soft pink..."

"Pink and blue?" Harry mused. "Whatever you say MamaKat..."

On Sunday morning, Harry met Jameson and Aaron at the little dock below the Livingson house, very early. In just a while they were joined by the surprised faces of George, White Feathers and Lawrence, who were ready to set out on their weekly fishing trip.

"Mind if we join you, Gentlemen?" asked Harry, smiling as broadly as Jameson and Aaron beside him.

White Feathers answered for his mates, "The more the merrier, but bring your own beer!"

"Already handled," Jameson patted the overlarge basket already stowed in the larger boat.

George and White Feathers arranged the rest of their gear and Lawrence took up a position at the stern at one of the oars. "Aaron, come on back here," he called, "I'm told you know a thing or two about how this operates."

Aaron's fond memories of his recent training in the canals of Venice came forward to add to his present glee at assisting in rowing the boat for such venerable personages. Jameson took the stern of the smaller sampan; Harry settled in the bow and they were off. Lawrence and Aaron settled into a cadence of strokes which both men could maintain without effort. And every so often one of them even called a 'shift,' which was executed flawlessly in tandem. If the rest of the day and night held no more for Aaron than this excursion, he would count himself one of the most fortunate of men.

The little flotilla made for land near the southwestern arm at the entrance of a few streams which drained into the lake. Once the boats were unpacked and tents erected, fishing rods were brought out and assembled. Harry handed Aaron a fly rod of his own manufacture. "This is a fly rod, Aaron." He put the pole into his friend's hands and methodically went through the process of instruction so that Aaron could repeat it easily, as needed. When they reached a bend on one of the streams and separated to take up their own waters for a while, Harry stayed with him and gave him some brief tips on how best to use his new tools. Before an hour was out, Aaron had his first fish on the line and was fighting it to the bank of the stream. The other men, near enough to see the spectacle, smiled

166

at the sight of Aaron beaming in triumph over the handsome rainbow trout in his upraised hand.

Jameson selected the best of the day's catch to clean and cook, the rest he let George and White Feathers clean and prepare for drying. Bottles of beer were passed around and the men relaxed into an engaging discussion of relative consequence; they were simply enjoying the company of like-minded companions and life at that moment was no more than that. When the fish was ready, Lawrence and White Feathers commented on the subtleties of the spices Jameson had employed, and the tenderness of the meat, "George, please learn how he did this so we won't have to endure your burnt fishes anymore," White Feathers chided his buddy.

"Burnt! I never burnt a fish!" he answered in kind, "Now, maybe one or two of them sat in the pan too long until you rescued them, but that's just because you're slow at most things anyway..."

They joked, laughed, sang a song or two for which they all knew the words and then their yawns grew more frequent than their words. Before they retired, White feathers as the eldest, spoke for his friends.

"A toast to our honored guests. You three men are the embodiment of all that we had hoped for in sons. We are humbled and proud that we have lived so long to see the fulfillment of this family's promise for the future, in our children. To Harry, Jameson and Aaron!" George and Lawrence raised the toast with him. "To Harry, Jameson and Aaron!"

On behalf of his brothers, Harry answered, "We are the humble bearers of truth and we stand in the shadows of the great men who have come before us. To George, White Feathers and Lawrence... long life and joy." Jameson and Aaron answered with him, "To George, White Feathers and Lawrence."

Aaron finally knew what it was to be surrounded by true men and he slept in the confident knowledge that his journey was directed by the sure hands of those who knew the way and that he, unquestionably, at last had the strength to follow.

Lawrence and George accompanied Aaron, Poly and Becky to Berkeley and helped them find the married faculty housing which had been arranged as their temporary quarters. After their trunks were deposited there, they looked along the streets of the northern end of East Berkeley for a suitable homesite until they found a lovely shaded site near the Codornices Creek. George made a note of its location and sketched out the interesting aspects of the surroundings noting the views and landmarks so that Harry would have something with which to begin a working plan. Before taking the train all the way to the Oakland pier, Lawrence took them on a short side trip to see the cannery. Again George sketched out the neighborhood; Lawrence assured him he could provide the existing plans for the factory. Then they continued on to the ferry to San Francisco. Harold, Chloe and Hannah met them at the landing and escorted them to dinner.

They ate once again at the 'New World,' and afterward they all went to the Pacific Heights house where they settled in the drawing room for a nightcap. Lawrence again commented on the curious arrow and ribbon 'trophy' which was so prominently displayed above the hearth. George looked at the item, turned to Harold and asked him directly, "Please tell me about this curious trophy."

Harold looked to Chloe and she put Hannah into Poly's arms, "Mr. Livingson, Mr. Spelman, Aaron, Poly, Becky... Harry bade us to be *very* careful to whom we should tell this story. It is not in his nature that anything he does be aggrandized in any way as you are no doubt aware. However, as you sir are the wellspring, so to speak, of our line, I think Harry would approve of his own father hearing the tale. Darling?"

Harold began, "It may take both of us to do it justice, dearest." He proceeded to recount the unbelievable story from beginning to end just as he had told Jameson in confidence a year before. After relating how Harry had not only caught the arrow in flight, but had retrieved the ladies' hair ribbons then put that 'trophy' into his own hands, Harold repeated Harry's final words---"...as serious as death, he said, 'Because your wife wished for you to see with your own eyes what is truly possible, in honor of her love for you, I condescended to make this little demonstration'." When his voice at last fell silent, the gaping mouths and wide staring eyes looking back at him were all the response he'd expected---all that could be expected.

Even George was agog at the tale of the arrow---and he had trained the lad himself. "I am speechless; other than to say, thank you from the depths of my heart,for keeping this treasure and giving me this story." He bowed; then all the others followed his lead They simply had no other idea how else to respond.

By the evening of the next day, Aaron and Poly were situated in their little house. Arrangements were confirmed for sending along more of their possessions---now that they could determine their exact space and needs. Lawrence and George returned to Tahoe. George gave Harry the sketches he'd made and Lawrence delivered the factory plans. Harry put them into his ever-enlarging queue and turned back to the tasks Kat had set him for the next few days. "I thought that being dis-employed, I would have more time on my hands..." he mused and cheerfully began painting the nursery.

The first visitors to the village for this Summer Season were due any day and Kaitlyn did what she could to assist Tania in the final preparations of the Bungalows. This also meant that the new theater season for the Tahoe Players was about to begin; this year's production was to be *Much Ado About Nothing*. Miss Sarah Bunker had leveraged the popularity of the village's acting troupe and created the Junior Players. Their inaugural presentation which was to run through the summer as a matinee to the Friday productions was *The Tempest*. The openings were to coincide on Friday next, and all shows were sold out. Several of the junior thespians were employees of the *Concession* and Jameson was happy to have them in costume, if they pleased, when they served at the restaurant on the evenings after their shows.

Aaron and Poly returned for that weekend, as did the Bessamers and Miss Backhouse. Belle and George entertained Poly and her

169

husband while Kaitlyn played hostess to their family from Pacific Heights. When the afternoon of that most anticipated day arrived and all was made ready, the audience began to gather at the school-theater entrance and in the *Concession*. The children had certainly outdone themselves in creativity. The sets were compelling though stylized, even extravagant. Only once did Caliban drop a line, but the actor quickly recovered. Since it was the 'drunken' scene only those thoroughly familiar with the play's script even noticed. When Prospero broke his staff and Ariel was at last freed, the audience rose in a resounding ovation which quite surprised the young thespians. Miss Bunker was presented a bouquet by her 'Miranda and Ferdinand,' and the curtain came down to the still loud applause of the crowd. Miss Bunker reappeared and reminded those of the audience who had tickets for the evening's performance by the Village Players, that they should return in two hours time to find their seats.

Kaitlyn and her sisters along with Jameson, all went forward to congratulate Sarah on her marvelous accomplishment and the abilities of her students. "High praise, indeed, coming you four," accepted Sarah, humbly. "You *will* be here this evening?"

Kaitlyn assured her they wouldn't miss it for the world and then promptly invited the cast up to the house for a party following the opening performance. Sarah said she'd pass the invitation along and would save them seats in the front for the show. The Livingsons, Connors, Backhouses and Bessamers adjourned to the *Concession* for a light meal and a drink before returning to the theater. Just after they had taken their seats for the play and before the beginning of Act One, Mr. Avery Goodman appeared in costume in front of the curtain and made an announcement:

"Ladies and Gentlemen, this season's inaugural performance by the Village Players is marked by a most auspicious circumstance. We are this evening honored by the presence of the founder and first director of our enterprise. A woman whose inspiration lent our fledgling company the courage and dedication of spirit to establish this village's tradition of thespian excellence. Will Mrs. Kaitlyn Elizabeth Speling Livingson please stand and receive our humble gratitude?"

Kaitlyn stood up in acknowledgement of the rousing applause from the audience. She was instantly presented with a most lavish bouquet from Miss Bunker who winked as she bestowed the flowers on her friend. Kaitlyn raised the gift for all to see, made a bow of her head to Mr. Avery and then in a dramatic flourish she presented the bouquet to Belle, for all to see.

Harry whispered to her, "...even though there aren't any musical numbers..." She blushed at that, but Mr. Goodman wasn't finished.

"With her this evening are also a few of our most distinguished founding members: Mrs. Hipolyta Livingson Backhouse, Mr. Jameson Connor and his wife, Titania Livingson Connor. Please join us in a hearty show of gratitude for their most valuable contributions to this Society."

Poly, Tania and Jameson stood and received resounding applause as well. Once the audience was settled again in their seats, the play began. The tale of the resolution of pride in Benedict and Beatrice and their story of love's struggles was a rousing success. After the cast and crew took their final bows, they all retired to the Livingson House on the hill for the cast party. Harry with Hannah in his arms played the charming host. They must've heard sixteen different stories of Kaitlyn's involvement with the company; each of them glowing and every one of them reminded Harry how utterly fortunate he was to have 'persuaded' her to marry him. He easily agreed whole-heartedly with each person's accolades proffered throughout the evening's revelry.

Harry and Kat went with the Bessamers and Backhouses when they departed for their respective homes in the Bay Area. He assessed the site previously selected for Aaron and Poly's new home and added his approving support of their choice. While Kaitlyn and Poly set up some of the furniture and things brought along from Tahoe, Harry and Aaron met with the owners of the property in question. During a brief negotiation over the price Harry established primary options for adjacent parcels and gave Aaron the necessary funds to proceed with the purchase.

Poly and he had discussed this point and Aaron told him, "Harry, this is very generous of you but once Poly and I have established ourselves here, I insist that you allow us to repay you."

Kaitlyn spoke for both of them. "Aaron, dear. Poly, my sister: Not a day goes by that we do not think of the happiness and well-being of our family. If *you* think it is *absolutely* necessary to do this, then I will tell you that those monies will be put directly into an educational fund to benefit all Livingson children. I remember that, as Backhouses, your own children shall be handsomely provided for from *your* family's Trust. That is a relief, of course. And, like that Trust, this one shall be for *all* Livingsons. Should you decide to contribute in earnest, it will be an honor to make those deposits on your behalf."

Aaron and Poly were determined that they should do so; then Harry introduced a second issue for their consideration. "The design and construction of your future residence is to be something of an advertisement in the Bay area for both my upstart architecture company, Sierra Architecture, and for the CANED Ltd. design company. So those costs will naturally be absorbed by those two companies. If you insist on paying for it out of your own pockets, you would be essentially repaying yourself, if you see what I mean."

Neither of them could take issue with that rationale and so the plans were laid out on the living room floor as they each offered comments and suggestions for tweaking Harry's drafts before finalizing them and set the date for ground-breaking. When Harry and Kat returned to Tahoe, he wasted no time making the final plans and forwarding copies to Aaron and to Becky. Then he enlisted Becky and White Feathers to assemble construction crews, which wasn't as difficult a task as it might otherwise have been. Becky needed only three or four master carpenters and masons with support crew of laborers; White Feathers easily found competent candidates, and that was that.

The summer was a great success for all concerned. The Bungalows and *Concession* were busy as ever. Tania also began spending more time at the Mercantile to relieve her father of his daily presence there, which allowed him time to work on special requests for his fly rods. Aaron's first term at the University was well attended and led to very full attendance for the Autumn Term. The Sutro contract was awarded to CANED Ltd. and so the three ladies split their time between that job and that of the Backhouse Residence project in Berkeley. Harold and Harry met with Mr. Tillman and settled on a scheduled and phased renovation of the cannery. Fred Tillman was elated that the factory would become the state-of-the-art facility he'd always hoped it would be. Harold recognized what an attractive selling point that renovation would be for future clients and growers as well as leverage in merger opportunities with other canneries.

As Kaitlyn's due date approached, Aaron and Poly took up residence in their new home. At Poly's insistence Becky also moved in, not as a temporary guest but as a family resident. All three Backhouses traveled with Harold and Chloe when they brought Hannah to Tahoe for her second birthday. All the family, then, was together when Kat went into labor. She was surrounded by nearly all the women she held most dear in the world, missing only Olivia Allcock and Mandy Hill. To everyone's surprise, she remained in absolute control of her household throughout the weekend of the birth. No one, save George and Belle it seemed, was privy to Kaitlyn's resourceful and unseen counsellors. Hannah, as she had begun to do since she could walk, followed her Uncle Harry wherever he went---much to the amusement and gratification of her parents.

Harry and Hannah were just finishing the final phasing plans for the Oakland Preserving Company when a voice, both familiar and clear, congratulated him directly on the birth of his oldest twin girl. Harry stopped mid-stride in route to Kaitlyn's side. "Great-great-uncle Fong Li, am I to understand you are *actually* speaking to me directly?!" he asked of his unseen ancestor.

Lizette responded, after Fong Li acknowledged the communication, "*Harry, you don't seem at all disconcerted at our direct participation in this blessed event...*"

Harry, with Hannah in tow, continued to Kaitlyn's side and responded to his Great-grandmama aloud, "How could it be otherwise, you have counseled my father and mother these many years; you must have, at some point, intended to introduce your succor to each of us in turn." He entered the room just as the second of the twins emerged into Belle's waiting hands. Kaitlyn's glowing face looked up at her husband's. When he knelt next to her and put his head near hers, they were both regaled by their ancestors' voices in congratulations and blessing. Kaitlyn thanked them very sincerely for their assistance over the last months. She was still looking into the eyes of her husband when he raised an eyebrow thoughtfully. For his part, Harry remarked that if they'd spoken any louder over the last several years, even ordinary folk would have been privy to their conversations. Lizette again had a question.

"*George Henry Livingson, how long have you been listening to us?*"

In answer Harry kissed his wife's forehead and said, "Great grandmama Lizette, since that August afternoon in the Midlands when Kat and Chloe began their journey---and you all had such wonderful things to say to mother and father about their family's future. As Great-great-great-grandmama said, 'Upon the birth of their first-born...' Well Chloe and Kat *were* my first-born!"

George, Belle and Kaitlyn had been following this conversation when at last Belle interjected, "So you knew, from that very day, what they said about Kaitlyn? I thought I alone kept that knowledge as a secret!"

Kaitlyn looked up from Belle to her husband's face, "What *did* they say about me?" Then, to her unseen counsellors she asked directly, "What about me was so important that you were compelled to inform Belle at the time?"

Harry's Great-great-grandfather answered, "*That your young and newly forming soul had absorbed so much of our Harry's spirit, it appeared that you would likely share all his own great depth of knowledge, understanding, and abilities, if you developed properly. That you were, in a word, his soul's mate. In a very real way: his other self.*"

Belle blushed when Kaitlyn looked up into her face again, "It's true," she admitted, "I knew you how very special you were, darling, before you ever arrived here."

Kat turned to her husband and asked, "And you've known this all along?!"

Harry looked deep into her eyes, "Yes my love---my *other self*. I cherished you those years, waiting for you *to take me* as your husband and acknowledge, once and for all, our very special bond. I couldn't, in conscience, even once nudge you into anything through any word or act on my part; it has always been up to you. Remember I once said: 'I can show you the path, but it is you who will have to make the journey?' You have done this. You once asked me how I did what I did and I said, 'Kaitlyn there is nothing which I have done or do that is outside your own reach, should you truly wish to grasp it for your own...' You have done just that."

Kaitlyn at once recalled those instances, "But Harry, I almost couldn't believe you *then*. It seemed like such a lofty and far-away striving."

Belle and George placed the twins in their parents' arms and left the room to keep the others in the house at bay for just a bit longer. Their ancestors, whose voices were filled with delight and pride, agreed "*...We knew he had gone further than any other upon the most vital of journeys...*"

"Sweetheart," Harry began, "you are *now standing* upon that once far-away and lofty peak and *that* is a fitting tribute to the success of *your own efforts*. I am your *most* proud and devoted mate. Now," he turned to his daughters, "which one is Hermia Belle, and which is Helena Belle?"

Hannah, who had been sitting quietly with them on the bed, smiling at the little twins, at once pointed to her cousins seemingly indiscriminately.

Kaitlyn smiled at each in turn as Hannah at last indicated each by name. White Feathers came into the room, walked over to the proud couple and reached for a twin, "I'll hold Lena first... No, you better hand me Mia as well. I'll present them to their family..." and he was out the door with the girls bundled into his massive arms; Hannah toddled after him.

Kaitlyn remarked as he went out the door, "Dear, you'd better follow him and keep up with which is which, now that *we* finally know!" Harry kissed her and passed *all* his sisters who were just coming into the room as he followed White Feathers out. He wanted to be there before his Great-uncle began switching them around like in a shell game, as he'd done with Poly and Tania so long ago.

White Feathers went straight to the center of the great room and said, "May I present," and he held aloft one of the girls, "Hermia Belle Livingson," then he held her sister up where all could see, "And her sister, Helena Belle Livingson."

The assembled family clapped and cooed at the adorable, wrinkled little bundles in his arms. Titania and Hipolyta came out of the bedroom, leaving Chloe and Becky with Kaitlyn alone for the moment. They rescued the girls from their Great-uncle's arms and with their heads near each other's, began to whisper things to the twins in their arms no one else could hear. They then passed the girls to Aaron and Becky who did the same while they went back to Kaitlyn's room. Once the private conferences were over, White Feathers again wrested control of the little ones and began pacing and dancing around the room with them.

George watched the interplay of all the twins with the babes, and surmised aloud, "Those two girls should never have to feel strange for being twins; it's the rest of us who may begin feeling a bit odd at *not* being so." The company laughed and chuckled at that. Harry held Hannah in his lap and watched White Feathers as he did, indeed, begin playing a shell game with the newest twins between himself and the rest of the family. An hour or so later, once no one else, it seemed, was able to say for certain which twin was which, Hannah went to one of her cousins and asked, "Lena hungry?" Then she went to her other cousin and asked, "Mia hungry?" She toddled to her Uncle Harry, who had observed the correct sorting and said, "Babies want MamaKat." Harry gathered up his daughters and returned them to their mother. All of the family nearest to hear her weren't able to contain their feelings of touching amusement and respect for their Hannah. Of course they just had to make sure everyone else was aware of her latest accomplishment.

Before all the family headed back to their respective homes, Tania arranged for the village photographer to come up to the home on the hill for family photographs: the whole family together, the individual families, the babies, just the women, just the men and the babies again. Naturally, it was Poly and Tania who decided the poses, the groups, the settings and the costumes. The photographer wasn't bothered in the least by the ladies' constant direction of his subjects, Harry kept him supplied with whatever he wished to drink and Jameson kept sandwiches and pastries at his elbow. When all was said and done, it was easily his largest commission during an off-season, ever.

By the end of September, once the Lodges were set for the autumn and winter, George and Belle with White Feathers and Lawrence came up the hill to visit to their grandchildren... and to see Harry and Kaitlyn, of course. Once the cooing, bouncing and cuddling had wound down, MamaKat began to feed them Harry read from recent letters he'd received from both the Allcocks and from Mandy. "It seems all is well across the pond." Harry added as he folded them and replaced them on the mantle.

Kaitlyn asked innocently, "MamaBelle, have you and George ever had a holiday from the store and lodges?"

Belle laughed, "Certainly not." Then seemingly a little vexed she asked, "George, why haven't we ever had a holiday from the store and the lodges?" passing the poser to her smiling husband.

"Well... we *have* taken long weekends across the lake, we have closed up shop for weeks at a time in the dead of winter... Do those count?" he asked facetiously. Lawrence and White Feathers chuckled.

Kaitlyn looked to Harry who was also smiling at the responses thus far provided. She followed with, "Would you *like* to have a bit longer holiday... perhaps visit faraway friends... see the world beyond California?"

Belle answered a little more seriously, "Kaitlyn, the need for an absence from our home and work has just never occurred to either of us." She looked at George for some explanation which was not readily presenting itself to her at the moment. "I realize to world travelers such as you all here that may sound a bit ridiculous, even provincial but honestly it hasn't occurred to me... George?"

"I have been to China. Does that count as traveling?" he countered.

Harry interjected, "A one-way trip *from* China isn't a holiday, it's a life decision. It doesn't count."

Kaitlyn pursued the thread of Belle's reasoning, "So, does that mean you are averse to traveling further than, say, San Francisco or the northern mountains?"

"I am not afraid of traveling; if that's what you're getting at." Belle responded and George chimed in, "Neither am I!" His wife continued, "But why would we want to go somewhere else? Our children and now our grandchildren are here or near. Our store and lodges are here. Our friends are here..."

Harry answered, "Mother, Father perhaps there are people elsewhere who would *like to see you* though. I know for a fact that Samuel and Olivia would be overjoyed to have you as guests for as long as you wished. I can say without hesitation that Mandy would be so thankful for a visit from you, she'd probably pee herself if you said you were coming..." White Feathers and Lawrence snickered because they knew he was right on that observation and it did conjure up a most humorous image.

George looked at Belle and she met his gaze. In an unspoken communication they seemed to decide upon something. Belle asked, "And who would tend the store? I know Tania has the Bungalows running smoothly already. What if...?"

George whimpered, "But darling, we just got more twins..."

Harry answered, "Mother I'll handle the arrangements for keeping the Mercantile open and running. And Father, we don't have to *return* Lena or Mia; we get to keep them---they'll be here when you get back." Again there were chuckles from Lawrence and White Feathers.

Lawrence straightened up and said, "I'll volunteer to make your travel arrangements. In fact, I'm rather interested in seeing the *Last Concession* myself and I know I'd love to visit with the Allcocks again in person. If you'll allow me, I'd love to go along."

Again, George looked at Belle and she met his gaze. He said quickly, "I've got dibs on Harry's trunk."

Belle rolled her eyes in amusement and answered, "I'm certain Titania or Jameson would allow me the use of one of theirs." She looked then at Kaitlyn. "Was that what they call a loaded question, dearest?"

Kaitlyn looked innocently back at MamaBelle, "Wow, I guess it turned out that way. I was just curious..."

Mandy Hill didn't *exactly* pee herself, not that she would have admitted to it in any event, but she was *very* excited at the news of their visit. The Allcocks were equally thrilled and as Olivia had not been on holiday since she was a girl, she decided for herself in the privacy of her thoughts that this was an ideal excuse for one. Aaron sent a letter to his parents informing them of George and Belle's travel plans. When they wrote back, it wasn't to Aaron or Becky, but to George and Belle directly, inviting them to stay with them upon their arrival in Liverpool and Manchester. Lawrence made their rail and ship reservations; he alerted the Chelsea House for the use of their suites. He was certain he could make the arrangements for transportation in Europe once they arrived.

The travel plans were the biggest news Tania and Poly could ever remember hearing from their parents; so naturally Poly came up from Berkeley and together they fussed over helping their mother and father pack for the once in a lifetime excursion. White Feathers gave George a few traveling pointers, with the caveat that whatever he said was likely woefully outdated. Harry and Kat sketched out all their previous touring destinations, the companies and hotels--- which to contact and which to maybe avoid. In a short two weeks, all the family who could be there were assembled on the Truckee platform seeing off Mr. and Mrs. Livingson for their first trip abroad, with the capable and resourceful Lawrence Spelman as guide and companion. Both the Livingsons wore their fur coats and hats. Belle at last looked *exactly* like the 'Russian Princess' Kaitlyn envisioned the first time she'd seen her in the photograph Harry showed her of his family when they first met. Fortunately for George, his oriental features could be explained away by his being in service to his companions and so avoided any scrutiny on the part of customs officials and the like. It wasn't ever easy in the States for an Asian man, and times weren't changing fast enough to suit anyone.

Jameson and Titania moved into their home behind the shop and promised to keep everything in perfect order: maintain the niches and keep the kitchen stores and medicines cabinet stocked. Jameson and Harry would fill any special orders for the shop, or for fly rods in George's absence. Kaitlyn couldn't promise that the girls wouldn't grow while their GrandMamaBelle and PapaGeorge were away, but she would make sure they were always reminded of their grandparents and that they would only ever be bundled in Belle's blankets and quilts, as if that wasn't going to be the way of it anyway.

About a week and a half after the Livingsons and Lawrence left Tahoe, White Feathers died. It happened like this:

He had taken to staying up at the home on the hill with Harry and Kaitlyn. He helped out by keeping the two girls in nappies and walking with one when the other was nursing. Sometimes he would just sit with them in front of the fireplace rocking them until they fell asleep---although it was usually himself who fell asleep first. So it was that late one evening, as he was rocking them in the glow of the fireplace, he fell asleep and didn't wake up.

Harry and Kaitlyn were in bed but were awakened by some very loud snoring. Harry got up to take the girls back to their crib and found White Feathers with a smile on his face, his eyes open and staring at the picture of all the family upon the mantlepiece. Harry quickly roused Kaitlyn to come and see. They stood there admiring the scene of the venerable old man and their precious girls. But even though his eyes were open, the snoring just got louder in their ears. Kaitlyn went to pick up Mia and Harry picked up Lena, but White Feathers did not rouse and his eyes didn't move from the picture.

Harry said aloud, "White Feathers! Wake up!" and all of a sudden they heard the snoring stop and his voice say, "*Oh sorry, I must have dozed off.*" His mouth didn't move and his eyes didn't focus. Harry reached over and closed his lids.

"White Feathers, I think you did more than doze off..." Kaitlyn pointed out.

"*Well, what do you know. My back doesn't hurt anymore; in fact I feel better than I've felt in decades!*" the old man declared.

Then a familiar voice answered his, "*Welcome at last Pompe!*"

"*Mother?*" he answered.

Lizette said, "*It's good to have you to talk to again Jean Baptiste...*"

"*Sister?*" he sounded shocked and delighted.

Harry said, "This is a most wonderful family reunion... and years overdue. But I thought Great-grandmama Lizette was... and that Great-great-grandmama Poriva was..." His confusion was evident, "White Feathers? I've been meaning to ask you for years---why have you always referred to yourself as my *Great*-great uncle and always followed your name with the initials: J.B.C.?"

181

White Feathers started to answer, but asked a different question first, *"Mother, can Belle and George hear us if we just talk to one another, or must I want to talk to them for them to hear me?"*

On a ship in the Atlantic, a hundred miles or so out from New York, Belle answered, "Uncle? Oh, my... Uncle White Feathers, I can hear you now!"

"Were you eaten by a bear or something?" George added.

"Okay, that answers that question," White Feathers remarked. *"This is going to take a little getting used to..."*

His sister provided a brief though complete explanation of their extraordinary communications and a few tips about directing advice which had been discovered and developed along the way. Communication, it appeared, could be personal but more often than not was general.

Lizette answered Harry's question first. *"Harry, Kaitlyn, George, Belle dearest, the man you have always called White Feathers is my brother, Jean Baptiste Charbonneau, known to his family as Pompe."*

Poriva added, *"Lizette and Pompe are my children, and the only ones to follow the work of the family."*

Belle simply said, "I'm confused. If you're not my uncle but actually my Great-uncle, then you weren't my mother's brother... White Feathers, Jean, Pompe... whatever I'm supposed to call you... who are you really?"

Harry was essentially asking the same question at the same time, not knowing his mother's confused questions were being posed also. White Feathers's voice rang out clearly to both, *"Let me see if I can talk to four different people in two vastly different places and make some sense for each of you. I will repeat any questions which Harry and Kaitlyn cannot hear Belle and George ask, and vice versa, but first let me make an overdue explanation to my Great-niece."*

He was quiet for a little bit, then began, *"I was born, as my little sister and mother have said, as Pompe---Jean Baptiste Charbonneau. I was essentially adopted by Captain Clark, mother insisted I have a good education, she returned a few years later and trained me properly in the family work. At age eighteen, I met Duke Freidrich Wilhelm, son of King Freirich I of Wurttenburg. While I was working at a trading post, he and my father Toussaint arranged for me to accompany him back to Europe, ostensibly to widen my horizons. I lived there for nearly six years and learned German and Spanish, adding to the French I already spoke. We toured north Africa and Europe, but then the Duke had an affair with a girl named Anastasia, and nine months later she had a son. I was standing right there when he gave my name for his own to the delivering doctor, 'to protect his family's name and honor,' he claimed. She was devastated, the child died soon after, and I had had enough. I returned to St. Louis, I signed on with a fur trading company, took to the mountains, and made life-long friends of other mountain men such as Jim Bridger ...whom George has met.*

For the next several years I hunted, led hunters and tried hard to stay out of battles, with some success. I scouted for expeditions, led wagon trains and supply marches, all successful. This sorta put me in good stead with the military commanders with whom I'd come into contact and some for whom I'd 'pulled their bacon from the fire' as it were. Anyway, I received an appointment as an alcalde of Mission San Luis Rey, a very unenviable position---as it turned out, very unpopular with the the governed. I had to resort to a trick I learned from the Duke when he was made to make multiple public appearances during times of unrest: I found a double, a poor sap who was my spitting image, and sent him into public when it seemed better I stay out of someone's gunsights. It was just then that I got word through reliable friends that Lizette's sixteen year old daughter, Alouette, had been, shall we say, 'lured' away from home by a smooth-talking devil whose intentions were not in the least honorable.

With barely anything to go on, beyond her description and name, I finally tracked her to a mining camp in Nevada, Alouette was just about to give birth. The scoundrel, who dragged her there, had abandoned her to her fate in the back of a makeshift camp saloon. She gave me his name before I had her tended to by a physician of my acquaintance, and then I went after the conscienceless wanton bastard. It took me two days to catch up to him in another mining settlement. Vengeance, it has been suggested, may belong to higher powers, but in this case it belonged to a three inch deep puddle. He evidently couldn't swim; he drowned.

When I got back to Alouette, she'd given birth to a weak but otherwise healthy baby girl, but my niece, Lizette's daughter, had died bringing her child into the world. I buried her with all due honor and reverence. Lizette had died two years before, and the family 'responsible' for Alouette, obviously wasn't. So, I took her little girl to the only person I knew for certain could bring her up properly: my mother. I named you 'Belle' and delivered you into her capable care.

There was a woman in her village who had recently lost her husband in raids. Mother instructed the widow to take you in and raise you as her own; meanwhile, Poriva made sure the training you would need was administered directly and indirectly by herself alone.

Belle, Sweetheart, that is why no one ever talked about who your father was; I was the only one who knew, and I refused to burden a sweet little girl with that pile of offal that was your father. Later, when you were older, it didn't seem to matter so much, so I forgot it as best I could.

I couldn't go back and resume my old life: it turned out my name was no good on two continents. That double I had installed in San Luis took advantage of his position and seduced a young girl, and she had a daughter. Later she was fortunate enough to marry a fine man who raised the little girl as his own. But the double went north, still using my name. At least he didn't cause too much more trouble. One of my old friends, Jim Beckwourth, heard that "I" was in the gold camps, and he went to find me and join up on a claim that was producing something, though not a lot. I was in the Sierras, and luckily crossed paths with him. I explained why I was where I wasn't and he took it with a grain of salt, good man. So, in the Sierras I stayed, and lived under the name of White Feathers. Mother had a lot of different names through her life, must be a family tradition.

Oh, and 'White Feathers' isn't for some noble Indian ancestor: I chose the name from a story a British lieutenant once told me while I was knocking around Europe. It seems a white feather was given a soldier, if in the crisis of battle, or some other needful situation, that soldier performed cowardly. I thought it was a fitting name for me as a man who would not return to his own life. As it happened, that usurper died in a river accident over twenty years ago, but by then I was 'Uncle White Feathers' to Belle, and most everyone else with whom I'd developed friendships....so White Feathers stayed close to Tahoe. Poriva moved further east after Belle was old enough and trained.

Harry, that is why I always signed notes to you as 'your Great-great-uncle White Feathers, J.B.C.' It's because I am your great-great-uncle, and, although I gave it up, my name is Jean Baptiste Charbonneau. Or rather was... is... uh, this is going to take some getting use to!"

The four listeners, two on the Atlantic, and two in Tahoe, sat whelmed at the tale. Kaitlyn was the first to speak. "White Feathers, thank you for that incredible tale, but as I only know you as my loving great-uncle, I shall continue loving you just the same. And you could never be called a coward: you gave up everything to save your niece and Belle. You are the most honorable man, next to my husband, I have ever known!"

And Belle, with tears in her eyes and her voice choked with over-powering emotion, simply said, "You rescued me..." she sobbed, "And gave me the life I know?" She almost couldn't command her own voice, "I have always thought of you as the father I never had... and now I'm more proud of you than ever..."

Lizette added, *"Darling one, that's why I could never tell you certain things. If my brother wished for you to know those things, he would have told you himself. You do understand? Don't you?"*

"Of course," was all Belle could manage.

The morning was approaching Tahoe, and White Feathers's empty body still sat in front of the embers in the hearth. Harry went down the hill to inform Jameson and Titania, then went to find the undertaker. White Feathers, through Harry, directed the arrangements of the ceremonies required for his own remains. All was done as he wished. White Feathers related the activities and what was said and such from the ceremony to George and Belle, so they didn't feel too absent from the occasion.

"Now," White feathers announced, *"I can see Europe again through your eyes... I am certain quite a few things have changed since Beethoven presented his Ninth Symphony in Vienna for the first time. That was a concert to be remembered..."*

Winston and Eugenia Backhouse were at the Liverpool docks when they arrived. They recognized George as the 'Oriental Gentleman,' and so recognized his companions, Belle and Lawrence by default. Mrs. Livingson introduced Lawrence Spelman to the Backhouses as their own best friend. After introductions, Winston helped George and Lawrence with the luggage as Belle walked with Eugenia toward the train station.

"You've never been away from home? Ever?!" asked Eugenia in surprise.

"George and I have always had enough on our plate to keep us quite busy and well, a trip anywhere was never something that crossed our minds. Then the children moved back and began taking over our responsibilities. So... here we are, ready to see the wider world," explained Belle. "Just the cruise across the Atlantic was worth it to me. I could *imagine* the vastness, but to be faced day to day with the *immensity* of that sea, the *endless* horizons... such stark beauty... it quite took my breath away."

"I must admit," began Eugenia, "I have only made the Channel crossing there and back again to visit Winston's cousins in Holland. The rolling waves were quite enough to put me off any thoughts of the larger sea."

The gentlemen joined them on the benches of the platform as they waited for the commuter train. Winston caught his wife up on his and George's conversation, "Genie, they plan to see Malvern..." Lawrence interjected that they weren't going for the waters, "...and Stratford before hopping over to the continent. Don't you agree they should see Bath. It is, after a fashion, on the way to Weymouth after all..."

"Oh, Belle, the city of Bath is a lovely place to be sure..." Belle glanced to George, who was watching her with a sly smile.

Lawrence caught their glances and turned the conversation, "Eugenia, Winston tells me you have turned your gardens into quite the showplace. I am most anxious to enjoy them."

186

"Winston always says such nice things and I am sure he is just trying to stay on my good side. The gardens are very average really, compared with the truly magnificent landscaping of some of our nicer estates, I assure you," she deprecated. Although her words were humble, the undertone of pride was clearly evident to her listeners.

"Nevertheless, *we* shall enjoy them, I am sure." George assured her.

The train took them to the station very near the Backhouse's Manchester home, and as evening had not yet fully dimmed their view of the neighborhood, it was a pleasant walk. Winston rented a trolley from the station assistant and promised to return it in the morning. The tourists enjoyed the walk and the discourse Winston maintained regarding the points of interest they passed near, or which were viewable in the distance. Belle certainly admired the parks and neat rows of great-houses they passed. The Backhouse steward and houseboy relieved them of their trunks at the door and Eugenia led them upstairs to their rooms. She must have been in very good physical condition because she did not stop her running discourse on the house, her children, the paintings and such all the way up the flight of stairs and down the hallways.

"I am certain you will be comfortable here. This suite was Becky's until she moved to Greengate and then to Berkeley... Aaron and Hipolyta wrote to say what a wonderful residence has been constructed for them... Did you perhaps bring any photographs?" she asked with a hint of sadness in her voice. "We shall enjoy your company in the parlor after you're settled. Dinner this evening will be a little later than usual; we should have plenty of time for a lovely chat." Then she led Lawrence to Aaron's old rooms.

George closed the door behind him and sat down. "Poly and Aaron weren't exaggerating; Mrs. Backhouse is a bit talkative, but she seems a nice enough lady. I am glad we brought so many photographs with us to distribute to these nice folks and to the Allcocks."

Belle nodded absently, she was setting up their trunks and

already pulling out the dress she wished to wear to dinner. "Genie has been abandoned by her children and she has assumed a new position in relationship to her husband. After her long history as the commanding presence in her own house, she is undoubtably still adjusting to those changes and if she seems to 'lead a conversation,' so be it." She pulled her hair down and began undressing, "I am eager for a good hot bath."

They met their hosts in the parlor and were greeted again with the same warmth. George presented Genie with three framed photographs. "This one is Becky, Aaron and Poly in front of their house in Berkeley." He passed the picture to her anxious hands. "This is Aaron in his professor's garb in front of the University. And this one is of Becky in the foyer of the Sutro & Co. Bank, in San Francisco, after she completed the renovation of the building."

Winston and Genie were near to tears seeing their children so successfully situated in their new home in California. "They really are happy, aren't they?" Winston asked.

Belle assured them, "Here is the last photograph we brought along for you; this was taken from Harry and Kaitlyn's house on the hanging deck. The view behind them is the great Tahoe Lake and our little valley." She handed the picture to Genie and sat next to her looking at the image. "This is George and myself, my great-Uncle Jean Baptiste, and Lawrence of course---Kaitlyn's father. Here are Jameson and Titania Connor. You met Harold and Chloe Bessamer and their daughter, Hannah, is in Harry's arms next to Kaitlyn. And naturally you recognize these three handsome people here."

"Oh, they do look so happy! This is such a wonderful gift. We can not thank you enough for bringing all these to us..." Genie began to tear up as she looked from one then the other of her children in their new lives among a larger and obviously loving family. "You live in this valley? It is like something out of a Bierstadt painting, almost too beautiful to be real!"

Lawrence had to concur and mentioned only that Harry had designed the entire house and its sweeping vistas *and all from only his*

188

memory of the hillside. "...Not only that, but he was finishing his education and apprenticed to a big architecture firm at the same time..."

Belle continued uninterrupted, "Yes, this has been our home for these many years now. Jameson and Titania are managing the Bungalow Lodges and the Grand Concession Restaurant. Harry is minding the Mercantile in George's absence. Naturally the tourist trade is lighter in the autumn and winter; we do get quite a bit of snow and ice through the colder months."

Winston asked George about his store and it was when George made a passing mention of his fly rods that Winston's interest truly was piqued. He pursued the topic and George admitted he brought along one of his rods on the off chance he might have opportunity to wet a line during their holiday. "Oh, I would dearly love to see it; my own father was an avid fisherman. Some of my fondest memories of him were our time spent on the rivers in the north country and of Scotland." George, Lawrence and Winston excused themselves and went upstairs like three boys who had slipped out of school lessons.

Belle's mention of their family's businesses introduced a topic Eugenia had wished to approach because she was hungry for more details but she couldn't decide how to begin... not wishing to appear to be prying... "Aaron mentioned that the Livingsons, that is, that *you* are proprietors of some note in the village on the Tahoe," she opened, "Is this area something of a tourist's paradise? This picture certainly reflects the beauties of the region... Who are your clientele?"

Belle began a most thorough description of the 'village' as well as their own role through the years in its progress and development. She explained how they accommodated the annual traffic of visitors from the great cities and towns of the three state area. Genie sat rapt in interest; she had been grossly under-informed of the breadth and depth of the Livingson presence in Tahoe. Belle did not spare any information or description, from any false modesty on her own part.

When she at last concluded her tale of their lives in Tahoe, Genie was without comment except to say, "Oh my! you have been very busy indeed, no wonder you've had no inclination to travel until now... When would you have had the time!" Belle chuckled and offered Genie an expression of resigned agreement.

The gentlemen emerged soon after; Winston had been assured by George that they should find time for an excursion. Dinner was ready and they adjourned to the dining room for a delightful repast.

Over the next couple days---having been well-supplied by their children with places to enjoy during their stay in Manchester---Lawrence, George and Belle visited the museums and galleries, Greengate and the pub where Aaron proposed, the Waterhouse offices and the University. They were heartily impressed by their offsprings' accomplishments and endeavors. "Kaitlyn didn't exaggerate in the least---if anything she was too modest, they were quite well situated here," Belle remarked as they returned to the Backhouse residence the last evening.

Winston and Eugenia each praised Harry for both his cordiality and his reason. "We were only invited a handful of times to Greengate, but each time we returned home more impressed with Harry's expansive generosity and taste. Both Aaron and Becky simply idolize him, and that is high praise indeed. My children are nothing if not brilliant when it comes to seeing the true worth of others..." Genie added. Then suddenly she remembered her caustic judgements and grilling of Hipolyta, her own son's choice for wife. The memory of herself then stood in such stark contrast to her own statements of her children's discernment, that she was chagrined and embarrassed by her private recollections. She atoned for her remorse by stating, "Our daughter-in-law is a grand example. She is easily one of the most gracious and beautiful women I have ever had the privilege of acquaintance."

George and Belle smiled and thanked Genie for her very kind accolades, then returned the compliment in kind: Belle enumerated Aaron and Becky's qualities to a most receptive ear. Winston seized the opportunity of Genie's good humor to make a proposition.

"Genie, George, Lawrence and I have not yet had an opportunity to go angling; would you wire your sister in Redditch to take us in for a couple days, so that we may all enjoy traveling with the Livingsons to Clive House?"

Genie was surprised her husband made such a request, considering his historic antipathy for visiting her sister and brother-in-law. "I shall send immediately." She called for the steward and dashed off a note to be taken and wired promptly to her sister. Returning to her guests, she said simply, "You have had a most profound affect upon my husband and myself; I hope it will not be an imposition that we should be your companions to Redditch?"

Belle assured her that it was in no way an imposition. Lawrence added that they would find Clive House most welcoming of guests, should her sister's family be indisposed at present. "Harry made it clear to me and Samuel, Mr. Allcock, confirmed by letter himself that Clive House is most available for guests. 'The more, the merrier,' he said. I have no reason to doubt it, Olivia Allcock took in Harry and Kaitlyn as if they were her own children. She is a most remarkable woman---the very soul of hospitality."

Winston smiled, "Good, it's settled then. Although I am sure Hermoine, Genie's sister, will be more than pleased to visit with her and make accommodation for our stay. Genie, dear, we should begin packing!"

His wife was so caught up in the moment she could only say, "We are seldom this spontaneous. In fact we weren't this impetuous when we were courting! This should be great fun!" She actually giggled.

Belle looked to George and smiled triumphantly. When they were alone in their suite upstairs, she told him, "I like Genie, she has the makings of a good friend. She just needed a good excuse to 'let her hair down' is all."

Olivia Allcock was indeed the very soul of hospitality. The

traveling party had no sooner stepped off the train at the Redditch station, than they were greeted most warmly by both Samuel and his wife. Although Lawrence had only sent a line to Samuel that morning, before leaving the Manchester depot, Olivia welcomed them all as if the Backhouses were awaited guests. "I am so delighted to meet more of our extended family. You must be ready for tea, shall we go inside out the chill and enjoy cake and biscuits?"

They walked the short distance to Clive House. Belle was instantly enchanted by the immaculate grounds. Even in the first cold winds of winter the beds and trellises, the bushes and shrubs were still well-manicured and prim. "Mrs. Allcock, you have very beautiful gardens."

Genie seconded her new friend's comments, "I have tried to keep my own gardens vital this season, but yours are simply thriving... and your roses, how lovely." The gentlemen maintained a healthy silence as the ladies showered each other with the social lubricant of complement until each were quite flexibly comfortable with the others.

Hamis, the steward directed the staff to take their luggage to their rooms, whereupon Winston mentioned to Mrs. Allcock that "...Eugenia's sister, Hermoine Grisham, would be expecting them."

Olivia surprised them all and nearly startled poor Eugenia into speechlessness. She announced that Mr. and Mrs. Grisham would be along shortly and would be joining them for dinner. "I count Hermoine Grisham as one of my dearest acquaintances. When she mentioned a visit from her sister in Manchester now entertaining in-laws from the States, it dawned upon me at last---it was yourself and the Livingsons to whom she was referring."

Genie replied in amazement, "My sister and I do not speak so often as I would like, so I am naturally unaware of all her connections here in Redditch. This is such an unexpected and wonderful coincidence."

Olivia enjoyed her moment of triumph in social arrangements, then changed tack. "Mrs. Livingson, I am more pleased than you can imagine to meet the mother of our Harry. I need not express to you how absolutely attached we are to your son and Kaitlyn."

Belle actually blushed, "Mrs. Allcock, I have been looking forward to this meeting for so very long. Not only your husband, but both Harry and Lawrence and our dearest Kaitlyn hold you in such high regard that I must admit, I have been a bit anxious over our first encounter..."

Olivia put her arm into Belle's, "No it is I who have suffered the greater part of insecurity at our meeting. Harry Livingson is more than a son here; he is a hero and cherished friend. That I should at last meet the woman who shaped and guided him to the greatness he has already achieved has been quite a daunting anticipation, I must assure you."

Samuel guided his friends, Lawrence and George, with Winston toward the drawing room, "The ladies won't notice we've sneaked off, unless they wish to certify some statement of genuine expectation or some fact they'll dispute with us anyway.... Name your poison: I have wine, beer, gin, you name it. Winston, I take you for a single malt man?"

Winston nodded, "Well spotted, neat, if you please."

"Wouldn't serve it another way. George?" Samuel turned to his long-time friend, "Our beer isn't near your own brew but it's dark and rich..."

"Thank you Samuel, I would like that very much," answered George with a smile and a stretch of his arms.

"Lawrence here's your gin and tonic with the twist of lime." Samuel had no need of inquiring after his friend's preferences, they had spent many secluded hours in this very room once upon a time. George looked around the Allcock drawing room, and there displayed prominently on the wall surrounded by pictures of Harold, Chloe and Hannah, was Harry's graduation photograph. It was set in a gilded frame and arranged on the wall in an obvious position of prominence. Samuel caught his friend's eye and walked to the photograph.

"You would have been 'busting out' proud of him that day. Olivia and I were in tears of joy the whole time ourselves; we're just that proud of our Harry." Looking at the photograph, he recounted: "Aced the entrance exams, finished in two years the studies for three, held down an apprenticeship with one of the major architectural firms in England all the while, and then became an associate director of that very firm within a year of graduation... It's more than remarkable, it's homeric!"

Winston listened, "Harry was *exceptionally* modest; this is the first I've heard this history. I knew he was greatly admired by Aaron and Becky, I don't imagine even they know that bit of background," he remarked with admiration.

"Nor would they have heard it from himself. George Henry Livingson is what every man aspires to be, whether they know the greatness of man's potential or not," Samuel announced. As if saluting the queen, he raised a glass to the image of his protege and friend on the wall.

Lawrence voiced a loud, "Here, here," to that.

The ladies found their way to the drawing room and joined their men. Samuel offered refreshments as Olivia described the protocols of their 'family' rooms, "So no 'Mr. or Mrs.' in here and other rooms out of sight of the public chambers. I am Olivia, and this handsome devil is Samuel." Her husband grinned and delivered the ladies' glasses. Eugenia introduced herself as 'Genie,' and her husband as Winston. Both George and Belle shared sidelong glances to each other at their new friends' candor and comfort.

"Pleased to meet you Genie," Samuel bowed, and Winston gave him a pat on the shoulder for his courtesy. Winston reminded George of their angling plan and invited Samuel, of course, to join them.

Samuel responded swiftly, "I can show you a few streams that are just now ready for a hook and I'll be pleased to introduce you to them. Winston, you *do* have a rod with you?"

"I'm afraid I do not. I haven't fished since I was a boy, but seeing George's gear brought all the most wonderful memories of my youth back to me and I am most anxious to relive some of them," admitted Winston. Olivia and Belle shared the same expression at those words, knowing full well what was likely coming next.

"Then allow me to outfit you." Samuel strode to a glass cabinet on the wall behind Winston and opening it, removed two of the finest rods his factory had produced. "One sister of this one," he indicated the long single-handed cane rod, "was a present to the Shah of Persia, just a two years ago." Winston and George both whistled at that and moved closer to inspect this most celebrated family of cane rods. The gentlemen occupied themselves in like manner until they were compelled to join the ladies in the foyer in order to greet William and Hermoine Grisham who had just arrived for the evening.

Dinner was a splendid affair and after Betty the cook had been properly congratulated and praised for her preparations, they retired once more to the drawing room well-sated and ready for relaxing conversation. William was also a fisherman at heart, so it was decided that all the men would assemble in the morning for their excursion and all the women would happily be left to their own devices.

Those many days at Clive House were most enjoyable and rewarding for the Livingsons who were very much part of the family already. It was equally fulfilling for the Backhouses. The relaxed intimacy of family, the mutual consideration extended to them made them feel so much at home they soon felt as if they, too, might like a trip to the continent. Lawrence felt as at home in Clive House as any place on Earth. Actually these days, any where he was became his newest most comfortable place to be. That new attitude did not escape Samuel's attention and so he asked his friend about this most remarkable transformation.

"It's not all so surprising, really," Lawrence began, "You've stayed with them in Tahoe. You, yourself came away renewed and awakened to some degree. I have had the benefit of their constant company and instruction these last few years and I am awakened to the world as I never thought, nor expected, I might ever experience." Samuel smiled and waited for him to continue. "Everything which we so admire in Harry, finds its root and life in that community of remarkable individuals... Oh, that reminds me. Our dear friend, White Feathers passed away just a week or so after our departure. He was a rare individual and a most instrumental guide for my own journey; I shall truly miss his company."

Samuel had received a wire from Harry about their friend's passing and put his arm around Lawrence's shoulders. "Yes, Harry told me as much. I was as singularly affected by that man's life as any one I am sure with whom he came in contact."

Lawrence continued, "Remember, I once told you snippets of my memories of the exhibition witnessed in Southern China of the Ten Tigers and my own near brush with that path when I was still young?" Samuel nodded. "Well the path, the stories were all true... but different than I had imagined."

Samuel then, without waiting for his friend to elaborate, embarked upon a most *extraordinary* tale of his own daughter's transformation and how he and Olivia made a clandestine viewing of an unparalleled feat in their *own* undercroft before Harold and Chloe were married.

Lawrence listened, smiling all the while then admitted, "Harold told George of that very encounter in my presence. So you see, my own renewal of spirit and perspective isn't all so surprising. I have made the efforts indicated by my guides and am a far different man than the fellow who arrived in Tahoe, aggrieved and disconsolate all those years ago."

Samuel and Olivia sat down with Lawrence alone during the last evening at Clive House. Olivia was curious about their itinerary and the anticipated duration of their tour. Samuel asked after the transportation arrangements. Lawrence became a little suspicious, but it wasn't until George and Belle, accompanied by Winston and Genie, joined them in the sitting room that their purposes were revealed.

Olivia announced, "Belle if you and George wouldn't be discomfited, Samuel and I would very much like to travel with you to Venice to see Mandy again." Before her new friend could answer, she hastily added, "Neither of us has *ever* had a proper honeymoon you see. Not during our previous marriages, nor after our own wedding. There has always been the business and seemingly no possibility of time away. Like yourself, I suppose: 'when has there been any opportunity'?"

Genie spoke up for herself and Winston, "Oh my, that's precisely what Winston and I were going to propose. Likewise, we are so enjoying this companionship; we have decided to beg a place in this touring company as well!"

They all looked at each other and simply laughed. Lawrence admitted, "How do you think I came to be here? Even though I knew I'd be a fifth wheel, as it were, George and Belle wouldn't hear of my not going." He turned to his dearest friends, "What say you, Belle? I can as easily arrange berths for seven as for three."

George smiled to his wife and Belle simply said, "I hope Mandy has room for us all. If not, George and I can sleep on the boat." That was greeted with more chuckles and laughter, although Belle had been quite serious. Lawrence realized it and promised to wire Mandy immediately.

They toured Malvern and at Lawrence's suggestion did not sample the waters. The College was just as they'd imagined. They were even admitted to Harry's old room in School House and no one impeded their perusal of every classroom, library or nook and cranny, as the Headmaster Rev. Mr. Grundy escorted them wherever they wished. He supplied a comprehensive history of Harry's activities, achievements and legacy at the college. As the Livingsons left the campus they were rivals of Samuel and Olivia in parental pride of their Harry. In Stratford they walked the lanes and visited *The Rooms* where Chloe and Kaitlyn had spent a year with Mrs. Smythe-Wilkins. She was most pleased to relate anecdotes of the ladies' time with her. They visited the Memorial Theater and were regaled by the Artistic Director, whom Kaitlyn had most impressed, regarding her skill and prowess in her every task during her time with the company.

At last they reached Bath and toured the white stone city with its many attractions. They took in the country side on walking tours before making the crossing from Weymouth to St. Malo. They acquired the same rooms at the hotel on Mont Saint-Michel that Harry and company had used during their own visit. Belle was enthralled by the deep sense of history which pervaded the very stones upon which she tread; it was for her hallowed ground---just knowing it was here that her own family had made such remarkable strides on their own personal journeys, and of course where her daughter and Jameson were married. She spent all of the last evening looking out toward the island of Tomberlaine and wept tears of great joy as she recalled Lizette's recounting to her of the blessed event. Then she remembered how they remained chaste for another week; Tania was so insecure in their 'right' to such happiness. It was heart wrenching. George assured her their family would learn from all their experiences and that the foibles with which they had inadvertently burdened their children would not carry forward to their grandchildren. "We did our best, my darling. They are the happiest of people in spite of our inadequacies."

"I know you are right, and their children will no doubt have similar misperceptions from their upbringing; I just wish we could have done better, that's all." They looked at each other tenderly; both acknowledging the superlative natures of their children. "I suppose when all is said and done, we did well by them..." she whispered.

"Yes, dearest. We did *very* well by them," replied George confidently.

Paris was a real eye-opener. The Eiffel Tower stood as sentinel to the city of lights and none of the company could get enough of it. They took the trip up to the very top and surveyed the course of the Seine as well as the vistas of the country side beyond, stretching out from the vast city. The galleries, the museums, and monuments to a proud people were icing on the cake of their enjoyment of the French culture. Belle and George surprised their companions at meals and on their walks of the city, by speaking in fluent French: White Feathers, in his new capacity, was certainly enjoying the tour as much as anyone.

Samuel and Olivia were, without question, most thoroughly enjoying their 'honeymoon.' During their walking tours Lawrence was repeatedly stopped in mid-comment offering some remark or pointing out a sight of historical or cultural interest while his friends were at that moment kissing or were in an intimate embrace. 'They *are* on holiday,' he reminded himself. Yet it was such a departure from his own stereotypes of the British people in general and his preconceptions of his friends specifically---who he thought he knew so well. He ultimately could only smile and mentally revise his own errant expectations.

The Backhouses were no different. Winston seemed to be using this excursion as an opportunity to take back his Genie and woo her as the attractive woman he had courted and married so many years before. If Samuel and Olivia surprised him, Winston and his Genie down right inspired him. They were as two teenagers again, constantly enamored of one another and all the while in such complete wonder at the sights and spectacles which surrounded them. To himself he concluded, "George and Belle have a most influential force on them in only the brief time since they met," he surmised. "But then who could resist the influence of two such remarkable beings radiating their calmness of presence and inner comfort?" As long as he had known them, George and Belle had never deviated from modeling sincerest affection and respect for each other and genuine respect and compassion for others.

"So..." his beautiful guest concluded, "we must get you to the place that you can do some inner world gardening. Separate the wheat from the chaff---Organic metaphors are very useful." The young man cocked an eye at her approvingly.

"To make use of the knowledge and tools at your disposal, you must remember what has been spoken of before---that is, that you must start with small things. 'Doing' always begins with 'un-doing' what is mechanical and habitual. Take some small thing which you know you are unable to do, at present, and focus all your energies on making a change in that. This is called setting yourself an aim. If you set a task for yourself too great for your present ability, you will not achieve it and you will instead, waste valuable time and energy, very likely making things worse in the end.

Remember those 'simple' experiments you undertook as a precursor to realizing your mechanical nature? Those were little things. Small efforts over time yield big results and the more we persist at something, the better, the more proficient we become. Let me illustrate my meaning.

When I was very young, I loathed the time I was forced to spend in the company of my mother's sisters. To me, they were frivolous, arrogant, undisciplined and intrusive. My attitude was the cause of more than a few of the problems that arose between them and me and the rest of my family. Later, when I at last turned my attention to overcoming my still strong attitudes regarding them, I had to focus upon a single manifestation, common to each of them---*one* instance from the categories of those manifestations so revolting to me personally and give that one thing all my attention and energy---in order to change *my behavior*, at least, regarding that singular issue. I knew from long experience what prompted that manifestation from them when in my presence and I first set about attempting to avoid 'pushing that button,' if you take my meaning..." He nodded in understanding.

"Careful as I was, that manifestation of theirs arose of its own accord without my assistance. I was back where I started. Next, I

200

attempted to practice, ahead of time, any response I could think of other than my habitual reaction of course which might lessen the impact of that manifestation upon me. I recited to myself each alternative before visiting them, so that I wouldn't be caught unawares in the heat of the moment. Gradually, I managed to replace my previous reaction with one or another response of my previous choosing, and my visits with them became a little more palatable." She paused and sighed as if reliving that first small victory.

"Over a *long* period of time, I constantly worked on my outward manifestations as well as examining my habitual attitudes and observing the subsequent postures I adopted around my Aunts. Gradually, I got to the place where I even didn't mind staying the weekend with them, if I so chose. Then it took me a while longer to go back and reassess my accomplishment so that I could apply those results to other of my personal flaws and shortcomings. Do you know what I found?"

The question hung in the air between them like a riddle. Her host shook his head at last, realizing it *hadn't* been a rhetorical question and that she was *really* waiting for a response.

"I found that we can not change an attitude---that is to say, bring forward a different emotion, at will, in the moment. *All* we can do in the beginning is to visualize ahead of time and *really try to feel* a different response or attitude. We must rewrite, or overlay a new emotion over the existing one until the new one comes as readily as the habitual one. In this way we can get a toehold on the root of *one* of our unpleasant manifestations at a time.

Now, I will admit that I could not have maintained my diligence in that endeavor had I not *known* objectively, *for sure, just how* my machine was constructed---*how* that attitude had taken residence in me and *how* my machine was *supposed* to function. I was forced to apply many cycles of the enneagramatic process in the pursuit of my aim and each cycle yielded for me more experience and enhanced my tools. Without an objective understanding it is very likely I would have given up after the first attempt. In this work, there is no room for speculation, conjecture and guess and without an objective foundation, *that* is all we are left with to confront those aspects of our own loathsome personality, or even to engage the world around us."

She suggested they stop early today so that he could digest all that had been said as best he could. "Who knows, maybe you'll try an experiment of your own..." Then, smiling fondly at him, she rose and walked toward the lane that would take her back to town. As she walked, she whistled and hummed a tune that seemed familiar and yet unfamiliar at the same time.

4

Perseverance

"Failure after long perseverance is much grander than never to have a striving good enough to be called a failure."
---George Eliot

T he morning was what anyone else would deem invigorating. The autumn air held the vitality of an emboldened thoroughbred; the first golden glints of light in the early dawn pushed away all hints of gloom in its path. Even the twittering birds seemed confident of their minor dominion. He rose troubled from a poor night's repose compounded by spilling coffee grounds all over the counter and floor in a fumbling attempt to load the coffee press and scalding his hand in the hot water trying to fill it. He settled into his chair on the porch and wondered aloud. "I thought wrong, Mocha, perhaps they call it 'the work' because it actually is and not just because the other clever names for the ways back to Conscience were taken."

Reflecting on his struggles the evening before and into the night trying to at once overcome his disgust for belligerent ignorance that he had encountered every so often by persons of his present acquaintance and in his past. He kept returning to such antipathy over the memories that he couldn't escape the revolving thoughts keeping him awake well into the darkness. "They say that if you are disgusted with someone else it is because you see yourself in them... I so hope that's not the case here."

Along the lane leading to his driveway came a tall woman striding in deliberate paces up the still steaming pavement. She approached the porch and with a smile asked why he seemed out of sorts already this early in the day? He told her of his epic struggles over the last eleven hours or so and almost whimpered his conclusions.

"Good," she answered brightly.

"Good?!" he responded. "Good, that I have been butting my head against a wall all night? Good, that I am so helpless in the face of this inner menace?!"

She soothed, "Good that you made an attempt. Next time instead of trying to drink the whole lake at one gulp, 'setting a task for yourself too great for your present ability,' dip out a glassful and drink until it is empty. This attempt of yours only cost you a night's sleep and not your future possibilities... so... Good!"

That was somewhat comforting, but his failure was still aching. "So if I perceive an attitude which overwhelms me and I lose all sense of myself in the emotions that follow that encounter, I can't do anything about it?" He moaned, "That sounds like hell!"

She tried again to reinforce the idea that it had to do with the scale of his attempts. "Try to pick *one* manifestation of *one* person which brings up in you that undesirable attitude---one glassful of the waters of the lake. You may naturally make the judgement that: because this undesirable attitude is irksome to you suggests it has its roots deep in your emotions. But you must sneak up on the sleeping giant by one small step at a time. Choose one small thing which you *can* overcome."

He still had that wounded and anguished expression. She wished to address those 'wounds' directly and proceed; she stood up, took his hand and walked into the yard, then turned with him to face the house. She commanded him, "Destroy this house!"

He looked at her as if she were nuts. She repeated earnestly, "Destroy this house! Don't dawdle, destroy it now!"

A light came on in his head and instead of the anguished look he'd maintained throughout his morning, his expression turned to embarrassment. He was embarrassed that he hadn't listened, really listened, to what she'd said about 'pick one small thing' and he almost laughed at *his own* belligerent ignorance in the face of her

204

first, very clear and reasonable suggestion: 'pick some small thing first!' He could only manage to respond with, "Oh, I see..."

"Good," she answered brightly for the second time that morning, and they went back up onto the porch to sit down again. "Now it is possible that you might find the *one key* pillar or post or joist that, if removed, would bring down the house all at once... but that is not generally how most structures are made, and for that very reasonable precaution. The strongest emotions and attitudes which we harbor inside our false personality are no different. They took a while to build, and they will take some time to dismantle."

She then gave the young man a list of degrees of response to the instances he would likely encounter on his journey. "The everyday sort of emotional disturbances, those which do not elicit in us 'great' emotional reactions, we must practice: active reasoning. That is to say, for example: 'You call me a fool.' I must realize that though you have that opinion does not mean that you are wise. Perhaps you heard it from someone else and are merely repeating it, and that produces in me pity toward you for being a slave to influences; I am not affected. However, perhaps I have acted foolishly; my aim is not to behave as a fool, and so I thank you for pointing out my foolishness; again, I am not affected." The host nodded, seeing the 'active' application of reason to this otherwise unsettling experience.

"Okay I see that, but what about an instance that would cause a stronger emotional reaction from me?" he followed.

"The infrequent disturbance which catches you off your guard. That influence for which you are unable, in the moment of its entrance, to counter with reason. You must, during the duration of the occurrence, refrain as best you can from *manifesting* any of the negative emotions evoked in you. Do not allow what is inside to make an appearance on the outside, if you will. You have heard, no doubt, the admonition to: 'count to ten,' or to recite 'Mary had a little lamb...' These are good---only in so far as you're doing *something intentional* against the mechanical reaction. It would of course be far better to recite something more inspiring or appropriate, but so long as it's intentional... it is something."

Her host interjected suddenly remembering, "Like what George told Harry and Hipolyta to do with their thoughts when faced with forces stronger than they could overcome: '...you must submit. Yet in your surrender, you must also not yield to the gnawing of fear and foreboding. The only way to do this is to send your mind to a place of comfort and security as a shield against the attack of doubt and anguish over your helplessness'," he seemed pleased to have remembered.

She glanced at him suddenly, "Good, so you *are* making some connections with this story after all!" She continued, "Then when such an occurrence envelopes you, remember how it happened and when you are in a calmer state, in calmer circumstances, apply active reasoning. And as was pointed out earlier, find some substitute attitude or feeling to overwrite that unseemly one. Always address one manifestation at a time... small things first."

He accepted the suggestion, but realized there were situations more pressing in the moment that made him 'crazy.' "I see. But what about those times when I just see red, and lose it?"

"Fortunately for most of us those instances are more rare, yet when they do occur the only thing left to you is to remember yourself: that *you* are not the emotion, nor are *you* the influence. Try to remember you, yourself, a part of but separate from what is around you: '*In the world, but not of the world...*' As I have explained to you and I should make even clearer: External impressions are harmless in themselves; it is we who decide to be hurt."

The young man probed facetiously, "So if a car is coming at me, it's really harmless and it's my choice to be hurt by it?"

"If it is a picture of a car, yes. If it is an actual car, it's not just an impression; it's a force. Forces are real and if you are under any confusing illusions about that: Try and stop the wind." She answered evenly not the least ruffled by his impertinence. "Impressions are merely the finer material food for our machine."

"How many foods are there?" he asked, forgetting the broader topic at hand.

"That is another discussion and we should have that dialog, too. It is more of the knowledge gleaned from our original symbol. But for now, and this discussion, try to anticipate what you will likely encounter in your next day and prepare yourself for the inevitable. In that way you may begin to observe even more of your inner world's curious construction and make some inroads into its renovation."

The host was unsure how to reply, "How can I anticipate what might happen tomorrow? Anything can happen?"

"In reality: *NO*; 'anything' can not happen. It should be fairly simple to recognize your own routines and to anticipate what occurs during your usual days. The Earth will still be turning around the Sun, gravity will still be in place, and your habitual behaviors and reactions will still be ready for the slightest nudge for them to come into manifestation. But, if you mean a meteor may drop out of the sky upon your head, or a crazy person will set off a bomb in your office or you may be struck by lightning: then this discussion will have been moot and you've no cause for worry in the least. You'll be dead. It is actually living that requires work."

She turned his attention to the story and picked up where she'd left off. He flipped to a new page of his notebook and readied himself for more notes.

"They arrived, naturally, well after scheduled into the Santa Lucia station in Venice. Lawrence wasn't surprised in the least. Samuel Allcock didn't even utter a single disparaging remark about the Italian railway and its lack of regard for schedules. In fact, he made reference to the pleasing appointments of the Venice station. The Backhouses were still so taken with the country side and their arrival in the city of canals, that time had no meaning for them at all anyway. George and Belle helped to load their trunks onto the trolleys as there were no porters at hand and the little company of honeymooners ventured out into the walkways of Venice. "The *Last Concession* should just be along here before long. Harry said just follow the main thoroughfare and we couldn't miss it." George encouraged. He was quite correct. Although time was a bit distorted, as it always is when venturing into unfamiliar territories, Mandy's Inn was on their left almost before they realized it.

A lady in an apron with her hands upon her hips was laughing heartily at something one of the men at the little tables under the awning was saying. She responded in a rapid description of some analogous situation and they laughed some more. Lawrence was accustomed to Italian, but less with the Venetian dialect. He was sure he heard something about drowning cats, or maybe it was opera singers; he was unsure. What he *was* certain about was that Mandy had thrived in Venice. She had made herself and her inn-caffè-restaurant quite a fixture in the hearts and minds of the local citizenry. He tapped the woman in the apron on the shoulder as he asked in rather good Italian: "Where can I find that beautiful American lady with the dark hair?" She turned to him and almost cried on the spot.

"Lawrence! Oh my! George, Belle..." she hugged them each and kissed their cheeks. "I wondered if you'd be on the morning train... and here you are!" She shouted into the front doors and Gio came out wiping his hands on his shirt. He saw the company of visitors and smiled.

"You must be the guests the lady has been talking about," he said in reasonable broken English. Mandy introduced George and Belle Livingson first. When he heard the name 'Livingson' he nearly genuflected, "I am met your son, Harry!" and he pointed up at the awning over the outdoor seating. There in bright letter's were spelled out: HARRY'S CAFFE. "A great man, very great man..." he continued, "Who are these others? They must be very special people."

THE THIEF

Lawrence smiled and introduced himself and each of their company. At the introduction of each person, Gio shook their hand very enthusiastically. When all the companions were thus introduced, he said, "My mother and father will be very delighted to have you visit them sometime during your stay. I tell them always of Harry and his American friends; they will want to meet you eaches." Mandy motioned for one of her young staff to take the luggage into the Inn and return the trolleys to the train depot. Then she took Belle's arm in hers and walked with them inside through the great entry hall into the courtyard. They sat at the little tables and she called for coffee and pastries to be brought out.

"I can't tell you how wonderful an event this is for me," she began to Belle. "Since I received the letter from Harry announcing your visit, I have been on pins and needles waiting to see you again." The wait staff delivered the requested provisions and she continued, "I understand you are a Grandmama now."

Belle blushed, "Yes and I am *so young* to have grandchildren!" They giggled at that. "Gio is still being helpful I see. Jameson made George create an alternative contrivance to make the wonderful coffee that Gio serves."

Mandy answered, "Yes, the dear has been like a man reborn. He has a steady occupation after years of struggle trying to decide how to support himself and his parents. He's here getting the Caffè ready before dawn every morning. I am sure that if Harry and Jameson hadn't made room for him to use his invention he'd be a most broken man by now. As it is, he is able to at last care for his parents as he's always dreamed he could and they are just that proud of him for his success... so long overdue." She paused to take a breath and sip the coffee, "I even think its given him the courage to court a girl he's known since they were young..."

She looked out the front door, "That's Varrissa just there," she pointed with her cup, "She comes by every morning about this time..." They watched as Gio went to a woman with a large basket under her arm. "Her parents have a fruit stand back down the way

209

there. They stop here every morning before setting up their stall and Varrissa, I think, is almost ready to tell them about herself and Gio." Mandy took another sip. "Everything here moves... well like White Feathers, very slowly and not before everything has been considered. Not at all the impulsive passionate people they are so often stereotyped as being... In most things that is."

Lawrence had been listening and asked could he direct his companions to their rooms, to allow them time to refresh themselves after the long train ride. "Oh thank you Lawrence! Where is *my* sense of time? Of course..." and she pointed up, "That suite there is for Sam and Libby on one side and there are equally posh accommodations for Winston and Genie on the other side of the same suite. The walls are thick and they will be quite insulated from each other. George and Belle and yourself have the suites on the opposite side over here," and she pointed almost directly above them. "I am sorry you all *have to have* the best rooms in the house. I am simply full up at this time of year. Everyone from the northern countries stream to Italy after September and they all, it seems, stop in Venice on their way south."

Lawrence answered, "We'll just have to make do. Thank you so much for making provision for a much larger contingent on such short notice."

To which Mandy responded, "Hell, I would have kicked the whole lot out if you'd brought more folks! Make yourselves at home; this is *almost* American soil after all."

Belle asked after her restaurant enterprise and they talked of Tahoe and the *Concession*, of Harry, Kaitlyn and Lena and Mia, Jameson and Titania. They were still sharing and catching up after the rest of the company had bathed, redressed and come back downstairs. "Well a fine hostess I must seem: sitting here gabbing while my guests fend for themselves," she announced to the company as they reassembled.

Lawrence stated simply, "We are grown adults, by and large. It's not like we have to be led by the hand..."

210

That got a chuckle from Mandy and a squeeze of her hand from Belle, who added, "Perhaps you'll suggest an afternoon's worth of destinations for our friends. I'll happily stay here; I do have a few other topics to air with you."

Mandy did make a few suggestions. A few of the choices were the notable locations all tourists flocked to when they arrived. "...But it's Friday, so you could see the artists who are usually around St. Mark's; they have a special showing at the Campo San Polo. There are musicians and stalls of merchants there. It's a very festive atmosphere..."

Sam and Libby Allcock agreed with Winston and Genie Backhouse that that would be a lovely afternoon's attraction. George opted to look over the Inn's boats for any needed repairs or re-varnishing. That seemed an attractive diversion to Lawrence as well and he followed George out to the canal. Mandy and Belle were again left to their conversation.

The sailboat was moored just outside the building and with both men's efforts, it was soon put on stands so that a thorough inspection could be made. As George went over every seam and plank, Lawrence asked a few questions that had begun to form in his thoughts about... things... "George, you've known Mandy a lot longer than I have; I don't remember her being, well, so alive. Her manner is easy-going, her eyes seem to see so much more, her voice is strong and her words are thoughtful and direct..." George halted his inspection and looked over to his friend.

"Lawrence was there a question in there somewhere? Harry and Kaitlyn were very thorough in her training and she has done very well indeed in the process of rearranging and purging her inner world, as have you, I might add. Is that all so surprising?"

Lawrence wasn't satisfied by the comment. "I suppose I mean to say: I hadn't noticed before just how incredibly attractive she is. Obviously she's always been a beauty, but I mean she glows from the inside out now... and..."

A little smile began to spread across George's face, "Dear

friend, are you finding that you have feelings towards our Mandy that you haven't had before?"

Lawrence was now the one who had to halt. He looked into his friend's face then into his own rising emotions. "I... feel... I... feel... I am startled by what I feel! My mind says, 'Here is Mandy, a remarkable woman in her own right and self-improved, if you will, upon an already sound design. Here am I, a widower and her senior by several years, but I am also improved over the man I once was... In fact, I am a new man for all intents and purposes.' George help me understand what I am feeling."

George pulled up a bench from against the wall and placed it where he could sit and more closely inspect the hull. It also gave Lawrence a seat near him. "Lawrence," he began, "...look at this boat."

Lawrence looked it over and answered, "Okay. It's a sailboat... so?"

"Ah, but it is a sailboat *now*. When Harry found it, it was a derelict rowboat which the owner had allowed to languish and decay. My son needed a vessel with which to train his students and to also provide transportation for the Inn's needs. This is a canal city, after all, nearly everything comes and goes over the water. With care, he stripped it to its basic constituents, removed and replaced broken and ineffective parts and pieces, then redesigned and rebuilt it. After all of that labor, not only is it now a serviceable vessel once more, but it also has new functionality."

He stopped his inspection for a moment and glanced to Lawrence. "Does any of that *resonate* with you?" Lawrence nodded, so George continued, "Whatever 'once were' your feelings for anyone, let alone our Mandy, *you also* have been stripped to your basic constituents and rebuilt. You can now capture the wind to propel you and are no longer driven by the physical beat of oars alone." He crouched beneath the upturned boat and examined her frame and ribs. "You are as much new a man as she is a new woman. *Naturally* you see more clearly all her very attractive qualities."

He tugged on the fittings he was inspecting. "Our feelings are like the wind and our mind: like the rudder and sails of a boat. There is no controlling the force of the wind and its direction, *but* you *can* turn and adjust your sails to use that wind. Of course there are times when winds blow so ferociously, you have to take down the sails or risk their coming apart. Strong emotions are a strong wind; careful attention and navigation are required to keep the boat in one piece. Lacking that care, you run great risk indeed. Now, upon the *sea of love*..." he leaned forward and looked directly into Lawrence's eyes, "...it is only the sailor with a *great respect* for the risks who can navigate the currents, winds and swells of *that* vastness safely. For on that sea there are always at least *two souls* at risk."

Lawrence was slow to respond. This was as close to direct advice his friend had ever offered him and it made sense. Like a man just released from prison will breathe the air of freedom with greater appreciation than other men; he was awakening to his emotions after their lifetime of semi-captivity. George added just one more thing for his friend to consider, "It is commonly said that women are fickle and ever-changeable. I don't think that is an accurate assessment. Women are just more like the wind than you and I; that's all," he finished with a wink.

After Mandy had been caught up to speed on the happenings in Tahoe, she veered the conversation in a direction Belle had not expected. "Belle, what sort of man is Lawrence Spelman? I know he came to Tahoe a widower and has enough wherewithal to have had a house built there and start over..."

Her voice trailed off a little and Belle watched her every expression. "He seems renewed, uh... reinvigorated. I'm sure that has everything to do with your and George's influence..."

Belle interrupted, "And White Feathers. He did more for Lawrence than any of us."

"And White Feathers." Mandy corrected. "I guess what I'm getting at is... well... what's he like?"

Belle took a breath to begin a response, but Mandy continued,

213

"He speaks Italian very well. He looks after his friends. I know, because he's been keeping me updated and informed about every little change or addition to your itinerary. Then when you all arrived, it was Lawrence who saw to your rooms---which is what *I* should have been doing. He looks younger than I remember too! There's a light in his face and an ease in his manner that just wasn't there before, to my recollection."

Belle was patiently listening with a little smile beginning to grow in her expression. Mandy persisted, "I never met his dead wife, but from what Chloe and Kaitlyn told me, she wasn't nearly the strong individual he has always been. I got the impression he tolerated her flights of fancy and self-centeredness on behalf of his daughter. Doesn't that speak well for a man, that he will abide the emotional trials besetting him to achieve a personally accepted aim---taking care of his daughter's well-being, I mean?"

Mandy stopped and looked up around the courtyard, then back to her friend who was still patiently watching her and listening. "I think I would like to have a good talk with him, maybe ask him to help me in the kitchen..." She caught herself suddenly, "Do you think after all the time he spent in the *Concession's* kitchens, he'd even consider that? Maybe I should find out what is his favorite dish and surprise him. Do you know what he likes?"

She looked at Belle's now smiling face. "What? Did I say something funny? You don't know what is his favorite dish? Why are you grinning at me!?"

Belle hesitated to be sure she *actually* would be able to speak and answered, "Sweetheart, I don't know what is his favorite dish. But I am absolutely certain whatever *you* set in front of him will be his *new* favorite dish."

Mandy cocked her head a little in an expression of confusion, "What? Will he eat anything, then? That is a good attribute too, I suppose... unless you need a considered opinion about something to include on a menu or not, then that's not so useful."

Belle continued to gaze at her friend, but now with an

expression of anticipation, waiting for Mandy to catch the meaning of her response. Mandy's eyes widened then, as it dawned on her what Belle had *really* said. "Ohh... Really? Do you think so?" and she just as suddenly became thoughtful again.

Belle kept her words as clear as she could manage, "Mandy, men are like dogs. Feed them and they'll always be at your door. Give them kind attention and they'll follow you anywhere. Even then if you kick them, they'll love you anyway. What you must *never* do is *treat* a man like a dog---they are far more fragile." Mandy continued to listen. "Dearest, if you have feelings for Lawrence, although you haven't said directly that you have, but if you do... I can tell you he is more worthy of your best affections than most any other man alive."

Mandy reached out to Belle, embraced her and whispered, "*That's* what I wanted to know."

When George had ascertained that the sailboat was sound and serviceable, he and Lawrence went into the Inn's great room through the side entrance to look over Harry's 'sempian' which still hung on the wall there. As they walked through the courtyard Mandy was just pulling a stray tress from her face and Belle was straightening the shawl on her shoulders. "Are you ladies near the end of your *initial* greetings?" Lawrence asked facetiously.

Mandy chuckled, "Don't be cheeky. We have actually thoroughly caught up on everything of importance, so there!" and she stuck out her tongue at him.

He answered quickly, "Be careful where you point that thing; it may go off!"

Again she was ready, "It's not my tongue you need worry about, it's my temper."

"Oh, come now..." he replied, "Surely you jest. How can anything unpleasant come from one so pleasingly winsome?"

"Belle, shame on you... You didn't warn me that he had a silver-tongue! You should at least caution your friends before they are taken in by his charms," rejoined Mandy to a surprised Belle.

"And since when is an objective observation become hollow flattery?" Lawrence quipped.

Mandy's widening grin was matched only by the depth of her curtsy, "I yield, sir. I am winsome and pleasant and shall always be so for you."

George and Belle who had known Mandy for most of her life, simply gazed in joyful confusion at her new-found playfulness and joie de vivre. Lawrence bowed in acceptance of her gracious offer and turned back to George to continue their inspection of the boat on the wall.

Mandy quickly cautioned, "Be careful of that treasure; it is my reminder---that I shall always have further to go upon my journey and must make the daily efforts necessary." Lawrence and George both bowed at that.

Belle remarked, "That's beautiful, dear. A very fitting reminder."

After a moment or two of quick scanning, George told Lawrence that he could see everything he needed to see while the boat was mounted on the wall, "Why don't you see if there is any beer in the pantry?"

Lawrence approached the ladies again. Mandy stopped what she was saying as he came near; she looked up to him expectantly. Her attention was so suddenly turned upon him, he couldn't help but reciprocate and they stared into one another's eyes.

"Uh..." he began, "Would you show me your kitchen, George would like a beer and I would like to light your fires."

Belle instantly cackled at that and Lawrence hastily added, "In your ovens... I'll warm your oven." This brought even more laughs from Belle and George could be heard unsuccessfully stifling his otherwise hearty laughter.

Mandy came to his rescue and said, "The kitchen is this way."

She rose and led him through the back double doors of the courtyard. White Feathers was heard to sigh, "*Here we go again... It's the camp store all over again. At least I'm not going to get dragged into it this*

216

time around."

Lawrence followed her to the pantry where she produced a few bottles of a locally brewed beer. She set them on the prep table and showed him the ovens.

"Actually, I *just* want to help," Lawrence began, "What *is* the menu this evening? I will be very happy to assist in whatever way I can. I am well trained, you know..."

Mandy started to say that she had thought Sardines in saor, and Poente and schie, with some potatoes, but he had only paused a moment and began speaking again.

"It's whatever *you* wish, of course." He sighed with a roll of his eyes in frustration, "*Honestly!* I haven't been this tongue-tied since I was a boy and had to choose between cake or pie! I'm not *really* the blathering idiot I appear..." She lay a finger to his lips to hush his rambling.

"Now, that's better," she said. She moved her hand to around his neck and pulled his face toward hers. "Just kiss me," she whispered. He obeyed without argument.

They didn't hear George and Belle enter, nor did they notice Gio as he brought in the daily groceries for the pantry and ice box. In fact, they were *so* willingly detached from the world around them, the applause they *finally* heard, they at first thought was the sound of their own hearts pounding in their chests.

"Brava, Lady, Brava!" cried Gio, still clapping with Belle and George. Mandy and Lawrence blushed to their toes. Mandy wiped a tear from her eye and Lawrence had to clear his throat before trying to speak.

George said simply, "It *is* much warmer in here with the fires lit and the oven warmed!"

Belle went to her friend and hugged her, whispering, "Now don't break him, dear. He's one of a kind."

Lawrence handed George and Gio a beer apiece and opened one himself. "Salut," they toasted and drank deeply.

Mandy then did the *second* thing she had never done before: she took a step back toward Lawrence, raised his arm and put it around her shoulders, then cooed, "Now! I am home."

"As am I dearest, as am I!" Lawrence answered, smiling from his very heart finally at peace, knowing that beside this woman he would *always* be home.

"Well," Belle announced, "You two were only *slightly* slower to break all barriers as George and I were the *very* afternoon we first met." She took George's beer, and raising it said, "To love and to those who bear it!"

Belle then asked, "Mandy I haven't seen the whole place yet; will you and Lawrence give me a tour?" George seconded that. His and Belle's trunks were still sitting inside the front door and he wanted to remove them to their room. He and Lawrence hefted them and followed the ladies up the staircases to the top floor and the suite arranged for them. With the trunks tucked away, Mandy walked them to the terrace first.

"This is a delightful retreat in the spring and summer. Just now it's a little chilly." Her friends and Lawrence looked out over the low wall at the plaza across the canal and the rooftops stretching away across their view of the city. "And just down here..." she led them to a stairwell off the terrace, "...are the owner's apartments. When Harry and the others left I still had not furnished them."

She opened a door and held it for them as they entered. The windows facing them on the opposite wall revealed an only slightly diminished version of the view they'd just enjoyed on the terrace above. Oriental rugs covered the floors and she had hung richly woven tapestries on the walls, along with some very appealing paintings. The settees and chairs were locally produced and so were the lighting fixtures which glittered with Murano glass.

"Here are the bedrooms and the bathroom; I have a little kitchenette not unlike what I had at the Bungalows... your bungalows, I mean." The bedrooms were sumptuous and inviting, the bathroom was tiled in an intricate mosaic on the floor and the walls were a single shade of rose that enhanced the floor's design without detracting from it.

Belle turned to Mandy and they whispered behind their hands. After the hushed conference, Belle told George to assist Lawrence in bringing his luggage downstairs and place it in here, she waved to Mandy's room. "And George, please bring the photographs we brought for Mandy." Mandy looked up at Lawrence in a very shy glance and he returned her somewhat self-conscious expression in kind. "Don't dawdle," said Belle, "there's no reason *everyone* need be made aware of their change of status this minute and our friends will be back momentarily."

"Just one look at them should do the trick, I should think…" George remarked under his breath as he and Lawrence hastily complied with his wife's injunction. Once his trunk was deposited, they returned to the kitchen and Mandy suggested what she thought they might serve for dinner.

"Fridays in the late autumn and winter the restaurant can't pay for itself with the other attractions of the day and all; so I've taken to not opening to the public. It's just for the guests."

Lawrence looked up as if through the ceiling and did a quick estimate, "Are the rooms double or single occupancy?"

"*We* have ten other guests just now besides yourselves," and she gushed, "I love the sound of that: 'we'."

"So, dinner for eighteen." Lawrence concluded. "George, will you lend me a hand rearranging the tables in the dining room? Sweetheart, I'll be right back to help with the cooking," he added to Mandy.

She smiled and sighed as she turned to Belle. "I am liking this already!"

The Allcocks and Backhouses did indeed return shortly and were informed of the approximate time for dinner. They retired to their rooms to freshen up and relax some from their stroll. George and Belle were shooed from the kitchen, while Lawrence and Mandy set about preparing their first meal together. Once all the dishes were only needing to be dressed and presented, Mandy took Lawrence by the hand and ushered him through a series of doors and unseen staircases to their apartments. "This place is full of little hidden passages..." she explained. Without even a sponge bath, they hurriedly changed clothes and returned to the kitchen careful not to arrive back downstairs at the same time, nor from the same doors. They set up the first course for presentation just as their company began to arrive in the Dining Room.

The Inn's guests were dressed formally and once they were seated, Mandy explained that the staff had Friday's off and that Lawrence would assist her in serving them for the evening. The Risi e Bisi was served first, a very tasty dish of risotto with pancetta and peas cooked with broth. Bottles of Pinot Grigio were at each table and the guests were encouraged to decant as desired. Breads and cheeses were brought to the diners as the next course was presented. Poente and Schie: small shrimp, fried and perched on a bed of white polenta. More bread and saucers of olive oil were supplied with the Venetian staple: Sardines in Saor, the little fishes marinated in vinegar with onions, raisins and pine nuts.

Empty bottles were replaced and George stood to offer a toast to their hostess. "On behalf of all of us, we wish to extend our heartfelt appreciation for this most exquisite meal and your generous hospitality. To the Hostess!" They all drank. Then Lawrence stood and cleared his throat to regain everyone's attention.

"This is a very special night for our little group of travelers. It was just a year and a half ago that Harry and Kaitlyn Livingson re-established and inaugurated this Inn with their companions and brought this lovely lady to this enchanting city," he gestured to Mandy who was sitting next to him.

She was listening most carefully, wondering what was coming next. "I have looked forward to this visit perhaps more than others, for this simple reason..."

He knelt, and took Mandy's hands into his own. "Miranda

Katherine Hill," Mandy's eyes grew wide at the sound of her given name, never uttered since her own christening and she was too young at the time to remember that occasion. "Will you offer me the grand privilege and honor of..."

She didn't wait for the rest, "Yes, I will! You most remarkable, wonderful man. I will marry you and shall give to you the love I never imagined I might ever bestow upon anyone!" She pulled him up from his knee to stand next to her, "Lawrence, you have made me the happiest woman in the world," her tears began to cloud her eyes.

Lawrence's grin was an odd contrast to his own tears streaming down his cheeks. The awed guests, once they regained their voices, clapped and cheered their elation at the couple's triumphant union. To the thunderous approbation of those assembled, they kissed for the second time that day. This time, as at the first, the sounds of the room faded to whispers as their hearts beat as one heart and their tears of joy mingled together in the rapture of the moment. A breath-taking several minutes later, Lawrence found his voice.

"Dessert will be served momentarily..." Miranda grinned and nearly skipped to the kitchen to begin the presentations of the dessert plates, her husband followed her and all the company noticed that his feet were barely touching the tiled floor in his passage

After the dessert plates were cleared and the other guests had retired, George whispered to Sam and they hopped up from their chairs, crossed the great room and carried the boat from the wall to the courtyard. George settled it sturdily on one of the water channels so that the water ran beneath it and barely wet the hull, then he took a position inside it near the bow. Belle and Olivia herded Lawrence and Miranda to the boat and George waved them into the midships. "As the father of the man who owns this vessel and in his absence, I assume the captaincy. Mr. Spelman do you have the ring?"

Lawrence fumbled in his vest pockets and produced a gold band, which he didn't know he had. George grinned. Belle had removed her wedding ring, given it to George and he had slipped it into Lawrence's pocket during the clean-up after the meal.

"Miranda Katherine Hill, do you take this man as your husband and promise to treat him always with compassion and love, whether you feel like it or not?"

Miranda said calmly and in a very deliberate voice, "I shall love him as myself, serve him when he requires it and guide him when he needs it."

"Lawrence Theodore Spelman, do you take this woman as your wife and promise to treat her always with compassion and love, whether you feel like it or not?"

Lawrence proclaimed aloud, "I shall love her as myself, serve her when she requires it and guide her when she needs it."

"As the living patriarch of the Livingson traditions---and present Captain of this fine vessel: which is the ever-present reminder that you shall always have further to go upon your journey and must make daily the enormous efforts necessary---I pronounce you husband and wife."

After the third kiss Miranda had ever had, George handed them out of the boat and suggested they return their treasure to its place on the great room wall, which they did gleefully. George followed them to the wall and just as it was secured in its place, he turned to the rest of the company and announced, "I present Mr. and Mrs. Spelman, who have made the *Last Concession* their own." Hands were shaken.

Then after hugs and embraces all around, Belle led the couple to their apartments upstairs. "It is a rare opportunity to give all that you are to another. You will do well to remember the first words of wisdom: *Know thyself.*" She kissed them each goodnight, and closed their door.

Once they were alone in their own sitting room, Miranda pulled her husband to her and whispered, "So, you haven't yet had even a shower?"

George was up very early. When he got downstairs, Gio was

already preparing the Caffè for the morning. George shook his hand, again, with a smile and asked him a few brief questions. Gio pointed up the way and gave what seemed to be clear directions. So George took a stroll on the thoroughfare following Gio's advised route. He came to where the fruit and vegetable vendors were setting up for the morning, and asked another question or two. He was answered with more pointing and broken English. After a walk of no more than thirty minutes through winding alleys and over a few canals, he stood in front of a most respected potter's house and workshop. He knocked and was led to the open work area where the kiln was being stoked for the day's firing. He made a drawing of what he wanted, sketched in its uses and indicated the number of items he required. After a brief discussion between the potter and his wife, they arrived at a cost for the items and George nodded. He gave them the address where they should be delivered and headed on to his next destination.

Through more neighborhoods and over more canals he reached the ghetto area and after back-tracking a couple times found the house of which he was told. The frail woman who came to the door let him inside and asked him, by gestures, to wait in the front room. Shortly she returned, followed by an equally frail old man. George explained what he wished to acquire and the old gentleman turned and started through a hallway to the rear of the building; the old woman took George's arm and led him after her husband. In a largish room, he was shown the selection of pieces they had left. George selected one, gave the old man the address to where it should be delivered. They then began the negotiations for the item, which he had been assured by the gentleman who had directed him to this couple in particular, would be along the lines of his own choosing. Once the smiling older couple enthusiastically accepted his terms, he was back in the lane once again. He looked up one way and down the other, shrugged his shoulders and muttered to himself, "It's an island, how lost can I be?" and he headed off on his best guess at the direction back to the *Concession* for his morning coffee.

Gio was waiting on the few earliest customers. When he saw George, he grabbed his hand and introduced him to Varrissa's mother and father who were at their usual table. George said as many wonderful things as he could think to say about the inventor and it was all received well by her father. When they left to set up their stall, he and Gio talked of Varrissa and her family, Gio's parents and his home, and that he hoped to purchase a little home with a workshop. "So that Varrissa's father shall see I am a man of properties..." he added.

"My wife and I will be delighted to visit your parents; would this afternoon be convenient?" George inquired.

Gio's face lit up and he nodded most enthusiastically, "I shall guide you there myself at two clocks, Okay?"

Smiling, George answered in kind, "At two clocks, Okay." He went to the kitchen and joined Belle, Miranda and Lawrence at the table. "Dear, we are going to be guests of Gio and his parents today at two clocks, okay?"

Belle reflected her husband's smile and nodded. She replied with a question, "Did you have a nice stroll this morning? You certainly were up early..."

George winked and admitted he did get a little turned around during his 'walk,' but that he was thankful it was an island. Belle then asked Miranda if the oven only used coal, or was there a source for chopped wood available and could the stove use either fuel?

"I suppose it wouldn't matter in the least to the stove, but the firebox isn't as large as those stoves designed for only wood... It would smell nicer, though. I have been wanting to have a brick oven built. I will most assuredly use only wood to heat that oven," she answered and looked to the vacant corner between the kitchen door and the window. "Lorenzo, darling, would you and George see if a brick oven is even something we can consider?"

Belle looked to George and mouthed silently, 'Lorenzo?'

Lawrence looked at the space and walked over to the corner,

made a few guestimates as to the area and volume. He opened the door and George got up to follow him out the back. "Do you suppose the floor would support the weight?"

George gauged the thickness and the height of the wall, "I suppose the floor will support a great weight. Harry was certain it was reinforced concrete. The hole for the flue will take a bit of chiseling and quite a length of pipe to breach the roofline. But I think you could have a brick oven in your kitchen in say... a couple weeks? Of course it will take a while longer for the mortar to cure out completely, so don't plan a new menu around it soon."

Lawrence smiled and led them back to the kitchen table. Belle and Miranda became suddenly quiet when the gentlemen returned. George cocked an eyebrow, but Belle gave the slightest shake of her head to ignore the abrupt silence. So George nodded for Lawrence to follow him to the sitting room. They went through the door at the end of the kitchen and George settled into one of the chairs near the fireplace. "My friend, I have taken the liberty of arranging for more furniture to be delivered this afternoon."

Lawrence was only mildly surprised at this, as his friend and mentor generally always had a very good reason for initiating any new activity. "Oh?" he replied, "And where shall this new furniture be situated?"

"Well, that's why I mention it. You know more about these things than I do, and it will wholly depend upon your own determination of its usefulness and importance." George answered cryptically. "I figured it would probably be in here."

Lawrence looked around at the few clusters of seating groups, and asked, "Am I to *guess* what this furniture is? Or, are you going to let it be a surprise?"

"I'm sorry," George replied, "Like I said, I don't know nearly enough about these things... It's a piano... and I only know what I could understand from the old man who told me about it: That it should not be placed against an outside wall, something about moisture and all. That it should be covered or kept at a reasonably constant temperature... and that it will probably require tuning every so often."

Lawrence's eyes were growing larger, "What kind of *piano* are we talking about here, George?"

George really didn't know any more than he was offering, "Again, I don't know about these things and I probably should have consulted you and Miranda first... but I thought if I didn't *push a little* it would likely never happen. The old man called it: a *Victorian Professional Grand Piano from the German factory of Steinway...* Do you know about that kind of instrument?"

Lawrence's jaw dropped, "George... *how much did you pay* for this?!"

George actually blushed, "Well, uh, that's why I brought this up now... *I* am only paying for it to be delivered... The terms of sale are: that you and Miranda shall provide meals for the seller... and his wife... for the duration of their natural lives." George winced and quickly added, "I estimate the old couple's age at about ninety, it won't be forever. But they don't get out much, so the meals will *have* to be delivered to them... uh... He said he'd tune it after it was delivered... but that's an extra fee..."

Lawrence's expression was still one of utter shock and awe. "You're telling me: that *you* traded a 'lifetime' of meals to an older couple..."

"Who have no children..." George interjected.

"...in exchange for a *piano*? Does that about sum it up?" Lawrence concluded, incredulously.

"Yeah," muttered George, unsure if he'd at last overstepped the bounds of their friendship.

Lawrence fell back into the chair, the edge of which he had been sitting at tensely. He repeated almost to himself, "Pasta and cannolis everyday for one of the *finest musical instruments crafted in all of Europe...*" He looked over at his friend, "Yes, George. I'd say this is a most welcome arrangement. Miranda and I will deliver their meals in person!"

George let out a sigh of relief and began again, "So, wouldn't this room be a nice sorta sitting room-music salon area?"

Lawrence was still gazing at the ceiling, "Just let me sit here and enjoy my amazement a little longer..." Then it dawned on him to ask, "What else have you been planning and arranging for the *Last Concession*?"

It was George's turn to look up at the ceiling, "Well..."

Belle and Miranda each went off to change for the day's activities. Belle dressed in clothes in which she expected to walk and work; Miranda put on a warm outfit for sailing. When she arrived back downstairs and found Lawrence and George in the sitting room, she announced, "I am so looking forward to this outing! I want to go to Burano and select lace curtains, table cloths and shawls... some for here, some for gifts to our family and friends back home. Is that alright, sir?"

Lawrence smiled, "Madam, your wish is my command. Shall we?" He turned back to George and winked, "Uh, I'm afraid we won't be back *until after* tea time, *or so...* Will that be an inconvenience?"

George smiled also, "Not at all, that *should* be just ideal!"

Belle looked at her husband as the newlyweds left the Inn, "Alright George, what sneaky things have you been up to now?"

Before he could reply, he was saved by Sam and Winston's greeting, "The ladies are adamant that they shall shop today, so we are off to the Ponte di Rialto and Piazza San Marco."

Winston added, "Right after coffee and cannolis, that is."

Belle wished them patience and fortitude and waved as they went out the front doors to the Caffè. "I suppose you think you've escaped..." She turned back to George and put her hands upon her hips.

"Darling," he began, "Do you think we could find a heavy duty sewing machine in this town?"

Their meeting with Gio's parents was a double blessing. Gio owned a very sturdy sewing machine, which he was more than happy to loan to Belle *and* it turned out that Gio and his parents lived very near the ghetto where George had acquired the piano. So after a lovely visit and a promise to return before they left Venice, Belle followed him to the little house to which he'd been so much earlier that day. The delivery men were just arranging the case and legs and such onto a massive cart, fastidiously supervised by the old man. George introduced Belle to the frail old man and then to his wife. Belle asked George how he knew them, and he gave a brief recap of his morning's adventures. When all was set, they followed the delivery cart to the *Last Concession* by a much shorter route than the one George had rambled earlier.

The little old man, with his wife on his arm, entered the Inn as nobility. He promptly began the direction of the instrument's reassembly: First by directing George to move one of the largest rugs to a place equidistant between the fireplace and rear wall, where he then had the pieces put back together on the rug. Belle sat with the frail little woman and they shared a filling lunch as the maestro tuned the instrument. Once satisfied, he tested it by playing one of the most energetic pieces of music George and Belle had ever heard. His frail little wife nodded to her husband and whispered, "Mozart," with a knowing smile. The master's hands moved so quickly and precisely over the ivories, George had to reassess the couple's longevity as he'd related it to Lawrence. As the finale was sounded, the little group applauded appreciatively. Belle gestured for him to sit and have a bite to eat which he most graciously accepted.

Gio returned about then, pulling his sewing machine on a little hand cart. "Where should you be liking to use thises?" he asked as Belle greeted him. She indicated the end of the kitchen which had space and light enough to work. He deposited it where she pointed, and, bowing, left to return home.

She turned to rejoin their guests, but as she looked over her shoulder at the machine she muttered to herself, "George, George...

what are you planning now?"

The elderly couple had eaten their fill and wished to return home. George assured them Lawrence and Miranda would be by later with their supper and they were off. He turned to Belle and said, "Alright, how would you arrange these seating areas to the piano's best advantage?" Belle began gesturing for this chair to move here, and that settee to be turned there, and after a little more than half an hour the resultant arrangement did indeed take full advantage of the fireplace's warmth and allow for clear views and hearing of the instrument.

"Oh this is nicely done George, very nice indeed. Miranda will be so thrilled; I am certain she is as yet unaware of *all* her husband's talents."

George was also quite pleased, "Well now, would you care to accompany me on a very brief walk... there is another piece of furniture I have my eye on..."

Belle laughed in answer and took his arm, "Your wish is my command!"

Everyone seemed to have magically timed there return to the Inn as if in response to George's satisfaction at the completion of the first phase of his additions. Lawrence and Miranda arrived first and she was thoroughly overwhelmed by the changes in the sitting room. Belle handed her a fresh handkerchief when her own became too moist for use. Lawrence then added the icing on the cake. He sat at their new piano and began playing his favorite sonata. Miranda's emotions were now in such a state; she was quite certain that if she learned he could also change water into wine she couldn't be any more in awe of her mate.

George went to the new bar which he'd *just* set up under Belle's direction of placement and poured drinks for the little company. As Lawrence began another piece, the Allcocks and Backhouses returned from their shopping adventure. The music drew them to the sitting room like an enchantment and they found seats as George served drinks to the new arrivals as well.

229

Lawrence reached the end of the opus and looked up at seven wide-eyed and very impressed people. He stood and took a little bow as they applauded his performance. Whereupon he sat back down and played another. Miranda walked over and sat beside him, put her head on his shoulder and sighed.

He remarked, "I haven't played this much in years and years. I'm so surprised my fingers know what to do." He lowered his voice and whispered to his wife, "I shall enjoy this very much..."

"Oh, Lorenzo, I *am* in heaven," was all Miranda could muster to say and she closed her eyes again with an angelic expression upon her beautiful face.

Genie commented to Libby that it had been years since she played well, to which Libby answered, "You? Me too!" She turned to their men and asked, "Do either of you play also? How many more surprises are we to experience before supper?"

Winston and Samuel looked at each other and they both nodded. Sam spoke first. "Libby dearest; I stopped playing when my oldest daughter was married and moved away. I am sure I am no where near the virtuoso Lorenzo is."

Although Winston hadn't played in an equally long time, he added, "Fifteen years of lessons and I bet I couldn't play scales, anymore."

Lawrence overheard a bit of the conversation and invited Genie to have a go. He and Miranda went to sit next to George and Belle. Genie sat at the piano bench, closed her eyes, placed her hands on the keys and proceeded to play Beethoven's Bagatelle in A minor--- Fur Elise. She blushed crimson when the company stood and applauded her. "Next?" she said meekly and hastily walked back to the waiting arms of her husband.

Sam was brave enough to approach the instrument next. No sooner had he sat down, than he was pounding out an adaptation of the final 'movement' of the fourth movement to the master's Ninth Symphony---the Ode to Joy. The company, who were enthusiastically

230

surprised at Genie's play, were now so whelmed at their friend's secret talent they positively held their breath. When the final chord was played, Samuel was almost standing at the keyboard; his hair was disheveled and his eyes were a little wild. He looked up to see Olivia in tears and clapping as if she'd no longer any feeling in her hands.

"I guess it all comes back to you... after all..." he said sheepishly, and ambled back to his wife's side and sat down. She climbed into his lap and cuddled him. She was, without a doubt, in bliss. He at last added, "Next?"

Winston rose without comment, although with considerable reluctance and moved toward the piano. He hummed a little and then began the first movement of Mozart's Eine kleine Nachtmusik. Again the company was in the throes of delight and impressed appreciation and again there was resounding applause. When he stood and pointed to Libby, still curled in her husband's lap, "All right, your up Libby!" She adjusted herself in Sam's lap and made to get up.

Olivia stood to her full height, and straightened her shoulders. As if in answer to the magic of the afternoon she walked to the keyboard, closed her eyes and in the most passionate rendition any of them had ever heard, played the Moonlight Sonata. There was not a dry eye in the Inn, nor at the front doorway where many passersby had gathered, nor upon the balconies of the upper floors. As the last few notes trailed hauntingly away to the final, near silent chords of release, the crowds erupted into an ovation that literally shook the windows. All in the sitting room were on their feet and they only realized so many others were cheering and applauding when Olivia bowed to those beyond the little group.

She walked back to beside her husband; he knelt before her and his tears spilt into her hands. She knelt down next to him and they whispered to each other of their mutual adoration new-kindled in their hearts. Genie and Winston were similarly engaged as Lawrence and Miranda turned to George and Belle and said, "There are not words for the joy you have brought to our lives... We are, and shall forever be, loving you." Lawrence returned to the piano and played just a melody he had always liked. Miranda went to prepare supper.

Belle whispered to George, "You have done well today George, *very* well, indeed," and kissed him on his cheek.

When the meal was nearly ready to serve, Lawrence and Miranda prepared dishes for the elderly couple. Lawrence added breads and cheese for their next morning's breakfast, told Miranda they'd be back very soon and followed George to their home. Taking the more direct route it was but a few minutes walk. After Lawrence made arrangements for his and Miranda's daily return during the weekdays, he asked if they would be amenable to being ferried by boat to the Inn on weekends, "...when it's warm enough weather for you to enjoy the ride." They grinned at the thought of being treated like special guests and assented. They bid the old couple bon appetit and returned to the *Concession*.

They assisted in serving the restaurant's guests and ate as they could when not delivering food or replenishing glasses. "You know," Lawrence commented, "it may be time to schedule a weekend staff for the restaurant and rooms."

Miranda replied to the comment, "The two young men and young lady who assist during the week have been asking for that opportunity and it's probably time we hired an assistant cook as well... As for the rooms and cleaning and such, I have been using two widowed sisters who come in every weekday morning for the laundry. Perhaps they know of someone who can do a bit of cleaning every other day or so?"

Sunday the company spent in the Inn. The gentlemen looked over George's plans for an awning over the terrace---its supporting structure and deployment. The ladies went about the sitting room, dining room and foyer deciding on table dressings, window treatments and wall decorations. Gio agreed to stay until evening, Varrissa was given permission by her father to visit for the afternoon, so Lawrence and Miranda went out with the company for a stroll, both to window shop and to generally become more familiar with the thoroughfares, canal network and bridges. As the late afternoon sent long shadows across their paths they turned back to the Inn.

By late Monday afternoon, the structure had been erected on the terrace. Belle made the heavy canvas awning, sewing on it through the evening before and into the night; the rest was completed during that morning. It was finally installed and secured. The potter arrived with George's order and the gentlemen helped carry some of them to the terrace while Belle arranged a few of them in the courtyard below. Wood was brought up, and the chimineas were inaugurated. The warmth and glow made the terrace and its vistas even more of an inviting retreat. In the courtyard the burning outdoor fireplaces became most attractive centers for gathering guests to relax and chat. Lawrence and Miranda took the time to sit down and compose letters to their friends and family announcing the joy of their recent union. The next couple weeks were idyllic for all at the Inn.

Olivia arranged for a photographer to capture their holiday company on film. She and Miranda proposed several vignettes around the Inn for their sittings and an equal number of group pictures for souvenirs of the holiday occasion. Every one ordered copies of the plates and when they finally arrived they packaged them safely for transport home. Afternoons and evenings were spent in conversations and storytelling, playing games and enjoying the music played by one or another of the pianists. Letter writing occupied the final evenings of their stay and the holiday waned to a close.

The days of winter began to descend with vigor on northern Italy. The Allcocks and Backhouses prepared to return home to England. Renewed in spirit and ready to step back into their usual lives. Sam and Winston went on a last walk with their lovely wives. In the morning, with trolleys brought from the station, they bid the *Last Concession* farewell and were escorted to the departing train by George and Belle, Lawrence and Miranda.

Olivia spoke for all, "We shall look forward to returning each year. And we've decided that perhaps we shall begin late next spring instead of during the colder months. The warm spring days should prove a more apt time for inaugurating our annual visits." Hugs and handshakes were made all around and they waved goodbye as the train pulled out of the station house. The Spelmans and Livingsons walked back toward the Inn.

Miranda asked innocently, "How long have you and George planned to stay with us... until our friends return in the spring?" she giggled.

Belle glanced at George before answering, "Would that be an imposition?"

Miranda stopped in her tracks, and gaped at her dearest friend, "I was jesting... You're really going to stay through the winter?!"

George smiled, "Traveling in such cold weather isn't very appealing. Besides, our Kat will think twice before the next time she suggests we leave for a 'little' holiday!"

Miranda took Belle's arm in hers as they continued, far more warmed than the chill air insisted and with the knowledge she needn't dread her friend's departure for several months. "And," Belle added, "if my Uncle White Feathers could learn five languages, I can at least pick up a third!"

They chuckled at that and George attempted a response in the little Italian he'd already begun to pick up. Miranda snorted a laugh, Lawrence corrected, "You probably meant you were as happy as a *clam*, not a *comma!* That *was* a good beginning though; your inflection is very good."

George grinned, "I like it here; what are the usual Yuletide traditions..."

"Oh that reminds me," Miranda suddenly exclaimed; we have a full house of guests arriving tomorrow! Belle dearest, you and George are gonna have to move into our apartments. Is that a deal breaker?"

Belle looked to George then back to her, "What!? Stay in the same rooms with you two?!... Just tell me I've died and gone to heaven..." she smiled.

A few days later, Miranda and Belle delivered the mid-day meal to the elderly couple, and Miranda engaged them in a conversation which she'd wanted to open for a few days. She explained how life-changing the addition of the piano had been for them and how she hoped the meals they brought were to their liking. All they had to do was just say what they wanted and it was theirs.

The old woman smiled and her husband was visibly flattered. They made it clear that the food they'd been delivered was the best they'd eaten in time out of memory; that they were pleased the instrument had brought such joy to them and they hoped it would be a lasting legacy in their family. Miranda blushed at that last and said that she and her husband did not have children. Belle interrupted and asked Miranda what had caused her to blush so.

She translated the last bit of the conversation; Belle touched her arm, "But sweetheart, you *are* pregnant; you'll likely have morning sickness beginning before long..."

Miranda's eyes grew round, and her face became pale. "Belle how do you *know* this? I haven't felt at all out of sorts or in any way different..."

"Miranda, trust this grandmama when she tells you you're pregnant. This isn't the first baby conceived while I've been privileged to be around the future mother." Belle secretly hoped that would suffice and she wouldn't be forced to invent any more excuses for her covert informants.

Miranda explained to the elderly couple what her friend had just said and thanked them saying: the music they'd introduced into their home would indeed become a legacy of which they were most proud. The old woman clapped as the old man simply wagged his finger at the expectant mother. The two ladies then begged their leave of the nice couple and started back for the Inn.

"Belle, you're certain? Lorenzo and I are *really* having a *baby*... a child of our own... *I'm pregnant*?"

"Miranda my friend, I could *not* be more sure. You and Lorenzo *are going* to be parents."

Miranda simply had to be nearly led the familiar walk back. When they returned and found George and Lawrence preparing the corner in the kitchen for the brick oven's construction, she couldn't contain herself. "Lorenzo! You're going to be a father again!"

Lawrence dropped the trowel from his hand and stood as a man in a spotlight on a stage. The grin that began to spread across his face said it all. "A baby?" He turned to George, "I'm going to be a father! We're going to have a baby!"

A messenger arrived at the front door and called for someone to answer. "Back here!" Miranda called absently.

The young lad brought a telegram and placed it in her hand. Lawrence tossed the young fellow a lira without a second thought. Miranda passed the wire to her husband, who opened it and read aloud, omitting the 'stops.'

"Lorenzo and Miranda, Harry and I are so excited for you we cannot contain our joy. I am at last to have a brother and you, my father, at last have the chance to raise a child with a most remarkable woman who is your very equal. Our love always, Kaitlyn, Harry, Mia and Lena Livingson. P.S. Tell 'Captain' George and MamaBelle we love them."

Miranda and Lawrence simply stood with the blank expressions one would expect from people who had just been told the world had gotten together and elected them emperor and empress for life. They mouthed the words, but no sound came out. George and Belle were chagrined at their children's letting the cat out of the bag so thoroughly. They looked at each other and proceeded to guide their friends to the table to sit down.

Belle opened, "This is going to take some explaining..."

There was no subterfuge she could spontaneously invent to explain away Kaitlyn's telegram. So without interruption and as comprehensively as she could, Belle gave the two eager listeners a history of the Livingson family secret. "...And that is why you hold a telegram from your very jubilant daughter in your hand."

Miranda simply mouthed, "A son..." she looked at her husband, "A son!"

Lawrence wasn't any more recovered from the shock than was his wife. George intervened, "There is no way of knowing if, when upon the birth of your child, you might also be 'inducted' as it were into the tribe. That is, I think, wholly dependent upon yourselves. You see Harry understands it this way and I have to agree: our ancestors are available to our minds and ears because the 'blinders' are off. That is to say, at a certain level of personal spiritual development there is nothing impeding the free-flow of communication with those of us *tuned* to hear the counsel from those who have gone before us... and who are still available for counsel, that is not yet too disinterested in their descendants. That's how Harry perceives it and my son has gone further than any in my lineage, or any other I dare say."

Belle announced as an experiment, "Well I know of *one* ancestor who would be most delighted to communicate, if it's possible..." and she said in a conversational tone: "Pompe? What do you think?"

The four sitting at the table, two of whom expected an answer, and two who thought they couldn't be more shocked, heard in a clear voice, *"Can you hear me now?"*

Miranda and Lawrence each responded so quickly and at the same time that their voices were nearly one voice, "White Feathers?!"

"At your service my dearest friends. Harry was correct in one regard; it does depend upon the ears of the hearer. In other regards, it has to do with family relations, and that is a situation I shall not begin to try and explain. Suffice it to say, you shall have my assistance and guidance in your every need"

Both the parents to be burst into laughter and tears; they were so numbed to any more surprises they simply surrendered to the reality they faced.

"Miranda, I like your pet name for my friend. 'Lorenzo' has such a good sound to it, and by the way, I was the one who told George your full name and he told your husband. Outside of that, I think you're up to speed."

Lawrence was caressing his wife's belly lovingly with her hand upon his. "We shall just have to start each day believing seven impossible things before breakfast; for I am certain we have fallen through the looking glass into another world," he remarked and Miranda nodded.

Belle answered decisively to that, "Do not *believe* anything. Remember, only what you can verify for yourself can be admitted as possible and practicable. The work we have begun does not disappear or evaporate at the introduction of new facilities or functions. It is incumbent upon us as the faithful and humble bearers of truth, to *always* remain true to the training which enables and empowers us to think, act and live as real men."

"I stand humbly admonished and reminded of our sacred trust." Lawrence answered for them both, "We are... well... surely *you* understand..."

Belle was as gentle as any mother, "Yes, dear ones, we most *assuredly* do understand."

The construction of the brick oven progressed steadily and at long last, after George was certain it was ready, Lawrence and Miranda baked their first loaves of bread. Then they made sweet cakes, then cookies. Their baking experiments continued much to the delight of the customers of the Caffè and restaurant---not to mention the elderly couple who were daily treated to the latest baked morsels. Lawrence was without question the more adventurous of the two and one Friday evening when only the Inn's guests were to be served, he made a variety of Neopolitan pizzas: recently mentioned by a guest from Naples in honor of Queen Margherita of Savoy. His own inclinations and tastes led him to add other ingredients than just the tomato, basil and mozzarella. He added sardines to one, to another he added crumbled Italian sausage, on another he laid prosciutto and then on another he piled the bits and pieces of vegetables left over in the ice box. The diners were so impressed by the selection and flavors that word soon spread as gossip in a village. So that the *next* Friday when the restaurant normally closed its doors for lack of patrons, Miranda, Belle and George had difficulty finding tables and chairs for the numbers of people crowding into the little restaurant. Miranda went to the kitchen and consulted Lawrence.

"Really!?" Lawrence answered in surprise, "Well I suppose since I have enough dough prepared we *could* set out the pies as a buffet and you could simply charge admission: say... so much per plate and let them find seats where they wish. You should probably make the sitting room off-limits though..." He took another two pizzas from the oven and put three more inside.

"Lorenzo do we have parmesan in the pantry?" He nodded as she fetched a grater. She mentioned "...and we will need more pepper grinders. I'd better start a list..."

Several hours later when the last of the dough was exhausted and the last guest had belched and left, the two couples plopped into chairs in the kitchen and reviewed the evening's excitement. "I'll need to have more dough ready, I'm sure," began Lawrence.

Miranda reminded him of the graters and pepper mills, then took out a pencil and paper to begin taking notes. It was George who began to organize their experience toward an ever more successful 'pizza night' for the following week. He ticked off on his fingers, "*One*: I must've answered the same three questions all evening---What's on this? Where can I sit? Is there more coming? We need signage. *Two*: The Caffè awning should be utilized; cloth walls can be installed for another seating area. Long tables and benches should suffice---it seems that buffets are social events. We can get more chimineas for that front area. *Three*: Beverages. We need the participation of a local brewery, or have pitchers and pitchers of tea... something to quench thirsts. *Four*: Special requests and salads. If you want to accommodate them, we need the requests noted early in the evening, not while poor Lorenzo is up to his elbows in the oven. We might as well just put a couple large bowls of salads and condiments out on the buffet tables. And lastly, *Five*: Pie pans, plates and utensils. Either we spend a lot of time cleaning and reusing, or we just get as many dishes, forks and knives as we can lay our hands on." He relaxed back into his chair and then remembered one more thing. "Oh, and I have an idea for cleaning plates and utensils enmasse. Once I hammer out the details, I think I can make that task easier, too."

Miranda went back over her notes aloud. Belle mentioned a supply of tablecloths and napkins, so that the tables could be stripped and recovered quickly. "I shouldn't be surprised, I guess, at the mess people can make while devouring food quickly."

Lawrence added that he felt sure, "Once our guests realize that this isn't a one time occasion, perhaps they will return to the relaxed tempo of dining we all have come to anticipate from Venetians. Honestly, Belle's right, the few times I peeked out the kitchen door, it appeared to be more of a contest than a repast."

They each nodded, hoping he was right. Sleep came easily that night. In the morning the ladies shopped for utensils, plates and very large salad bowls, bolts of fabric to make tablecloths, canvas for the awning walls, graters and grinders and heavy paper for the notes and signs they would prepare. George returned to the potter's workshop and ordered a few more chimineas, then he went in search of a metalsmith. Lawrence, after taking a survey from some of the morning clients of the Caffè about their preferred brews, was interrupted by Gio. "Lorenzo, you are asking about beer brewers?"

Lawrence explained the dilemma encountered on Friday night and their tentative solution. Gio beamed, "But I have a good friend in Udine, Luigi Moretti, he has a brewery! We served in the wars together; we are like brothers---we used to joke: he brew beer, I brew coffee... we brew up a storm!" he laughed and Lawrence laughed with him at the play on words---in Italian, that is. "I can wire him. How much do you want? When?"

When George finally returned, he was pulling a cart with a

rather large metal box, assorted rectangular plate metal and coils and coils of copper tubing and valves. Curious, Lawrence had to ask, "Uh, an anchor for the boat?"

George smiled, "No, next question..."

Intrigued, Lawrence asked, "Warming table?"

George nodded, impressed, "No, but that was a better guess..."

Lawrence tried one more, "A still!?"

George laughed, "No."

"Okay, what is it?" Lawrence asked as he helped carry the pieces through the back door and into the kitchen. George went to the sink basin and beside it he began assembling a frame, added the pipe legs and fastened the lipped metal plate to the top of the frame. Upon that he set the metal box and said, "Well at least it all fits together; kinda surprising as the old guy just had my sketch to go from... good craftsman there."

Lawrence looked the contraption over and as he had simply to rely upon George's comments the previous evening, "How is this supposed to wash dishes?"

"Good," George said, "at least we're on the same page. Now..." And he began to describe his idea: he held up the copper piping and moved to the brick oven. He made some gestures to indicate how the piping would go in and come out, run back to the 'box,' "...and clean the dishes; at least that's the plan."

Lawrence reviewed the idea aloud, to be sure he hadn't missed anything, and then asked about soap, pressures, the temperature of the waters and a few other aspects which occurred to him. He and George set down with pencil and paper and began to flesh out the concept and the prototype. They were still in conference when Belle and Miranda returned with the last load of necessities from the shopping expedition.

Belle separated out the fabric and set herself to hemming large squares and rectangles for tablecloths. Miranda measured the front awning and returned with sketches and dimensions for the hanging walls. "Lorenzo, will you come and help me decide what sort of framework we might need, if any? I don't want to overburden the awning's structure." He told George he was on his own for a while and followed his wife to the front of the building.

Belle looked up from the sewing machine and saw George's 'box,' "What are you up to Captain?"

George smiled and answered, "Just realizing that our Lorenzo has a good mechanical head on his shoulders! He has streamlined my ideas for the dishwasher. I just have to go and get a few more items from the fellow at the metal shop. I'll be back soon."

When Miranda and Lawrence came back to the kitchen, he was looking for George. Belle said he just missed him, "He's off to the metal shop again..." Lawrence bid the ladies a quick adieu and hurried to catch up with his friend.

"What was that about?" Belle asked as she finished another tablecloth.

"He has envisioned a very clever support system using very few struts and such. He thought narrow metal pipes would be best for them... I suppose we won't see the boys for a while." Miranda laid out the canvas on the floor and began marking and cutting the panels for stitching. "I had no idea a brick oven was going to be such work!" She muttered through the pins held between her lips, "I just wanted to bake fresh bread..."

Belle smiled and answered, "That's how it all begins. First it's wheels so you don't have to drag the box. Then there's a bigger box to carry more. Seats to ride on the box, instead of walking beside. Get an animal to pull it, instead of yourself. A roof to keep off the rain... and before you know it, you're at the center of an industry making carriages and trying to imagine how to do it without the horse..."

Miranda laughed, "You make it sound inevitable and so simple. How about this one: What about people sending a message to the *Concession*, request their pizza and have it delivered to their own door!

242

That'd save us from this 'pizzeria renovation' we're making." Belle stopped her sewing and Miranda looked up at her, "What?"

Belle asked, "Why not?"

"Why not, what? Which?" Miranda asked, then picked up on Belle's thought. "Well for one thing, if they take the time to deliver a request, why not sit around and wait to take it home themselves."

Belle's mind was racing, "But if they are like our little old couple in the ghetto, they can't get out so easily. What if they are sick or disabled in some way? People have to eat..."

Miranda answered, "We did that one winter in Tahoe for all those greenhorn families that weren't prepared for the ice and snow. *But,* there we knew where and who they were. How are we supposed to detect housebound people in the neighborhoods of Venice? Who also would like pizza? *And* know what they are ordering? *And* who's going to deliver it?..."

"Perhaps we're thinking of this from the wrong way cut. We don't *have* to do special requests; we could set it up like the hot dog vendors in New York. The cart comes around; you know it's hot dogs. The only question is: how many? If we sent a cart into a small neighborhood, it would still be delivery and we wouldn't have to know ahead of time where or who specifically wanted or needed it."

Miranda mused on the idea. "It wouldn't be long before we knew which households were in dire need and which... just liked pizza... We wouldn't have to limit it to pizza either, but the selection would need to be relatively small." She thought some more, 'Belle? Do you think we might need another oven already?"

Both ladies giggled at the direction their visions were leading and both continued to hash out for herself the parameters and considerations of such an endeavor as feeding those in the most need. George and Lawrence returned with bundles of pipes and tubing in their arms. "How about a beer George?"

Lawrence then recalled his meeting with Gio that morning and related it to them all. "So, Birra Moretti is our new house brew it would seem."

Belle finished stitching the canvas panels and adding their ties to attach to the awning frame. Lawrence installed the corner and intermediate poles, which as Miranda had noted, simply reinforced the existing structure and allowed the hanging walls something to which to tie at the middle and bottom of the panels. The doorway was the cleverest part of the design. One end of the enclosure was left half open, then recessed several feet and offset from the opening was a wider panel. Once it was hung, it created the entry way into the canvas room proper such that breezes could not easily whip directly into the room. A chiminea was placed just inside the entry to create a barrier of warmer air.

"Good." Miranda and Lawrence stood back and admired the quickly erected addition, "A sign of some sort and the 'patio' is ready for tables and benches." Lawrence said that he'd arranged for them to be delivered in the morning. They untied the sides of the panels and rolled them up individually into the overhang of the awning until Friday when they'd just drop them down and re-fasten them together. Meanwhile in the kitchen...

George fashioned a tray-rack to hold plates and utensils that would slide in and out on rails affixed to the inside walls of the dishwasher. He ran the copper tubing into the brick oven. He left many coils of the tubing inside of it, before routing the line out again to make the connections to the box. Inside the bottom of the box he mounted a hub on which a finely perforated pipe would rotate and spray the hot water up into the rack. He teed in a tube that would carry a squirt of soap into the hot water line, and then tied into the water supply to the sink with its own shut-off valve for the new line. By that evening he was ready to try it out. Both men applied themselves to the additional shelving attached to an empty wall near the pantry to store all the surplus flatware, plates, graters, grinders, cutters and the pie pans for delivering pies to the buffet or for serving. Lawrence acquired two more oven paddles that looked like very broad bladed oars, and a stiff push brush for cleaning the oven bricks. He installed pegs in the wall near the oven on which to hang the new additions.

After dinner was delivered to the elderly couple and the restaurant was closed for the night, they gathered in the sitting room. Lawrence sat at the piano and played one melody after another, each one leading smoothly into the next. Miranda and Belle outlined their ideas for delivering meals not just to the elderly couple they knew, but to others who were surely in the same state of need. When there was a pause in the discussion, Lawrence struck a few resounding chords and said, "And how about our new dishwasher!?"

There was a little clapping and George took a bow, "I just want to thank the people who made this all possible: Benito, the metalsmith," Lawrence struck the chords again, "Lorenzo: the mechanical genius," again the chords, "And the multitudes who love our pizza. Without them the need would not have arisen!" and Lawrence played a finale in the musical accompaniment.

They laughed and clapped a bit at that. "Belle," Miranda said, "I noticed some children playing on the lanes, marking out designs on the walkways with chalk while we were shopping today. Instead of making placards for the menus and such, why couldn't we mount a chalkboard at the entry and note the evening's bill of fare?"

Again the piano sounded a triumphal chord. "That's brilliant darling. Did all of you note how from the mind of my brilliant wife comes idea after idea... She's a genius, I tell you, a genius!" Miranda giggled and both George and Belle chuckled their approval of the pronouncement.

George changed the subject, "Miranda shouldn't you have a central desk, or counter thingy for the Inn check-ins and check-outs? Something that could also serve the restaurant? Just like the counter-service area for the Caffè area over there?"

"That's a good thought. *I've* always been the desk and register for the operation," she rubbed her belly and looked up at the others again, "I suppose I should shed a few of those hats I've been wearing and as you say, centralize it. It would make several little chores of my day run more smoothly."

George continued, "If you'll make a list of those 'little chores' and anything else you can think of which can be 'centralized,' we can sketch up what might accommodate those needs in terms of a front desk installation."

Lawrence took that opportunity to remark, "And it's contagious! She's even infected our George. Brilliant, I tell you!"

Sunday morning, when weekend guests usually checked out and simply piled their luggage at the front door while they had a last cup of coffee and pastries, Miranda stood in the sitting room near the fireplace and did some very creative visualizations. Gio brought her a cup of coffee, "What are you thinking so strongly about, Lady Spelman?"

"I am trying to imagine all the activities and uses a registration desk would serve." She replied, still staring at the vacant front corner where the sitting room ended and the great entry area overlapped.

"That is something very good! All the fancy hotels and ristorantes have bold, impressive front desk areas... The *Final Concession* should also have this impressive furniture. Besides, Lady, it will keep the guests from simply tossing their things in inconvenient places..." He nodded to the piles of baggage and luggage sprawled around the entry way. He went back to the Caffè service counter and continued what he was doing. Miranda envisioned all the luggage on trolleys, a polished wood counter and desk, backed by wooden pigeon holes---one for every room, menus neatly stacked on one end of the counter, shelves of stationary, baskets and bins each in their own cubbies under the counter---out of sight of the guests, and a leather bound registration book. She sighed, made some quick notes and went to the kitchen. Belle and George were chatting with Lawrence as she entered, "Alright Captain, get out your sketch pad; let's get this show on the road!" The rest of the morning was filled with desk designing.

When Lawrence and Miranda arrived with the basket of food for the elderly couple's luncheon, they knocked and waited. A young

246

man came toward them, staring. As he joined them at the door he asked cautiously what business they had with the maestro. Lawrence explained their routine of bringing meals to the old man and his wife. The young man's eyes widened a bit and began a running chatter of praises which he'd heard from the maestro about them: their kindness, good conversation and of course the delicious meals. "Truly, sir, you have meant the world to himself and his beloved wife."

There was still no answer at the door; the young man knocked again, "I am very early for my appointment..."

Miranda asked, "Oh, you are a student of the piano then?"

The young man looked at her as if misunderstanding her words. "The maestro doesn't teach the piano. He was and is the greatest conductor in all of Venice! He was Maestro di Cappella when my mother was a girl. She is from a wealthy family and they were patrons of the maestro for years. My father also believes him to be one of the last great men to occupy that esteemed position. I was privileged to be his only and last pupil. Now, I am abroad in study, but when I come home I always visit him for guidance." He distractedly knocked on the door again. "I do not understand why they do not answer the door. It is very cold this morning isn't it?" He added as if making conversation.

Lawrence had begun to sense something wrong when the door was not answered the first time they knocked. It usually always was. He reached for the door latch and tried to open it. The door opened easily and the three went inside.

"Maestro Benefiero?" the young man called out. No answer. Miranda took the basket to the kitchen where they usually sat, served and kept company with the elderly couple. Upon the counter, next to an empty bottle from yesterday's dinner was an envelope. In an unsteady hand was written "Lorenzo and Miranda Spelman." Curious, she called to her husband who came into the kitchen followed by the young pupil.

"Look, this was next to the empty bottle from last night." She held it out to Lawrence and the young man glanced at it, "That's the maestro's hand; it was once much bolder."

Lawrence opened the unsealed envelope and extracted the folded paper within. They gathered around him to read along:

"Our caring friends and saviors, Julieta and I have been renewed in our belief in the goodness of others through your faithful administration of our agreement. Many would have shirked the simple burden we set before you, considering it trivial or beneath them somehow. Yet you and your beautiful wife have not only fulfilled the daily ministrations to our physical needs but nourished our souls with your company and laughter..."

The young man's eyes teared up, "Signore, he speaks from his heart... it is so beautiful..."

"...This winter has been far too harsh on these old bones, and neither Juliet nor I have any more winters we can endure. You are an honorable man. We have no children and at our age, good food and friends to enjoy it with are worth more than gold. You and your beautiful wife have provided both. We end our sojourn the wealthiest of people. Please dispose of my estate as you see fit, and arrange our interment. May you be blessed as you have blessed our last days. ---Maestro Lucio and Julieta Benefiero"

The young student sniffled and wiped his eyes. Miranda and Lawrence simply stood in silent respect for the elderly couple they had become so close to over the last months. "Well, I suppose I shall have to go up the stairs and look in on them," Lawrence said at last. "Young man... what is your name?"

The maestro's last pupil straightened up and answered, "Giorgio Polacco, Signore."

Lawrence said in solemn tones, "Giorgio, would you please find a physician and bring him back here as quickly as you can?" Then he turned to mount the staircase, leaving the letter with Miranda. In a little while he came back down, shaking his head he said, "They do seem very peaceful. It's as cold as ice in that room; no doubt they let the winter at last win the battle for their lives... hypothermia."

Georgio returned with a professional looking gentleman behind him, who introduced himself as Dr. Abramo. Lawrence told him what he'd seen at the top of the stairs and the good doctor went to verify Lawrence's conclusions. When he returned, he corroborated the observations and sat down to write out an account of the event for a proper and lawful medical rendering of the situation of their deaths.

"I shall register the certificate; you shall no doubt be informed of your responsibilities regarding the maestro's estate. This is an additional record of what Giorgio has described as the events of the morning, Signore Polacco, please sign hear as the witness." Giorgio did so. "And Signore Spelman would you and your wife sign here, indicating your receipt and possession of the last will and testament as witnessed by Signore Polacca?" They did so. "Very good. It is best in these situations to make certain of all parties consonance in the observation of the protocols; it will make the magistrate's duty very straightforward." He put away his things and stood to leave, "My heartfelt condolences at your loss," and he was out the door.

Young Giorgio walked with them to the *Concession* and was persuaded to have a bite to eat and a glass of wine. He spoke of the maestro's life and of his wife's care of him through the years. When Giorgio's spirits were sturdier, he thanked them most humbly for their kindnesses and promised to return for a visit when next he was in Venice.

A couple days later an official summons came to Lawrence and Miranda for the disposition of the Benefiero estate. Lawrence was no stranger to judges and courts, whether they were in Europe, America or most any other place; his previous life's occupation required that familiarity. Something surprising from the proceedings was the addition of the adjoining house to the Benefiero's home, which was also part of the estate. They had kept it as leased apartments and it was the old couple's only stable source of income. The last tenants had left five months before and so it had remained vacant; no others applied for residence. *That* was what reduced the Benefieros to the condition of having no income and which led to their bargaining with George for their last hope of any sustaining connection with the world.

The 'family' at the *Concession* had some decisions to make. "I can see several things occurring to make the most of this situation..." George began, "The instruments and his personal papers can of course be donated in their honor to the church and chorale." Lawrence and Miranda both agreed that would be very fitting and an apt tribute to the maestro.

George then made a suggestion which was near to the heart of each of those assembled. Once they all considered the implications and ramifications, they all agreed and Lawrence went out to the Caffè. He asked Gio to join them in the kitchen. When he arrived, he immediately went to the dishwasher again.

"You know, from one inventor to another... this is very nice, very nice workings." George thanked him again. Miranda asked him to have a seat and he did so. Lawrence explained all that had transpired and then introduced George's thoughts about the disposition of the estate. Gio remained expressionless; his mind was reeling with the information. The kitchen was so quiet, all that could be heard was the slow drip of the faucet into the basin.

"Lady, Lorenzo, what you say is making my heart to swell. I am not having the words to saying the fabulos... the gratitudes... this is most great news." Tears trickled down his weathered face.

Miranda patted his hand, "Giovianni Francesconi, without your help over the last year and a half the *Last Concession* would not be the thriving enterprise it is today. This estate is certainly your just reward for the time spent here and the years of struggle you have already endured. May I suggest that Varrissa's parents, Signore and Signora Sarpini will look with new eyes upon your suit for her hand in marriage."

Gio was way ahead of her on that score. "And both my parents and her parents can be moves into the apartmentses? They have such a little homes, only two roomses."

Lawrence answered, "Signore, how you manage the estate is up to you; if you accept it."

George and Belle had listened to the interchange and although they were only able to catch phrases and snippets of the dialog held mostly in Italian, the pathos and the gratitude were clearly conveyed despite any language barrier. Gio extended his hand to Lawrence and shaking it, said, "I most humbly accept." He shook every person's hand enthusiastically. Then grinning broadly, "I must go and tell my parents this most wonderful newses."

Belle whispered something to Miranda and she was reminded to tell Gio, "We shall have the houses ready for you by the weekend. And if you don't mind our intrusion, we insist that we host your wedding here in the *Last Concession*, provided all goes to your and Varrissa's advantage."

"Glorioso, Bella Dona, glorioso!"

So, after the instruments and Maestro Benefiero's personal papers were graciously received by a legate from the cathedral and chorale, the houses were put in order for Gio and Varrissa's homecoming. Many of the maestro's furnishings were split between the two houses, which then left plenty of room for the possessions of their future occupants. All was cleaned and an awning was erected over the adjoining entrances to the residences which renewed the facade and gave it a new brighter character.

Signore and Signora Sarpini were at last proud to give their daughter's hand in marriage to the man they had so long respected for his industry and creativity. Needless to say, Varrissa was ecstatic at the news. Gio's parents and Varrissa's parents were amenable to the idea of relocating next door to their children and they added, *grandchildren!* They took possession of the large house's separate apartments. The wedding was a beautiful affair and after the reception Captain George rowed them to their new home through the canals from the Inn... he took the long way around.

In the interim between the wedding and the holidays, Miranda and Belle used the heavy marbled paper to make little tent-shaped placards for the tables of the restaurant. They hoped that the carefully worded solicitation for the whereabouts of the 'homebound' would yield results they could act upon in their determination to carry on the Benefiero's alternate legacy. They were not disappointed. The responses they gathered at the end of each week allowed for elderly couples, widows and other homebound people of Venice to at least have a meal and company during their days. Gio was so inspired by the endeavor he built three 'heated' carts for transporting the meals and then, offering an honorable wage, he found willing hands among the younger Venetians to make the deliveries.

When the Inn returned to its previous more sedate tempo of activity, the Christmas season was upon them. The Livingsons' spoken Italian became very good and often days went by in the Inn when not a word of English was uttered. Belle and her Captain were like children again; they cheerfully put up decorations around the Inn and walked through the streets of Venice admiring the festive change of face the city put on for the holidays. They often strolled to the Campo San Stefano where the Christmas market was getting into full swing. Many of the very most expensive hotels' and restaurants' workers were leaving the city for their homes throughout the rest of Italy---leaving the lanes and canals less crowded than usual. The *Last Concession* wasn't immune from the closed tap of tourists which allowed for lovely days and evenings almost alone with each other.

Something that resulted from the absence of boarders was the opportunity for them to get to know Varrissa much better. As it happened she was a startlingly good cook and they had found an assistant chef at last. Varrissa's first change to the operations was to insist upon tailoring each of the 'Benefiero' requested meals to the actual needs of the individuals receiving them. The fledgling program was such a boon to the recipients during the harsh cold of that winter that whole families began to have at least one dinner at the Concession Restaurant during the week. They wished to show their gratitude and support for the Benefiero Program in general or for their own homebound relatives who had received those benefits directly.

The front desk was installed and although it couldn't be put into use at full capacity, due to the lack of tourists, Miranda and Lawrence were to be found behind the polished wood counter every morning as each day at the Inn began a new life. Miranda's idea of having the *Concession's* own luggage trolleys was also realized. George and Lawrence had a good time constructing them from hard copper piping, rather than simply purchasing already made one's from the depot's old stock. They were a very attractive addition to the receiving area at the front of the Inn and were useful as blockades during Friday pizza nights. The other addition to the Inn was a new, much larger iron stove. Its firebox was large enough to take wood or coal and the oven chamber could handle two large pans of lasagna and three loaves of bread at the *same* time. The best part of the new fixture was the stove top which allowed for several large pots at once and greatly increased the capacity of the kitchen's utility.

The little company of six went together to the Christmas concerts held around the city. On Christmas Eve they gathered with what felt like the rest of Venice's population inside Basilico San Marco for the mass. It was the first time either of the Livingsons had ever stepped into a church for any service at all. They were overwhelmed at the ceremony and the glittering gold mosaics, icons and dome of the richest of Italian churches. It seemed that even the air around them glistened from the candles held by the thousand others crowded into the space. A very few flakes of snow fluttered down on them as they made their way back home. Belle and George were nearly beside themselves with laughter to see the overreactions of native Venetians worriedly trying to protect themselves from the unaccustomed 'snows.' Because so many ristorantes were closed, the *Concession* restaurant was full to brimming with the few remaining tourists in the sparkling winter jewel that was Venice at Christmas. St. Stephen's Day followed and then not long after: the New Year's celebrations. Bundled in furs, the Concession Six went out to ring in

1890. Fireworks, Prosecco and kissing were the entertainments of the night and everyone went home warmed and festively happy.

Belle also used the time to bring out the small medicines chest she brought on the journey; every day she and Miranda discussed the properties, usefulness and application of each packet. By the time Belle exhausted the stores she had brought, Miranda was far more confident that most any health concern which she, her son or Lawrence might encounter, short of a major disease, could be dealt with swiftly and effectively. This had a two-fold effect on the new mother: the knowledge increased her already confident and independent nature and more importantly it opened her eyes to the vast variety of troubling ailments and debilitations to which humans succumb. There was a balance established between her knowledge and her being that evoked a wholesome respect and greater understanding of herself and the world around her.

Meantime, Captain George assisted Lorenzo in installing rain gutters and a run-off collection system to prevent the seasonal inundation of the courtyard. After that was accomplished they turned to building a gondola-like boat. The need was present for a craft which could more easily navigate the canals, carry weighty loads and at least six people comfortably and safely. It had to be no wider than a traditional gondola, and like its cousin, would be oared from a position on the stern. Both Lawrence and George preferred the squared stern and platform of the sampan, allowing the yuloh-method of oaring, but both men were drawn to the high prow of the gondola, so useful for mounting a lantern, tying off the boat at mooring and the practicality of its offsetting the weight of the rower in the balance of the craft. Harry's sailboat, the *Little Tigre*, was nearer the model on which they decided to build. Although the Tigre was well-suited as a sailing vessel, it lacked the sleek maneuverability required for constant canal use. The sempian, given Harry by the old forcola carver and which presently hung upon the wall of the great room, was simply too small for their needs, though it was ideal for single-handed excursions on unencumbered errands.

They constructed the forms, built the frames and began planing and fitting the planking. It was a laborious process and took most of January and February. When it was lacquered and varnished, fitted with seats, hardware installed and an oar fitted to it, she was yar and winsome. Belle and Miranda wished her to have an awning with sides that could be rolled up and down. After an integral frame was installed the ladies created the canvas cover to match the awnings at the Inn. Her maiden voyage on the occasion of her christening: *Grande Tigre Femmina*, was to ferry the company to the Giardini Pubblici, still under development but a very pleasant sanctuary from the paved city.

With the warmer weather came tourists and the *Concession* was once again the busy center of visiting traffic. The chimineas were still lit on the chilly evenings and the front tented awning was revised to allow direct entrance through the front entry, but with a chiminea on either side of the canvas doors as a heated barrier to the cooler breezes. The Caffè habitues were sheltered and the patrons of Friday Pizza night were accommodated generously. Lawrence played every evening in The Salon, as the sitting room/bar was renamed, and there were always appreciative ears for his melodic renditions. Varrissa ruled the kitchen as her own domain, but with a velvet hand. She was the rival of Belle and Miranda for getting an activity performed with the most willing assistance of others; all the while having the absolute last word on how a job was done—a benevolent empress. Miranda was able to turn her attentions to management where her native talents lay. Lawrence was of a similar cloth: well-considered decisions and direction were his forte and his manner was always conciliatory so that he empowered rather than commanded. Belle and her Captain tended to odd jobs and hospitality as they wished... holidays *were* holidays after all. They received a package of photographs from Harry and Kaitlyn from the Christmas gathering in Tahoe. There were so many of them even Lawrence was going to say something of the expense until in the enclosed letter, they read that Harry had purchased an amateur camera which started a landslide of picture taking by the ladies... so, more pictures would follow. Miranda and Belle selected several and added them to the Salon wall with other of the Inn's prized photographs.

Lorenzo and the Captain were sitting with some of the old-timers at the Caffè, when the topic of the Acqua alta, the infrequent flooding, came up. Both men were captivated by the tales and the city's countermeasures. It seems while the greater threat was from the seasonal tides and the scirroco winds which kept the lagoon full instead of allowing it to drain normally, unseasonably high rainfalls worked the same effect from time to time. George and Lawrence set their minds to protecting the Inn from flood damage.

They walked the perimeter, noted with relief the lack of possible ingress through structural breaches, but realized standing water for any duration would find its way through the plaster and block construction---not to mention through the front, side and back doors. Miranda and Belle were made part of the deliberations and after several preventative measures were discussed it was Lawrence who ultimately arrived at an alternative which made the most sense.

Over the next week and a half, low walls of about two feet in height were constructed. In the front they followed the outside perimeter of the massive awning. The inside edges of the walls, at the three wide openings for passage, were slotted to allow solid panels to be slid into them like sluice gates on a canal lock. The same arrangements were fashioned around the entrance areas of the other two doors then all the exposed walls of the building and the shelter walls were thoroughly tiled, grouted and sealed up to three and a half feet on the building proper. Miranda and Belle chose the tile and design scheme. Once all was completed they took a second look at the front awning configuration.

"You know..." George observed, "with the foundation wall in place it wouldn't be difficult to install a structurally sound roof and a series of pivoting glazed panels between the eaves and the new wall... the three entries can be fitted with dutch doors, and..." Miranda and Belle leapt at the suggestion and showered Lawrence with appeals to begin the design at once.

"Okay, okay... let me and the Captain sort out the particulars," he pleaded. After a brief sketch of the basic construction, he looked up at the terrace awning and said, "It is a design that we could replicate up there and turn the terrace into a conservatory, a banquet room, meeting hall or a dance floor... you name it."

That prompted the ladies to begin a train of thought which opened up vistas of possibilities. Over the next several days as the warmer weather persisted, the designs and purposes for the enclosures became further resolved. In the first week of March Lawrence placed orders for all the framed glass panels required. Before they arrived the gentlemen constructed the frameworks and roofed the front entry to match the Inn's existing tiled appearance, while the terrace roof, as had been decided, would be patterned upon a conservatory scheme.

The existing canvas that had served as a shield against sun and rain would be recycled and used as retractable shades under the terrace-conservatory glass roof. Likewise, the canvas panels of the front enclosure were recycled as roman shades for the glass windows there. When the glass panels arrived, on boat from Murano, all the brass fittings and latches were affixed and the doors were installed. The interior wall of the conservatory was assembled of hinged frames of glass panes so that entire sections could be folded back to open the room to the courtyard below. A dumb waiter was constructed and installed so that meals could more easily be delivered to the terrace when it was in use for parties or banqueting. After all was in place, the new entry to the *Last Concession* and the conservatory were practical, elegant and presented a palatial quality to the Inn that was not lost on its patrons and guests.

They next built overhangs over the side and rear entries to shelter those enclosed areas and prevent them from becoming flooded in the rains. Miranda and Varrissa talked Lawrence into not just covering the rear area, but installing a greenhouse so that there would always be fresh herbs, some tomatoes, onions and garlic and various greens for the kitchen. Once it was installed they wasted no time planting seeds and potting plants. The terrace conservatory housed a lovely selection of irises, lilies and tulips, in addition there were palms and ornamental trees which were rotated throughout the Inn for decorative purposes. Planting boxes were mounted along the balconies where Belle encouraged mint, clematis, and swedish ivies.

March became April, and Olivia wrote to announce their intentions for their annual visit to commence in the early weeks of May. Rooms were set aside and confirmations returned. The more pleasant days also got them out on the boats more often and they set themselves the aim of visiting the surrounding islands. George and Lawrence caught and cleaned fish, while the ladies strolled the markets and shops. Belle was delighted to find a shop that catered solely to providing fresh and dried herbs, flowers and roots. She and Miranda spent hours in discussion with the proprietress who rarely had such knowledgeable customers as these. When they returned home that day, Belle and Miranda's medicines chests were fully restocked and new items added that were unique to the Mediterranean. Varrissa was curious about the various herbs and plants since some of them hung in the kitchen for further drying. Whereupon she too was introduced to the plant and herb lore to which Miranda had so recently been exposed. She was also a quick study, and when next they visited that island, Varrissa was welcome company.

The Allcocks and Backhouses returned on the second of May and the first thing they noticed was Miranda's now growing belly. A gathering of all the women of the Inn was a foregone event and to the surprise of all, Varrissa had just found that she, too, was with child. Nothing will keep women together and talking longer than the sharing of stories and advice about birth and babies. The gentlemen went fishing.

They brought the day's catch home for a welcome seafood feast and delivered dishes to the ladies, who were still in conference in the conservatory. The men retired to the Salon and enjoyed cigars and drinks. The music of the piano at last lured the ladies from their discussions and all were once again gathered in the comforts of the sitting room. Miranda pointed out the photograph collection of their families arranged upon the mantle and mounted on the walls either side of the hearth. She said, "We are always reminded of our brothers, sisters, families and friends and our other homes---far away from Venice but near to our hearts."

Varrissa invited them to visit their home the next day and yawning, excused herself. Gio thanked the gentlemen for such a wonderful afternoon and evening of good company then walked his lovely bride home. Genie and Winston said good night, followed soon by Sam and Libby which left the four of them sitting together again as the last up at the Inn.

Lawrence mused, "I think I'll invite them out for a tour of the Grand Canal tomorrow, I've absorbed so much history and information on the palazzos and churches, I could give the local tour guides a run for their money."

Lawrence did offer and they accepted, saying to Varrissa that they would go with her to visit her and Gio's home when they returned. The ladies saw them off from the dock and went back inside. Miranda watered all the Inn's plants and joined Belle and Varrissa in the courtyard for tea. As the ladies enjoyed a chat, George began making lists of tools, inventions and widgets that they had run across during their travels. He intended to gather contacts and resources for the items and have them either in his store back home or recommend their use for others as need be. He also began sketching out a type of pedaled boat, using a gear-driven propeller with power introduced by a flywheel which gained its momentum from the pedal's revolution. He calculated gear ratios, flywheel weights and the question of twin propellers versus a single one. Some people doodled; George invented."

His guest reflected on his continuing questions and responded, "You are right in a sense... that we are bombarded daily with impacts and it seems as if they are coming out of nowhere. When in truth, it is only the tunnel-vision with which we live our lives that makes it seem so. Let me add to your perspective by introducing context to the octave we have been studying thus far in isolation. Perhaps after this explanation, I can explain about 'those other foods' you asked about earlier." The guest looked at her host in patient expectation of a response.

Just finishing his narrative journal, he replied absently, "That sounds great to me," and he brought out his other notebook, the one in which he had been jotting down notes about the structure of things... separate from the Livingson tale. "Okay, shoot."

She sat up and said, "Let's look at that first octave that we initially derived from our symbolic enneagram. The three forces which became aligned with the octave's notes DO, LA, and FA inside the first octave in the universe are forces in their own right but can only manifest inside the constraints of the fabric in which they exist. So: LA and FA, in order to be fulfilled, as it were, must initiate new octaves. LA becomes a DO and an octave descends from that point... FA becomes a DO and descends from that point."

The guest interrupted, "You are no longer describing an inner structure... Right? Because in inner octaves: DOs stay DOs, LAs become FAs, and FAs stay FAs..."

"Correct. Instead of an octave's inner construction, we are going to explore the outer world of an octave---the Universe, if you will."

"Thanks, okay... and?" the guest acknowledged, ready now to continue.

"Draw a series of two octaves in succession as they would appear if the first octave simply just descended into half of itself. Let's start with a large number as the top DO, say: 1296." The host did as indicated and his guest continued. "Now at the LA and the FA in the original---the top octave of the two, draw a horizontal line a little ways out from each and label them as DOs at the vibrations from which they emerged and share. Now fill in the descent of those two new octaves." While her host calculated those two octaves' descents, she added, "This is going to get confusing in just a little bit unless we make some decisions now."

And as he turned to look at her once the calculations were completed, he listened closely. She began, "We will continue this downward creation of octaves until we reach the bottom of the initial octave's complete descent, Okay?"

He nodded making horizontal lines out from the new LA's and FA's.

"And we are going to find that: new octaves begin from the LAs and FAs of all created octaves. Look at the LA of that second created octave: it begins at 900, which is before we have descended to the FA of the initial octave where it can sound the first note of its *own* new octave at the new DO, 864. What I propose is that we begin to assign 'family' names to these newly created octaves as they connect back to the initial octave---whose family we'll call Supreme. And like a family---father, mother, daughters and sons---we will be able to map these relationships, after a fashion anyway. Inside one octave's descent, the LA will be a daughter and the FA will be a son. Outside that octave, the octaves created from LAs will be females: mothers or daughters, and those from the FAs will be males: fathers and sons... This is just to get a handle on the larger family connections you understand... they aren't actually gender related *at all*."

The host nodded again, while looking down at his initial four octaves which were not in a nice even descending order...they were beginning to hop up and down in the order of creation. His guest assured him that this would require a first draft, then a final version for him to have a workable model.

"With the second octave created from a LA then from the next created LA, a daughter, comes a new family name. Just as in life: my daughter will arise from my husband and myself, but when she marries she will take the new family's name. The second family must begin from the LA of that second octave created, mother to daughter if you will. We will call this the Prime family, because they were the first family created after the Supreme family in the Universe and can claim a direct lineage from our first family. In the continuing proliferation, the family name will continue through the line of the sons. So at this point we have the first Supreme, 1S, a second Supreme, 2S---with a direct connection to the initial octave. Then we have the daughter of 2S---that one who changes family names, and we have the first of the Prime family---the second family---we shall refer to its initial member with their family ranking: 2, so the 2P is created. Then another Supreme, the one from the initial octave's FA, the 3S. So far we have the 1S, 2S, 2P, and 3S. Now continue to allow other octaves to come into existence and we will organize your results into a constant descension in the sequential order in which they were created. The families still to come can be Distant and Final by the way... for the obvious reasons you'll soon uncover."

The host became absorbed in just calculating octaves from the forces, then from the new octaves created and those new forces, until he arrived at the bottom vibration of the very bottom of the initial octave's lowest octave's note. "Okay... Well this is a mess!" he commented as he looked over the page.

"On a fresh page, write in our first four octaves for which we *do* have the order established," he began to do so, "and you can begin adding to the list in the order you sort out from those others created."

He organized: "1S, 2S, 2P, 3S, 3P, 4S, 3D, 4P, 5S, 4D, 5P, 6S, 4F, 5D, 6P, 7S, 5F, 6D, 7P..."

"Good. If we go ahead then and complete each of those octaves' *ascensions*, we can see some interesting things emerge. Now you'll notice a few things straight away: the Supremes can all trace a direct connection back through their REs to one of the notes of the 1S. The same is true for the Primes, they can trace a direct connection to the 2P, which connects to the Supreme family only through the 2S. All of the Distants can trace back to the 3D, which connects to the Prime family's 3P---to the 2P, and on to the 2S--- hence Distant. Lastly the Final family, both members connect back through an equally convoluted path to the 2S, and are also the last family to sound a DO in the Universe. Nineteen Octaves."

The host nodded, satisfied. His guest still had a few questions. "Look at vibration 540. How many notes are at that vibration?"

"La, Do, Mi, Sol, Ti, Re..." he answered as he ran his finger across the page.

"And at the vibration 450. How many notes are at that vibration?"

"La, Do, Mi, Sol, Ti, Re..." he answered again.

"Do you see a pattern, here? Are there any other patterns?"

J. L. LAWSON

5

Exploration

"In wisdom gathered over time I have found that every experience is a form of exploration."
---Ansel Adams

Her host began to marvel at the woven vibrations and notes generated by the sounding of those initial forces as they descended into the Universe, creating for themselves their own Laws of Three and of Seven. His guest continued, "Now, with the realization of a cosmic weave of octaves, and always at least six other octaves sharing the same vibration, or position we also are occupying, we can investigate those three foods of man. Look at the 5S, 4S, and 3S octaves... perhaps you should reconstruct them on a new page of their own; we are going to make a few notes about just their relationships."

The young man opened to a new page of his 'structural' diary and prepared those three octaves for investigation. "Alright..."

"You will notice a few things straight away: That the relationship between these three octaves are in an interesting ratio. Look at the DOs, and jot down their values." He did. "Can these be reduced?"

The young man did so and came up with, "Twelve, Ten, and Eight."

"Correct. In the Great Knowledge it is suggested that a real man must equal a thirty. A curious statement at first blush, until one sees this pattern in the octaves you see in front of you. Food, Air, and Impressions---eight, ten, twelve---Physical, Astral, and Mental---First Story: Instinctive-Moving, Second Story: Emotional-Intellectual, Third Story: Higher Emotional-Higher Mental. We have stumbled upon another connection to the structure with which we are already becoming familiar."

The young host accepted the plausibility of the inference. "I think I'll need an explanation here..."

The elegant lady smiled and continued, "Yes, let's begin with the foods, or as understood in the Great Knowledge---the Diagram of Nutrition. At that lowest vibration of DO in the 'eight octave'." The host located the vibration indicated. "As omnivores, a wide range of 'foodstuffs' enter. Anything from near wood, up to the weakest broth of near water enters and through a process of just blending, the masticated and swallowed bits go to RE, then to MI. Again, thus far, just the blending involved in internal processes is sufficient. Then there comes a place where blending alone will not suffice. At what vibration is the MI of the eight octave, and also the DO of the ten?"

"Uh...at the same vibration..." he answered.

"Good, 'For this purpose, Nature in her beneficence has made such propitiation that the air we breathe should provide the necessary force,' or shock, to allow the incoming coarser digesting foodstuffs to proceed passed this gap it otherwise would not be able to pass on its own. And the new octave joins with the first, and they run together. A second food has now entered the machine---Air. It can be thought of in this way: if one man can not pass a barrier with his own strength and momentum, a second man may join his efforts. Together they can overcome the barrier and their fates are now intertwined." The young man recognized this as a useful analogy.

"The second octave is now in its own process of blending that occurs between DO-RE-MI at the start of any octave, and for the first octave its FA-SOL-LA experiences the same 'just by blending' phenomenon. Herein lies the dilemma: while the first octave can pass all the way to its TI, the second octave meets the gap barrier and can not continue. This presents a problem for the newly federated movement of the two octaves and more importantly the progress of these two foods. It is now up to the first octave, the eight, to take advantage of its own resonance with the twelve octave's DO at its own SOL. The entrance of impressions---which can be thought of as the smallest increment of a sense, feeling, or thought---is unlike the first two octaves. Impressions simply enter into the progress of the other two with its DO of assistance. To move to its RE requires one of two things to occur: either an accidental shock---such as laughter, or sudden trauma---or an intentional action on the part of the individual---the act of self-remembering. Otherwise what occurs at that vibration is what the ancient sages refer to as: 'pouring from the empty into the void'."

"The eight octave continues on to TI and stops, the ten octave continues on to its LA and the twelve octave will only assist to allow those events to occur and rise to its MI, nothing more for itself. Three foods: the things we take in our mouths, which we can live without for a substantial period; the air we breathe, which we can last for several minutes at the most without; and the impressions---which if we were bereft of them, we could not last a moment."

She sat back as her host sighed, "Shall we continue our story?"

"Harry and his family had not been idly awaiting the return of their parents from their long holiday. Mia and Lena were sleeping through the night, which allowed Harry and Kat to also return to more normal daily rhythms. The girls were crawling after each other through the house by May with the result that walking through any room now took greater care to avoid colliding with them in their sudden stops of curiosity. Titania managed the season's series of lodge guests with only one miscommunication over bookings. It seemed one couple from Silver City had requested three weeks in June by sending three separate booking requests, one for each week instead of one request for three weeks. The result was that they had to move to a different Bungalow for the final week of their stay. They had a suite booked, just not the same suite. They were almost reasonable about the mix up. It certainly helped that Titania took all the blame upon herself for their compulsive reservation-making and also persuaded Jameson to provide complementary breakfasts for their final week's stay.

The *Grand Concession* was running smoother than ever. The

young staff of servers were responsible and covered shifts for each other when their schedules didn't work out as they'd planned each week. His kitchen help were aspiring young cooks, dedicated and proficient. There was one young woman, however, who started the year assisting with baking then later decided she wished to specialize in pastries. That she also wanted to arrive at ten in the morning, not at four when the pastries were made for the day, didn't work out so well for her. She decided assisting with the routine baking was all right after all.

The Tahoe City School, next door, had a burgeoning enrollment with all the new families moving to the area. The *Concession* still catered all their breakfasts, at least for those who required them, kept spaces reserved for the schoolchildren to sit down for lunch and hosted all the school events which included food. The students, it turned out, had better table manners than most of the Summer Season visitors.

Harry or Kaitlyn opened the Mercantile every morning and locked it up every evening. During the early months of the new year Harry had begun training two young graduates of the Tahoe School to tend the store. One of the young men would finally be leaving for College at the end of August, while the other had not yet decided what he was going to do 'when he grew up.' So the daily business of the store was tended by one or the other of these two lads. Titania checked in on them often since the Lodges' bookkeeping was still conducted from the Mercantile's office. Harry duplicated his father's workshop in the home on the hill so he could watch the twins while building fly rods to fill special orders. Jameson had less time to devote to that enterprise, but he still managed to construct one or two a month as needed---Titania did most of the assembly and finishing.

Aaron was to have his first Summer Term off so Poly and he planned to come to Tahoe very often and wanted to stay with Titania and Jameson in their parents' home. Becky and Poly had two contracts underway in the Bay area which kept one or the other of them, or both, in Berkeley when they would rather be in Tahoe with Aaron and the family. After the newest twins were weaned from MamaKat milk, Kaitlyn joined their efforts on-site as she could. When Harold and Chloe decided to sell their Pacific Heights home and move to Berkeley closer to the Cannery, CANED Ltd. and Sierra Architecture would have a second residential 'calling card' on the ground advertising their talents. The Bessamer House project gave the women another cause to spend more time together, and Hannah with Mia and Lena.

When they received the letter from MamaBelle at the end of last November announcing their intention of staying through the spring, they were all relieved but each for their own reasons. Harry and Titania were working on a renovation to the store and wanted it to be finished before 'Captain' George returned. The owner of the millinery shop next door to the Mercantile sold her inventory to the Goodmans at the haberdashery---who expanded their operation to handle women's fashions also. She then accepted a reasonable offer from Harry for her empty shop. Titania began at once to draw up layout after layout to best take advantage of the additional space. Harry made suggestions as her designs unfolded and they were still in the conceptual stages by the December holidays.

Kaitlyn, Poly, Aaron and Becky were relieved by the extended stay in Venice because they didn't like the notion of the most important members of the family making the journey home through the harsh and hazardous conditions of mid-winter in the northern hemisphere. All of the family, Livingson, Connor, Backhouse and Bessamer were not just relieved, but delighted that 'Captain' George and Belle were staying with Lorenzo and Miranda for as long as it took to allow the newlyweds time to settle into their new relationship and responsibilities. Then with the news of the Spelman's new son on the way, they were all quite sure they wouldn't see them until at least the next autumn.

Olivia Allcock sent a letter to Harry and photographs for every one around Christmas. Her letter so touched his heart, that when they all gathered for the yule celebration, Kaitlyn read it aloud.

"Dearest Harry and Kaitlyn,

Samuel and I are privileged to have been present at the union of two such fine people as we have ever met. Lawrence is so changed in habit and demeanor that we almost would not have recognized him as the same man with whom we were acquainted years ago. Miranda is likewise so renewed and jubilant of spirit it is remarkable to see her growing almost younger, daily, before our very eyes. The inn is more than prospering under their careful administration and we were blessed to have been witness to its thriving.

All of this is but a prelude to the intention my correspondence. Several years ago, during the holidays before Chloe and Harold were wed, Samuel and I missed you four after breakfast one morning and went through Clive House in search of you. We were therefore secretly present for a most remarkable demonstration in our undercroft, and that event so changed our perceptions of our world we were quite untethered from our confidence in the reality we once held so securely. Samuel then explained, to the best of his knowledge, about the activities of the 'Sisters of Mercy' and your hand in the remarkable transformations of our Chloe and of Kaitlyn. Henry Livingson we owe you so much that it is not within our means to ever repay you in kind.

For my own part, I have witnessed my husband cry three times since I have known him. The first time was after he returned from Tahoe many years ago and related to me all that had transpired concerning his folly and redemption, then sought my support in the bargain he struck with Belle. The second time was after your graduation from Malvern. We were so proud of your accomplishments, we readily pledged our ardent support of you and your endeavors. Truly, we could not love you more if you were our own son; you are as dear to us as Chloe, Harold and our granddaughter Hannah. The last occasion was during this last month. We had just returned from sightseeing with Winston and Genie, and were greeted by music at the inn. Lawrence was playing on a most beautiful piano, which the Captain had arranged to have installed that very afternoon. I, for the first time, heard my Samuel play that instrument with such virtuosity I was moved to tears of joy and pride. When it was my own turn to recollect a composition, I chose the Moonlight Sonata which had always resonated in my heart for its undercurrent of struggle and perseverance of vitality. When the last chord was sounded, Samuel's eyes met mine and for only the third time in the whole of our marriage, tears fell from that great man's eyes and this time it was for love of me!

We are as newlyweds ourselves. The flickering flame which you lit amongst the kindling of our old lives has sprung to glowing warmth and burns with a passion we have not known before. For your, and your family's friendship, we--- like Lawrence, like Miranda, like Chloe, like Harold, like Aaron, like Becky, and by the way, like Winston and Genie---hope to live our lives as tribute to, and in honor of the faith you have demonstrated in our potential to become greater than we have been.

Your devoted and Loving friends,

Olivia and Samuel Allcock

There wasn't a dry eye in the house. Even Hannah and the twins were affected by the contagion of tears in the people around them. Nor was Harold immune from the touching correspondence and for once he had no words to prompt anyone's distraction from the heartfelt appreciation delivered through the letter. Kaitlyn refolded the letter and put it back in its envelope, then she went to the mantle where they kept their most cherished treasures and set it prominently next to the photograph of the *Final Concession*, with the three smiling couples looking out at her from the front of that special place in Venice.

Next, she distributed the other photographs Olivia sent from their time in Italy and they all smiled and laughed at the comical settings and silly poses of those 'respectable' people that were their parents. Becky laughed through her tears, "Mother looks so incredibly happy! And I never remember daddy calling her 'Genie,' they must be so very different than we remember them."

Poly was looking over her shoulder, with her arms around her, "So very happy... so very different..." she whispered.

Chloe had the biggest shock seeing her step-mother curled up in her father's lap like a school girl... and her father with that silly grin on his face, like the cat who just ate the canary. "Are we sure we know these people? They seem familiar, but this is not the mother and father I knew!" she remarked suspiciously.

Harry could only say, "It appears a holiday was exactly what they all needed."

Hannah and the twins weren't nearly as interested in the pictures as they were with the wrapping paper and envelopes that Hannah donned and also dressed the twins in as hats, dresses and shoes. Hannah toddled around the room and pulled Mia and Lena behind her, leaving a tattered trail of brown and white paper in their wake. While the girls were capturing everyone's attention, Harry slipped to his office and came back out unnoticed. He had an oblong box in his hands and he proceeded to pull a string and press a button on the box every minute or so. Before long, Aaron looked up and spotted him, "Harry, is that what I think it is?"

Everyone looked up and another 'click' came from the box in his hands. "If you think it's a camera it is," he answered, "I thought it would be fun to take photographs of us, while looking at photographs," and at once everyone else wanted to take pictures too.

That is to say the five women were anxious to set up shop and began to nominate settings, poses and scenes. The gentlemen were more interested in the technical achievement of an amateur camera and the relatively little time required for returning the camera to the factory to develop the film and the processed photographs to be returned to the photographer---with the camera reloaded and ready to go again.

Harry added, "I think it should be a useful and fun device. This first round of snaps will be a trial to see if the quality of the results are worth the six week wait and the one-time twenty-five dollar expense." The little girls continued their parade and play, uninterrupted by the excitement around them until their mothers and aunts dragged them away from their paper odyssey and subjected them to the their whims of photographic adventure.

Harry spoke up again, this time to the ladies, "The operating instructions suggested very well-lit conditions and to avoid movement while the shutter snaps..."

The ladies took some notice of his recommendations, but were already well under way using as many of the one hundred exposures as they pleased. Becky wondered what the quality of the processed photographs would be and: did Harry think taking photographs of their completed design projects would be something they might want to do, "...whether we use them in a brochure, or just for archival purposes, it seems to be a brilliant opportunity."

That sparked another round of enthusiasm and neither Harold nor Jameson were immune from contemplating the usefulness of photography in augmenting and enhancing their own endeavors. This left Aaron and Harry standing in the kitchen together watching the holiday circus unfold.

Harry turned to Aaron with his glass raised, "Cheers, Mate!"

"Indeed, 'Cheers' it is," he answered and they drank to the holiday none would forget.

When Titania and Harry at last agreed on how best to use the added space for the store, they turned to CANED, Ltd. to make their desires a reality. Titania exclaimed, when they presented the project to Kaitlyn, "I am so excited that your three will have an example of your work right here in Tahoe City! This is so exciting!"

Becky and Poly wasted no time in coming up to Tahoe and the home on the hill in early February when the no-bid contract was awarded to CANED, Ltd. for the Livingson Mercantile Renovation. Poly, easily as familiar with the hardware store as her sister, truly appreciated the innovative design requirements her brother and sister had provided. "And look," she pointed, "there is an entire section just for fabrics and notions and a whole section for 'sporting' gear and..." she gasped, "a section for arts and crafts!"

Kaitlyn raised an eyebrow, "Do you suppose Titania wants to capture the school supplies market out from under Jake Hasting's nose?"

Poly laughed at the mention of the name, remembering Titania's interrupted window shopping so many years ago and just *who* had interrupted her. "Last I checked, it's a free market! And Jake Hasting isn't any more a real businessman than his father was. Just because he was 'apprenticed' to keep him out of school doesn't mean he learned anything useful sitting in his dad's store day after day, swatting flies and making change. His father was foolish to turn it over to him in the first place."

Becky listened, then said, "That is exactly the ilk I was up against in the construction business with the subcontracting companies attached to Brown & Backhouse. A long string of inept fathers passing their inexperience on to incompetent sons and all of them *still* making enough money to keep their wives in nice houses and furs. It wasn't every one of them, mind you, but the pattern was there for all to see."

Kaitlyn pulled some vellum over the two stores' footprint and began sketching in the distinct sections indicated by the design requirements. "An inviting entry, smooth transitions and a free flow between buildings, ladies that's what this calls for..."

She was joined promptly by Becky and Poly in brainstorming over just those few initial criteria. Like all contracts, they were to have final plans in the hands of their client by a certain date, in this case, a *very* certain date. Harry wanted to have the new Mercantile ready for the Summer Season, which meant the doors open and the shelves stocked by no later than the end of May---at most, one month's planning and two months' renovation and restocking.

The Connors sat out on the back deck looking over the Tahoe one evening and Titania reviewed the design requirements with Jameson, which she and Harry had worked up for the store. The air was crisp and the days had begun to lengthen a little; the nights began early and were still long and cold. The last rays of the sun were making the lake sparkle on the furthest shore, but the long shadows chased the glitter off the waters and up onto the mountains' evergreen shoulders. "...And there will be a separate office for the Lodges in the corner of the building nearest the bungalows."

"That is superlative, sweetheart," he responded. "With all the other additions to the store's offered inventory and the increase in customers for that inventory, do you think *you'll* have enough time for running both the store *and* the lodges over the summer? Harry could get another commission at any time you know and leave you to handle it all by yourself..."

She looked up at the bare branches of the tallow trees, "When Mama ran the lodges she almost always had some help... maybe I should think about hiring some assistants..."

"As I remember, you and Poly were her help. If you want assistants, maybe we better get busy and make you some. You'll have to wait a while before they're big enough to train and be useful so maybe we should get started *very soon*."

Her attention turned instantly from the tallows and snapped to focus on his face. "Really?!" was all she could manage.

He stood up and held his arm for her, "Shall we go try and make some assistants?" She blushed and took his arm as he added, "If it's twins, I get dibs on one for the restaurant..."

"Deal!" she announced and put her head on his shoulder as they went into the house out of the chilly early March evening.

It was during the planning process for the new Mercantile that Harold and Chloe approached Harry and CANED Ltd. about their wish to relocate to the other side of the Bay. While Harry was nominally just the 'client' for the store renovation, he took on the project. On the same weekend that the final designs for the store were presented to Titania, Harry met with Harold and Chloe to interview them for their requirements in a home which would best accommodate their particular needs and lifestyle. One thing which became apparent in their discussions was the desire both of them had for a connection between the outside of the house with the inside, not just easy access, but the idea of a lack of visible transition from one to the other.

"Like in your and Kaitlyn's home..." Chloe verbalized.

It was from this discussion that Harry was prompted to return with them as far as Berkeley to look over the few selections they had settled on for the new homesite. Each had advantages for accommodating their wishes, but it was the site not six hundred yards from the Backhouse residence which, in Harry's mind, could ultimately offer the most complete satisfaction for all of their stated requirements. He paced off a footprint for the house and then repeated the process at a few other logistically sound locations within the site and one of those felt ideal to both Chloe and Harold. Hannah had been riding on her uncle's shoulders and when he stood in the middle of that last possible footprint she eagerly pointed and shouted, "Look Uncle Harry, look and see the boats. They are floating on the trees like big birds!"

Sure enough, when they each got up to *her* eye level and looked out in that direction, it did look as though the ships in the harbor were perched in the old growth trees with the bay beyond just an extension of the sky, like so many herons flying about and nesting. Harry said to her, "Hannah, where PapaGeorge was a boy, they call them ba-ahk-lo-uh."

Hannah tried the sounds in her own mouth and it came out: 'booklove;' her father and mother laughed. Harold announced, "Booklove it is then. Harry please use this site as the basis for the Booklove House plans."

Chloe added, "And be sure we can see the 'herons' from the front rooms!"

When he got home he told Kaitlyn about the site, the views and Hannah's naming of the future house. That inspired Kaitlyn; she began sketching furniture and window designs which sprang from the floor like trees, but which supported billowy shapes of forms in flight. So it happened that when Harry was ready to present the architectural designs, Kaitlyn presented the designs for the windows, doors and major furnishings. The Bessamers fell in love with the plans and couldn't wait for its construction and furnishing. Which, of course, they *had* to wait upon, but only until the next August three weeks before Hannah's birthday.

Before a single change was begun in any project going forward that spring and summer, Harry took photographs of the original sites, stores and Lodges. The trial photographs had come back of sufficient quality to encourage the camera's use in, as Becky had mused, archives and brochures. He documented all the design and architecture projects that had already been built, constructed or installed, as well as the views of them in the context of their environments and the views *from* them *into* their environments.

The Mercantile renovation only just missed the season's first week of the Summer Season trade, but it more than made up for that week in sales over the remaining season. There were now two broad arched passages between the showrooms that allowed easy transit from any point in the store to any other area. The original office was doubled by mirroring its space on the other side of the former dividing wall. The counter now stretched around the entire office area and through the front-most arch,like the disc of Saturn's rings. This allowed customers who were only interested in merchandise on one side of the store to enter, shop, pay and exit through that side only if they so wished. Yet seldom did any customer tarry only on one side of the Mercantile. The 'departments' had signs suspended over them from the ceiling and where practical the walls were adorned with samples and examples of finished projects or other representations of the department nearby. Skylights were introduced into both ceilings, so the natural light of day better illumined the store's wares much better than the mere front window light they once relied upon.

The other innovations which Becky, Poly and Kaitlyn incorporated were in the shelving itself and in added seating. The islands of shelves were still capable of bearing as much as their predecessors, but appeared less bulky and heavy. The lowest shelves throughout the store allowed for cleaning beneath them and for the store cat to retrieve any prey unimpeded. Fastening hardware was still in bins and buckets, but now was appended to walls rather than stand-alone shelving and the same was now true for the paint supply section and other heavy merchandises. Benches were installed, integral to some of the island shelving which served as a place to sit, but also as makeshift counters for customers arranging their purchases in visible assemblies. It was a sales gimmick; other customers had the opportunity to see the arrangement of 'doodads,' and the power of suggestion took over from there. Catalog stations were also incorporated into these 'nooks,' which served a dual purpose: they allowed customers to browse longer in the store and 'suggested' ideas for the purchase of items other than just those the customers originally entered the store to obtain.

There was even a section devoted to children's interests near the school supplies and other arts and crafts. There were kits for assembling wooden toy carts, kites, boats and houses, there were balls, blocks, and most popular of all with the kiddos: rubber bands and toy balloons. Above those baskets, Titania and Harry made a lengthy list of all the enhanced toy applications which could be used with them. The other staples in this section were bundles of dowels, balls of string and magnifying glasses.

A new door was added at the corner of the building which led into the new Lodges' Office. Shelves of books were appended to the wall next to its interior door leading into the store proper. All were paperbacks which any customer could borrow or trade for with another of their own. The offices themselves underwent a transformation. Pigeon holes were mounted over the desks, other shelving spread from these and ran the circuit of the inner walls. Most importantly, transom windows above the doors could be opened for ventilation and clerestory windows were installed in the external wall for additional light. These few modifications gave the offices a greater feeling of lightness and space, so important in relieving the tedium inherent in their purpose.

This had been the most successful summer yet experienced for the Livingson Mercantile, the Grand Concession, the Bungalow

Lodges as well as for the firms of Sierra Architecture and CANED, Ltd. In their honor the Bessamers hosted the next families' gathering. At the end of August and before Aaron had to begin his Autumn Term, they all came to visit the successfully completed Booklove House.

The Connors came with a success story of their own--Titania was pregnant.

As soon as Titania made the announcement Hipolyta shouted, "You're kidding me!" and she turned to Aaron, "We thought *we* had the only grand announcement...I'm pregnant, too!"

The Bessamers then had a third surprise, "This is a multi-fold celebration," Harold began, but Chloe finished, "We're pregnant, too!"

The celebration that was held by the families made holiday celebrations of years past seem dull. Jameson had closed the *Concession* for two days and a night and brought a smorgasbord of platters of foods. Through it all Harry and Kaitlyn stayed mum in the knowledge they had of the babies' sexes, even to the point of avoiding comments on colors for the nurseries. That the Connor's child had been conceived in George and Belle's room, even in the same bed where each of the Livingsons had been born was not lost on any one in attendance.

Poly commented, "I'm surprised just sleeping in their bed didn't lead to an immaculate conception!"

Titania quickly answered that this was *definitely not* an immaculate conception; she mentioned to Jameson quietly, "In fact, we still need to replace the lamp we broke..." The unabashed laughter and cleverness which answered her overheard aside, became a running joke the rest of the night, from 'illuminating' commentary, to 'lighter' conversations; in a group of individuals such as those, the play on words seemed unending.

When they returned to Tahoe, the Connors came to Harry and Kaitlyn with a request long anticipated. Jameson spoke for them both, "Harry would you build a house for us down at the turn in your driveway? Every time we pass that little stand of trees and the glade beside it, we have imagined our house right there."

Kaitlyn answered, "I don't suppose that when Harry originally made the plans for this house and its grounds, *and specifically* directed that that space be cleared and left as it is---could possibly have been *un*intentional."

Harry added just emerging from their studio-office, "The pipes for septic and water supply are already in the ground and here are the plans I first imagined for the cottage there... Of course you'll need to make adjustments to them..." He produced the roll of plans he'd been carrying around with him for all those years.

Two letters arrived a week later, each with birthday cards for the twins. In the one from her father, Kaitlyn learned that she did at last have a little brother, Jean Baptiste Spelman, born August twenty-sixth. MamaBelle sent the other which said that she and George would be leaving Venice in mid-September and should be home no later than the second week of October. She added that Harry and Kaitlyn should give the Backhouses and Connors their love and congratulations and to tell Titania and Hipolyta they would be the same age when they gave birth as their Great-grandmama Lizzette was when Belle's own mother, Alouette, was born.

Jameson and Titania made minor alterations to Harry's designs for the cottage and after Mia and Lena's first birthday celebration, the construction began immediately. They were all trying to have the Connors in their own home before Belle and her Captain returned. Titania made sure all was as they had left it the year before so when they stepped into their own home again, the house at least would be the same. Neither Harry nor Titania mentioned the Mercantile renovation to their parents. Harry had his photograph of the original store enlarged and framed, then he hung it over the counter on the office wall for all to see. They were hoping against hope that George would *really* like the major changes.

George and Belle did *really* like the changes, both to the store and the Connors' new home half way up the hill to Mia and Lena's, at least that's the way they referred to it. They brought more photographs of their family in Venice. At their welcome home party, held in Jameson and Titania's new home, they caught up with every one about the last year's various endeavors and excitements. Both Belle and the Captain lapsed every so often into Italian as they became excited about some topic or other being described from Venice, much to the admiration of their children.

Kaitlyn gathered Mia up from George's lap and said, "If I'd known ahead of time that you and MamaBelle would practically turn your 'holiday' into a year's absence, I don't think I would have said a word..."

Captain laughed at that, "Belle didn't I say that? I said that. When we decided to not get on the train with Sam and Winston, that's exactly what I said..."

Belle took Lena from Jameson and replied off-handedly, "Yes, my Captain."

George looked again at the before and after pictures of the Mercantile, "Harry, you and Titania planned the renovation better than I would have. It would not have occurred to me to add some of the departments you did and I certainly would not have done as good a job in the design and execution as Kaitlyn, Poly and Becky did! Inspiring, very well done indeed."

This was the first time Kaitlyn could remember getting such a direct complement from her father-in-law, "My Captain, I can't tell you how much it means to me for you of all people to say so. We did put our best efforts into the job as we knew you would do if you were here to do it."

Harry pulled out the photographs of Booklove House and the Bay area projects CANED had completed over the last year. George repeated the word he thought he heard, "Did you say booklove or baahklouh?"

Harry laughed and told the story of the house's naming, then showed the photograph of the view. George looked at it carefully, "They do look like herons flying and nesting! Remarkable."

Mia and Lena escaped the laps they were in and toddled off toward the rug in front of the fireplace where they sat and shared a cracker. Titania put her hand to her belly and furrowed her brow, then asked a question she'd been meaning to ask. "Mama, you said in your letter that Poly and I would be the same age as your Grandmama when she had your mother Alouette? Why is this the first we've heard that name?"

Belle sighed and Harry stepped in to answer. "White Feathers and I had a conversation on the day he died and I asked him about the letters he'd sent me and the inscription in the watch he gave me---why he always signed J.B.C." Harry pulled out his pocket watch, opened it and set it on the table in front of Tania. He told me a most remarkable tale of his life which none but himself ever knew. His name was actually..."

Harry related the entire story verbatim as White Feathers had told them just one year before. When he finished, Jameson and Tania were both in tears---Out of joy for MamaBelle and in solemn respect for the Great-Uncle they only knew as White Feathers.

Jameson cleared his throat and said, "From the time I was little I always thought of him as the greatest man I ever knew and I tried to imagine what he was like when he was younger... but this? He was legendary beyond my wildest imagination."

Tania nodded and added to Belle, her eyes still wet with her tears, "He rescued you! So in a real way, we owe our lives even our very existence to his courage and determination! And he was so humble... always so happy to help with any little thing..." She burst out crying some more. Jameson put his arm around her and hummed a tune he learned from his adoptive father when he was still a little boy.

Belle heard the first few notes of the melody, "That's Beethoven's Ninth Symphony! Where did you hear that?"

Jameson told her and a smile spread across her face as White Feathers spoke in her ear, "*I told you, it was truly a concert to remember...*"

With their mouths full of cracker crumbs, Mia suddenly said, "Consher," and Lena answered, "Bember."

Belle and Kaitlyn gasped, George and Harry looked at each other while Titania and Jameson just giggled at the girls making words, "That's so cute!" Titania cooed and her sobs diminished at once. However, this wouldn't be the last time the twins somehow seemed to overhear conversations they couldn't possibly have heard.

"He was holding them when he died; you don't suppose they somehow..." Kaitlyn suggested to Harry after they tucked the girls in for the night.

"I *don't* suppose." Harry replied abruptly, "If they can hear our forebears as we do and this was not just an odd coincidence--which it may well have been; we will have to make some very solid explanations to them and take some extraordinary measures to keep them from feeling freakish as they grow up." Harry mused.

"And what if they *can* already hear White Feathers and Lizette and Fong Li and the others... how are they ever going to have 'normal' lives?" responded Kat.

"Their lives *will* be 'normal' for *them* sweetheart. I have been listening in on stories and advice for years now, which our ancestors had not anticipated... and look how 'normal' I am. And you *certainly* can't imagine you're still on the same playing field with any woman on the street..." kidded Harry.

"Okay, normal's not the right word," agreed Kat, "All I'm saying is that if Mia and Lena are in some way taking the family's legacy to the 'next level,' won't that affect how we raise them? Are we prepared to raise and educate children who have the wisdom of millennia at their beck and call? How am I going to discipline them when they're naughty, or explain to them how to behave in public, or..."

Harry giggled, "Or explain to their grade school teacher how the girls were right about some historical event on a test and the textbook was wrong---because they spoke to the guy who was there, and he said so!"

Kaitlyn had to giggle at that, too. "I guess I'm making way too much of this, but that's my job isn't it? I *am* the MamaKat after all."

Poriva offered a story to help put Kaitlyn's mind at ease.

There once was a girl who lived in the northern land above the big lakes. She was at a marriageable age. As time went on, more potential suitors were proposing to her and making promises of loyalty and wealth to her parents. One day two different men went to her house to propose. The first man was from a tribe in the east. The eastern tribe was very wealthy with goats and sheep and tilled lands, but all of them were very ugly. The second man was from the great western tribe, and like all of his tribe, he was very handsome, but all of that tribe was also very poor; they lived off the land, merely hunting and gathering the wild roots and grasses.

Thus arose a problem, which family, and which man? Her parents discussed it all day and at length they realized the problem should also have her opinion. Hearing her parent's explanation, she was silent.

Her parents realized how difficult this decision would be for her, and said, "If you are embarrassed to speak your thoughts you may point using your hand." Tentatively the girl raised her left hand indicating the Eastern tribe, but then suddenly she also raised her right indicating the Western tribe.

Her parents were bemused, "What? You can't marry both of them!"

"No," she replied, "I was going to eat with the Eastern tribe and sleep with the Western tribe."

Harry smiled at the story and nodded his head. "You see Kat, maybe they'll come up with solutions of their own for themselves which neither you nor I would have even considered."

Kaitlyn was mollified, "Thank you MamaPoriva, that did help... a lot. We'll just have to get used to the extraordinary, I guess!" she said it with a straight face. Harry almost doubled over in laughter until Kaitlyn could no longer maintain her look of nonchalance; they both realized the whole conversation had been, essentially, splitting

284

hairs. There was nothing completely normal about the Livingsons' lives other than their trying to appear normal to the people around them. And that was that.

George spent a few days in the *Concession's* kitchens installing a larger version of the dishwasher he'd fashioned in Venice. Instead of running a coil of copper tubing into an oven, he invented a water heater of sorts that did still utilize the coils of copper tubing, but relied on burning fuel to heat the water. It was a most welcome and successful addition to Jameson's kitchen and besides the water heater and dishwasher he was very interested in the brick oven. George drew up the plan which he and Lawrence had worked from; within a couple weeks the *Concession* had its own brick oven and as fate would have it---pizza and baked lasagna were added to the menu.

Harry began to re-organize his daily routine after the girls were born the year before. In the morning after they all had breakfast together, he went down to the store and did whatever was needful. In the last couple months the twins went with him. He walked at their pace---very slowly. There were even some mornings they just didn't make it all the way down the hill. In the early afternoon he worked at whichever designs and plans he'd contracted to produce and by evening he was ready to help Kat with supper. Once the girls were in bed he and Kat would just talk or sit on the hanging deck and listen to the valley. Once the girls were big enough to make the walk all the way to the store every day, a new era in the Mercantile dawned.

Mia and Lena typically investigated all the aisles and the offices before settling in one particular department of the showrooms. The arts and crafts area was perhaps more frequented than other areas. While Harry caught up the accounts and inventories, the twins pulled out one wooden kit at a time and often made something other than what was intended by the manufacturer. They added sticks and rubber bands to toy boats to make ducks, the toy carts became trains, horses and dogs. One time they pulled out a kit kite and the resulting object came soaring across the store and flew up on top of the open transom window in the office where it stayed for a few days unnoticed. PapaGeorge was the first to see it. He got a chair and retrieved it from its 'nest' above the door. After a careful examination he launched it through the air; it glided in a circle and settled on the counter in front of him. He adjusted part of the intricate structure and tossed it again. It flew in the opposite direction, but still came to rest back on the counter.

Harry and the girls came in as he was about to try another adjustment. "What has PapaGeorge got there?" Harry asked looking at the twins.

Mia said, "Lena's bird." Lena nodded her head solemnly, confirming her sister's statement.

PapaGeorge said, "Lena's bird is it? Harry watch this..." and he launched the object a third time; as before, it soared in a great circle and landed again on the counter. Harry looked from the 'bird' to Mia and Lena, to George and back to the 'bird.'

"Lena?" Harry began, "did you and Mia build this?"

She shook her head and said, "No, Mia made it for me. I got to throw it first and it got up there..." she pointed to the transom, "so we made something else..."

"Mia?" he turned to his other daughter, "can you make another one?"

"O.K." she said, and the two girls toddled over to the arts and crafts area. Harry and his father examined the object some more. The balsa kite struts were all there, just rearranged, and the paper was torn and shaped so that instead of a diamond, it was a triangle. Rubber bands held together an under-structure and the cloth for the tail was missing entirely.

Mia and Lena came back in a little while with another contraption. "Here PapaCaptain," Lena said and handed George a variation on the original. The two men looked back and forth between the two versions.

Mia said, "Lena helped."

286

Smiling, Harry launched the second object. It flew in a wide arc, then turned in the air, a kind of aerial pivot and traced its previous path back to where they stood. Instead of landing on the counter, it flipped up at the end of its flight and landed on the floor in front of them, pointing at the ceiling. "Girls, what kind of birds are these?"

Lena and Mia each pointed to one of their creations, Mia's was a "eagle," and Lena's was a "baby eagle," they said.

"Eagles," Harry repeated. "And where did you see eagles?"

They ran to the window and pointed up to the flagpole across the street over the post office. "Auntie Tania said it's an eagle," Lena answered and Mia said, "And she showed a picture in the book." There on the tip of the pole above the fluttering red, white and blue flag was perched a triangular shaped bronze eagle with its feet and talons extended as if landing. The men looked from the flagpole ornament to the objects of paper. Each was a remarkable facsimile of what the girls saw on the flagpole... and no doubt of whatever picture Titania had found to show them---but how could they also fly?

Their father asked, "Girls, if I give you a picture of a another kind of bird, can you make another model?"

Mia looked at Lena who looked back at her, they shrugged. Harry sketched an albatross and omitted drawing the feet. Lena took the picture and they toddled back to their 'workshop' again. George looked over the construction of the second flyer, 'the baby eagle,' as he asked, "Why an albatross, Harry?"

"Well," Harry answered, "it *should* have a different flight..."

The next creation was different from the previous two. Its wingspan was greater and when Harry launched it, it flew as straight as an arrow for the back of the store and hit the back wall. "Oops! bird fall down." Lena and Mia said almost together.

When Harry and the girls got back up the hill and home, Kaitlyn came out of the studio where she shared a design table with her husband and asked how their morning went at the store. Harry made a bite of lunch for his daughters as he answered. "Remember how... uh... 'concerned' you were a while back about... uh... 'normal' things?"

His eyes glanced quickly to the girls and Kat nodded in understanding. "Yes dear, I remember..."

"Well, you don't know the half of it!" and he proceeded to tell her about the eagle and baby eagle and the albatross... "I don't mean to add fuel to the fire, as it were, but they were able to repeat the process, twice, right there on the spot. The odds against making the same 'accidental' construction twice aren't so great, but then to 'accidentally' make a third, on a different design plan, that also performs as the real thing... I think we'd stand a better chance of roast pigeons flying into our mouths!"

Kat took his hand and led him to the girls' room. "Look what I found under their bed." She pulled a few loose papers from beneath the bed frame. Harry held them and whistled. On the first paper was a diagram of the village with all the streets and buildings in the right spots. On the second page was a drawing of the Tahoe with the mountains, valleys and streams all in the right places. On the third paper was a drawing of the 'eagle' model that had been out of their reach on the transom until this morning and on the fourth page was a curious depiction of what looked like their Aunties Tania and Poly with babies in their bellies which were clearly boys.

Harry just stood looking out the window, the papers hanging loosely in his hand by his side. Kat took them and put them back where they had been under the girls' bed. "So, I wish I could say I was surprised at their model building..." she soothed and went back to the kitchen table to the twins.

Harry tried to reason out how any of those images in his daughters' drawings could have gotten into their heads, but he was at a loss. To account for them logically stretched his imagination further than simply acquiescing to, as Doyle had propounded through Holmes, 'Once you eliminate the *impossible*, whatever remains, no matter how *improbable*, must be the truth.' The sticking point to that perspective was that a great deal of how the Livingsons conducted their lives already verged upon the impossible by ordinary standards. And beyond that even if the twins had been listening in on their ancestors' dialogs, it wouldn't account for these drawings or the bird models.

When he came back out to the main room again he asked them, "Mia, Lena look down there at the river," and he pointed through the window to the valley floor at the Truckee River. "Where does it go?"

The girls looked at it then their gaze followed it around the last bend in sight and still they kept gazing. A little while later Mia said, "...to another lake," Lena nodded in agreement, "...a big lake." Surprised but undaunted, Harry tried another one.

He fetched a deck of playing cards and strew them across the floor in front of them. "Girls, these cards are not in proper order; can you arrange them so they make sense?"

Harry and Kat sat on the settee and watched as their girls began forming an arrangement already *very* familiar to their parents. Mia said, "Need more cards."

Whereupon Harry said there were more in the sideboard, "...over there," he pointed generally.

Lena went to the sideboard and stared at it for a second or two, then she pulled open only one of the cabinet doors and reached into one box on the bottom shelf. Harry's eyebrows rose into his forehead and he sighed at the sight. Kaitlyn's eyebrows were similarly raised, but she *was not* sighing. Lena brought back two more decks of cards and the girls returned to their arrangement. When they sat back and looked at what they'd done, they looked up at their father and mother and smiled, "There!" they said almost at once together. Kat tried another poser.

"Girls?" she crossed to the piano and began, "Come over here, please." They toddled over to her. She ran her hand across the entire length of the keyboard striking all the keys; then she played just one note: a 'C.' "Are there any sounds that go with that sound?"

Lena pulled out the bench and helped Mia get up on it, then Mia pulled Lena up so they sat next to each other at the keyboard. Harry was instantly reminded of his sisters at that age---climbing on and over everything in their path. Lena pressed the key her mother had just pressed and Mia pressed the key an octave above it. Kaitlyn thought, 'Well that's easy enough, they look just like the same note just moved up on the keys...'

Then Lena pressed the 'D,' then the 'E,' and the 'F.' Mia pressed the 'G,' 'A,' and 'B.' They looked up to their mother grinning.

"Good!" Kat said and pressed 'B flat.' "Now, what goes with that sound?"

Again, Lena pressed the first three keys: 'C,' 'D,' and 'E flat,' then Mia pressed the next three: 'F,' 'G,' and 'A,' then played the 'B flat' again to end the octave.

"Very good!" Kat praised them again, "Now, what goes with this sound?" and she played 'G flat.'

Lena played: "A flat,' 'B flat,' and 'B.' Mia finished with 'D flat,' 'E flat,' and both 'F' then 'G flat' an octave above where it started.

"Very well done, girls!" Kat congratulated them, "Shall we have some pie now?"

The twins scooted off the bench and toddled to the kitchen and climbed onto the chairs Harry had made for them which got them to the table surface for meals. Their father sliced little pieces of the apple pie, one for each of them and put small glasses of milk in front of them. While they were enjoying the snack, he turned to his wife and said, "Well, there *is* probably *something* they can't do... yet. I don't mean to sound like one of those proud parents who see only their kids' abilities and ignore their foibles, but these are two of the brightest and best girls with which a father was ever blessed!" Mia and Lena grinned up at their parents, each wearing a milk moustache.

Kaitlyn giggled and answered, "Hopefully, like our counselors, they can't see the future or any such nonsense. Although I wouldn't be surprised if they could anticipate as well as you or me once they have a bit more experience with the world around them." She thought a little more, "Darling isn't it about time we took out the sailboat?"

During the Christmas holidays, when all the families gathered for the annual reunion, Mia and Lena in spite of their parents efforts to avoid any displays of the girls' uncanny abilities, told Tania and Poly they were having boys; not only that, but what color hair each had and that Poly and Aaron's son kicked more than Tania and Jameson's... "...because he likes his father's singing," they said.

Aaron looked at Poly and said, "You said you wouldn't announce that I like to sing to the baby at night!"

"I told you I wouldn't, even though it was silly you asked, and I haven't told a soul," she replied.

Mia said simply, "He just likes it and you sing pretty Uncle Aaron."

Flummoxed, Aaron was urged to sing for every one, which he did. Harry commented, "You do have a pretty singing voice!" Aaron smiled in spite of himself.

Then Hannah asked *the* question, "Mia does MamaKat sing?"

Lena answered for her sister, "MamaKat sings all the time. She's singing right now... don't you hear her?"

All eyes turned to Mia, Lena and Kaitlyn. Kaitlyn giggled and sputtered, "I think we have some explaining to do... Harry?" and she went to the kitchen and fussed over something cooking on the stove. Harry could feel his family's eyes on him. He closed his eyes and tried to think of the best way to phrase the difficult explanation.

Hannah asked, "Uncle Harry, are Mia and Lena just like you and MamaKat?"

Pleased for the assistance, Harry replied, "Just like me how, sweetheart?"

Hannah looked at her mother and back to him, then said, "Well, like the way you walk through walls and can be in two places at once?"

If the pressure of the stares on him were noticeable before, now they were almost palpable. "Darling, when have you seen MamaKat or me walk through walls, or be in two places at once?" he stalled.

Harold asked the same question of his daughter, "Yes, HannahBelle, when did you see Uncle Harry or MamaKat walk through walls, or be in two places at the same time?"

Hannah answered matter of-factly, "Uncle Harry, you do it all the time! Show them!"

"Hannah darling when we do that it's not for show, it's... Sometimes it's just the simplest way to get what we want done, done... Do you understand?"

"No, Uncle Harry, I don't understand. How come only you and MamaKat do it?" she was almost pouting, "I've seen you! And Mia and Lena see it too!"

Harry looked around the room at the blank faces of his relations. "It seems this next generation are a bit more capable than any of us anticipated..." He turned back to Hannah, "What are Auntie Miranda and Uncle Lorenzo doing right now?"

Hannah looked out over the lake through the window. "Auntie Miranda is asleep and baby Jean Baptiste is in Uncle's arms asleep too. But Uncle Lorenzo is humming a song and rocking in the chair." She looked at her Uncle Harry, "Aren't they!"

Chloe's breath was shallower, but she had enough presence of mind to do some quick calculations, "It is almost two in the morning, tomorrow, for them." Harry assured her it was precisely as Hannah had said was.

Aaron was near speechless; he looked at Poly and then at George and Belle, "I knew when I joined this family that remarkable things were your stock and trade... but this is a little beyond the pale..."

Belle answered quickly, "Don't look at us! Neither George nor I have any specially developed abilities... at least not anything like this..."

Aaron looked to Harry again, "So where is this coming from?"

Harry let Hannah crawl up onto his lap and Mia and Lena too, until he almost couldn't be seen behind them. "Well... I think it's like this..." As he was beginning his explanation, George began to light his pipe, one of the one's White Feathers used to puff on. Only his attention was distracted by the discussion and the match was burning down to his fingers. Kaitlyn was instantly at his elbow and, holding his hand, blew out the match. Before he could thank her, he looked up toward the kitchen and there she was still stirring the saucepan.

He said aloud, "Yes, please do tell me how you think it is that Kaitlyn can keep my finger from burning *and* still be stirring the saucepan? I'd like to hear this!"

The others looked at him instead of at Harry. George reiterated what had just happened. Everyone looked back at Harry. He tried to smile. "Having children isn't what we thought it would be... it really challenges you."

Harold contributed, "So all those times Hannah has told me what her Uncles and Aunts were doing and I thought she was so cute exercising her imagination; she wasn't imagining?" Harry nodded.

Then Chloe asked, "And when she told me about when she and Kaitlyn had just left the house and she told Kaitlyn the water was still running in the bathtub; she could see it running? *And* when she told me MamaKat ran into the house to turn it off, did she mean without using the door?"

From the kitchen came Kaitlyn's apologetic, "Sorry!"

Harry looked at each of the girls in his lap and each looked back at him, "We only do these things to protect ourselves and others. Not just to show off! Do you understand why?" And the three girls shook their heads. "Hannah, what happens when use a piece of bread as writing paper?"

She giggled and said, "You can't do that; it just gets holes in it!"

He pressed another question, "Right, that would be inappropriate. Okay, what happens when you try to use a piece of paper to make a sandwich?"

She giggled some more, "You can't do that; paper tastes bad and it's hard to chew."

Harry added, "Well spotted and from the voice of experience it appears. That would also be inappropriate. So we don't do these things when it's not appropriate... only to protect ourselves or others... when it is appropriate. We always see and hear, but we need not act upon what we see and hear... all the time. Does that make any sense?"

Hannah nodded at last, but asked, "But you and MamaKat don't just see and hear things; you can *do* things too."

"And when you are a little older and have shown that you can behave appropriately almost all the time, you shall be trained to do more than you can do right now. Deal?"

She smiled, "Deal! See Mia and Lena, we have to be 'propriate!" The twins nodded and the rest of the company could not be sure if the toddlers *really* knew why they were nodding; given the strange turn of events this afternoon.

Harold and Aaron were the first to recover; Harold went first. "I know I am in no position to train someone who is already *way* beyond me..."

Harry replied, "Sure you are, or will be when the time comes. Hannah and the little one on the way are *your* children. Who better than their parents is there to continue their training. You're doing marvelously so far!"

Then Aaron said, "But I am still unclear on this... How is it that these children are... well, uh... gifted?"

Harry then had to put forward a hypothesis which could in no way be verified---something he clearly preferred to avoid *ever* doing. "...And I can't say it is, or it isn't: but it may be the same phenomenon that has allowed Kaitlyn to progress further than others who have been on this journey as long or longer: *Me*."

For the most modest of people this was easily one of Harry's most difficult moments. "For whatever reason, beyond the obvious singular dedication to which I have applied my every effort, I affect people with whom I am in constant and intimate contact. Some to a greater or lesser extent than others, but that has more to do with the individual rather than my influence." He mused, "Which explains Kat. It explains why Hannah was as an infant easily affected. And of course Mia and Lena, that would seem to be a straight forward example; what with the combined make-up of both Kat *and* myself..."

Poly and Tania were now very curious, "Harry? Can you really walk through walls?"

"Uh... it's not walking from my perspective, nor do they appear to be walls..." He took a deep breath and admitted, "but yes. And no I will not demonstrate; that would be setting a very poor example for Hannah and her cousins, don't you think? After what I just got through *trying* to explain to them..."

"Yes, but it also sounds like an evasion." Tania commented evenly.

Harry didn't even smile, "You can't goad me, darling. Suffice it to say though should you ever find yourself in a situation that I perceive requires intervention, I shall not hesitate. 'Always only what is necessary,' is a very good rule of thumb."

Titania then did what she perhaps should not have done. She went through the door onto the deck and went straight to the balcony; she peered at the twenty-foot drop to the ground below. Both Jameson and Harry watched her and suspected the next move. Kaitlyn called to the girls to come into the kitchen and gathered them behind the counter. Tania turned to face the house and with everyone looking out at her, pushed herself over the railing.

In the living room there was a sound of rushing wind through a not quite closed window. When they looked around, Harry *appeared* to still be sitting in his chair but Jameson wasn't in the room. Poly rushed out to look down over the railing; she was followed instantly by the others. When they all looked down, there was Jameson holding Tania in his arms as if about to carry her across a threshold. His only bewildered comment was, "How did I get *here*?"

As Harry then rose to walk out onto the deck, Kaitlyn said quickly, "Darling..." and she flicked at her shoulders. He looked at his own shoulders and brushed off the few snowflakes dappling his coat.

He went out and peered over at his sister and brother. He simply said, "Nice one sis!" and went back into the house. Jameson was *trying* to describe what had just happened from his own vantage point but it was confusing at best. He carried Titania back up to the front door and didn't put her down until they were next to the fireplace again. He looked at Harry, "Really, what just happened here?"

Harry replied evenly and he ticked off on his fingers as he spoke, "One: Titania has always been a most thorough student and has never believed anything without verifying its validity. Two:" and he looked directly into her eyes, "You are carrying a very important passenger there and you should be considerate of *his* future as well. Three: White Feathers was right---'Time is the uniquely subjective phenomenon.' It took me years to fully grasp the implications of it, but it is more true than most people imagine."

Titania looked right back into his eyes, "George Henry Livingson if I couldn't trust my child's life in your hands, what use would a demonstration be anyway? Besides if it weren't for my *passenger* you probably would have let me hit the ground."

"Me? It was your husband that kept you off the ground..." Harry responded coyly. The others were so amazed there simply were no words to begin to express their condition.

Kaitlyn announced quickly, "Dinner's ready, grab a plate and get what you wish."

Hannah made sure Mia and Lena were served first, then only after she had seated them and they began to eat, would she get a plate for herself. The display did not go unnoticed by anyone and there was a sense that perhaps, as strange as the future may seem to be becoming, their children *would be* good people. Harry made the mistake of, for the second time, innocently asking, "Would someone *just* pass the nuts?" Some jokes are just good no matter how many times they are told. The laughter in the house could likely be heard a long way down the narrow little valley.

As they settled under the covers that night Kaitlyn asked Harry, "Why didn't you just put Tania back on the rail yourself? Way take Jameson along for the ride?"

"We already know how those sort of antics affect children; look at all the time you and I spent with Hannah when she was an infant, and need I mention our own little cherubim?"

"Good point," she yawned. The holiday snow fell on the valley, and the sound of every flake that dropped was marked by the two little angels laying awake in the room next door as they peered through the window at that most ordinary of scenes which for them was a symphony of sight and sound.

The interesting thing about traveling abroad is that the traveler can become used to conveniences found elsewhere that are not available at home. Such was the case with the Livingsons. Harry had been gathering trade journal articles, catalogs and following developments both back east and in the Bay area of the installations of electric power. His own experiments forced him to conclude that the only viable, and by 'viable' meaning practical for him to install, system would be a wind generator and battery storage system---very similar in operation to Charles Brush's laboratory in Ohio. As he was reading about a windmill and battery system in the issue of a trade journal to which he subscribed, Harry happened across an article referring to a recently published book; soon to be in its third edition, *How to make a dynamo: a practical treatise for amateurs*, by Alfred Crofts. Without hesitation he ordered a copy; Harry had always had a penchant for gleaning the most useful information from texts.

He ordered a large number of batteries from the National Carbon Company, then ordered a dozen or so fixtures and light bulbs just for his initial experiments. He decided on utilizing the Aeromotor designed tower and vane configuration, knowing that the Sierra storms could ravage a lesser adaptable design---as they discovered over the last several years with the constant repairs to the old Halladay tower at the Lodges. Before the summer was out he had a working dynamo-generator mounted in a weather-proof housing on top of the windmill tower behind the house. He ran copper pipe from the tower housing to a brick shed he constructed to house the batteries. From there more conduit was laid to the two houses and down to the restaurant. His first installation of just lighting was down in the *Concession*. Jameson agreed to the experiment willingly, hoping to reduce fuel costs for the lanterns and so transfer the savings to the more vital and direct expenditures of his enterprise. He directed Harry's installation of the fixtures: several in the kitchens and pantries with the balance in the dining rooms and sitting room-saloon. In addition to the incandescent lighting Harry installed six Diehl-manufactured ceiling fans, two in the kitchen and four in the rest of the building.

On an evening in early April, before the first wave of visitors began filtering into the village for the Tahoe Tournament, a very round Titania threw the main switch for the *Grand Concession's* new lights and the restaurant was illuminated without oil or kerosene lamps for the very first time. Any passerby might have marveled at the way the staff and customers stared up at the lights in the restaurant all evening as if they'd never seen a lamp or a ceiling fan before. After a week or so of checking voltages and currents, battery charge levels and such, Harry was ready to increase his bank of batteries and begin adding fixtures to the two houses. When he wired the the buildings he continued the use of copper piping as conduit, and since they were visible in the rooms where light fixtures were installed he was sure to polish the pipes and apply a wax finish to them, both to minimize corrosion and to keep them shiny and attractive.

George instantly asked to have the store and the house lit, Belle wanted the Lodges wired and lighted, and each of the women in the affected households wanted a new electric iron. With his father's assistance the tasks were quickly accomplished and before the Connors', Backhouses' or Bessamers' new bundles of joy began to arrive in May, both sides of Main Street and Lakeside Road at the entrance to the village were lit and ventilated by electricity. Harry purchased arc lamps and erected them on poles on either side of the street at the Mercantile, the Lodges, the Concession and School House,so that the late evening visitors to Tahoe City were bathed in the warm glow upon entering or leaving town along the River Road. Kaitlyn and Titania persuaded him to also add lights to the driveway from beside the restaurant all the way to the home on the hill. Over the years Harry made amendments and additions to his 'grid' as technological progress provided efficiencies unavailable at the time of the first installations.

First came James White Feathers Connor on May second; a very healthy red-headed boy with an equally healthy appetite. Before the week was out Belle and Kaitlyn were on the train to Berkeley for the arrival of William Henry Backhouse born May eighth. Aaron couldn't have been a prouder father; Poly, Belle and Kaitlyn had to vie for time with the boy as his father monopolized all the time when the infant wasn't nursing. What neither pair of parents anticipated was the sudden and somewhat shocking newly established communication initiated with the Livingson ancestors. It was one thing to have their immediate family congratulating them, it was quite another to receive those felicitations from the voices of the most wise and ancient. Jameson and Titania were most gratified that White Feathers would always be close to them and that he was honored to have their son be a living bearer of the name he'd carried through the remainder of his life. Aaron and Poly were likewise humbled and gratified that they should have such considered assistance going forward in their new lives as father and mother.

The final visit by the stork was to the new Booklove House and the arrival of Oliver Henry Bessamer on the sixteenth. Hannah was at last a 'big' sister, and at three and half years old she kept her little brother in her lap and guarded him like he was her own possession. Chloe remarked that if her daughter could nurse, she'd never get to hold their son. Harold was more than delighted and took photograph after photograph with his own new Kodak of his children for Chloe to send to their parents in Redditch. Kaitlyn and Hannah, with Mia and Lena in tow went on walks during their visit. MamaKat wished to reinforce Harry's injunctions of appropriate behaviors to which Hannah responded, "Father and Mother remind me all the time... but..." and after Hannah's moment of hesitation Kaitlyn asked, "What is it dearest?"

Hannah looked up at her and admitted, "I only like seeing what Uncle Harry and MamaKat, you I mean, and Mia and Lena are doing... sometimes."

Kaitlyn smiled, "We are happy to have you watching over us, sweetheart. That makes me feel very loved indeed." HannahBelle grinned and took the twins' hands in hers for the rest of the walk.

The Livingson women went back and forth between the two homes for another week before returning to Tahoe. Harry and George had spent almost all their time at the Connor's cottage and looked forward to their wives' return so they could make the trip to Berkeley as well. Before long, after all the visiting and photographs were exhausted, life in the village shifted to the rhythms of the Summer Season. Belle made a mock up of a brochure for the Lodges using actual photographs, and highlighted the electric lights and fans as well as the new water heaters for the bathrooms which George had constructed and installed. Kaitlyn and Belle spent a day or two over the designs which resulted in three main advertisements: one for newspapers, one for travel related publications and magazines, and a folded version for train depots, restaurants and such.

Mia and Lena made daily visits to the Lodges and the Mercantile. At the Lodges their mother, grandmama and Auntie Tania enlisted their 'help' in the maintenance of the plant beds and grounds chores. At the Mercantile, as Poly and Tania before them, they were let loose to wander the aisles, bins, baskets and buckets of an unending world of doohickies and thingamabobs to their hearts content. George confided to Harry that he was convinced it was the time spent in the store when they were little that cultivated their mechanical sense and creativity; Harry had no argument there---his own fondest memories of his childhood were in this store. Jameson, Harry, Belle and Titania tilled the little field behind the restaurant for a garden to support both the Connor home and the restaurant kitchens. The idea was contagious and before Harry knew it he was terracing and tilling the hillside next to their own house for Kaitlyn. Lena and Mia were more like dusty and muddy urchins than the cherubs their father usually referred to them as, and they wore their soiled clothes in preference to any other outfits in their drawers.

However, the girls' chief entertainment and occupation was 'playing' with little James, whom they insisted upon calling Jamie. At meals they were full of stories about how Jamie did this and Jamie thinks that... until at a certain point it dawned on Harry and Kat that their girls may not be imagining *all* of what they related about what Jamie was thinking. Their uncanny talents had not diminished as yet; they were remarkably consistent about their cousin's wants and needs and accurate as well it turned out. Many times when the baby wouldn't stop crying, as babies are wont to do from time to time, it was a suggestion from Mia or Lena that, if acted upon, calmed the child's distress or at least explained his initial disturbance.

Harry decided to learn to play the piano. He was 'assisted' in this endeavor by Mia and Lena who sat on either side of him as he played scales upon scales to get his fingers familiar with the instrument. The piano practice was usually followed by reading time and Harry opted for the same reading material he and his sisters began with reading---*Shakespeare's Complete Works*. Whether the girls understood the plot twists and characters wasn't material, that they began to recognize written words and phrases every now and again was. Of course it helped that he had a different voice for each character. Kaitlyn told them stories every night which were in large part reiterations of tales and fables told to her by their unseen counselors.

The summer's warmth was furled into the arms of an approaching autumn and the march of cold air gradually drove the leaves from the trees as winter crept through the valleys. Birthdays were celebrated and the Yule holidays were upon them again. Becky decided this year she would be the grand organizer of the feasts and gatherings. In this capacity she was helped and guided by Belle who had taken her under her wing and was determined that she always felt as integral to the life of the family as any other siblings. This holiday there were six children to accommodate in the plans. At least three of them were in someone's arms all the time, but the other three made themselves 'junior directors' under Becky's administration and followed her everywhere. They set tables, helped clear dishes, decorated mantles, trees and shelves as well as counters, doors and windows at the store. While they couldn't reach everywhere nor carry much, they were praised as 'the most wonderful helpers' Becky had ever had.

Perhaps because of Belle's influence, perhaps because of her brother and sister's new capacity as parents, Becky stayed in Tahoe City after the holidays were over and moved into Tania and Poly's old room with George and Belle. She became their newest daughter and neither George nor Belle spared any moment giving her the attention and additional training they had lavished upon their own girls; Becky was a sponge. When she needed a drawing table for design proposals, she used Harry and Kaitlyn's. Then she and Kaitlyn would spend as many hours as necessary hammering out ideas which were then forwarded to Poly. As the weather warmed, Belle took 'her girls' out on the Tahoe for entertainment and for the opportunity for Titania and Kaitlyn to offer further encouragement and direction to their 'sister.' It was upon one of these excursions that Titania mused about Sarah Bunker's departure from the school.

"I can't imagine *who* the School Committee will find to replace her. At least the lessons and schedules are well established; whoever it is shouldn't have a great deal of difficulty picking up the baton."

Becky was curious, "How long was she here?"

Titania answered that, "Although she was initially hired on a temporary basis, she stayed for six years and I suppose if she hadn't met Mr. Ivory she'd be here still. Poly and I assisted at the school the first couple years. Those were two of my best dressed years..." The other ladies laughed knowing Titania's preference for just throwing on 'something' to wear and getting her day going.

Kaitlyn added, "She was very good to work with at the start-up of the Theatrical Society, she will be missed."

Becky sat silent for the rest of the trip back. Before supper that evening Becky stopped in at the Tahoe City School House after the children had left for the day and introduced herself to Miss Bunker. They chatted about Becky's upbringing in Manchester and her previous career. Sarah told about her own education in Massachusetts and her move to San Francisco and her ending up here.

"I really intended to just get the school up and running, but one thing led to another and well... it's been a lovely several years .. very, very rewarding. I shall miss the village and my students."

Becky then asked an odd question, "Sarah are there specific credentials required to teach here in California?"

"That's a can of worms! There was a time when the state had a certification process; several years ago the legislature adopted a new constitution which essentially did away with many of the standards that were once in place. Amendments have been proposed but we have not recaptured our previous standing. Why do you ask, Miss Backhouse? Could you be considering a career change?"

Becky blushed, "As a matter of fact I am investigating the

possibilities."

Sarah made a final comment as they parted, "I have not had any children of my own, yet I have had hundreds whom I *consider* my own. Short of inventing a cure for the common cold, providing a remedy for ignorance has been the most rewarding activity of my life. I highly recommend it." She pressed Becky's hand in farewell, and Becky went to talk to Belle.

At supper she asked for some more advice, "MamaBelle? Do you think I would make a good teacher and role model for children?"

George and Belle put down their spoons with stew on the way to their mouths. "Rebecca Jane Backhouse, you are one of the most capable and successful women I have ever met; what would come into your head to ask such a question? As a role model, you are exemplary. As a teacher, I have watched you with Hannah and with the twins; you are patient, thorough and clear---what else must a teacher need be?"

The Captain then had to ask, "Sweetheart are you considering taking over for Sarah?"

Becky said with much more confidence than she felt, "Yes." Then she added more than a little concerned, "I just hope Poly and Kat won't feel that I have abandoned them... which I guess I am essentially doing."

Belle got up and put her arm around Becky's shoulders, "Dearest they *do* have their hands full, you've noticed; perhaps CANED Ltd. should become the design arm of Sierra Architecture. You all will still have design work, but without having to devote so much time to making proposals... I don't know much about these things, but isn't that actually how it has worked out on a few of the projects already?"

"Yes that is how it has happened," Becky was somewhat relieved, "and with some success I might add. So as soon as I tell Kaitlyn and Poly, I'll put my name in the hat with the School

Committee." Becky Backhouse had always been one to make decisions which affected not only her life, but the lives and livelihood of others, and she always came to the best solution for all concerned. This was no exception. Kaitlyn and Hipolyta were both excited for her and very encouraging; while Harry was relieved his friend was confidently making a new way for herself in her new home.

It was mid-spring, and the Tahoe School Committee was overjoyed to have an applicant for the position before they had to spend any money advertising for a replacement. Miss Rebecca Backhouse was formally invited to accept the position by letter a week later. Sarah Bunker began to include Becky in lesson planning, tutoring and last but not least, in the support and organizational activities for the annual Theatrical Society performances. Kaitlyn and Titania were *very* supportive in the latter. By the time the Spring Term was near complete so were the preparations for the new season's productions. One of her duties in the theatrical endeavors was as liaison between the school and the Players' director, Mr Avery Goodman; he was very excited, and truth be told, very relieved that such a capable individual was to assume the reins of the School. The productions this year were: for the Junior Thespians---*Romeo and Juliet*, and for the Players---'that Scottish Play' (*MacBeth*). Surprisingly, it was Becky who drew the company's attention to the superstition of never mentioning the title of that play once performances were staged---the legend of tragic accidents and such. The Players warmed to her immediately as one of their own.

For Mia and Lena this would be the first play that they could actually appreciate, at least to some degree. But for their cousin Hannah it was the *most* exciting event. Her exuberance infected the twins, especially when they got dressed up for the opening performance. Any observer would suppose they were attending a Broadway premier for which the three girls were the proud producers, much to the enchanted pleasure of their elders. Seats were reserved on the front row for the 'little producers' and they were the model of childlike wonder and decorum during each presentation.

"And we get to go to the cast party afterwards, and meet all the actors, *and everything*..." Hannah informed her tyro cousins who followed her around like goslings after a goose.

While they were in Tahoe for the annual event, Harold and Chloe, with little Oliver in her lap, sat in the home on the hill and approached Harry and Kaitlyn with a proposition. Chloe had just conveyed their approbation of Becky's career change, "...for the best I'm sure and it makes Harold and I even more certain of something we have been deliberating. The Berkeley schools aren't dreadful but some of the children are, and their parents aren't much better. So it occurred to us to ask you and Kaitlyn if perhaps you would consider..." and she took a deep breath, "...allowing Hannah to live here through her school years, attend the Tahoe School and at the proper time receive her other 'education' which Harold and I believe would best come from yourselves." She let out a sigh, as if she'd wanted to give the entire appeal in one breath lest she loose her resolve by merely breathing.

Harold bolstered the request with, "Hannah Belle loves you all so dearly; she watches you all the time, she says, and we will of course provide for her financially whatever she requires. We don't mean this to be in any way a charity on your part or a burden in any fashion..." They were so imploringly humble in their request, it struck both Harry and Kaitlyn how very unlike either of them this approach seemed.

Kaitlyn answered for them both, "Hannah is always welcome wherever we are, as she has always been. I would like to make a few things very clear, however..." and both Harold and Chloe stiffened. "One," and she held up a finger so like Harry and his father in manner, "We will absolutely *not* take a single penny in her support; it is unnecessary. Two," a second finger was raised, "...we absolutely applaud Becky's choice to take up the reins of the Tahoe School. Just as it has for you, it has made our outlook for Mia and Lena's early schooling even more acceptable. But it is of no matter in what environment our children are schooled, in the end it is their training and socialization which is actually at issue---not so much the data they absorb. So in that matter we applaud your decision. Three," and a third finger went up, "her 'other' education should best come from yourselves. However, as only Chloe has had the closest brush with that experience from the instructive side, we will accept the responsibility of her real education. It is *most* vital that you understand this: You must know that in this matter there is no turning back; it would not only be confusing to her, but in a very real way, destroy any of her future possibilities and *that* is simply *not acceptable*." She relaxed into the chair in which she was sitting and took Harry's hand back into her own; they waited for Harold and Chloe to digest their terms.

"We expected no less," Harold answered, "and we absolutely accept these terms." Mia and Lena emerged from their room at that moment to show off the costumes and jewelry they'd contrived from the assorted bric-a-brac in their room.

"Well that's settled then." Harry announced, "Let's go see Papa and Grandmama shall we?" and he scooped up Mia in one arm and Lena in the other and propped them on his shoulders.

"Wheee!" they yelled as they bestrode their father and waved for the others to come along---looking all the while like princesses in a carriage waving to their adoring subjects. The image was not lost on Kat who assured Chloe and Harold that *all* their children would be most evenly adored how ever her girls seemed to behave at present.

Chloe just laughed; Harold answered, "Uncle Harry is just Harry no matter with whom he is, that person or those people are the most important to him at that moment. It's a gift and I've tried to cultivate it in emulation."

Miss Rebecca Backhouse spent quite a number of weeks that summer with Poly and Tania reviewing all that lay ahead of her in her new profession. Her brother was so pleased that she was pursuing her new vocation with the same zeal she'd applied to every of her other endeavors he could hardly keep from mentioning that 'his sister was the new teacher in Tahoe City' to very nearly everyone with whom he came in contact over that season. Of course that was when he was around anyone to hear him. He spent a lot of his time with George on the lake, or in the streams fishing, wandering the mountain trails hunting or just riding. Although lumbering of the forests around Tahoe Lake proper had reduced whole slopes to stumps and undergrowth, the Sierras west and north were still just as wild and beckoning.

When the Autumn Term ended in late November Becky and MamaBelle sat down and reevaluated the results of her decision of the year before. "Honestly it's almost like dealing with a bunch of construction workers... having to practically hold their hands and walk them through the same steps over and over---only the very youngest ones I mean. At least with all my students older than six I usually only have to give instructions once; in many ways they are all a lot smarter than the clot of laborers I once managed and far more cooperative. Of course there was some unruliness in the first week or so, but we all came to an agreement very early on: 'I wouldn't torture them, and in turn they wouldn't cause me any headaches,' that seemed to do the trick. I think having an accent different from theirs helps a little in a way; some of the older ones have even taken to using my voice when instructing the younger ones---at least when they need them to understand something important."

Belle kept smiling, and nodding and listening, enjoying every moment of Becky's descriptions.

"And if I didn't know better, the parents seem to take whatever I say as gospel with regard to their child's progress or lack thereof. I am sure Sarah's counsel had the same effect, but it's such a relief to not have to 'convince' them of anything. They just hear it once and that is that. And the children's comprehension is just so incredible. We went over the oceans and major currents once one Tuesday and when I asked about the Gulf Stream on the next Friday every one of their little hands were in the air anxious to be the one called upon to respond. Oh, speaking of that, do you still have Poly and Tania's tests from several years ago? We just received new final testing and as I have never seen the previous version---I was in Berkeley winding up my affairs when Sarah administered them last spring---I am wondering what might have changed."

Belle went to the room behind the workshop and came back with the three envelopes containing the 'first graduates' tests and results. "Here you are. I read through the tests after I first received them. I must say... well... my children have always surprised and amazed me with what they know, and do not know..."

Becky took out one of the examinations and looked over it, "Actually but for a few dates, and some wording regarding world locations' naming and such, it seems to be essentially the same test. Here's the new one; look for yourself," and she handed Belle a few officially printed forms for 'Graduation Examination' candidates.

Belle looked over the 'new' testing:

Grammar (Time, one hour)

1. Give nine rules for the use of Capital Letters.
2. Name the Parts of Speech and define those that have no modifications.
3. Define Verse, Stanza and Paragraph.
4. What are the Principal Parts of a verb? Give Principal Parts of do, lie, lay and run.
5. Define Case. Illustrate each Case.
6. What is Punctuation? Give rules for principal marks of Punctuation.
7-10. Write a composition of about 150 words and show therein that you understand the practical use of the rules of grammar.

Arithmetic (Time, one and quarter hours)

1. Name and define the Fundamental Rules of Arithmetic.
2. A wagon box is 2 ft. deep, 10 ft. long, and 3 ft. wide. How many bushels of wheat will it hold?
3. If a load of wheat weighs 3942 lbs. What is it worth at 50 cts. per

bushel, deducting 1050 lbs. for tare?

4. District No. 33 has a valuation of $35,000. What is the necessary levy to carry on a school seven months at $50 per month, and have $104 for incidentals?

5. Find cost of 6720 lbs. of coal at $6.00 per ton.

6. Find the interest of $512.60 for 8 months and 18 days at 7 percent.

7. What is the cost of 40 boards, 12 inches wide, and 16 ft. long at $.20 per inch?

8. Find bank discount on $300 for 90 days (no grace) at 10 percent.

9. What is the cost of a square farm at $15 per acre, the distance around which is 640 rods?

10. Write a Bank Check, a Promissory Note, and a Receipt.

U.S. History (Time, forty-five minutes)

1. Give the epochs into which U.S. History is divided.

2. Give an account of the discovery of America by Columbus.

3. Relate the causes and results of the Revolutionary War.

4. Show the territorial growth of the United States.

5. Tell what you can of the history of California.

6. Describe two of the most prominent results of the Bear Flag Revolt.

7. Who were the following: Morse, Whitney, Fulton, Bell, Lincoln, Penn, and Howe?

8. Name events connected with the following dates: 1607, 1620, 1800, 1849 and 1865?

Orthography (Time, one hour)

1. What is meant by the following: Alphabet, phonetic orthography, etymology, syllabication?

2. What are elementary sounds? How classified?

3. What are the following, and give examples of each: Trigraph, sub-vocals, diphthong, cognate letters, linguals?

4. Give four substitutes for caret 'u'.

5. Give two rules for spelling words with final 'e.' Name two

exceptions under each rule.

6. Give two uses of silent letters in spelling. Illustrate each.

7. Define the following prefixes and use in connection with a word: Bi, dis, mis, pre, semi, post, non, inter, mono, super.

8. Mark diacritically and divide into syllables the following, and name the sign that indicates the sound: Card, ball, mercy, sir, odd, cell, rise, blood, fare, last.

9. Use the following correctly in sentences, Cite, site, sight, fare, fain, feign, vane, vain, vein, raze, raise, rays.

10. Write 10 words frequently mispronounced and indicate pronunciation by use of diacritical marks and by syllabication.

Geography (Time, one hour)

1. What is climate? Upon what does climate depend?

2. How do you account for the extremes of climate in the regions of California?

3. Of what use are rivers? Of what use is the ocean?

4. Describe the mountains of N.A.

5. Name and describe the following: Monrovia, Odessa, Denver, Manitoba, Hekla, Yukon, St. Helena, Juan Fermandez, Aspinwall and Orinoco.

6. Name and locate the principal trade centers of the U.S.

7. Name all the republics of Europe and give capital of each.

8. Why is the Atlantic Coast colder than the Pacific in the same latitude?

9. Describe the process by which the water of the ocean returns to the sources of rivers.

10. Describe the movements of the earth. Give inclination of the earth.

When she had quite completed her perusal, she handed the sheets back to Becky. "Yes that does seem to be very similar indeed to what I heard day in and day out from the three of them for the few days leading up to examination day."

Becky sighed, "Well good. I was a little worried only because consistency should be maintained from one year to the next at least in so far as we can at the same time keep up with changes in the world in which we live, and our increasing understanding of it."

Belle couldn't help noticing how her adopted daughter had become so 'maternal' over the last few months and it caused her own heart to swell in the knowledge that not only had Tahoe City benefitted immensely from her decision to change careers, but Becky was without a doubt the greatest beneficiary of the situation, second only to her students it seemed.

Hannah, her little brother Oliver and their parents returned in May for the annual productions that inaugurate the Tahoe Summer Season. This year Harold and Chloe stayed the whole summer in Bungalows Seven and Eight nearest the *Concession* and the Livingson house to make Hannah's transition to Tahoe a real family affair. With the Bessamers there, all the family was in residence for the summer and the children went everywhere, generally as a group, but always 'upon an expedition' it seemed. James, William, and Oliver---who quickly became Jamie, Will, and Olly---followed their older cousins as best they could. More often than not one of the girls would have a boy in hand as they went about their adventures: climbing, hiking, playing in the store, holding formal teas at the *Concession*, playing pirates in the sailboat (drawn into the shallows for the occasion) or even farming the vegetables for Jamie's father and the restaurant.

Hannah was nearly convinced the entire summer was for her benefit exclusively and she was a most benevolent empress. While the Vanderbilts enjoyed their newly opened Marble House that summer in Newport, the seventeen members of the Livingson clan in Tahoe relished every day they were together and always kept their absent loved ones in England and Venice near to their hearts. With each household now in possession of a camera, or two, the entire summer was most thoroughly documented for posterity and naturally for their absent family. At the end of June the first of the initial series of photos returned, which was of course another cause for a 'gathering.' By then a 'gathering' needed no excuse in the least.

The six women maintained a moving tea party nearly everyday of the week, and a few times out on the Tahoe itself in the two boats. The five men tried to go fishing every weekend at least. During two weeks of that summer when they rested from repairing the Connor pastures' fencing, they wet their lines in the creeks running down to the Truckee River or in the river itself. The Squaw Valley pastures were an inheritance from his father; Jameson and Titania still pastured their horses up there in the summers.

After they celebrated Jean Baptiste Spelman's third birthday, in absentia, the summer wound to its natural conclusion and the Berkeley families made ready to return home for the autumn. Harold and Chloe sat with Hannah in her new room and offered her some final words of encouragement and caution. The now larger Livingson family waved farewell to the Bessamers at the bottom of the driveway next to the *Concession* and then went inside for brunch. Hannah suddenly looked troubled. Harry noticed and asked, "What's the matter Hannah Belle? You look as if you have misplaced something."

"I can't see Mama and Father," she said evenly, but with a hint of sadness.

Kaitlyn looked to Harry as he answered consolingly, "Sweetheart it may be that you are just growing up and you will have to wait until you are a much bigger girl before your sight returns. You were very lucky to see the people you care for anytime you wished. With special efforts you will probably be able to have that ability again someday. There is nothing wrong with you at all. You're just growing up... I promise."

Hannah smiled a little and repeated, "I'm growing up..."

Kaitlyn offered, "Darling you are almost the age when I first learned how to play piano; would you like to learn how to play the piano with Uncle Harry? He's learning too?"

She looked at her uncle and in a voice of awe she uttered, "Uncle Harry? *You* don't know how to do something?"

Harry laughed, "That's correct Hannah Belle. There are things I do not yet know how to do. But I can learn, just like you can, and Lena can, and Mia can. Even MamaKat learns new things all the time." He added with a wink, "Although MamaKat doesn't have too many things more to learn... She's very, *very* smart."

"Your Uncle Harry is partial. Of course I have a lot more to learn. For example: Why isn't a beautiful girl like you married already?" Kaitlyn asked with a serious voice.

Hannah laughed out loud, "MamaKat, boys are silly! And I'm not old enough to marry somebody! I'm not patient enough..."

Harry and Kaitlyn had to laugh at that, "That sounds like your mother talking alright. Did she tell you that?"

Hannah shook her head, "Father said, 'Mother had to have a lot of patience to marry him because he was so silly.'"

Kaitlyn was still chuckling when she said, "Well there you go; I didn't know that before! I just learned something new! Hannah when you start school next week I hope you will tell me about everything *you* learn so that *I* will learn more too. Deal?"

Hannah was well over her minor bout of sadness by now, "Deal!" Mia and Lena wanted to hear all about what she learned at school too. They were just that much envious that their cousin was already going to get to go to school and they still had to wait until they were bigger.

"We almost read a whole page by ourself with daddy the other day!" Lena crowed to let her cousin know that they were worthy to also hear about her school lessons.

Miss Backhouse introduced all the new students to the returning classes, and introduced her previous students to the new arrivals. Hannah made friends quickly with several girls in her own entering class who had older siblings in the school already. After the first day she was feeling right at home in Tahoe. When classes were let out for the day she went next door to see Uncle Jameson, as she was supposed to, and waited hardly any time at all for Uncle Harry or

MamaKat to come and walk her home---'just until she get more used to the routine.' That didn't take but a few days. Tahoe City had been Hannah's second home for years now and she had walked all over the village herself before now. Kaitlyn just wanted to have the whole family used to the schedule that Hannah followed before she left Hannah to her own decisions about what she did after school--- so long as one of the family knew where she was at all times.

Every morning Lena and Mia would hurry into Hannah's room and help her choose what to wear then after breakfast they walked with her to the school house. Then they went to 'help' in the *Concession* kitchens, or tended the gardens until one of their parents or other family would walk with them to the store where they were now in charge of sweeping and stocking. Sometimes they went with Grandmama to help Auntie Tania with chores at the Lodges. They were beginning to believe Hannah's school days were even more glamorous than ever. In the late afternoons Harry and the girls would sit at the piano and each would take turns practicing scales, arpeggios and chords. After a month or two each of them chose a composition to learn. Then at the supper table almost every evening Hannah would regale her wide-eyed cousins with the amazing things she'd learned just that day. In turn the girls would supply Hannah with the news of the Mercantile, the restaurant and the gardens, or other notable events. Every Friday evening there was letter-writing to Berkeley. Hannah seized upon the notion of addressing her letters to her little brother, Olly, since "...Mother or Father will have to read it to him anyway, so everybody will hear my letters."

The rhythms of the village rose up to the holiday tempo as the end of the Autumn Term wound closer. The Livingson house sported the same decorations as every other house in town with school children. After school let out there was a new industry of paper chain construction in reds and greens. Jamie got involved in this enterprise by being the official gluer... he even got some of it on the paper. The girls 'chained' the house, then the store, then the restaurant. After the paper chains came popcorn strings and ornament creation, then the inevitable Christmas present production. No one in the clan was omitted and the first gifts completed were sent off immediately to Venice and Redditch so they would have theirs in time. Wrapping the masterpieces was nearly as much fun as any of the other activities and here also the girls worked at making the wrapping of each gift as unique and elaborate as the special creations inside.

When the family gathered for Yuletide and New Year's the girls made sure each guest was made fully aware of where each of their gifts were located under the tree; it was all they could do to keep from telling what each was and how it was made; secrets were just not their strong suit---but they managed. Hannah showed her parents all her school work and was properly applauded for her dedication and scholarly behavior. The children made snowmen and had snowball battles, although the boys were mostly consigned to manufacturing rather than lobbing the projectiles themselves. That separation of work didn't last long and the girls got as 'pelted' by their little cousins as they did by each other. It was a free-for-all.

The routines established during the last several months continued as the spring brought warmer weather at last and the school devoted more and more time to the preparations for this year's thespian productions. Now instead of attending the performances, Hannah would be on the stage and nothing short of playing all the parts herself could have made for a prouder little girl. The Junior Players were staging *As You Like It*, and Hannah was to play Audrey. She did not have many lines, but to be up on the stage with an audience looking up at her---she was in heaven. The Village players were to perform *Anthony and Cleopatra*, and since Hannah was in the first play she was not obliged to assist in the preparations for the other. She was determined to be as involved as she could be, and so helped to make all the sets.

After the opening night at the cast party, Kaitlyn asked Hannah loud enough for her mother and father to hear, "I thought you told me you weren't old enough to get married, and there you were tonight on the stage: getting married! You *must* be old enough now!"

Hannah squealed and giggled, "That was only make believe MamaKat! Besides Touchstone isn't a real person and I was acting. I still don't have the patience to be really married!"

Chloe and Harold laughed at her answer; chagrined at the knowledge of the source for her 'patience' reference. They asked Kaitlyn how the subject of marriage had ever come up anyway. Kaitlyn told them about the 'brunch discussion' after their parting at the end of last August. Hannah was sad over her lost sight but Harry and she distracted her from any serious sorrow over the loss.

"She just stopped seeing? Just like that?" asked Harold, a little startled.

Harry was nearby and explained how he'd wondered: as the girls got older, if bit by bit their certain 'talents' would diminish or disappear entirely. "That they were able to do what they did was inexplicable, save through a kind of imbued or associative vestige of a past connection with someone who already *had* developed those abilities---like myself or Kaitlyn for instance. The only abilities which are our own and inalienable to us are those we gain through our own efforts---*that* is the reality. The 'talents' they exhibited simply weren't their own. Perhaps with proper efforts they shall be able to reclaim them since they seem to already have tendencies in those areas... time and their *own* efforts will tell."

What neither Harry nor Kaitlyn mentioned was how some of Lena and Mia's savant abilities were actually, however gradually, still developing; their talents no longer extended to the extrasensory depth Hannah's had been.

Chloe was visibly relieved and Harold added that Oliver had not shown any similar special-ness as was so strong in Hannah. "Just a happy go lucky lad, sharp as a tack and precocious only in the mischief he can wreak on his knees and elbows."

Poly and Tania vouched for their boys' similar aptitudes and the parents shared stories and anecdotes while the little cousins dashed around the celebrating cast and friends playing games interesting to themselves alone.

When the summer season opened Harry discussed with Harold and Chloe the likelihood of beginning Hannah's training very soon. "My sisters were trained later than this, and I was trained earlier; it just seems that she should have it sooner rather than later. This will also insure that the information she gathers while in school over the next seven years can be assimilated appropriately for what it is."

Kaitlyn entered the conversation by adding, "And then there is the consideration of her growing desire to be the center of attention. It's relatively cute now but it was also cute when I was like that at her age; that is a road down which I would caution everyone I love to avoid."

Chloe agreed and Harold only asked: when in particular Harry considered beginning. "That does depend upon Hannah to some degree. She already has much of the internal organization necessary, and as Kaitlyn pointed out, that could dissipate---so the sooner the better." He turned to Kaitlyn, "When are you taking her out on the boat, dear?"

At breakfast the next morning Kaitlyn announced that she and Hannah Belle would be going out for a special trip on the Tahoe. She left specific instructions for Chloe, then remembering the picnic basket and her fishing rod, walked with Hannah to the little boat dock below Grandmama Belle's house. Hannah settled into the bow of the sampan; Kat took the oar and began to row them onto the Tahoe. When they had gotten quite a ways offshore she began an introduction to what lay in store for her adoptive daughter.

"Your Uncle Harry trained your mother and father how to become all that a person can become. Uncle Harry was trained by his father, Grandpapa George, and he was trained by his Great-uncle Fong Li, and he was trained by his father and on back into the mists of ancient times. That I am able to be who I am is a debt I owe to that long, long line of Harry's ancestors. From the shadows of the great ages past with few interruptions the great knowledge has been

318

passed down. This you must remember: "Once upon a time there was no donkey in the Guang. So someone from the Heavenly Court sent one there, but the farmers and peasants finding no use for it, set it loose at the foot of the mountain.

A tiger ran out from the mountains. When he saw this big tall thing, he thought it must be divine. He quickly hid himself in the forest and surveyed it from under cover. Sometimes the tiger ventured a little nearer, but still kept a respectful distance.

One day the tiger came out again. Just then the donkey gave a loud bray. Thinking the donkey was going to eat him, the tiger hurriedly ran away. After a while he sneaked back and watched the donkey carefully. He found that though it had a huge body it seemed to have no special ability.

After a few days the tiger gradually became accustomed to its braying and was no longer so afraid. Later the tiger became bolder. Once he walked in front of the donkey and purposely bumped it. This made the donkey so angry that it struck out his hind legs and kicked wildly. Seeing this the tiger was very gleeful, 'Such a big thing as you can do so little!' With a roar he pounced on the donkey and ate it up."

Kat finished the story and then she began the same explanation always conferred upon the child before a decision should be required of them. "We master the art because: in order to be able to unite the machine of a human, all her lower centers must be active, strong and willing to surrender to the higher center's will. This must be trained in a person, it can not be left to chance. Otherwise she will be like the discarded Guang donkey, helpless before the forces of nature, and never recognized as the helpmate to mankind she was meant to be. We are the faithful, and humble bearers of truth. The wall around the house isn't only for the thief or the tiger, but to keep honest men from the temptations of riches they can not bear unassisted."

They continued in silence until they reached the other side of the lake where they anchored and Kat opened the basket, offered

Hannah bread and cheese, then began to fish.

Hannah listened to MamaKat carefully and finally asked, "What training must I have; and how shall I build that wall that keeps out the tigers and protects honest men?" Kaitlyn was again awestruck at how many generations of Harry's family had asked those very questions, and she swelled with pride and resolve that their family would carry on the new traditions of so remarkable a lineage. She began the explanation of the state of man's being and of the structure of man's machine; that it was a microcosm of the great world, and how it was supposed to function. Then she detailed the necessary steps which enabled it to perform as intended. At length she sat quietly as Hannah absorbed as much of the information as she was able.

"When may I start?" Hannah asked at last.

"Your father and mother, and Uncle Harry and I have seen to the foundations of your internal training; you may begin external training when you wish." Kat then cautioned her sternly, "But it is not an everyday wish like: 'wishing for more pie.' It is a wish that must command your whole attention." She looked at her adoptive daughter, "When you decide to begin, there is no turning back; it would waste what you have already acquired and endanger your future desires."

"Today, we shall begin today," was her resolve in response.

"Very well, you shall row us back then," she answered. Kat demonstrated the proper grip, stance and stroke she expected her to emulate, 'just so.'

The demonstration having been given, Hannah traded stations with her and set herself to the task. She dipped the blade in the water and pushed the handle out, then pulled it back. "Wait," Kat stopped her. She got up behind her, and reaching around her, placed her hands near Hannah's, then went through the movement once more. This time the young girl could feel the boat propelled by the strong force of each push and pull of the oar's motion. Kat sat back down and let her continue unassisted.

She pushed with all her strength keeping her hands and feet 'just so.' Then she pulled back with all her strength, carefully watching that her body kept its posture and position. It wasn't easy going at first; gradually though, she maintained a rhythm. After a while her legs and back ached, and her arms and hands were sore.

Ahead of the prow, she could see the tiny dock with Grandmama's house in the trees beyond the edge of the lake. She pushed herself to greater efforts and finally reached the dock. MamaKat commended her strength and spirit before they walked up off the dock. As the long shadows of evening allowed them a dimmed view of their steps up the graveled path and across Main Street they walked slowly up to the house. Hannah slept very well that night.

The next morning before sunrise MamaKat roused her from sleep, told her to splash cold water on her face, arms, and legs and meet her at the boat. She walked back down the driveway and down to the dock, packed the basket into the boat and waited. Soon Hannah joined her, took up her position at the stern and set her hands and feet into position, then commenced to row them away from the little dock.

Kat instructed, "Aim for those two large boulders at the foot of that Aspen copse just there; she pointed." Hannah sighted along MamaKat's arm and began the steady push and pull on the oar; always keeping the craft headed for the two boulders.

Kaitlyn, as George had done years before with Harry and Belle had done with Titania and Hipolyta, lounged in the bow feigning sleep under her parasol; but she kept careful vigilance on Hannah's form and progress without her pupil noticing. They finally reached the boulders. Kat pretended to rouse herself and pointed to another spot even further up the lake to which she would next like to go. After the briefest rest and only a bite of bread, Hannah was compelled to begin rowing again, but this time with the oar on her left side instead of the right. A few moments of adjustment to the new position and she was making for the next destination.

Once again they arrived and as before, Kat roused herself and pointed to another spot further up the lake to which she would next like to go. And again after the briefest rest and only one bite of bread, she began rowing once more, this time with the oar back on her right side again. Three more destinations and three more changes from right to left and left to right, three more bites of bread, and all the while with MamaKat seeming to doze in the bow. Then at last they were back at their little dock. It was only a bit after noon and Hannah was famished. She was very ready to have some lunch. When they went into Grandmama Belle's house her father provided her: a piece of fish, a hunk of goat cheese, and a small potato. Hannah was too ravenous to question the menu; she set upon it at once and devoured the meager morsels.

Chloe came in just as Hannah finished and asked her daughter to come and help with Uncle Jameson's gardens. She led Hannah back down to the dock where she indicated four buckets and two poles. Chloe dipped each bucket into the lake to fill them, then slipped a pole through the handles of two buckets, indicating for Hannah to do the same.

"Unfortunately the irrigation piping for Uncle Jameson's gardens isn't functioning just now. Until it is, we shall need to bring water to the gardens by bucket." Placing the pole across her shoulders, she started up the hill toward the gardens behind the restaurant on the other side of the street.

Hannah followed her mother's example and with the buckets balanced on the ends of her pole across her own shoulders she also made the trek up the hill toward the gardens. When they arrived Titania and Hannah's younger cousins were beginning to plant tomato seedlings up and down the rows on one side of the large garden plot. Chloe poured her buckets of water into a large tank at the head of the garden and Hannah did the same.

Then her mother said, "Dear we'll need more water to fill this tank. Please fetch more water until this tank is half full; that should suffice for today's planting."

Hannah lifted the empty buckets on her pole and headed back to the dock. After a while she returned carefully balancing the pole and buckets so as not to waste any of the water she'd brought with such effort. Once the buckets were emptied she looked into the tank, sighed aloud and headed off for another trip. Before she was out of sight her mother called, "Talking to the empty buckets won't put more water in the tank."

The weight of the water buckets and balancing the pole across her shoulders began to bow her back after a few trips. Her mother again commented, "You are doing splendidly; keep your back straight, dearest." Hannah straightened her back and returned to the lake. On and on she carried full buckets up the hill and empty buckets down. Until, as the long shadows of evening at last began to stretch across the gardens, the tank was half-filled and Hannah set down the buckets against the tank and started to follow the others up to the house for supper.

Chloe called over her shoulder, "Hannah Belle, bring the buckets and poles up to the house so they will be ready for tomorrow when you go down to the lake."

Hannah turned back and arranged the two poles on her shoulders, balanced all four buckets on them and finally arrived to the house for supper. A plate of food was set out for her. Ravenous, she picked up her fork, raised a mouthful to her mouth and savored the anticipated bite of food. She straightened her back and shoulders filled another forkful, began to raise it to her mouth and fell asleep... the forkful of food suspended before her drooping head. Kaitlyn and Harry smiled at each other. Harry put her fork down, picked up his niece and carried her to bed. After tucking her under the covers and closing her door, he came out to the great room and sat with Kat looking out over the darkening valley to the lake.

"She did very well today," MamaKat commented.

"I almost thought she'd get that second bite of food... I was really pulling for her," Harry replied, and they smiled with the pride they felt for their adoptive daughter's achievements of the day.

The next morning, and the next morning the routine repeated. Until on the fourth morning when MamaKat went to rouse her, Hannah was not to be found. She didn't need to search the house; she went from her room and walked down to the lake. There was Hannah waiting for her on the dock, her hair still wet from the cold morning water. She mused as she went down to join her, just as each teacher had marveled before her: how many times these same activities had been performed with nearly the same schedule and expected results over the countless generations before. Kat walked down to the boat, took up her position in the bow, and they started off toward another part of the lake.

Before they had gotten too far, as the training dictated: without waiting to arrive where the boat could be steadied, Kat told her to shift sides of her oar. With an anticipated bit of fumbling and rocking of the boat, Hannah switched to the other side of the oar. "Wait," MamaKat said aloud, "Shift like this." She traded places with her and demonstrated the fluid movement she expected her to perform. It was a smooth and seemingly effortless transition in which: during the pull stroke she lowered her body with her back held straight, swiveled on the balls of her feet and rose up on the other side of the oar without the boat wobbling, without a splash or even the blade losing its powerful stroke through the water. "Here," she said simply, and they traded places once more.

Hannah took up her position, made a couple usual strokes and at Kat's command she shifted sides nearly as she was shown. "Almost," MamaKat observed. "Set your feet first; then be sure as you make the shift so the oar doesn't notice you've moved. Try again." This time she complied smoothly and was on the other side of the oar with as little wobble as Kat had executed. "Better," she commented. "Watch where you're going," she added as they were naturally drifting quite a ways off course. Hannah had no sooner brought the vessel back onto course than Kat called out, "Shift." Hannah made the maneuver as smoothly as before and resumed from the new side. MamaKat settled into her usual posture and position in the bow, and every odd moment or so would call 'Shift;' to which Hannah would readily comply.

The tank at the top of the gardens was finally filled; later that same afternoon the irrigation piping was miraculously 'repaired.' The next day when they arrived back to the little dock, and after Hannah ate her meager meal, Chloe informed her that they would need to prepare the other half of the garden for planting.

"It needs to be tilled before we can plant the herbs and other vegetables." They went up to the large empty side of the garden area which had lain fallow last winter. Chloe picked up a couple hand trowels and demonstrated how Hannah was to turn over the soil. She squatted and made efficient sweeps of her arms and hands with the trowels held 'just so.'

She said, "This side of the garden will be as fertile as the other side in no time." She put a hand trowel into each of her daughter's hands; watched her begin the process and said, "Wait." Hannah sat back on her haunches and looked up at her mother. Chloe adjusted the girl's grip on the tools saying, "...hold them 'just so,' darling." Then she turned and went down to the restaurant and into the kitchens. Hannah moved along the ground performing the odd but efficient motions up and down the length of the plot. It took all afternoon before the top half of that side of the garden was tilled completely; she looked back over her handiwork and smiled. She carried the trowels to the water tank, cleaned off the residual soil so that they were shiny and bright once more. She carried them up to the house, set them with the buckets and went in for her supper.

"Tomorrow will be the second half..." she reminded herself as she walked in deliberate strides with her shoulders back and her head held higher.

The afternoon of the day after the garden had been tilled, Jameson brought out flats of seedlings and bulbs for planting. Hannah stood looking at the plethora of plants as her uncle began to indicate where each of the groups of seedlings were to be planted.

"Around the border are all the garlic bulbs and inside those will be the onions and chives. This large area here should be planted in rows of herbs," and he carried each tray of plants to the areas he'd indicated. "The basil here..." and he waved his hand in lines along the 'rows' he wished the seedlings to be installed. "The parsley here, the sage here, the cilantro here, the rosemary and thyme will bush out a bit so they need to be over here." Hannah knelt next to the first flat, and with a little stick made a hole and put in the first little sprout.

Uncle Jameson said, "Wait. Here is how this task is done." He took a hand spade and held it in a certain fashion. He made several holes at a time, reached to the flat, deposited little plants in those places, pressed the soil down around each with his open palm then moved on; squatting all the while and moving quite low to the ground. "Now, unlike when you tilled and kept changing directions, as you plant, always keep facing the back of the restaurant when you move down and then up the rows you create."

Hannah imitated the method she witnessed; her uncle set the spade in her grasp, 'just so,' and he turned to go back into the kitchens. Over his shoulder he called, "Be careful not to squish the little plants when you're going backwards; and switch hands every dozen seedlings..."

Hannah squatted over her first intended row and began. When those trays were emptied, she began backwards up the next intended row weaving a little from side to side at first until she realized that: like in the boat, if she kept her eye on the end of the row and a distant object in the same line she kept in straight lines. The little seedlings were spared squishing, and the rows she planted were beautifully aligned. She switched hands as instructed, and soon did not have an unsoiled hand, wrist or forearm to brush her hair from her eyes. She got to the top of a row and went to the tank of water, rinsed her hands, wet her hair and went back to planting. Now she remembered to keep her back straighter and chin up so as to keep her hair from dangling so much in her eyes. Hours later she stood from the last emptied tray; looked at the fully planted garden and made a feeble smile. She went back up to the tank, cleaned the spade, gathered the flats and trays and baskets, carried them to the potting shed behind the restaurant then headed for the house and supper.

The next day when they were docked for the morning, and after her she had eaten the meager lunch, Chloe walked her up to the hanging deck at the house on the hill. She put sanding blocks in each of her hands and said, "The weather has been hard on the deck planks, but before we can re-varnish them they have to have all the rough spots and old varnish smoothed off."

Hannah got to her knees and started to push the blocks in her hands pell mell over the planks. "Wait," Chloe said. Hannah stood back up with her shoulders sagging already. Her mother borrowed her blocks and demonstrated the posture and motions she expected her to use. She then placed her daughter in one of the corners of the deck, and like the 'frog work' in the gardens, she squatted and made large circular patterns with the blocks over the deck's surface. The right hand: clockwise; the left hand: countering in alternating cadence in front of her as she moved very, very slowly away from her corner down the length of the deck. "Good," Chloe announced once she began; then she said she'd need to help PapaGeorge mix the varnish and she left Hannah to the task.

The next afternoon, with more of the deck still to be sanded, Chloe set her to task once more. This time she positioned her in such a way that she covered narrower stretches of the deck and so had to start a new direction more frequently. Chloe watched for a moment, and when she was sure that Hannah would continue always facing the same direction, she left her to the remainder of the task. Once the deck was completely sanded, next came the varnish. Now Hannah was supposed to use the squatting position from the sanding and gardening chores, but with a heavy towel grasped in both hands in front of her. She had to push forward almost as far as she could reach without collapsing face down on the planks, then pull back to her starting position. Forward and backward across the deck she pushed and pulled like a giant inch worm rubbing the thinned varnish into the grain of the wood, always being careful not to step on the deck planks already coated. Unlike the sanding, the varnishing was completed in one afternoon, at least for *that* deck. Auntie Titania met her after her little lunch the next day, and they walked to the decks behind PapaGeorge's and Grandmama Belle's. The outdoor furniture had been removed, and the sanding blocks were waiting...

The days passed, tasks were accomplished and still every single morning she was out on the lake rowing and 'shifting.' The only task she seemed to have genuinely enjoyed thus far was the one in which she was still engaged---picking up twigs. That had begun when her mother met at the dock one afternoon and as they walked to the house for Hannah's little meal, Chloe did a few handsprings on the way. Each time she gathered twigs in her hands as she made the forward leaps.

After lunch her mother had said, "So that Papa George and Grandmama Belle have plenty of kindling for next winter, you shall gather enough to fill these buckets." She set the four big wooden buckets at the foot of the deck. "You saw how to collect them as we walked up from the dock... off you go then," and she left her to the task. New to handsprings, it took Hannah a few tries to begin landing on her feet, let alone remembering to grasp twigs in the process. Needless to say, it took several days to fill even the first two buckets.

Once the first two buckets *were* filled and taken into the house, Chloe met them as they came into the dock at mid-day. When Hannah began the new day's gathering, her mother called, "Wait." That always boded ill... Hannah stopped where she was. Chloe smiled and encouraged, "You're doing so well..."

Hannah tried an uncertain smile waiting for the other shoe to fall, "...but do it backwards until the last two buckets are filled." Her mother went into the house. Hannah just stood there looking at her receding figure and mouthed the words, 'Go backwards?' 'Do it backwards' she repeated sullenly. 'How am I supposed to see what I'm aiming for if I spring backwards?' she mused.

She looked over her shoulder at the ground behind her. She fixed on a twig and leapt. Then she tried again. And again. And again. Although her first several attempts were miserable, she tried yet again. She looked over her shoulder once more; after so many repetitions of going forward, she at last relaxed and let her trained gaze spot a succession of twigs amidst the chaos on the ground which would be in her path if she began to spring a particular direction. She leapt in a back handspring; a twig was under her left hand. She sprang again and another was in her right; she shifted the twigs to one hand in mid-air and grabbed the next one with the free hand then landed. She looked into her hands at the twigs and smiled. She was still springing around the yard backwards and forwards, squat-walking a bit between and leaping off on another tack when Chloe called her in for dinner.

The next few days were, as has been said, her favorite thus far and perhaps because of the disparity between the excitement and sense of accomplishment in this last task versus the monotony of the rowing, something at last snapped in her resolve. Her elders had all been monitoring her progress and knew it would happen any day now. Each morning they expected would be THE morning and they were ready.

Sure enough, the next morning when MamaKat strolled to the little dock to begin her rowing practice, Hannah didn't get in but stood immobile not letting Kat pass to the boat either.

"MamaKat," she began, having absolutely decided that she was not willing to row another stroke, "...what is the point of 'rowing the boat' and 'just so,' and 'shift'?" She punctuated the commands in a vague imitation of MamaKat's voice.

Kat didn't answer. She turned to the side of the little dock and grasped the fishing gaff leaning against a pier post. She held it by the gaff end with the handle pointed at Hannah's stomach. Hannah didn't know what to expect. Kat shoved the butt end of the handle into Hannah's solar plexus in a sudden and very quick short jab. The girl winced and bent over. "What did you do that for?" she exclaimed.

"Let's try that again," said MamaKat calmly and without expression. "This time 'row the boat'." She jabbed again and said loudly, "Row the boat." Hannah's right arm deflected the wooden handle aimed at again at her chest. Kat didn't stop there; she jabbed at the girl again, "Row the boat," she called and Hannah deflected the pole again but from the other side. Kat pulled the gaff away and made a swinging arc aimed at Hannah's head; once more she called aloud, "Shift." As the pole slashed at her, Hannah went through the motion of shifting from one side of the oar to the other, her hands caught the arcing pole and she tossed it harmlessly to the side. Kat swung quicker this time, calling "row the boat," again it was deflected. The gaff in Kaitlyn's hands became a blur of jabs and arcs and heavy blows; each time she called out, "shift," or "dig garden," or "pick up stick," "sand the floor," or "pick up stick, backward."

Hannah was leaping and twirling, deflecting, blocking and dodging with every new onslaught. The rest of the family stealthily gathered on the deck behind Belle and George's to watch the performance. Hannah noticed them, but she was far too busy protecting herself from the serious damage MamaKat would inflict on her if her guard dropped for even a moment. When after half an hour or longer, MamaKat at last paused and set the gaff back against the pier post. Hannah stopped too; still poised, balanced on one foot atop the last pier two feet above the deck of the little dock with the lake washing rhythmically below her. Her breath came in ragged gasps trying to keep enough air in her lungs to maintain her defense.

"That's the point," said MamaKat without any inflection of emotion. She bowed to her adoptive daughter, turned and walked back to the house. Hannah blinked; followed her with her eyes up to the deck and suddenly recalled that all her relatives---her family---had been watching the whole scene. They all bowed to her at once as one person. It was only then that she realized her precarious perch and stepped down still stunned at the morning's developments. She steadied herself, went over to the boat, stepped into her usual position and cast off for a point of her own choosing across the lake---every now and then: 'shifting.'

The crowd on the deck were so moved at her accomplishments, and that she was at last beginning the journey of her lifetime; they sat down where they had stood and gazed out at the lake to the receding figure of a girl making strong strokes with an oar on a course of her own choosing. Chloe and Harold were the proudest of parents and the humblest of people.

The only thing that made the summer's end more complete was Kaitlyn's admission that she was in fact going to have another child. The clan was therefore even more impressed, were that possible, that she had so thoroughly and methodically conducted Hannah's training *while pregnant!*

She responded innocently, "It's not an intrinsically debilitating condition you know..."

The host finished scribbling his notes from this last installment and before he closed his notebook, said triumphantly, "I think I am finally getting it!"

His guest looked him in the eyes and asked simply, "*What is it* you finally *get?*"

"That this story *and* our conversations about reality and work---man's inner world, reclaiming Conscience---This is all the same story! It's different sides of the same thing: knowledge and being---the duality of man's possibilities..." he answered excitedly.

She smiled. "How can you be sure?"

J. L. LAWSON

6
Expansion

"Ever since I was a child I have had this instinctive urge for expansion and growth. To me, the function and duty of a quality human being is the sincere and honest development of one's potential."
---Bruce Lee

"I can prove it," the host exclaimed, "that's how I can be sure. All our own conversations and dialogs have been to point out and explain the reality of man's situation---*my situation.* The great knowledge which can change a man, the actual mathematically verifiable structure of the inner world of man, the proper process of *really* thinking and planning. Why no one makes much headway against their own emotions without real knowledge of their own machine's construction and function. That our mechanicality is both our nemesis *and* our only salvation." He paused to see if his guest was still smiling, or not. She was and he continued emboldened by her presence.

"If it weren't for our innate ability to make the simplest routines habitual, we wouldn't have the possibility to replace poor habits and actions with sound ones. While at the same time it is the existence of those very habits which prevent our seeing the world around and inside of us for what it actually is! The story of the Livingsons is the tale of all of that in the actual lives of people who live those truths. They are not just philosophizing or theorizing about the *notions* of man's possibilities---they are *actually* living them. It's here in every episode and chapter. Right here, and it's been staring me in the face the whole time!"

She patted his hand, "Well done. Yes, our mechanicality---our habits *are the true thieves.* They protect our self-delusions and inhibit our movement toward change. Well done indeed. Shall we continue?"

"Once all the Tahoe visitors returned to their homes, towns and cities, the village returned once more to its usual rhythms. The Autumn Term began. Homes and businesses prepared for the sedate pace of the off-season. In general the inner-life of the town resurfaced and it resembled any other remote village. Over the next several years each of the Livingson clan's children reached the age of training and their parents administered that rite of passage according to the same paradigm that Hannah and all before her had undergone. Mia and Lena were trained by Harry and MamaKat the next summer just before the twins began school. Jamie received the same when he was of age, as did Will under the aegis of his parents: Aaron and Poly. The Bessamers were unsure if they would be able to introduce little Oliver to the training as tradition allowed.

What would later be recognized as spinal polio, disabled Olly for quite a long while during his toddler years. Although his recovery left him without any *truly* debilitating atrophies or deformities, the lack of normal exercise for the term of his bed-ridden period left him weak and fragile. His parents made every effort to restore their son to the state of capacity to which they were sure he might have otherwise attained. Chloe massaged his legs vigorously twice a day, his meals were as healthy as they could contrive, and although it was a tediously slow endeavor, they encouraged him to walk as soon as was practical.

The entire ordeal naturally took its toll on Harold and Chloe. They were not wholly immune from the questions a parent will inevitably entertain when their child has been thus stricken. Harry spent a lot of time at the Booklove House over the months of Olly's illness and gradual recovery; not so much for the boy's sake but as a sounding board and whipping boy for his dear friends in the extremity of their desolation. Harry's sacrifice allowed George and Belle to serve as counselors and guides. As with all challenges to hope: that dark night of the soul was inevitable even for those most resolute individuals of Conscience. However, the observation: that which does not destroy us makes us stronger---could not be more aptly assigned than in this instance. Although both Chloe and Harold questioned even their own existential relevance when in the depths of the despair which overwhelmed them---the gradual realization of the perspective of scale in all things at last turned the tide. Yes their son was afflicted when so many other children were not. Yes it seemed unfair that the innocent should suffer. Yes they had self-recriminations---What had they done or not done? In the end they were left with the nakedness of reality itself, and from that vantage they surrendered to the actual; leaving forever behind the *what if*, and *what might* of futile imagination.

To say the entire clan was affected by the woeful intrusion would be an understatement. No other group of individuals exemplified more the words of the poet after his own bout with near total incapacity: *No man is an Island, entire of it self; every man is a piece of the Continent, a part of the main; if a Clod be washed away by the Sea, Europe is the less, as well as if a Promontory were, as well as if a Manor of thy friends or of thine own were; Any man's death diminishes me, because I am involved in Mankind; And therefore never send to know for whom the bell tolls; It tolls for thee...* A renewed resolution of unity, of absolute communion pervaded their intercourse after the debacle and never lessened. Later, Oliver finally became stronger---just in time for his schooling. Aaron and Hipolyta followed the Bessamer's example and also enrolled Will in the Tahoe school with Becky; then they each would be left with their nests emptied for the duration of each school term.

Aaron's undergraduate classes in Culture and Literature were, as during every year, the most sought after and filled the capacity of the lecture hall. Each year they began with the introduction to *Beowulf*, and depending on the discussions evoked by the subject matter, sometimes the entire semester was focused solely upon the Skandinavian verse. Aaron had through the years worked on a translation that would convey the beauty of the poetry---working from the the Thorkelin Latin manuscript. He taught from one of the Kemble editions, but continually added his own more powerful language whenever he felt the passages under consideration by his classes were more apropos with the added force.

Outside the University he and Poly accepted memberships to the Berkeley Club and the Ebell Society, respectively. The weekly gatherings offered an outlet for and an exposure to the pulse of intellectual debate amongst their peers. Hipolyta was less enchanted with the Ebell group for their constantly returning to the issue of suffrage---as a guise for bashing masculinity while promoting femininity---which for Hipolyta was something truly uninteresting. It was her opinion that those women who were closest to self realization were the *least* likely to harp on and on about equality---having already succeeded where their lesser sisters had not begun an effort. However when not in the throes of gender-adulation, the discussions which occupied the meetings were quite entertaining, even thought-provoking, which was the *only* reason she maintained her membership.

The Berkeley Club was a curious invention to Professor Backhouse. His own experience during University in the Cambridge Union, with whom he had enjoyed membership, contrasted sharply with the timbre and tone of *these* gatherings. There were the same open discussions of almost any issue, yet the depth and potency of the arguments and stances assumed were a bit more shallow than were his previous engagements at the Union. Aaron therefore had less to contribute now than once was his wont. Before his life-changing experience during the 'continental tour' culminating in Venice, he would be foremost in any dialog or debate---if only to reduce the opposition to babbling---which he was quite capable of doing still. Yet the over-arching precept of the work was to refrain from calling men 'slugs,' to not contribute to their 'sleep-walking,' to, in short: live and let live.

This position did offer him a unique advantage. There was always a plain dinner as a rallying point for social communion, then a paper presented by one of the membership, followed by a discussion during which every member could speak without reserve, freeing his mind as far as possible in the time allotted. There was no limit to the range of subjects brought under discussion: philosophy, history, political economy, physics, biography, government, law, ethics, higher education, finance, literature, the culture of manhood, or the culture of a rose, the evolution of an eye, the transit of Venus, the occultation of Mars, or the microscopic world which the tools of science had revealed.

At least once in every discussion 'the Professor,' as his colleagues regarded him simply, would proffer a perspective which either turned the conversation to a new tack, or caused introspection on the part of the author of the initial contribution. More often than not Aaron's interjections were in the form of a question, or he might posit the logical extrapolation of a given argument to its unforeseen conclusion. While these participations did not endear him to all the membership, he garnered their respect and was often approached for advice when outside of the Club's confined meetings.

That he was younger than the general membership was not readily apparent. Hipolyta had encouraged him to grow a beard; she said she liked the look of it. To his way of thinking it merely offered her something to run her hands through and purr during their quieter moments together. Whatever the reasons, he did not look the part of the youth he still felt. His appearance also enhanced his image among his students---whose stereotyped perceptions of a University Professor naturally included the 'beard of wisdom.' Harry, who could not grow a beard due to his heredity, often made *generally* respectful remarks about the new growth on his long time friend; it was a continuation of the same satirical banter they had always maintained since their first bonds of friendship. Will was delighted in his father's whiskers and couldn't pass a mirror in the house without checking to see if his own were yet coming in---so that he could *not* shave like his father.

After Will's fifth birthday, and during his last autumn at home before Tahoe schooling, Aaron completed his Beowulf translation and submitted it for publication to a reputable publisher in San

Francisco. When the spring term began, his own text on Beowulf became the auxiliary required textbook for his classes. His career as an author slowly became an almost viable third income for the Backhouse family. Any stresses they had once anticipated over finances, at last very gradually diminished into a non-issue. It had taken eight years since they decided he should not take receipt of any of the Backhouse Trust funds for them to at last begin to secure their economic future to a much greater degree, especially once other colleges and university programs picked up the use of his translation. This was just in time; Hipolyta was pregnant with their next child and they had been duly informed that it was a healthy girl. Poly's dreams had come true, her own daughter---at last!

Hipolyta and Kaitlyn maintained CANED Ltd. most effectively under the umbrella of Sierra Architecture. As a matter of fact it was Hipolyta's proposals which brought in the bulk of the contracts to both companies after Becky's career change. She sat for long hours some days in the studio: drafting, sketching and redesigning interior after interior. Will spread sheets of butcher paper over the floor behind her and with his pencils and colors: mapped out elaborate scenes for his toy boats and carts and horses to venture through. On other days they spent time visiting Chloe and Olly, walking in the park, going out on errands and appointments, or when raining--- reading from poetry and plays, and of course from Aaron's *Beowulf.* Will was getting as much an advanced upbringing as either Poly or Aaron received at his age and he was just as curious and precocious as they had been.

By February Professor Backhouse had finally reached his stride as a teacher. Although a fellow instructor, Prof. Gayley, had opened *his* lectures to the public and garnered the approbation of the masses; Aaron Backhouse had the stalwart devotion of an ever-growing student body. Most of them had not only learned an appreciation of early English Literature, but they had in many respects awakened to the broader world of academia and to the wider world around themselves. Professor Backhouse not only encouraged individual reflection and initiative, it was virtually demanded if a given student wished to do more than merely warm a seat in his classes. For example...

The professor opened a discussion after a reading of Beowulf's second battle, that of the fierce underwater contest against Grendel's mother. "Mr. Connoly, why is it Unferth who offers Beowulf the sword: Hrunting? And why has the poet next described Beowulf's instructions to Hrothgar about the disposition of his men and rewards?"

The selected student, Norris Connoly, instead of being expected to answer from his own rote memory, was required, in Professor Backhouse's class, to solicit as many views on the topic as possible and synthesize a new perspective. Norris at once began to survey his fellow-students for a consensus upon which to build a satisfactory response. After the brief congress Mr. Connoly answered the second question first: "It was the responsibility of the leader to see to the security and protection of his followers, and as the outcome of any mortal engagement could not be successfully foreseen, Beowulf made certain that in the case of his own demise those who had pledged themselves to him at the outset of his adventure would be provided for as well as any of Hrothgar's own warriors---which included the disposition of all the rewards that been been promised Beowulf personally."

"Alright if that is the situation, what can be said of the king's leaving at the ninth hour *leaving only* the Geat companions still on the shore awaiting the return of their hero? And I'm still waiting on your views concerning Unferth and the offer of the sword: Hrunting..."

This time students from across the hall came to convene with the knot around Mr. Connoly. The only result being that they were stumped as to the significance of either instance under consideration. "Professor Backhouse, we don't know," came the plaintive response. In the Backhouse courses that was also a most acceptable answer.

Aaron then employed his usual recourse, "If this poem is a

reflection of their culture in particular, and an exposition of the human experience in general, can you resolve these passages along those lines of inquiry?"

The congress widened as the mass of students gathered in a much louder debate as to the significance of one or the other of the examples in regard to the criteria set forth. Professor Backhouse made only passing comments: encouraging some lines of thought and investigation and discouraging others until at last the hour and a half was near an end. Mr. Connoly announced, as spokesman for the assembly, their conclusions. This in hand, the professor made the next class's assignment---a brief essay covering the findings they had derived from this class to be handed in upon their next arrival. The students left the lecture hall confident in their ability to accomplish this meager task and maintained no small anticipation of the next class's adventure. That was a more than typical scene in Professor Backhouse's 'lectures.'

After the publication and inclusion of the texts of his own translation, in which he had brought the alliterative voice of the saga into English with as strengthened a palette of color as the original afforded---his lectures were able to expand the considerations by his students into other realms of investigation. For instance he began one term by reading aloud...

> *"To him an heir   here afterward born,*
> *a son in his halls,   whom heaven had sent*
> *to favor the folk,   feeling their woe*
> *that erst had lacked   an earl for leader*
> *so long a while;   the Laird endowed him,*
> *the Wielder of Wonder,   with world's renown."*

"This is but the introduction, if you will, to the poetic quality of the anonymous scald's tales. What are those qualities? Miss Humphreys can you determine a few of them and explain their utility and import for the storyteller?"

Ada Humphreys then became the focal point for the cadre of collegiates around her as they inundated her with observation after observation. At length she stood and made a broad statement regarding the use of poetry as a mnemonic device for the transmission of oral literature. Then with a short list of the examples provided by her 'ad hoc committee,' she enumerated a few: "The usefulness of a euphemism, or literary trope, allows the poet to make substitutions of regular nouns---both to add color and spice to the account, but also to continue: line after line, the alliterative nature of the poetry. Where later English poetry emphasized end rhyme, this culture seems to have preferred the rhyming quality of the phrases themselves---as revealed by the caesuras also present in each line."

Professor Backhouse was sometimes delighted by the responses of those students who were most able to enter into the discussions he'd preordained for each class session. Miss Humphreys, and those nearest her to offer input, just happened to be among those rarities. "The only addition I would like to include for your notes," the Professor responded on this occasion was, "those literary tropes for the skald are called: 'kennings'." It made the time pass almost much too quickly for anyone's taste, but that was one of the alluring and paradoxical qualities of Professor Backhouse's courses---never enough and always more.

This was the same approach that Aaron employed in his participation at the Berkeley Club gatherings, as well as in the disposition of mentoring his own son, Will. No longer was Aaron Backhouse the arrogant know-it-all with something to say about everything that occurred around him---as was his former self's disport. He was an empower-or of thought, not its distribution hub. The foretaste of reason that had caused Hipolyta to tarry and withhold judgement about him all those years ago, at last had borne the fruit of her faith and she felt the most blessed of women for it.

Aaron's next enterprise in authorship was to make a translation of the *Epic of Gilgamesh* in the footsteps of George Smith: the first English translator of the epic only twenty years before. Because of western culture's dependence upon the Judeo-Christian traditions, he wished to look behind the arising of those faiths to the antecedent literature and histories which he was certain shaped the root and source of both those religions and also western civilization. His familiarity with Akkadian as a language of literature was in need of refreshing which he did as he awaited the arrival of his ordered texts and manuscripts. He had never entertained notions of acquiring a facility in the Mesopotamian tongue of Sumerian, but since the Assyrian versions were the only extant manuscripts (hence: Akkadian), he didn't feel the need to do so. The library at the Backhouse home was nothing if not eclectic.

"Aaron! when Will and I get home from our outing this afternoon we will be in the studio; so please think of what you might prepare for dinner tonight. Remember Chloe and Olly will be over..." called Hipolyta from the conservatory as Aaron was gathering his notebooks and texts for his morning classes.

"I haven't forgotten. I think fettuccine and prawns with pesto will be on the menu; ask Chloe if that's acceptable. If so, will you be able to go by the seafood market?" He answered absently, patting his pockets to be sure he'd gathered his usual personal effects.

"Yes dear. Have a wonderful morning..." and she emerged to kiss him goodbye, potting soil still clinging to her gloves and apron. "I'll also check at the post office for the parcels you're expecting 'any day now'."

He bowed, "You are too good to me." Will ran to the door as his father opened it, potting soil covering his hands and knees. "And you too Biggun. Take care of Mummy while I'm out! And leave some of the soil in the conservatory for the plants."

Poly and Will finished their morning chore and she sent him to the bathroom for a good cleaning before they rejoined in the studio where she had to put the final touches on a new proposal. They left the house and walked the block and a half to Booklove House to see Chloe and Olly for coffee. The boys toddled off to Olly's room while Poly and Chloe sat in the front room with coffee and croissants. After catching up Poly on Olly's progress in the last few days, they chatted about other things. "I suppose since I'm now in the rotation for the Ebells, I had better figure out where everyone might sit!" mused Chloe.

"If everyone sits at once, which I've yet to see, we could bring out a few chairs from the drawing room. And by we I mean Aaron and Harold," replied Poly absently.

They were both looking through the bay window out over the tops of the oaks into the bay and across to the Golden Gate just as a tall ship was rounding the Marin peninsula into the strait. "I wonder how Jean Baptiste is... we haven't received any word from Miranda since New Year's.. he'll be seven this summer; does he have a school in Venice? I can't remember..."

"Nor do I; but between them I'm sure little Jean will have an exquisite knowledge of two languages, plenty of mathematics and geography no doubt. I know he's playing the piano, sailing and cooking---a fine education, really," assured Poly. She then remembered, "Aaron asked me to ask you: if prawns and pasta will be a satisfactory menu for this evening; I'm not certain what he expects the boys to want to eat. Will sometimes turns up his nose at shrimp, or crab or lobster---strange for a boy grown up on the Bay."

"Olly will eat anything, fortunately. It wasn't even a serious transition worth noting when calf's liver had to be a staple of his diet for a while back there..." she sighed a little and offered a feeble smile to her dearest friend.

Without hesitation, Poly put her hand onto Chloe's, "He's just that sturdy a fellow, our Oliver, tough as an old tree and funny.." she giggled at a particular recollection, "Anyway, he's almost as tall as Hannah and smarter than most other boys his age; I told you what Mrs. Hamlin said when I picked them up from the birthday party..."

"No. You mean she actually had a pleasant word for someone else's child?" Chloe answered astonished, "You know she still thinks you're our hired nanny. She has repeatedly asks me how much I pay you!? What did she say?"

Drawing her face into a fair imitation of the pinch-nosed mother of their boys' playmate, Poly said, "Oliver has made this little soiree most pleasant; when the other children nearly bowled through the house after cake, Oliver picked up the plates and utensils and asked 'Could he put these in the kitchen, mum?' Such a pleasant young boy..."

Chloe almost chuckled, "Well good for Olly! Already impressing the ladies; he certainly takes after Harold!"

"I hope his taste in women will be as refined..." Poly quipped quickly.

The chat went on a little while until Will and Olly came out and asked could they both go with Aunt Poly to the Library and Market, please? Chloe glanced to Poly, who nodded, and so she approved the venture. "But you must come along when Auntie Poly is finished with her meeting; we do want her to leave a good impression with her future clients. Is that clear?"

The boys both nodded and went to put their shoes back on and select hats. That was the other thing the boys had in common: they loved wearing different hats, and each already had quite the collection. This morning they selected berets. Poly gathered up her satchel and drawing carrier, and said they'd be back around one or two. The pace of their walk wasn't noticeably slower. Although Olly's left leg was slightly splayed he could keep up with even his father's long strides. When the boys walked together anywhere they were always slower than the grown-ups because they kept up a running discussion about whatever happened to be the topic du jour. Today it was pirates. Hipolyta smiled as she caught snatches of the dialog and herded them along the edge of campus down Oxford to Allston and the library.

After the boys were settled with a large book of sailing ships (pirate ships), Hipolyta notified the librarian of her appointment with the Director and waited patiently in one of the seats outside the offices. Dr. Kelsey invited Mrs. Backhouse into the office and Poly made the CANED Ltd. proposal. Her designs allowed a smooth

344

transition from the 'Fireside' hall into the library proper. Although she'd substituted oak and cedar for the teak and rosewood she would have preferred, she was still daringly close to the stipulated budget for the project.

"If there were a proper renovation, the lighting could be suspended as in these drawings, but since the structure will not support them at this time we have made *this* arrangement---keeping in mind your desire for indirect lighting where possible, but with good lighting in the reading areas..."

She elaborated on the dual utility of the lower shelving designs, and the inconspicuous dais at the hearth for a speaker's platform. Then she arranged the swatches of fabrics for the seating, window dressings, carpets and wall hangings.

"The sound dampening qualities of these hangings is far superior to acoustically neutral wallpapers, and the installation time is also minimized. It is the very same treatment we used in the Sutro & Co. Bank Project several years ago. It has therefore proven its effectiveness and durability over that time..." Poly couldn't help but drop the names of a few of their more successful and high profile projects; it was just good salesmanship.

Dr. Kelsey accepted the designs and promised to return with a recommendation from the Committee as soon as possible. With a warm smile and handshake the meeting was completed; all Poly had to do now was wrest the boys away from the book on sailing ships. She approached them unnoticed; both their heads were pressed together in an inspection of the tall ship they were most impressed with at the moment.

In a low voice Poly said, "I think the *Novelty* is moored near the fish market..." The boys nearly sprang from the chair. They carried the book back to its place in the shelves, and like little gentlemen followed Poly from the library.

"Oh Boy, the *Novelty*!" Olly crowed.

Will asked, "Mama, how do you know it's the *Novelty*?"

"Well how many four-masted schooners *are* there on the Bay?" she answered easily.

"Oh Boy, the *Novelty*!" Will crowed, "Do you think they're loading?"

Hipolyta glanced over at University Blvd. by which they were walking parallel and noticed logging carts trundling down to the quay. "It may just be..."

Hipolyta set the boys at a good vantage point to watch the lading of the great schooner, and also where she could keep an eye on them from Spenger's as she made prawn selections. While she was at it she decided a pot of chowder would be good for lunch, or maybe for tomorrow's dinner. She bought a few dozen clams and shopping was complete. With the boys in tow, and each now carrying a package from the market, they rounded the bottom of the town nearest the wharf and went up Virginia Street toward home, stopping only at the Post Office on the way. The boys carried their loads easily and without complaint even though it meant they couldn't skip along as they would otherwise have wished. Skipping was one thing Olly had gotten *very* good at since his recovery and it didn't take much coaxing for him to demonstrate.

Chloe had baked three date and walnut cakes while the others were out and about, expecting to bring one along for after dinner. They all settled in the kitchen. Auntie Poly set the chowder on the stove to heat it back up while the boys applied themselves to drawing the ships they'd seen that morning. Keeping to today's theme: each flew a Jolly Roger. They set down to a late lunch and afterwards Chloe and Olly went with them back to Will's house. Poly put away the seafood and took her drawings to the studio. Chloe joined her and sat in the large leather chair by the windows where she could watch the boys in the yard. She gathered up her knitting and continued the sweater she had begun for Hannah while Poly began work on the next proposal. The Longfellow Society were trying the waters for a permanent home instead of the constant moving from parlor to parlor as they had always done. Harry had sent along some elevations and a sketched floorplan to which she was giving life and color.

The Professor came in through the back door with two boys hanging off of him. He'd sneaked up on them playing; they made a swift counter-attack and now had him right where he wanted them.

"Hello, the house! I am ransoming two pirates today. Do I have any takers?"

Chloe set aside her knitting to see them disentangle themselves from Aaron's clutches, which took a little while, for as one would get an arm or leg loose he'd reach across and grab another limb. It looked more like he was a piece of playground equipment rather than a captor. She went back to keep Poly company in the studio. Aaron put aprons on the boys and they helped him make noodles for the fettuccine and pesto---fortunately they had plenty of the pesto already made.

Hipolyta's idea of a conservatory's usefulness wasn't along the same lines as a wealthier family with a conservatory. Where they might house exotic vines, trees, palms and orchids; Poly grew herbs, tomatoes, garlic, onions and even---her latest experiments: potatoes and strawberries. They had already harvested the basil to make the pesto after the holidays; so now she had just this morning begun the crop of strawberries. Aaron sent Olly to fetch some rosemary from the 'garden' and set Will to pounding the ball of dough and rolling it flat, while he set up the mangler and cutter.

When the drawings were as far along as she could contrive them for the moment, she and Chloe went to watch the boys make noodles. "When will Harold be back from Chicago?" Aaron asked as they settled in the breakfast nook to oversee the pasta project.

"He wired this morning to say: probably by Sunday on the morning train. He just wanted to make a stop in Tahoe and see Hannah before coming on home," answered Chloe while admiring the way the lads were applying two rollers to the same flattened ball of dough. "He will likely be thin as a rail. I do wish he'd eat better when he's on the road..."

"Becky said Hannah is way ahead of her class, and will probably be taking the exit examinations two years before the rest of them. I suppose she'll decide it's time to go to Europe on her own after that!" Aaron joked, but not so very far from the truth of the matter. Hannah was as headstrong and determined as her mother when she got a notion into her head *and* had worked out the details for herself.

"Harold and I have been thinking that very thing. If she would just decide to take courses right here first, so she can get a few more years behind her, we'd be far more inclined to take her to visit Lawrence and Miranda," stated Chloe.

Poly added, "So long as it'll still be safe to travel in Europe by then; all I read in the papers is the German and British naval build up, and factories springing up to build armaments. It's more than a little distressing."

The room was quiet for a little while except for the sound of the mangler and cutter Aaron was cranking. "Lay them out on the table boys as they come out..."

Will and Olly carefully laid the bundles of strips on the prep table and at last there was quite the mound of fettuccine ready for cooking. They helped clean up after the noodle making and got ready for cooking and peeling prawns. The boys were as adept at the processes of the kitchen and the meals which came out of it as were their mothers. Truth be told, they almost had as much experience. Every time they were in Tahoe, if they weren't being dragged hither and yon by the girls, they were in Uncle Jameson's kitchens. All those tools, and pots and pans... it was a *very* exciting place. They really envied their cousin Jamie since he got to be there all the time!

Aaron announced, "Alright, who's going to boil, and who's going to help me peel?"

The ladies went to the conservatory to gather tomatoes, cucumbers and chives for a greek salad. "Ooh, I do hope this experiment is successful! I so love strawberries!" Chloe commented when she saw the plantings in the strawberry pots along the south windows.

"I hope so too..." Poly answered as she selected several of the ripest tomatoes and put them in her basket. "And I am very interested to see if the potato experiment produces anything bigger than a walnut."

February became March, March became April and the end of the Spring Term drew nearer, which meant they were just that much closer to the boys' last days at home for a long while. Although the baby wasn't due until July, she would have to sit out the summer's anticipated training of the boys. There were plenty of guides available and she wouldn't miss a day of being an active observer. Aaron had been looking forward to this summer more than he'd admit. His own son was to be put through the rigors he had once endured, and he himself would get to administer them. He was going to be a father again, and of a girl---life just couldn't get better than this!

Harry accepted the training of Olly; naturally Jameson and Titania dealt with Jamie. Belle helped cover the restaurant in the mornings, while George---the proud Grandpapa---oversaw the development of another generation of Livingsons and their promising futures.

Alouette Belle Backhouse was the noisiest baby any of them had yet met---but they kept her anyway. Born in the same room as her mother and Auntie Tania, Alouette was a red-headed, green-eyed spitfire from day one. Jameson and his son were overly pleased that there was *another* red-head in the family. She was attended by not only her Grandmama Belle and her mother's sisters, but also Hannah, Mia, and Lena who were *very* fascinated by the entire event to say the least. She had a good appetite. So much so that Poly began to wonder if the girl would ever do anything but yell and eat. The girls took turns rocking the infant any time she wasn't nursing, which was not as often as they would have liked. Before the Backhouse's prepared to return to Berkeley, Alouette had begun to only cry, a little whimpering actually---when she was hungry----a great relief to both her parents.

Miss Becky Backhouse welcomed three new boys among the fresh crop of students that autumn. Hannah, Lena and Mia couldn't have been more thrilled. As the eldest, Hannah made sure her cousins were in the study group for which she was the responsible seventh grader. Although she was ten and nominally in the fifth grade, she had surpassed her entering class and was now in her penultimate studies at the Tahoe School. Lena and Mia were in the same situation: studying fifth grade materials at only eight years of age. The boys were duly informed of the high expectations placed upon them to excel in their studies and maintain the family traditions of academic excellence. Fortunately they were so whelmed at being surrounded by so many children their own age for the first time, the weight of the mantle they were to wear wasn't in the least cumbersome... at least for the first few weeks. Olly stayed at the house on the hill with his sister Hannah, the twins and their two year old little brother George Lawrence, so he got the brunt of tutoring. The girls simply occupied his every waking hour with the studies and skills they had already mastered---They were only too pleased to lavish their hard won knowledge upon him.

Will and Jamie weren't off the hook by any stretch of the imagination. If they weren't sitting with their heads in a book or writing out lessons, they were assisting at the kitchens or the Lodges: learning the bookkeeping and maintenance of both businesses. The girls and Olly weren't immune to the extracurricular lessons either. Harry and Kaitlyn guided them through engineering and construction, PapaGeorge utilized them at the Mercantile for everything his own children had been responsible when they were that age. So when they *were* rewarded with the occasional weekend off, they almost didn't know what to do with themselves. Almost.

Back in Berkeley, the Backhouses were to host the annual, informal back to school faculty gala. About twelve of the Culture and Literature department faculty and their wives had returned RSVPs. Harold brought cases of beer and wine, whiskey and gin, and made sure there were buckets of ice in the kitchen. Chloe had been baking from the day before. Jameson had put together pastry dough for Poly to roll once more, cut and bake, so she made canapes and croissants, cooked shellfish and carved meats. They were prepared to set out an extensive smorgasbord. Aaron and Harold smoked three salmon over a pit in the back yard and brought them in for Chloe to prepare for presentation. Hipolyta was fortunate enough that Alouette nursed just before the appointed hour, so the small company relaxed in the front room.

"You look fabulous Poly... I mean Hipolyta..." Chloe corrected herself quickly. "I'll remember during the soiree, I promise."

Aaron quipped, "Yes, we mustn't seem *too* casual..." and he winked at Poly who had asked that her friends please use her given name. "...At least until they start slurring their words anyway," he finished.

Harold chuckled, "You've probably been to as many of these as we have---So long as the bathrooms are always available, and I know there's enough food, all should be well. My only concern is that I have something nice to say to Professor Gayley. I sat in on one of his *public* lectures, and if he's the same in his private capacity... this'll be a great evening of *work* for me."

Chloe patted her husband's knee in support, "At least you all have been to University; I'm just a wife and mother with a background in hotel management. What am *I* supposed to chat about? *Work* is *all* I'll be doing this evening."

Aaron and Hipolyta assured their friend that her own Reason would be far superior to the inanity of a lot of what she might need to respond to this evening. "Besides, we have the advantage." inserted Aaron, "I am constantly amazed at the balderdash most Americans are willing to swallow when it's presented with a British accent..." They all had to laugh at that; each of them had witnessed that very phenomenon.

"Okay, I'll just try not to be too ridiculous," finished Chloe.

Hipolyta made one last request, "Once Alouette is put to bed, please let's always keep one of us near the entrance to the hallway here leading to her room... and keep our ears open for her. She can be a little restless; it may be nothing, but better safe than sorry."

They all agreed to keep notice that one of them would remain 'on-post' and at that there was a knock at the door. They put on their 'party faces,' and greeted the first round of their guests. Chloe and Hipolyta with Alouette in her arms, went to begin a small fire in the hearth. Hipolyta had dressed Alouette in a miniature version of her Auntie Chloe's elegant dress---which both flattered Chloe and allowed for the tiny girl, with only red fuzz for hair, to be as feminine as possible... by proxy.

After the initial cordialities, the gentlemen went on a little tour of the conservatory, the library and some of the rose garden. Their wives enjoyed oohing and cooing over Alouette, then they also received a brief tour of the house. While they were thus engaged more of the guests arrived and introduced themselves into already begun conversations; later they were also led in a repetition the 'tours.' The attraction which captivated the ladies most were all the photographs Hipolyta and Chloe had mounted into albums. There were all the pictures of Venice, Manchester, Redditch, etc. and an abundance of Tahoe photos of the family. All captivating and in *such* quantity it quite impressed them. That would prove unfortunate for their husbands when they would soon be 'encouraged' to make Kodak purchases of their own.

The four or five gentlemen still looking over the plantings in the conservatory were discussing the state of California produce. Harold had just concluded expounding on his forecast that in a very short time, a consolidation of growers, packagers and distributers would come to dominate the exports of Californian produce and leave little or no room for small independent organizations to participate in any meaningful way, save locally of course---which was vital to neighborhood cafes and restauranteurs not to mention the soup kitchens. To which the gentlemen listening had mixed reactions: some nodded in agreement and had a certain appreciation for his foresight; others however, pleaded the case of the nobility of the independent farmer, the enterprising canner and the unlikelihood of any one conglomerate ever rising to such a dominant position---such as Mr. Bessamer espoused.

One gentleman remarked, "Although, truth be told... to think that somehow the state of California should be the exception to the modern trends of monopoly and trusts, *is* a bit more than *I* can swallow. Why shouldn't even the produce industry go the way of: oil, railroads, and electricity generation?"

That discussion proved less factious than others that evening. Aaron moved to near the hallway to take up the position Chloe had just vacated---just as Professor Gayley placed himself in the position of defending his notions of the utility of a thorough grounding in the Classics. Then the topic of the future of the telephone came up between himself and some of the women around him.

"Nothing will *ever* replace the value of the written word: the consideration of how to form a phrase, a sentence, even a letter of correspondence will *always* be the highest personal requirement for effective communications. Mere quick snippets of communication through stretches of wires is at best a *raging fad*---nothing more; it will pass!" he concluded; Aaron proposed an alternate perspective.

"If that is so, and I hope your words are prophetic, then the advent of this device will likely be relegated to its primary use among the representatives of the corporate world... As an effective and most expedient means of carrying on their interests in the expansion of financial empire-building. This would naturally suggest that the device will, at least, proliferate among the business-minded. However, as the volume of those sales and installations increase to accommodate the demand, the costs will come down, the infrastructure to support it will expand... And *then* ladies, and sir---At what point will mothers *demand* to speak to their sons and daughters away from home at University, or wives to their husbands abroad upon company business, or grandparents to their grandchildren... friends to friends separated by great distance? It would seem that, if the history of other conveniences, such as the toilet for example, is any indicator---average people will not sit by as *passive have-nots*, leaving efficient and immediate communication to be the sole domain of the *haves* in big business. That would be counter to logic as well as to the nature and history of human expression." Aaron's argument was truly appreciated by the women and they turned to Professor Gayley for a rebuttal. Gayley shrugged and shuffled off to fill his plate with more food and his glass with more wine.

The women in the dining room were also caught in a dialog about the ever-growing progress of technology and invention. Professor Hillard's wife, Lois, was praising the dictaphone-phonograph advances. "Honestly, although Horace doesn't share my enthusiasm, *I* am of the opinion that to have recordings of great concerts, or operas, or of sermons and lectures may prove the *end* of public social intercourse! But it should bring some much needed culture to the under-classes." A few of the ladies nodded, however Chloe had a slightly different take upon the likelihood of the phonograph pushing public performance and social intercourse into the domain of the dodo.

"...The recordings you speak of must be first performed! And there is *no reason* to think that *those* performances will suffer in the least in attendance. In fact, it would be *more* likely that instead of diminishing social participation, recordings could bring *more* people to those events. As 'handbills' for any performance, they will probably serve more the role of advertisements for the great virtuosos, lecturers and pastors, rather than as their surrogates. It is *far* more likely indeed that the 'under-classes,' as you've called them, will *not* be as taken with the phonograph---until mass-production brings the device into the reach of their *pocketbooks*. Once *that* is accomplished, and it seems inevitable, human culture may find itself absorbing an entire subculture devoted solely to increasing the quality of *those recordings*. While the rest of us will continue to enjoy the social *and* personal experiences of *live* performance. Humans *are* social creatures essentially..." She became as quiet when she'd concluded as before she had expressed her views. The other ladies and the few gentlemen who had wandered near nodded to the reason exhibited. Mrs. Lois Hillard ended up being one of those ladies *most* enthusiastically nodding in *agreement*. It probably *wasn't* the accent...

In the conservatory another group of fellows were discussing the isolationist tendencies of the Monroe Doctrine, and its hampering of free commerce, and the free flow of intellectual exchange. Harold and Aaron were the only members of the group who could offer a Euro-centric perspective. While others at the university had studied and received degrees abroad, they were not themselves so immersed in the native mindset of the European.

Harold offered, "To be able to see the topic from the combined perspectives of North American and of Imperial British is perhaps most useful. It should not come as a surprise that the industrialization of the western powers has made some of this discussion moot. The constant inventiveness of western civilized peoples has caused the world to *shrink* rather than grow insularly. That being said; the threat doesn't appear to be so much to commerce and intellectual exchange, as much as to the peace and security which afford the conditions for those enterprises. The seas are *far* more dangerous as a result of Bismarck's Germany... not that he is preparing a militant state, but to challenge the naval power of Britain has required a massive build in vessels and armament over these last few years. The fragile treaties which keep the Balkans in check, and France at arm's length, coupled with a dire underestimation of America's growing capacity for any industrial application---*will lead to trouble*. Gentlemen I assure you: if the fuse is lit in the Balkans, it will be the German's who will fill the vacuum after the explosion."

Aaron joined that little gathering after Hipolyta relieved him at the hallway, and so he caught just the tail end of what Harold was saying; he wished only to add:

"...that while the peace is *presently* secured, it would be wholly

J. L. LAWSON

worthwhile to improve the economics of tourism here and abroad. The benefits would not just be the financial security of otherwise insecure areas without the advantage of industry, but it would further encourage the aforementioned free intercourse of intellectual pursuits and commercial opportunities. It would be most prudent," he went on to say, "that clear and equitable immigration policies should be internationally agreed upon in order to underscore the secure nature of free travel in general."

That set off a tirade by a couple of the faculty who had long been vocal advocates of a supremely 'white' America, and the dangers of sullying that (assumed) purity. The guests around them began to edge away, and remove to other areas of the house and grounds---hoping to distance themselves both in proximity and in association with the blatant expressions of bigotry.

The evening's discussions culminated in a general dialog about the automobile and its being either: a curious fad, or an omen foretelling the demise of the horse and buggy for private transportation. It was not a topic about which any of those present had the slightest investment; that made it the ideal subject for closing the debates of the party on a note of common interest. It was generally accepted that, as with other curiosities of the last decade, the automobile would have to find a ready and receptive customer base to become anything more than the novelty of the wealthy it was already. The ladies entertained the ideas of adventure and independent travel, the gentlemen explored the necessity of mass production and the attractive prospect of cleaner streets. The Backhouse's guests began to make their several farewells.

The four who had sat in anticipation of the party's onset hours earlier sat down once again in the front room to recuperate from the evening's exercises.

Chloe stretched, "I don't know why I was anxious... they were a jolly crowd."

"All but for that crack about white supremism..." mentioned Harold, to which they all nodded. "Always a bad apple..."

356

Aaron stood with his last glass of wine and made a toast, "To Mrs. Hipolyta Backhouse, and Mrs. Chloe Bessamer, well done. Well done indeed!"

Harold shouted, "Here, here," and the ladies stood and took blushing bows.

All was not merely business for the two households, the other activities which occupied the two families were sailing---hence Olly and Will's attachment to sailing ships---and golf. It was not unusual for them to pack up and sail the Bay in the *Victoria*, now moored in the Berkeley Marina closer to home. It was on one of those junkets that the fellows discovered a golf course in Belvedere down on the end of Tiburon. So on their next trip across the Bay they were sure to bring along their clubs. Aaron and Harold enjoyed the first round of golf either of them had played since college in England, and promised each other it wouldn't be the last.

Poly had of course grown up on the Tahoe sailing with her family and was no stranger to the waves. As it happened, more often than not she'd take the helm on their weekend excursions; in time Chloe became comfortable manning the tiller while Poly trimmed the sails as needed. Since Chloe's first trip in the *Victoria*, when she and Harold brought her up from Monterrey Bay several years earlier, she had determined that anytime the boat went out, she wanted to be aboard. There were some weekends when they dropped the men at the golf course and went on to Sausalito for a bit of shopping and a bite to eat. Whenever Kaitlyn, Titania or Becky were able to get to Berkeley they were wholly enchanted to be out on the water, whether just for the voyage, or to visit the other marina areas around the Bay.

It was upon one of those rare occasions when all five women were in Berkeley and made a voyage on the Bay when a conversation that began between Tania and Poly was joined by the other ladies. Poly was at the tiller and they were on a broad tack across a gentle wind, she wondered aloud about where Will might attend college if he chose somewhere other than the University of California. Tania was sitting in the stern with her sister and mused about the eligibility of future mates for their sons. Poly was still formulating a response to that eventuality when Kaitlyn and Chloe threw in their two cents.

Kaitlyn suggested, "There are good people in the world and many who are seeking to become more than they are at present. Our boys, and girls for that matter, will no doubt encounter some aspiring young ladies and men who will become curious enough and dedicated enough to pursue the path..."

Chloe said, "Harold was a labor, but he came along beautifully when presented with evidence of the value of this journey. Besides the possible pairings of our children, which should be a few years off yet---What about our Becky?" At the sound of her name, Becky's attention was wrested from the view of a ferry making weigh out of the Hyde Street docks and now also turned to the conversation.

"What about me?" she inquired not having followed the dialog until then. Tania reiterated the gist of it and Becky rolled her eyes, "Don't waste time matchmaking on my account. I am absolutely content to be unencumbered at present and I do not anticipate that condition to change any time soon."

Chloe replied, "I didn't mean to say you should; I was just pointing out to these ladies that if we were to muse over viable mates for others---we might begin where there is a more presently available individual rather than our young children."

"But..." Becky began, then caught herself and decided to join the speculations---as an exercise in reason rather than any genuine attempt to discard her status as a single woman, "Very well. If I were to be on the lookout for a promising candidate for my attentions, I suspect I should need to begin by..." and she faltered; it had just not occurred to her before now to consider the issue and she was stumped.

Kaitlyn interjected, "That illustrates my point precisely. There should be no such endeavor as 'searching for a mate' where we are concerned. And by we: I mean those on the journey of this *work*. If in our progress along the lines we have intended to pursue, a person presents his or herself as wishing to 'travel' alongside us, *then* it would be incumbent upon us to take notice and make due consideration. Those are essentially the circumstances around each of our own stories, aren't they?"

Poly quickly pointed out that Tania and Jameson's story was a bit different in that they were childhood sweethearts and had never given any thought to any alternative but that they would be married someday. "And speaking of that, has any one else noticed how much attention Mia and Lena lavish upon Olly to the exclusion of any other boys or girls?"

It was Kaitlyn's turn to practice her eye rolling, "Harry has noticed and has specifically asked me not to interfere. I just hope it's a phase; as all children are apt to go through..."

Poly then interrupted, "They are the same age as Tania and Jameson were when the sparks took hold between them and grew!" Tania looked at Kaitlyn and Chloe then sheepishly nodded her confirmation of her sister's point.

Chloe almost gasped, "Oh my..."

Kaitlyn was silent but her expression said volumes. Then she ventured, "I wonder which of them is the one attached, and which is merely supporting her sister?"

Tania made an observation in response, "Um, MamaKat darling, they *both* hold his hands and they *both* dote upon him. I haven't noticed a diminishment in *either* of their attentions where Olly's concerned." She paused, then added, "What if it should be that *both* of them... and... Olly doesn't... What if he... and they..."

Chloe looked at Kaitlyn, and they both looked to Becky who had hoped her opinion wouldn't be sought.

"Well..." she began hesitantly, "I have tended to think of them as inseparable---in an innocent sort of childhood friendship kind of way---But if what Tania has corroborated, and what other's have noticed as well is true for the Livingsons in general..." and she couldn't form the words around the relationship which they all had begun to fathom.

It was quiet for a while and only Poly had something to readily distract her from those considerations; she made ready for a starboard tack and warned her passengers to duck the boom. When they rose up again and looked to port, now that the sail had closed their view of Fisherman's wharf, there in the direction of Angel Island were a pod of dolphins cavorting and dancing on the water's surface in their own apparent festival of play. The ladies followed their movements and interactions completely fascinated by the very intelligent creatures before them. For a moment, they let the previous topic lay un-deliberated.

Chloe at last broke the silence, "Olly's letters home *are filled* with descriptions of his studies, adventures, and responsibilities... and in *every single activity:* one or the other twin figures prominently..." She also looked a little sheepish at acknowledging the evidence. She turned to Kaitlyn and nodded encouragingly but without conviction, "Maybe it's a phase?"

Kaitlyn openly addressed the elephant in the room, "Okay ladies, what if it is not a phase? And like our Tania and Jameson, this bond turns out to be a lifelong attachment? There I've said it. What should we think about Olly with *both* Mia and Lena?" That was a conversation stopper.

Kaitlyn, Tania and Poly heard Poriva and Lizette's comments on the matter, "*Almost all tribes have this practice of many partners. I myself was one of several wives to Toussaint, my children are still my children. It was only when the European Christians came to this land in great numbers that there was ever any issue about it. It is they who have the problem with more than one partner...and that has more to do with property rights than people and reason.*"

Lizette added, "*Of course this is a different society than our ancestors developed, and to publicly counter their ideas of relationship and marriage is tantamount to spitting in their face. All we can offer you in guidance is the reassurance that there is nothing objectively bad in this.*"

Becky made the observation that, "If they should find each

360

other as suitable partners for the long term, well, Mia and Lena are extraordinarily identical... I could see the three of them maintaining an illusion for nosy neighbors if it came to that. They each are *remarkably* intelligent you know; they shall likely surpass my ability to *teach* them *anything* before very long..."

The others looked at her suddenly, she added, "What?! Did I say something out of place?"

Poly replied, "For a woman who claims to have no conjugal aspirations---probably because of that I suppose, you sure do have an interesting take on relationships... 'An *illusion* for nosy neighbors'?"

"But that's all this boils down to isn't it?" responded Becky evenly to the comment. "Societal judgements and prejudices. I mean there is nothing objectively odd about the situation... unless I'm missing something. They're not *actually* related in any way... no complications of in-breeding or such---just nosy neighbors and a government that's *too involved* in the private lives of its citizens."

Chloe had always had the utmost respect for Becky's judgement and decisions, and could not find fault in her thoughts on this matter either. Kaitlyn resolved aloud to follow Harry's advice and avoid interference with the children's friendships. The other ladies agreed with that stance and offered further suggestions for at least ensuring that the three of them realized what was in store for them---if what this group foresaw came to fruition.

"It could be accomplished passively; you wouldn't have to sit them down and lecture them or anything," Becky began, "I suppose you will have to point out the inadequacies of those characters in Utah who have made a militant stand on the subject... Otherwise, I think history is by and large on *their* side in this."

Both Chloe and Kaitlyn ended with, "It may just be a phase, but it was a good exercise in 'what if.' *And* if it does turn out that our children follow in Jameson and Tania's footsteps, well this discussion was well made."

One of the byproducts of that day on the boat was that it became ever more difficult to watch when Mia, Olly and Lena were together, which *was* really *all* the time, and not be vividly reminded of that earlier afternoon on the Bay.

Hannah graduated a year earlier than her thirteenth birthday---the usual end of eighth grade. She had begun to blossom into a most attractive young woman, just like her mother in many respects. When after the ceremony for graduation she announced that she would very much like to attend Malvern Girls School, Harry and Harold could not have been prouder.

"Another Malvernian in the family! This is just brilliant." That was all either of them could discuss for several days.

Harold procured an application and entrance requirements for the Senior School, and after returning all Hannah's transcripts, letters of recommendation, and fees, her admission was easily secured. The question then arose: would Harold and Chloe follow and take up residence in the Midlands again? Harold had just the month before liquidated all his and Lawrence's holdings in the cannery, save their considerable stock options. The 'California Packers Association' formed under the aegis of Fred Tillman and others. The new entity used the Del Monte brand as their flagship logo, and 'California-Grown' became a reality. The Spelmans and the Bessamers were now *very* well off, indeed.

After much discussion and some very tense moments for Mia and Lena, it was decided that Hannah's parents would set up residence in Redditch and Oliver would complete his studies at the Tahoe School---essentially as an adoptive son of Harry and Kaitlyn. They put Booklove House on the market as a rental and Poly agreed to oversee the management of the residence. The *Victoria* was transferred to Aaron and Poly and by the end of July, they were ready to make the journey back to the home of their youth and to University for Hannah Belle. The going away party was a splendid gala, not a tear was shed; until Mia and Lena had to say their final farewells, for a few years at least, to the dearest girl they'd ever known. Hannah had been both their hero and dearest friend. They were determined that one day they too would follow her to Malvern and take up their rightful place in the town of their father's Alma Mater. First on the agenda however was finishing their education in Tahoe.

Other changes were in the wind that summer; a man named Bliss decided to throw his future in with Tahoe City and arranged financing for the construction of a spur from the railway in Truckee right into the heart of the village. But that wasn't all... After the demise of the Tahoe Inn a few years before in the fire, the vacuum for a new full-service hotel needed to be filled. The Lodges were at a premium but even they could not accommodate the numbers of visitors, nor boast of an enclosed dance hall. Sierra Architecture and CANED Ltd. provided plans for the new Tahoe Tavern, and Harry even resurrected his father's water supply plans from all those years ago in order to provide for the enormous needs of the new establishment. The tracks were laid and tourists began to pour in. At first they came just for the sights and a steamer trip on the Tahoe. Later some stayed for weeks at a time as the town's former regular visitors had once done; but most were day visitors.

By the time the twins had graduated the Tahoe School, been studying for a year on their own at home---their choice, ostensibly to enter Malvern Girls College as near complete Senior students---Olly and his two cousins were in their anticipated last year of studies. The Tahoe Tavern broke ground and was scheduled to open the following year; the same year Alouette Backhouse was to spend her last spring in Berkeley before her transition to Tahoe, training and school.

While one day the children are gathering flowers and making mud pies, the next it seems: they're grown and collecting college hours and making a new life for themselves."

The long days were waning and the longer nights began to impinge upon the two figures sitting on the porch that autumn evening. "Whew! That was the end of the nineteenth century and a new era for the Livingson legacy begins..." commented the host.

"Yes those were busy times toward the end of that century. Now before we stop for the evening, what questions do you have?"

The young man flipped through his notes and was again impressed by the amount of knowledge that kept coming from that one symbol they'd begun investigating weeks before. "Can you explain how I can use this diagram of nutrition? It makes sense and all, but what's the significance of there being three foods?"

The guest set her head back on the cushion of the chair and took a deep breath. "There. I have just taken in food intentionally."

"Uh, you breathed... we all breathe... all the time. What's so special about that?"

She looked at him, then to the pond and swaying willows, then up at the now rose-colored clouds. "There, I have just taken in food intentionally again."

The young host was not getting this 'obviously' important lesson and said so, "I'm sure you're demonstrating something; but I don't get it."

She smiled, "What is the difference between mechanical and intentional?"

"Well mechanically we do things without any thought at all... it just happens; the intentional occurs only when we decide to make an effort---Sometimes... rather... Mostly *against* what would otherwise *just happen* through us?"

She smiled again, "Good answer---but without the question mark." She elaborated, "Once we realize how our machine works: what are its needs, and how to get the most out of the energy we have; we can begin to make even the smallest act more intentional. For example: when you eat a meal, you could also recognize that you are taking in a second food---Air---and make that an intentional meal as well.

You might additionally, as you savor each bite and breath, recognize what it took for that meal to get in front of you to eat--- the husbandry that raised the cow, the butcher who prepared the cut... the farming process that supplied the grain and the bakery that made the bread... the gardening that raised the produce and the grocer who made it available. All the while, you are chewing and swallowing, breathing and savoring. Make the mechanical more intentional by acknowledging your participation in your own thoughts and acts. Coarse food, air, and impressions are going to get in anyway, *but* we can decide to make the efforts necessary to lift those things *out of* the mundane and routinely mechanical."

The young man tried to grasp this; he repeated her illustration in his own words to be sure he understood. "So, if I eat slower so I can recognize that *I am* eating, rather than wolfing down a meal. If I notice that *I am* breathing as I do that; that the air itself is another food---rather than panting to keep up with how much I'm shoveling into my mouth. *And* if instead of going blank while masticating, I acknowledge that what I'm eating didn't *just show up* on my plate--- that my surroundings *are* where I am at that moment---recognize that impressions are a food, too---Then I will be more of a participant in my own activities. In fact it sounds to me like I will be a participant for the first time... I don't remember *ever* making those sorts of acknowledgements before when just having a sandwich."

"That's the gist of it," she agreed." Of course at first no one is going to be able to maintain that level of attention all day, or for several hours, or even for more than the duration of a meal. It takes practice and effort and the ability to avoid leaking our energies wastefully. Take some small thing and bring all your attention to accomplishing that one thing. No effort is in vain, and everything we practice---we will improve upon. In its simplest formation to be intentional is simply the attempt to bring attention where we have not brought it before. We know how our machine is supposed to function; it follows then that we should operate it intelligently---

intentionally." She sat back again and returned her gaze to the deep colors of the dusky sky.

"We are apart of all that surrounds us... that is an impression which should be foremost in our attention---anytime we remember it, that is..." She rose, stepped off the porch, took a couple steps toward the lane then turned back to her host, "Enjoy your dinner!"

7

Practice

"In theory there is no difference between theory and practice. In practice there is."
---Yogi Berra

M orning coffee steamed a little more in the chill air of autumn and the early shafts of sunlight made the frosted ground and leaves dazzle his eyes. As his guest made measured and deliberate steps toward the house from the lane, he noticed again how almost like a dancer she was in her simplest movements. Her every gesture and posture positively emanated confidence and surety: flowing through the space she inhabited, not battling through it as so many people seemed to do. He ducked inside and returned as she was mounting the steps, he handed her a cup of coffee and she asked, "...And how was your evening's repast?"

The young man smiled and related to her the experience "Well for one thing: I ate a lot slower but I still was filled in about the same amount of time I usually take to eat." She nodded encouragingly. "Secondly, while I am pretty sure I couldn't actually tell that I was 'digesting' second and third foods, I *know* that they were entering, and I *knew* that they were assisting what I was chewing and swallowing because it just... well... tasted better. Does that make any sense? It wasn't a different recipe or anything, just my usual hot chicken salad, but it *really did* taste more... uh... well more of itself. I mean I actually tasted it more thoroughly I suppose." He paused, not sure how to describe the experience in terms that conveyed the depth of it.

"That's a fair assessment, at least as far as I can corroborate it from my own experience. All that we do intentionally, however incremental or modestly we begin, always brings more energy. There is an aphorism: *The energy spent on active inner work is then and there transformed into a fresh supply, but that spent on passive work is lost for ever.* Your meal last evening was a real foray into that reality. So 'you were filled in the same amount of time,' you 'tasted it more thoroughly,' and because you *knew* that you were taking in more than just what you were chewing, and probably watching *yourself* in your own act of eating at the same time, impressions were able to pass from DO to the RE above and so allowed air to pass its barrier as well--- Transformed into a fresh supply as it were." She glanced at him for a sign of his understanding. His brow was only slightly furrowed, but he was rubbing his chin and nodding at the same time---always a good indication that knowledge is being digested.

She added, "Now, what would *really* make this as beneficial as possible for your machine, would be to also diminish the leaks of energy which still persist. In that way you can begin to accumulate a greater store of that energy and apply it to make even greater efforts. We are a factory for the transmutation of energies. When the factory is not losing its precious products through needless waste, the benefits begin to mount. Our being increases and with it our ability to expand our knowledge---which leads to greater understanding--- is likewise increased."

Her host finally tried to verbalize what he believed he understood of what she'd said, "So, while our mechanicality creates a downward spiral of losses, our attempts at intentionality encourages a gradual spiral of gains. To the extent that we inhibit the one, the other becomes greater---a balance of sorts?"

She nodded, "Balance in the sense that its a self-contained system, and nature abhors a vacuum... something will always 'fill the space.' It is up to us to fill it intentionally," and again she sat patiently for any more observations or questions he might offer. The young man mused over his recent experiment and the explanation she'd offered, wanting very much to keep it as clear in his mind as he could. This was another real example of the practicable methods his guests had been expounding since that very first encounter, and he really didn't want to lose anything of the small gains he'd made thus far. He reached for his pad and pencil and she took that as a signal that he was ready to continue their story.

"Jamie, Will and Oly had just the one year left at the Tahoe School; while they weren't the age of the other eighth graders, they made up for their youth in the meticulousness they evinced in their school work and in sheer enthusiasm. Their two younger cousins, George Lawrence, who was beginning his first year, and Alouette who would be coming to Tahoe the next year, were all that was left of their generation to pass through the Tahoe School. So the three boys were at the top of the heap and they were a benevolent triumvirate---Mia and Lena saw to that. George Lawrence entered as a third grader in studies---his own training under his father had instilled in him a seriousness towards schoolwork. That was not to say he wasn't clever and funny... he was... he just set his priorities and stuck with his plan of accomplishment, which did not preclude him joining his cousins on the Tahoe.

The older boys had priorities too: any afternoon they weren't required at the Mercantile, *Concession* or Lodges, they were sailing on the Tahoe. For Will and Jamie *that* was a priority. George Lawrence was almost always with them on the boat. Olly would drag Lena and Mia along on some of those voyages, but when he could not persuade them he stayed behind and turned his attention to whatever they decided to do---which often entailed poring over the University texts and examinations which Uncle Aaron had provided. They were determined to repeat, as closely as they were able, Harry's career at Malvern---except that they would be younger than he was when he made that plunge.

The examinations which Uncle Aaron provided contained sections on English, French, German, Latin, Greek, history, mathematics, chemistry, and physics. The test was not multiple choice but instead was evaluated based on essay responses as *excellent, good, doubtful, poor*, or *very poor*. Naturally, what had the girls and Olly stuck were the topics which were not covered in their last six years of subjects... particularly Latin and Greek, the chemistry and physics were essentially more in-depth versions of the maths and sciences they already had. Examples:

Latin --- Advanced Latin Composition

1) Write the rules for the following constructions and illustrate each by a Latin sentence :

    a Two uses of the dative.
    b The cases used to indicate the relations of place.
    c The cases used with verbs of remembering.
    d The hortatory (or jussive) subjunctive.
    e The supine in um.

2) Translate into Latin:

"I see," said Cicero, "that the faces and eyes of all of you are turned toward me. Your good will toward me is truly pleasing to me. But I can see what is to my advantage much more clearly than you can what is to the advantage of the state. I shall encounter a storm of wholly undeserved odium: but it is worth my while to be called a tyrant if only this be driven from the city and the danger of this war be averted from you. But, since I must live with those whom I have conquered, it is your duty to see to it that my deeds may never harm me or mine. I have made it possible that those who are fighting for our country in foreign lands may have a place to which they may return as victors."

3) Change 2 as far as the words "But since" into indirect discourse depending on Cicero dixit.

Physics

A

1) A balloon contains 300 cubic meters of hydrogen, each cubic meter of which weighs 90 grams. The material of the balloon weighs 250 kilograms. Each cubic meter of the surrounding air weighs 7290

grams. How many kilograms in addition to its own weight will the balloon lift?

2) Describe a method of finding the specific gravity of a solid heavier than water; of a liquid.

B

3) A cylindric bar of uniform diameter and 1.5 meters long has a strong ring fastened to each end and another at a distance of one meter from one end. Show by three drawings how this rod may be used as a lever with each ring in turn serving as a fulcrum. What weight in each case (the weight of the bar itself being neglected) applied to one remaining ring will balance 25 kilograms at the other?

4) A steamer is moving eastward at the rate of 240 meters per minute. A man runs northward across her deck at the rate of 180 meters per minute. Show by a drawing his actual path and compute his actual velocity in centimeters per second.

Uncles Aaron and Harry were invaluable assets in the pursuit of these subjects and it wasn't just learning the tests, their tutors intended them to have a thorough grounding in the disciplines themselves. Both their mentors agreed and told them so...

"A most complete understanding of the principles and concepts involved in these studies will yield a greater return in the long term than any one-time triumphant passing of a single test."

The three university-bound pupils still had time for the occasional voyage; of course they often occupied their time on those excursions: calculating wind directions, velocities, moments of inertia and force, etc. Will, Jamie, and George Lawrence enjoyed their company anyway. As the school year progressed and the weather kept them closer to home, the boys began formulating plans for a post-graduation enterprise involving the *Victoria* on the San Francisco Bay.

Will pointed out that, "Dad has said it often enough, 'If those students had a little more experience with the real world, they'd appreciate the studies they are supposed to be pursuing,' so why

371

J. L. LAWSON

shouldn't we contribute to that real-world experience..."

Jamie added, "And it wouldn't be too much of a stretch to include a deluxe meal or two on the junkets... it'd be a regular 'cruise on the bay,' and we could log all that time toward captaincy... *if* we can get a captain to oversee us for a couple years."

That was a sticking point but it wasn't a deal-breaker. Professor Backhouse had contacts throughout the University and societies with which he was associated, and promised to find an amenable overseer. Meanwhile, they acquired the written testing for licensure. A little chagrined, they were soon joining Olly and the twins learning advanced maths and physics. All the parents were pleased that their children were finding relevant uses for the knowledge they were acquiring, especially since they were acquiring that knowledge to achieve their own goals. The school year ended. Jamie and Will's success was toasted, and they received tokens of esteem. Oddly, Harry's gift to Jamie was more curious than the others, but Jamie decided that anything from Uncle Harry was a treasure.

After their graduation parties several things happened at once it seemed. Lena and Mia weren't sure Olly was as ready as they had hoped him to be to take the examinations for placement at Malvern, although they felt pretty confident in their own preparedness. Jamie and Will were itching to be out on the *Victoria* for some trial sailing all the way around the Bay with Aaron or Poly, or somebody else on board just as a precaution. George Lawrence didn't want to miss sailing on the Bay with his cousins, nor did he wish to leave his parents, grandparents, or Aunt and Uncle. A family conference was called in the *Concession* during the last week of May to decide how to handle the variety of needs now plaguing their younger generation. Belle, Kaitlyn, Hipolyta and Titania sorted out the individual needs, wants and desires of each young lady and young man, including George Lawrence, and even of five year old Alouette, who wouldn't be left out of the deliberations.

It was Hipolyta who guided the debate and ultimately offered the resolutions they would agree upon. "The Booklove House has been the transient residence of visiting Professors and Lecturers, and can easily be held 'vacant' for the Summer. Here is what I propose: Harry and Kaitlyn with their present household should occupy that house as a summer residence, whilst Aaron and I will host Jamie with Will and Alouette of course. Lena and Mia can continue tutoring Olly---I am sure Aaron can arrange for you all to even audit a class or two over the summer at the University. Jamie and Will, under one of us in supervision, can begin their sailing career---" and she leveled her voice at them exclusively.

"But I have to say this boys: there's more to tending a ship than manning the tiller and trimming the sails. You *shall* become intimately familiar with every line, sheet, boom, sail, brass work, block, hackle, and pin on that boat. You will keep it ship-shape and in Bristol fashion or you can kiss your *aspirations* goodbye---Is that clear?" They had no choice but to agree, and they did so with George Lawrence's enthusiastic "You bet..." chiming along with their own.

"Now as to Alouette---Dearest, I hope you will accept the position of Assistant Director of activities for the summer, MamaKat and MamaPoly are going to need your help... is that okay with you?"

The little girl beamed at the honor of helping her mother and MamaKat run the houses for the summer and said simply, "Yes Ma'am!" She grinned at her cousins as if she'd just been made rear admiral of the fleet; they all responded with congratulations and applause---she grinned even wider.

George and Belle sat quietly through the discussions and final announcements and after all was said and done, she asked Titania if she could spare her for a few weeks at least... "Just long enough to see my grandchildren doing all the grown-up things they have planned?"

Tania rose and hugged her mother, "Mama you may have all the time in the world to do whatever you wish to do... Everything will be right here when you get back. Unless the Tahoe Tavern takes over the Lodges too, in which case I'll be joining you in Berkeley!"

George and Jameson made them all promise to take plenty of pictures, and write home often. Jamie looked at his Dad and said, "We're just going over to Berkeley Dad; it's not like we're going off on a circumnavigation or anything..."

Jameson chuckled, but repeated... "Write home often and take plenty of pictures; this'll be the longest you've been away from home... your mother worries."

At that, although across the room, Titania quickly turned her head to her husband and son not sure if she'd heard what she thought she'd heard... '*I worry*?!' she mouthed incredulously.

Harry took as long to pack for the trip 'just over to Berkeley' as it took him to pack returning from Europe---much to Aaron and Poly's amusement. They had been making this trip every summer since they could remember and offered a bit of advice for Harry, Kaitlyn, and Belle's preparations and packing.

"Uh... by the way Harry, the Booklove House *does have* all the conveniences of your home here... Remember, you designed it? I don't think you'll need to lug along the kitchen sink..."

Harry chuckled but packed his drafting supplies anyway, *and* his rod-building gear, *and* his trade journals... Aaron just kept smiling as another, and another box or crate came out to the staging area in the great room.

Kaitlyn took one look at the mass of 'stuff,' and could only shrug as she placed her own valise and George Lawrence's bag on the pile. Mia and Lena took more after their father, but hadn't had the years of accumulation he'd had. When all was said and done, and with Kaitlyn staring at the whelming stacks, Harry sheepishly began putting some of his things back until he had the pile down to his trunk and a single oblong crate. Aaron and Poly simply applauded when he emerged from his studio empty-handed at last.

Professor Backhouse was asked to fill in for another professor's classes for the first month of the summer, with the promise that there would be a replacement forthcoming. This turned out to be a convenience rather than a burden; he was able to escort the twins and Olly to the campus every morning and return with them in the afternoon. Harry or Poly went with the other boys to the docks every morning where for the first couple weeks the *Victoria* never left her slip. The three young mariners polished, scrubbed, mended and refitted where needed everything on the boat that would bring it up to ship-shape condition. Before they were allowed to even cast off from the marina the first time, Poly made an inspection tour and promised to repeat it every week.

Naturally Poly had sailed as much as anyone in her family, but she did not assume that she knew how to make a meaningful inspection. So while the *Victoria* was being readied, she met with a retired sea captain of Aaron's acquaintance and asked a thousand questions of him. Since she was eager to learn and very pretty, and because he was retired and had a lifetime of experience to pass along to a willing ear, they spent hours at a time over days and days. Poly was sure she could not only inspect a ship, but could rig, run and repair anything on the *Victoria* herself. Captain Thomassen was also willing to occasionally preside over the boys' excursions---a necessary part of their licensure process.

Harry was glad he'd brought along his rod-building equipment. After a few days at the docks, he decided he needed a very sturdy rod for boat or pier fishing. He looked over the gear used by some of the old fellas on the pier. After purchasing two level-winding reels of sufficient capacity for the heavy linen line, he set about building rods that would accommodate them. The butt blanks he'd brought along, once ferruled and mated, made stout poles able to bear the tension of large blue water fish. He made the guides and reel seat from brass wire and stock and was ready to wet a line after Poly gave the go ahead for the young mariners' first voyage on the Bay.

It was an event. Jamie and Will waited for a day when the whole family could come aboard. The sixteenth of June, a Saturday, arrived and the family made their way to the marina. Will and Jamie were already on board making last minute adjustments to the rigging for the winds and currents they expected in the afternoon up across the Golden Gate and back again.

Olly and the twins, with George Lawrence, stepped alongside the *Victoria*, "Permission to come aboard..." George Lawrence asked on behalf of the group. Their uncles, aunts and Grandmama were behind them and just coming onto the docks heading down to the slip.

Will answered, "Mr. Livingson, come aboard, you'll crew the mainsail and maintopsail, if you please." To which George Lawrence grinned and hopped to a position in the cockpit.

"Mr. Bessamer, come aboard and please take a position to crew the foresail and foretopsail... and would the Miss Livingsons care to assist at the foresail? Or you may use the rattlins to go aloft if you wish. Mr. Connor and myself have replaced the rope rungs with oak. You may also assist with the jibs and staysail along side Mr. Connor---as you choose."

The three of them smiled and answered, "Aye, aye Mr. Backhouse."

Once the crew was set, Harry, Aaron, Belle, Kaitlyn and Poly holding Alouette's hand, asked to come aboard. Mr. Backhouse answered, "Come aboard, please. Stow any items below that can't be lashed down on deck; we'll be getting underway shortly."

They were handed on board; Harry and Aaron stowed the rods and food baskets below in the aft saloon and marveled at the shine and polish of all the brass and woodwork. The ladies found comfortable places along the starboard cockpit nicely appointed with generous cushions, the uncles took places opposite them with Alouette in her father's lap.

Aaron said, "Mr. Backhouse, the cargo and passengers are secure sir."

Will nodded and called forward, "Mr. Connor, cast off the bow line and prepare to raise the the fore jib to starboard; we'll ease her out of the marina. Will the Miss Livingsons cast off the fore and aft spring lines. Mr. Livingson cast off the stern line, if you please... and George Lawrence," Will whispered, "coil it nicely on the cockpit sole."

The crew confirmed the mooring lines were stowed and then the moment came, "Mr. Connor, raise the jib and staysail. Mr. Bessamer, Mr. Livingson, prepare to raise foresail and mainsail."

"Aye, ayes" came wafting back to the cockpit from forward. George Lawrence unfurled the mainsail head and spar from the boom and stood ready at the belayed halyards, just as Olly was preparing at the foresail. The *Victoria* was moving slowly out of the marina into a quartering west wind. "We'll be making for the Tiburon peninsula on the first leg of today's cruise, then we'll swing around Angel Island for the Golden Gate, drop down toward Goat Island---Yerba Buena---and then back here. Sound good?" asked Will of his passengers. They were just delighted at the efficiency shown thus far in managing the sails by the 'crew;' all nodded, smiling.

He turned back to the crew, "Hoist the foresail, Mr. Bessamer, and once it's set and trimmed prepare the foretopsail."

Olly pulled on the throat halyard until the gaff head was set, then he raised the end with the peak halyard. "Foresail raised; ready to trim," he called.

Will then asked Mr. Livingson to hoist the mainsail, which George Lawrence attempted with some success. It just took a little while longer than Olly had taken with the foresail. Once the throat was up, and while he was raising the peak, Olly trimmed the foresail to match the jibs' alignments Jamie had set. The *Victoria* was beginning to move swiftly into the Bay.

George Lawrence called out, "Mainsail raised; ready to trim, sir."

Will answered, "Well done; trim to a close reach on this port tack, sir," and he added in a low voice, "George Lawrence, match Olly's trim on the foresail, and prepare the topsail for raising."

"Mr. Bessamer, raise the foretopsail. Mr. Livingson, raise the maintopsail."

"Aye, ayes" again came wafting back and Will added, "Mr. Connor let fly the jib topsail, if you please."

Jamie called back, "Aye, aye," and raised the third jib, secured the clew sheet once trimmed and sat down on the prow with his legs dangling either side of the bowsprit. Mia and Lena did climb a little way up the rattlins just for the view, but soon descended and sat flanking Olly who was leaning back against the foremast, gazing out across the turquoise bay.

Will always kept one hand on the tiller; they were well under way making maybe five up to six and a half knots close reach into a fifteen knot wind; he made course for the north end of Angel Island. "Uncle Harry, Dad, you can fish now if you want to; we won't need to change tack for an hour or so."

Harry went below, brought out the rods and tackle box and handed one to Aaron after he'd sent Alouette across to her Grandmama. They selected lures and let out plenty of line.

"Mama if you wish, now is a good time for the picnic baskets." She nodded and fetched up the food. Will called forward, "Lena, Mia would you distribute the meal to the rest of the crew?"

They hopped up and gracefully maneuvered their way to the cockpit. MamaKat made little bundles for the forward crew and the twins delivered them, keeping their own and eating with Jamie and Olly at the bowsprit.

The ladies and every one else for that matter had noticed the twins' outfits: full length harem pants in dark blue, tied at the waist and ankles, and striped sailor's 'shirts.' Kaitlyn also noticed when the wind lifted the bottom hems of their blouses, that her girls had been into her bureau and found the modified camisoles she and Chloe designed years ago, because it certainly appeared they were wearing some just like them but perhaps of their own manufacture.

Poly made the comment that she should like to make some pants like those, and Belle had just said how adorable the sailor stripes were on them, when a gust of wind brought some spray up over the prow and wet the deck to midships. The ladies eyes opened wider---one of the twins was *very* dampened; her clothes were clinging to her skin---she was quite clearly *not* a darling *little* girl any longer. Her curves and blossoming endowments made her look even more like her mother. It was a stark contrast, one twin---sodden and revealed; the other---dry and still camouflaged.

When the ladies looked away from the twins and back to each other it was Kaitlyn who began, "Oh my, poor Olly..."

Belle added, "our Olly doesn't..." then Poly finished, "he doesn't stand a chance!" They ate from the baskets and reveled in the girls' maturity and foresaw with reluctance how they would affect Olly and other young men.

Aaron got a bite and began fighting the line, reeling in as quickly as he could. Harry brought in his line since they were almost to the island any way and went to assist Aaron. "Looks like a good sized halibut, buddy, bring her on in and I'll get the gaff."

Harry looked around, Will pointed to the deck above the companionway and said, "We've got a generous ice box below if you want to store it." Aaron got the fish close up beside the boat, the ladies moved to the other side of the cockpit and Harry gaffed the large fish and dragged it into the sole of the cockpit.

"Nice! Another one or two like that and we have dinner for tonight and tomorrow to boot!" Aaron commented and handed it to Harry who took it below.

Will called out, "When we clear the island we'll get a big gust; prepare to come about on my mark."

Will and Olly handed their food bundles to Lena and Mia then made ready to adjust the sheets of the sails for which they were responsible. George Lawrence did the same with the main, after he gave his mother his little bundle. They came out of the strait between the peninsula and island and sure enough they got a big gust directly off port. Will shifted sides and pushed the tiller to starboard, the bow eased more to port and just as the wind gust settled, he called, "Come about!"

Jamie loosed all three starboard jib sheets and began hauling in the port sheets starting with the staysail and working out to the flying jib. Olly and George Lawrence loosed their booms and they swung to port. Fortunately George Lawrence ducked only just in time as the main boom swung at his head; he made a defensive 'shift' move to avoid it, *but* instead of merely deflecting it, he grabbed the spar and was carried right passed the ladies' stunned expressions out over the rail---dangling there with a bemused look on his face. The ladies gasped and Will grabbed the boom sheet, calling out at the same time, "Mr. Livingson, stop showing off and get back in the boat; you're throwing off our balance!"

George Lawrence came hand over hand along the boom back to where he could swing a leg over the rail and come back down to the deck and into the cockpit. He looked up at Will, took the main sheet into his own hands and said, "Sorry skipper, wrong reflex; it won't happen again." He trimmed the mainsail to align with the foresail. The ladies were speechless.

Harry came up from below, "Oh, we've come about. Pretty smoothly done; I didn't really notice too much shifting below..." Aaron whispered to Harry about the off-balance antic, while Will glanced at George Lawrence and winked.

They continued the starboard reach for another half an hour until they almost reached the Marin Headlands. Will called out, "Prepare to make a beam reach as we cross the Golden Gate." He turned to his Dad and Uncle Harry, "We won't dare the currents through the strait, the current's almost max flood and although we'll be broadside of it, we wouldn't make progress too well dead into it anyway."

"Give her her head boys; set a beam reach!" The crew let out the sheets until the sails filled with the near following wind, then they adjusted them from the mainsail forward. George Lawrence kept easing the boom sheet in a little at a time until Will nodded for him

380

to cleat it. "The wind is stiffer here... Mr. Bessamer, trim the foretopsail; Mr. Livingson trim the maintopsail." They rolled with the waves to which the *Victoria* was parallel, and Will initiated a long arcing course to minimize the bucking, while the crew adjusted sails to match the wind.

"Mr. Connor we'll be in a broad reach shortly; prepare to set the spinnaker." Jamie hoisted the socked sail up to the top of the forestay and was ready.

Will called out, "Set for a broad reach. Mr. Connor fly the spinnaker." Olly and George Lawrence let out the foresail sheet and main sheet, as Jamie pulled the sock down from the block on the forestay; the spinnaker billowed open and Jamie kept a hand on the clew sheet to offset any sudden gusts. Every one felt the *Victoria* nearly leap forward as they sailed broadside of Fort Mason and on to pass the Fisherman's Wharf. The twins, both on the starboard rattlins above the deck, waved to the fishing trawlers and ferry passengers along the shore and wharf. The *Victoria's* spinnaker was striped with deep red and white across the lightweight canvas. Between the twins' apparel, their hair flying in the wind, the spinnaker and the *Victoria's* red striped gunwale topped by her bright brass rails... well she was a beautiful sight.

Unbeknownst to the passengers and crew aboard the *Victoria*, photographers from the Morning Call, the Examiner and the Chronicle were on the waterfront to photograph a piece on a visiting celebrity author for the next day's issue. What they also got were pictures of the *Victoria* in the background as she flew by the wharf. Jameson was going to get more than the family photographs he'd requested.

A while later, Will called out, "Trim your sails gentlemen; we're making for the south of Goat Island on this leg," and he pushed the tiller a little more to port. As she headed around Telegraph Hill the wind dropped a bit. The crew trimmed the sails; Will made a beeline for Alameda Island.

In short order, Yerba Buena was off the port bow and Will

called out, "Prepare to come about!" The twins climbed down from the rattlins and sat next to Olly. Jamie pulled the starboard spinnaker sheet a little tauter, and gathered the other jibs' sheets into one hand while George Lawrence and Olly got set for the booms to swing.

As they came abreast of the island, Will called, "Come about!" At the same time he pushed the tiller over, now onto a broad reach to port with the prow pointed directly at the Berkeley Marina, then he switched seats to the port side of the tiller. The girls climbed back up the port rattlins and waved to the Naval Commandant's house as they sped by.

The last six mile leg allowed Harry and Aaron to fish a little more. Aaron got another halibut a bit bigger than the first. Harry was satisfied that the rods he'd built were appropriate to the task and looked forward to another excursion just for fishing. As they neared the marina, Will called out, "Mr. Bessamer, Mr. Livingson, prepare to drop the foresail and the main sail on my mark. Mr. Connor douse the spinnaker, then the jib and staysail, please."

Jamie released the sheets and pulled the sock at the head of the sail back down, gathering the spinnaker as it came to the deck, then he lowered the jib and staysail and tied off the bundles to the bowsprit. Will called for the sails to be dropped, and the crew gathered and battened the canvases around the booms. At the same time he pushed the tiller over so that the *Victoria* pointed into the wind, as her stern swept by the end of the docks and righted, Jamie used a whisker pole to hold out the clew of the remaining jib.

The boat crept backwards towards the dock; Will called, "Set the mooring lines at your leisure." Mia and Lena hopped to the dock when they were close enough, caught the lines thrown them and the *Victoria* was back in her berth. "We'll tidy up here if you would like to get those fish cleaned and ready for supper," said Will calmly to his parents as they stood to disembark.

The crew's elders were very pleased with their handling of the ship and the smooth efficiency of their methods and movements. Aaron and Harry said admiringly, "We look forward to another fishing trip on *your* ship gentlemen."

Belle quietly said to George Lawrence as he handed his grandmama off the boat, "You were quite acrobatic; I very much enjoyed the show." George Lawrence started to say how he hadn't intended to fly with the boom, but she chuckled and he just blushed instead.

Hipolyta took one last look at the *Victoria* as she and Kaitlyn left the dock, "It appears that our children are destined for the sea..."

Kaitlyn put her arm in her sister's and consoled her with, "Yes, and very likely greatness to boot; we'll get used to it, dearest. You set the bar very high for them and they o'erleapt it with ease. We can't expect them to not behave as Livingsons."

The crew, with assistance from Mia and Lena, furled the sails and fitted red sail pocket-covers over them. The jibs were furled and stuffed in color coded bags then stowed below with the spinnaker sock and topsails---also color-coded. They then carried buckets of fresh water from the tap at the head of the dock and rinsed the decks and hull, rubbed all the exposed brasswork and woodwork with oil cloths and locked down the companionway. The sheets and halyards were coiled and tied off with colored ribbons, which elicited from the twins, "Ooh, that's such a pretty touch, all those different colored ribbons..."

Jamie answered, "I suppose, but they're actually coded for each sheet and halyard's use. Did you notice the ends of each are whipped with different colors, too? If we could have the whole length of all the ropes different colors... *that* would be the *best* solution. You know---line management."

Will added, "With so many sheets, halyards, lines, stays, shrouds and such on a boat this size, it can easily get to be a mess really fast on the water."

The result of all that was that Mia and Lena had a little project they set for themselves before the summer was out, and naturally they conscripted Olly, George Lawrence and Alouette into their plans. First: they went to their mother and father for financing; second: they had a long talk with Grandmama Belle. She of all people would know the answers they had to find before they could get their project off the ground. Belle was more than just helpful with information, she went so far as too help them set up the particulars of the process. In no time at all, the back garden of Booklove House was a covert processing plant for dying ropes... *lots of ropes*---and in the only colors they could make permanent: red, black, blue, green, amber orange, and a purpley color that looked like slightly faded eggplant, a dark violet. They figured they would need six colors per mast: the two halyards for raising and lowering, port and starboard sheets for trimming, and the halyard and outhaul for the topsail. That could be replicated at the foremast, then the six colors for the port and starboard sheets of the three jibs---the jib halyards would still need to be simply whipped with bands of color for reference, but this was a good start. The standing rigging needn't be a consideration, because... well... it was just standing there and could be whatever color it was; the same was mostly true of the anchor rodes and mooring lines.

By the last of July they were ready to present Jamie and Will with the color-coded ropes---all labeled by use and length. It was a ceremony of sorts after supper one evening. Belle set them in two chairs in the front room and blindfolded the lads, then the twins carefully laid out the ropes in proper order of use from the main mast forward. The black, blue, and green were on the starboard sides, and the violet, orange and red on the port sides. When the lads were allowed to pull off the blindfolds and looked at the display on the floor before them, they were actually in tears they were so overwhelmed by their family's concern and provision.

Lena said, "But that's not all..." to which Mia called, "Olly, George Lawrence?" Out came the other boys with woven fenders for the *Victoria* in red to match her main colors---three for each side, two for the stern, and a bow collar.

Then as if Will and Jamie could have taken more surprises that evening, Harry brought out new mooring lines: on the dock ends were eye-splices for the dock cleats, and side-spliced monkey's fists for heaving the lines.

Then came Aaron and Hipolyta with the pièce de résistance. "Gentlemen, this way if you please..." said Poly and she held her arm toward the back door.

Wiping their eyes and having no idea how this evening could possibly get any better, they walked into the back garden and there behind Aaron, hanging on davits (secured to the ground for presentation) was a dinghy. Not just any dinghy, but one painted in imitation of the *Victoria's* own colors and sporting a yuloh oar setup just like the sampan on which they had been trained.

Will's Dad simply said, "Tada!" and the boys were frozen where they stood. They looked at the boat, looked at their family's smiling faces, and renewed the tears which had not yet completely abated.

Harry added, "Your father and I crafted the davits' mountings to install at the only structurally sound positions on the stern; I hope they won't spoil the sleek lines of the *Victoria*..."

Will and Jamie were now utterly speechless. George Lawrence said, "Even though it started as Lena and Mia's idea... we all helped!" and the twins made deep curtsies to their cousins as a final show of honor to the family's mariners.

They added, "And none of this would have been possible without the consent and assistance of this summer's Assistant Director..." and they motioned for Alouette to come stand near them, "Alouette Backhouse!"

Applause, hugs and kisses followed with cake and ice cream to round it all out as a most successful ceremony. The seamen were up before dawn to cart their new treasures to the dock and begin installations. No one was surprised in the least at their absence from the breakfast table; it had been anticipated. Olly and the twins took a basket of food down to the boat slip before their day's classes and were delighted to see that the davits were already being installed.

Aaron and Harry had been very thorough in their measurements and had not only provided the necessary hardware, but had penciled in the mounting positions, which neither of the lads had noticed until they made a preparatory inspection.

Olly said in parting, "We'll be back this afternoon to help with anything you might need more hands for, but George Lawrence will be down soon with Grandmama anyway." Sure enough, on their walk back up towards campus they passed George Lawrence and Belle heading the other direction.

After they all waved, Mia commented, "Just two weeks of classes left. I sure wish we could have gotten credit for these courses; I think we've done quite well."

Lena and Olly nodded, "Well at least we have college experience, even if there're no transcripts to show for it."

Olly remarked, "I have really enjoyed being in two different classrooms, with two different instructors. It's such a change after so long at the Tahoe School."

Lena added, "A year from September second, we'll even have a change in student populations... I wonder if Mia and I will pick up British accents like Dad did when he was there?"

Olly replied, "Well, whether you do or don't, at least we'll be in the same town and have each other as support. I can't imagine going anywhere without you two, even if my folks *are* there."

That got a squeeze of his hand from each of the young ladies, and a promise of eternal devotion... "No matter what!" they added.

Oliver Henry Bessamer *really* never had a chance, as his aunts and grandmama had observed, but it had never crossed his mind to need one. Their courses were a struggle, in spite of their brave facades; they were the youngest in the lecture halls and it didn't help that they out-performed the enrolled members of the classes. They weren't welcomed with the warm open arms they had at first hoped to encounter. None of the other students bothered to speak to them; nobody invited them to a study group. In fact they were essentially ignored by everyone... except the professors, who were truly delighted to have such capable students. They represented a glimmering promise that maybe the trio's curiosity and intelligence might somehow be infectious. It wasn't.

When they returned that afternoon and neared the boat slip, they could see that the dinghy was hanging proudly from its davits and the lads were just replacing the port and starboard sheets for the jibs---the last of the re-rigging. All the halyards were in place and the mooring ropes had been changed out; Alouette and George Lawrence were sitting in the cockpit and with a pencil and paper in front of him. He was recording ideas for the dinghy's name at christening.

Will called, "How about: the *Donkey*?" George Lawrence wrote that down on the list after *Little 'Un*, *Victoria's Girl*, *The Belle*, *The Poly*, *The BabyKat*, and *Bay-bee*.

Jamie said, "Or maybe the *Mule In Rouge*?" Again George Lawrence began to write the name down, but everyone else was laughing and he suddenly wasn't sure if it was a serious candidate.

He looked up at his cousins, "Why is that funny? A mule is a beast of burden, like a dinghy... except it's not really a beast. And rouge means 'red,' which is the *Victoria's* color; it seems like a very good name!" That just coaxed a few more laughs from the company.

Belle, who was sitting opposite him, explained, "It's also a play on words George Lawrence. There is a famous cabaret in Paris, near where your mother and father defended their friends on one of their visits, that is called the *Moulin Rouge*... it means red windmill."

George Lawrence muttered, "Oh," then insisted, "Well I still think it's a very good name. Besides, a dinghy is for leaving an anchored ship to go ashore... maybe even to have a good time! It is a *very good name!*"

From the bow came two clear voices, "Alright George Lawrence, alright. Mule In Rouge it is."

Jamie added, "And *you* shall break the champagne bottle on her prow at the christening. *What do ya think about that?*"

That one phrase, uttered by Samuel Allcock upon first meeting George all those years ago had become a part of the family's colloquial heritage, and it still elicited chuckles when used appropriately, which it always was.

Still giggling, Lena called, "Permission to come aboard?"

The lads on the foredeck waved them aboard, and Will asked, "What do you three think? She looks better than ever doesn't she?"

Olly nodded and said, "She's brilliant, simply brilliant. Say, when are you planning the christening? That sounds like another excuse for a good party..."

Jamie said, "We thought we'd have it at sea, out on the Bay I mean. Maybe Saturday or Sunday when everyone can come out again. We just haven't decided who should be the first passenger and who the first pilot."

Mia spoke up, "We volunteer! Olly can row us back to shore, or around the *Victoria* a couple times, or whatever you think her maiden voyage should entail, and Alouette should naturally be seated in the bow." Alouette clapped at that.

Will liked that suggestion and Jamie was satisfied, too. "There's just one thing left then," commented Belle, "What should you wear?"

That got another round of laughs; everyone of them were finally realizing how meticulously planned the twins wardrobe actually was, especially after that bow spray incident during the June run on the Bay. To avoid any suspicion that they had *ever* made *any* such particular preparations in apparel (to always look the same age as Oliver) they put on their serious faces and sat with Grandmama Belle to discus their options. George Lawrence couldn't have been less interested and got up to search for the paint can and brush, he wanted to begin the lettering on the *Mule In Rouge*.

The next Sunday, again with fishing gear and picnic baskets in hand, the family went out on the *Victoria* for the christening of her new baby boat. George Lawrence had done a superb job at matching the lettering style from the transom of the *Victoria* in lettering the transom of the *Mule In Rouge*, and also in the same black paint with red shadowing. It really looked good and everyone commenced him for it. When they had gotten a few hundred yards offshore from the marina, the ceremony began. Jamie untethered the dinghy so that it swung free of the *Victoria*.

George Lawrence kneeled over the stern rail and said in a loud voice, "As first mate of the *Victoria*, I christen thee, *Mule In Rouge*!" Then at the same moment, he smashed the champagne bottle against her prow and Jamie let her drop the rest of the way to the water. The company aboard clapped and cheered and were served from an unbroken bottle of champagne by the twins. A series of toasts were made for both the *Victoria* and her new dinghy, as well as for the skippers and first mate. Jamie then lowered the stern fenders and the trio with Alouette descended the boarding ladder to the launch. Olly took up the oar and rowed them around the ship several times to the applause and further cheers of those aboard. When they were ready to re-board, the twins attached the davit cables to her bow and stern and made fast docking lines to the cleats installed for that purpose below the *Victoria*'s transom, and climbed back aboard after Alouette followed by Olly---once he had stowed the oar once more in her sole.

After the *Mule In Rouge* was again secured, Will and Jamie made for an anchorage near San Raphael Bay so that Harry and Aaron could fish. Will went below and came back up carrying a great brass bowl with a shallow lid on top of it. The passengers around the stern could only stare at the object as he mounted it to a receiver on the port stern railing; he lifted the lid and said, "Tada," in a very good imitation of his father. "Captain Thomassen said this was the easiest way to cook aboard ship... so Jamie and I are going to inaugurate it today!"

"It's an oven?" Belle asked.

"It's a grill, Grandmama, and it uses wood, coal or charcoal.

Captain Thomassen suggested charcoal, so we bought a sack of it from the blacksmith in town."

Will pointed, "Look, it has two grates inside: one for the fuel below, and one for the cooking surface---here on top." Then he added a little louder, "Now all we need are some fish!" Harry and Aaron had been listening to the explanation but instantly turned back to their rods and looked busy.

Jamie brought up a bucket and a cutting board that also mounted to the railing next to the grill. "All that's left now is: how do you start the charcoal burning?"

Will was ready for that too, "Captain Thomassen used wadded up newspaper below the charcoal, it seemed to work for him just fine."

Down below, Mia and Lena were assisting their mother with chopping vegetables and slicing fruits for salads. "Mother," Lena asked, "How long is the trip from Tahoe all the way to Redditch?"

"Oh," MamaKat began, "The Overland train is about a five or six day trip to New York, then the Atlantic passage is seven to nine days, then from the docks in Liverpool by train to Redditch is only hours... so anticipate anywhere from twelve to fifteen days as an estimate. Why do you ask dear?"

Mia replied, "We know it's early to begin preparing, but it's one less matter to consider later on as the arrival of Uncle Harold approaches. It's interesting, the longer we have to just think about something, not calculate or anything, just have a thing in our minds, the answers or arrangements or whatever are just there waiting when we need them... Does that make any sense?"

MamaKat smiled, "That's precisely how your father has always used his mind, and how he taught me to use mine. You two have never seemed to need instruction on that score. It's always come as second nature to you. You both are very unique, and if I may say without any symptom of modesty, most extraordinary young women." The twins kissed her cheeks and carried the platters of food up to the dining table mounted in the cockpit. They got George Lawrence and Olly to help with the folding deck chairs, which they arranged on the deck above the companionway in front of the deck house.

At least this time around Harry did catch a fish and it was enough for the entire company. With Aaron on the gaff, they brought aboard a thirty-six pound striper; it took both men to clean it at the rail-side cutting board. Will started the charcoal and by late afternoon no one could eat another bite. The grill was a success. They came back into the marina before evening and were home before sundown---another great day on the Bay.

As September neared, Jamie wrote his father and mother one last letter for the summer, requesting to stay on through the autumn and spring to continue their apprenticeship with Captain Thomassen and study for the licensing examinations. Harry sent along a letter also, with the newspaper clippings and other photographs of the *Victoria* and her skippers. When they arrived back in Tahoe to bring Alouette for her first year at school, and hopefully for Jamie to pack up his other necessities for staying in Berkeley, Jameson and Titania met them at the Tavern Station with a large sign reading: "*Temporary housing* for the Skippers of the *Victoria*: This Way." Will and Jamie could not have been more jubilant.

Alouette was shown to her room, Jamie's room, which had been redecorated for a young girl's tastes. She was so thrilled with her new quarters she exclaimed, "Oh MamaTania, this is as wonderful as my room back home. Thank you, thank you, thank you," and she started putting all her things into drawers and arranging pictures on the bureau, setting out her shoes and the hundred other things little girls are wont to do when playing houses. Poly was just as tickled with her sister's careful preparations.

"I am so glad that you get to have a girl in your house for a change. And if you decide she needs to learn to ride a horse, or roll in the garden as well as you... be my guest. My daughter is your daughter," and tears were welling up in her eyes. Titania was just as affected and they sobbed their mutual joy on each other's shoulders before returning to join the rest of the family downstairs.

Jamie had mixed emotions about the transition and his father took him aside for a chat. "I know you would like to have the entire world at your fingertips right now, but like the saying goes, sometimes you can't have your cake and eat it too. Alouette is overjoyed to be in her cousin Jamie's old room and you will always have a home here... just not in that room while Alouette is in school."

Jamie felt better, "I know all that, but it's one thing to know something and another thing entirely to experience it. I guess I'm just growing up a bit all of a sudden."

His father replied, "I don't think there's anything sudden about your aging, son. Your mother and I have had to anticipate your leaving the nest ever since you and Will and Olly spent all your time that last year in school on the Tahoe sailing. You and Will will do magnificently in your plans for the *Victoria*. Your mother and I do have one request, however..."

"Name it, Dad," Jamie answered without reservation.

"When you *do* go on a circumnavigation, we'd like to go along. I can cook, you know, and your mother can do just about anything except not be near her son on a grand adventure. Deal?" Jameson held out his hand.

Jamie took it and gripped it firmly, "Deal!"

Aaron and Hipolyta prepared to return to Berkeley with Will and Jamie. They had just said their goodbyes to George and Belle, when Kaitlyn and Harry came to walk them to the station. "You'll probably have your hands full for a bit," Kaitlyn began, "but if you get around to it..." and she handed Poly a roll of plans for three more projects around Tahoe. "There are a number of wealthy folks moving up to this area and our reputation has preceded us. Just get back to me when you can with these. There are two new residences in very picturesque locations, and one renovation---the Goodman

Clothiers."

Harry asked for an invitation to come down to Berkeley and go out on the Bay with Aaron again in the autumn sometime and hopefully in the spring. Aaron gave each of them a hug in farewell, they boarded the train and were off.

For the trio, the autumn passed quickly while they were busy with not only the continuing studies, but also the widening range of responsibilities they were now given. The twins spent school hours assisting Becky with the younger children, whose numbers had increased as younger families moved into the area. In the afternoons after school they managed the Mercantile's inventories and special orders. On the weekends they served at the *Concession* for the early risers through to the lunch crowd, which left them Saturday and Sunday afternoons for their only moments of recreation. Kaitlyn occupied that time often with their piano practice or gardening chores.

Oliver was as busy as his counterparts with tasks and chores for the Lodges, deliveries for the *Concession's* growing catering activities and weekends he went with Jameson and Harry to tend horses in the Connor pastures, sometimes bringing back stock for the Livery. Now, these full schedules weren't *specifically* designed to give the trio time apart, it just happened that the three of them were not in each other's company save at evening meals at the home on the hill.

By the time the holidays arrived, the Livingsons and Connors were far more interested in staying indoors, reading and inventing games and toys. One long afternoon, Oliver and George Lawrence sat in Harry's workshop building a model airplane from balsa and paper with twin propellers driven by rubber bands. The trick in flying it was getting the 'engines' tuned with the same number of turns. Encouraged by this experiment, Mia and Alouette made a wheeled vehicle, also rubber band driven, and Lena fashioned a flying machine that resembled both previous models, with a large horizontal propeller. When they flew Lena's contraption, it fluttered around the main room erratically until Olly and Mia added a lateral secondary propeller to keep it from gyrating quite so much.

Chess, Chinese Checkers and Reversi were the strategy games played most often, games of chance simply weren't very interesting to them. A good series of backgammon certainly held the whole family's interest, as did charades and other parlor games. The 'dictionary game' was only fun if Harry didn't play... he knew more obscure words than should be right for a person. They took turns reading from world history texts, sometimes trying to imagine themselves in this or that epoch: what would they eat, how would they get from place to place, what would they wear... all the questions which could spark their interest in some otherwise stale descriptive passages. Then there were all of Harry and Kaitlyn's trade journals filled with engineering and architectural designs, drawings and constructions. So building models of the grander designs was on the list of favored pastimes as well.

By late February when the days became a little brighter and longer, but the snow was still thick on the ground, they ventured out onto the hillsides on sleds or large boiler lids---essentially shallow bowls that were a bit more treacherous because they couldn't be steered. They even erected a loop line strung between blocks on the storage shed at the top and to a tree at the bottom of their favorite hill so that they could slide back up the hill instead of climbing. That really became popular after Harry added a small electric motor and geared it to continuously loop the line. All a sledder needed to do was hold onto the ascending line until they reached the top of the hill again then let go. When the snows finally began disappearing, the former schedule of responsibilities resumed, but the fond memories of that winter lingered through the spring.

Uncle Harold wrote to say that he would be arriving a little later than planned... everything was fine, no worries... he just wanted to come over on the maiden voyage of the newest White Star Line ship, the *Celtic* (II). The return was scheduled to leave New York on the twelfth of August, and could he meet the trio in Buffalo; there wouldn't be enough room in the schedule for him to make the trip all the way to Tahoe and back. Olly was delighted at the delay, as it meant a few more excursions on the *Victoria*, and the twins were happy that he'd have time with fellows he knew before being thrust into making new male friends.

When Will and Jamie got back to Berkeley, they headed right down to the marina. Captain Thomassen was on his skiff mending nets; he offered a wry smile and said, "She's still where you left her, lads." The boys weren't self-conscious of their excitement in the least and asked when the captain might go out with them next.

"I've been considering our junkets..." he began, and his tone boded ill to the boys' ears. They winced involuntarily as the captain continued, "...it seems to me a bloody waste of my time to babysit you two on the *Victoria* until you've accumulated the regulated time asea..."

Now it was really sounding hopeless. "So, I've come to a decision." They held their breath for the coup de grace... "You two pass that paper test they give and I'll sign off your hour logs. I've sailed with the finest mates on three oceans and most of the seas, and I never encountered such natural born mariners as you two. How does that sound to you?"

There was only the sound of pelicans and gulls to answer him; the boys were astonished. He added quickly, misjudging their silence, "I know it's not *exactly* copacetic, but the licensing board doesn't know you as I do and haven't seen you sail as I have. Once you take me out in a storm and show me you can handle yourselves like sailors. Then, I'll sign off on you."

Will spoke first, "Captain Thomassen, we will not disappoint you! We still have some studying to do for the test... really technical stuff mostly about international regulations, but we *will* pass that test..."

Jamie enjoined, "Bet your life on that!"

"Good it's settled then," replied the captain. "You fellas keep coming down here every morning and we're bound to have some inclement weather before the month's out."

Will and Jamie shook his hand on the deal and went aboard to make some modifications they'd considered while away. Jamie proposed a method of color coding the jib halyards so they could reach for the correct one every time and he pulled colored waxed thread from his duffle to begin that addition. Will had a hint from Uncle Harry that he was interested in fitting the *Victoria* with a wind generator so she could sport the required lighting they'd need in blue water cruising. He just wanted to have all the measurements for a generator mast on the stern, the wiring to the masts' spreaders, the bow and running lights all written and diagramed to sorta remind his uncle of his once mentioned thoughts. The evening was coming on and they had to wait to complete the rest of their activities in the morning. After checking the fender heights and mooring ropes one last time, they headed home for supper and to tell their folks about Captain Thomassen's offer.

In preparation, they constructed two drogues and a bridle for the stern. They practiced reefing the main and foresails, and were again appreciative of the color-coded halyards their cousins made for the *Victoria*. They found sou'westers and converted one of the lazarettes for just storm gear. The *Mule In Rouge* was measured and fitted with a cover to keep her from getting swamped while on the davits, then while they were in covering mode they made a few others. The hatches got fitted covers as well as the winches---those weren't actually for a storm, but for long mooring spells. They rechecked all the seals around the companionway and hatches, then caulked and varnished where needed.

In a flash of insight during a test run, Jamie asked, "Won't the deck be even slipperier with the rain and the higher waves? Remember when we went climbing with our mothers and we always had a belay line in case of a missed hand or foothold..."

Will was on that thought like a bird on a june bug. He clapped Jamie on the back and grinned, "We can rig a constant belay to a running block on the main topmast stay and leave enough line to get to the far stern and the far bow; we might fall overboard, but we'll have a built-in life-line already. You are brilliant, sir... Brilliant!"

"We can clip onto belts on the outside of our raincoats and won't even have to give them another thought, except not to get tangled in the forestays. Otherwise there shouldn't be any hinderance to going anywhere on deck! Let's rig them and try 'em. This could even be fun!" Jamie added excitedly. They did just that, and they were still adjusting the lines to the 'perfect' lengths when another evening caught up to them.

An afternoon storm did indeed blow in a week or so later. They were coming up from the lower San Francisco Bay after sailing to San Mateo beach, when darkening skies to the north heralded an oncoming autumn storm. There are always choices to be made. How much time does one have before a storm eliminates some of those choices? That was the real question. If they ran for a harbor below Alameda, they *might* make it to safety, but if they misjudged the travel time they couldn't make it into the harbor safely without hitting something, *and* they'd still be under sail and have to reef or douse sails in that instant. They could begin reefing now, keep the *Victoria's* prow pointed up at the storm by setting the series drogues then just wait it through. Or, they could beach the *Victoria* and never go to sea again---well *that* just wasn't going to happen. While they disagreed on the precise time it would take to make Alameda, they agreed that reefing and setting a sea anchor was inevitable. That's what they did.

The stern bridle was fitted and the drogues were deployed, then they began taking down canvas: topsails, followed by reefing main and foresails. At last all but the fore jib was left, which Jamie trimmed and ran the sheet back to the cockpit. With their sou'westers on, they clipped onto the belay lines and waited. Captain Thomassen had remained silent through their deliberations and preparations; he just filled his pipe and took a seat in the port stern... watching them as calmly as you please.

When the lads were finally seated near him and the first pelting drops hit their faces, he said simply, "As the old saying goes, 'The first time you think of reducing sail you should, and when you think you are ready to take out a reef, have a cup of tea instead,' Well done lads, you might not have to put on a pot for tea just yet, but you can get out the pot and secure it to the stovetop. Good practice being below decks during a blow... *scary*, but good practice."

The cockpit was self-bailing. After four hours or so, the storm abated; a cold north wind blew crisp on its heels. Captain Thomassen smiled at the lads and said, "Now, about that cup of tea...?"

A package arrived for the lads a week and a half before Thanksgiving. Whether Will's diagrams for wiring were necessary or not, Uncle Harry hadn't forgotten about the wind generator he'd contemplated. They opened the package and stared at the components for the device. Aaron reached in and pulled up a sheaf of papers. On the cover was a note: *Gentlemen, I thought it would be best if you assembled this yourselves, as I will likely not be around if it should require repair at sea. Always know your ship and its equipment! Uncle Harry*

Aaron smiled; he turned to the next page and the next. They were filled with detailed assembly drawings and specifications. Hipolyta asked if they wanted her help with the puzzle Uncle Harry had sent for them, to which Will and Jamie replied, "No, Uncle's right. We'll figure this out and we'll know it as well as if we'd designed it ourselves, or we won't install it."

Fortunately, Harry also told them where to obtain batteries locally, as well as how and where to best install them below deck. The next several days were spent putting the generator together and taking it apart again. The local battery supplier had already received a letter of introduction from Uncle Harry about the boys' requirements and the proper selections and quantities were waiting for them when they arrived. The proprietor then showed them a lamp configuration of his own design: he had replaced the kerosene reservoir and wick in the bottom of a brass sea lamp with a socket and bulb, a very clean design and weather-proof. He then pointed them to a lantern shop just down the street, "The owner and I have the same interests and you can get the sockets from him as well," he added with a wave.

Jamie mounted the bank of batteries under the mid-ships salon seating and installed the light control panel over the navigation station across from the galley. Will was still trying to figure out how to run the wiring through the ship and also up to the spreaders so that it wouldn't impede any of the rigging. It also had to be accessible for repair when needed. He brought up the topic at dinner that evening and got more suggestions than he bargained for---some were even good ideas. When all was said and done, thin-walled copper tubing was the choice which met all their criteria of: waterproof connections and joints, ease of running wire, easy access, nominally light weight and as Hipolyta said---'pretty.' On top of all that, mounting hardware for copper pipe didn't need to be re-invented, just purchased in quantity and installed. Which they did.

The wind generator-trickle charger, or 'aero-dynamo' as Jamie and Will liked to call it, was mounted on its own short mast above the starboard stern rail next to the starboard davit, and the little streamlined propellers whirred in any breezes strong enough in which to sail. On the eve of Thanksgiving day, the family went down to the marina. Will and Jamie went aboard. Will went below and threw the main switch for all the lights at once; the dock and surrounding waters were aglow all around the perimeter of the *Victoria*... it was a glorious sight.

When January was nearly February, their results came back from the San Francisco Regional office of the National Maritime Center. Aaron and Hipolyta were prepared and truthfully it was hard to say who was watching for the mail more closely and with more anticipation. When William Henry Backhouse and James White Feathers Connor opened their letters and held up their certificates, they were each 'crowned' with captain's hats and a celebration, which had long been anticipated, began and lasted into the night. The event was immortalized in photographs, speeches and a poem Aaron had prepared. Jamie and Will slept very well... once they could at last go to sleep.

When the end of May rolled around, the captains had already hosted a dozen excursions for college age folk and tourists on day-cruises up and down the length of the San Francisco Bay and San Pablo Bay. They had even been hired for delivering newlyweds to their honeymoon cottage on Bodega Bay. One of the additions to the *Victoria* as a result of her frequent pleasure trips and request's from so many female passengers for deck shade was the construction of a bimini frame. The boom crutch between the davits provided a solid stern frame, so the captains duplicated that construction in two more positions culminating over the companionway. They sewed up a canvas cover which could be furled and lashed at the peak, or unfurled all the way down the sides and tied off like a tent. The *Victoria* was rapidly becoming a very popular local attraction and Professor and Mrs. Backhouse were their best promoters.

All their Tahoe family arrived at the end of the term, including Jameson and Titania, Grandmama and PapaGeorge---they just shut down the Mercantile, *Concession* and Lodges for a couple weeks to come and celebrate the mariners' accomplishments. The *Victoria* had carried up to eighteen passengers before, so fifteen with a few of them as crew wasn't a problem at all. As soon as everyone was settled in, they would take them out on the Bay. This was to be a special excursion under a full moon; it was their first overnight on the water with their family.

Belle and George were shown to the port forward stateroom and next to them, in the starboard forward stateroom were Harry and Kaitlyn, a head and sink were between those cabins just as there was between the aft cabins. In those were Aaron and Poly, next to Jameson and Tania. Becky had the saloon bunk, and the kids would be able to sling hammocks wherever they wished. Will and Jamie acquired the hammocks from a merchant on Fisherman's Wharf who had a plethora of gear and equipment from the clipper ship trades. The woven yucatan hammocks were very easily stored and came in handy, not just for numerous sleeping accommodations, but also for holding cargo below when necessary. The kids were delighted and each tried to locate their own 'best' spot to sling their bed.

Before dusk, with the *Victoria* anchored off the islands in San Raphael Bay, her captains lowered the *Mule In Rouge* for little runs to the nearby beaches. Jamie and Will had filled their freshwater tanks and stocked the galley, so the family was well-provisioned for a much longer voyage if they wished. The adults on the decks were enjoying drinking and snacking, swapping stories and sing-a-longs, while the younger generation walked the beaches, or swam in the warmer shallow waters between the two islands. It was a clear night so the brightness of the moon was sufficient to illuminate the deck and surrounding waters without needing to turn on the ship's lighting to see well. However, the mast lights had to be turned on as a courtesy to other sailing vessels, so the family members on the beach always had sight of the *Victoria* as they walked, splashed and explored the little shores.

The tide was out which exposed enough sand for George Lawrence and Alouette to build castles, Olly and the twins searched for unique shells and driftwood, while Jamie walked the shore with Becky and talked about their very different experiences over the last spring. As the moon rode higher, they all gathered back on the boat. The kids got situated in their hanging cocoons, the trio were stacked between the two masts, Alouette was comfortably situated in the dinghy with cushions and blankets, George Lawrence, Jamie, and Will slung their hammocks beneath the bimini frame. Their uncles, aunts, and grandparents went below just sitting with each other, sometimes telling stories, sometimes just sitting quietly together. Gradually all the crew and passengers drifted off to bed and sleep.

Will and Jamie setup the grill in the morning and prepared sausages and boiled eggs, then set up the cockpit table for a buffet. Once the adults began to stir, Jamie went below and started the unending coffee production. Early morning swims were the morning attraction for all, with a good freshwater rinse off at the bow when they came back aboard. The sun was rising warm over the north bay and the day promised further adventure. After the meal was finished and everything was stowed, the *Victoria* headed for Sausalito. They moored in the marina and walked the streets, window shopped, enjoyed a late lunch at a marina-side cafe, then boarded the *Victoria* and headed to the San Mateo beaches. They spent another very enjoyable and comfortable overnight anchored off the beach and the captains were even more proud of their ship as a voyaging vessel.

George Lawrence stayed in Berkeley with his cousins when the rest of the Livingsons returned to Tahoe for the twins and Olly to pack for their departure. Oliver had grown taller and like the other men in his family, Samuel and Harold, he already had the beginnings of whiskers which he kept shaved close. He had to buy new boots for his growing feet and two new suits were purchased at Goodman's. Olly's growth spurt finally made him just a bit taller than the twins and they were relieved that now they could dress as the young women they were grown to be.

The evening before they were to board the next morning's train, Kaitlyn had them dress in their traveling clothes, pack their trunks and pose for photographs. Harry and Kaitlyn were so proud and impressed with their 'children,' their manner, demeanor and appearance were those of very capable young adults, but even that didn't make it easier to see them off on the train and say farewell for who knew how long.

They were provided with enough cash in hand to comfortably accommodate their travels and situation in Malvern. Harry sat down with them and explained the family's assets and what he and Kat had made ready for their children's schooling. Mia and Lena were informed of the access they had to additional funds while away and they promised to be wise with their expenditures, and as frugal as they had been raised to be. All the preparations having been made, Harry and Kat, George and Belle waved goodbye as the train chugged off toward Truckee and their connection with the Overland

Route train to Omaha, then to Chicago, and on to Niagara Falls near Buffalo. There they would join Oliver's father, Harold, and on to New York City and the *Celtic* for Liverpool and Redditch. The Miss Livingsons were the picture of elegance and they carried themselves with pride and dignity, as did Oliver in his new suit, boots and hat. They were a very attractive little group, always together and always cordial and courteous to the other passengers.

The four and a half days to Buffalo went by quickly. When not at meals, they were in one or the other's cabins studying or just reading to each other. The mountains of the west gave way to the prairies of the great mid-west and it all rumbled passed their windows, each of them were personally whelmed by the un-bounded immensity of the land that was the America of their birth. When the train arrived in Buffalo, Harold was on the platform awaiting them. Lena and Oliver descended from the carriage first as Mia directed the porters to their cabins and trunks. They noticed Harold still looking up and down the passenger cars trying to catch sight of them. When Mia joined her companions, they casually strolled toward Olly's father with the intention of passing behind him; still he had not noticed them. Once passed, they halted and in a louder and deeper voice than his father knew he had, Olly initiated a conversation about the possible direction of the Falls from the station with Lena, who responded, also in a louder than necessary voice, and then Mia chimed in, matching their volume. Harold caught a bit of the dialog and knowing how best to direct *these tourists* behind him, he turned to offer advice. He looked Oliver in the eyes and stopped. He looked at the twins and a grin spread across his features as a laugh erupted inside him. "I was looking for children! How foolish was that?!"

Oliver tipped his hat and the ladies curtsied as Harold stood back and got a good look at the three of them. He was trying to believe his own eyes... his son was near grown, dressed for business or travel, the cut of his suit disguised his swayed left leg so he looked every bit the dapper young collegiate And Lena and Mia were already the very image of the beautiful women their mother and grandmama were---and, he noted, dressed to accentuate their femininity. He sighed and extended his arm to one of the twins. (Still, after all these years, it was only Harry, MamaKat and Oliver who could reliably tell the twins apart.)

He explained as they led the porters to the waiting carriage, "I think you will enjoy the Falls very much indeed. I have only seen them myself once before, and I am anxious to view that grandeur again. We have rooms near there, so we can take our time: have a lovely supper and be off on the morning train for New York and the Celtic which sails the day after tomorrow."

Once the trunks were installed in their rooms they made the short trip out to the Falls. Just as Harry had been so breath-takingly impressed all those years ago, each of them carried away their own lasting memories of the extraordinary force and majesty of the natural wonder that was Niagara. They purchased post cards and after writing encouraging notes to their folks back home, sent them off in the post for Tahoe. Dinner was delicious and before they retired that evening, Harold commented again upon their poise and sophistication, adding that he was most honored to be accompanying them upon their voyage to England.

They arrived mid-day at the Chelsea House, after taking a carriage ride through the Central Park. Their family history in this place was almost palpable; Mia and Lena went to every special nook and room of which they had been told all their lives. They were even staying in their father and mother's room, naturally---the Spelman and Allcock apartments of the Chelsea. They ate at a charming restaurant which Harold had discovered after his arrival days earlier and then walked the lighted streets and avenues until it was quite late and they had to retire to get a fresh start in the morning.

The *Celtic* was boarding when they arrived at the pier; they were whisked to their staterooms and installed well before the ship was to sail in the afternoon. They made an inventory of the shops, boutiques, salons, sitting rooms and dining rooms as they followed

Harold on an initial tour of their decks. The *Celtic* was a massively enormous ship and its accommodations were luxurious and extensive. Each of their cabins had its own bathroom and views of the ocean from their windows. The staircases between decks rivaled any they had seen in grand hotels and there was always music playing.

The twins dressed for dinner in the first dresses they had not made themselves. When they emerged from their rooms to join the men, they caused every head to turn as they walked to meet them. Even Oliver, who had known them from birth, stared with his mouth almost agape. Their evening gowns were high-waisted and low-cut, their hair was piled in curls up on their heads and their slippers, barely showing beneath the hems of their dresses, sparkled when the light caught them. They had spent nearly an hour applying make-up, in an effort to appear as though they weren't wearing any, and the effect was stunning. Each of them took an arm of one of the Bessamer men and they entered the dining room, where again, heads turned.

As the evening grew into a starlit wonderland of sea and sky, they strolled the deck and listened to the waves and last cries of the seabirds. Music from the halls below wafted into the night air, and Oliver hummed along with it as they walked, then added words to the odd melody:

> *Full fathom five thy father lies;*
> *Of his bones are coral made;*
> *Those are pearls that were his eyes;*
> *Nothing of him that doth fade,*
> *But doth suffer a sea-change*
> *Into something rich and strange.*
> *Sea-nymphs hourly ring his knell:*
> *Ding-dong.*
> *Hark! now I hear them — Ding-dong, bell.*

Lena cooed, "How enchanting Ariel's song is once set to a melody."

Mia asked, "Has PapaHarold retired for the night?"

Oliver nodded that he had. Lena asked, "Are you willing to stay up and walk with us a while?" Again he nodded and continued to hum.

Mia asked, "Did we overdo our outfits this evening? We simply wanted to be *very* feminine tonight."

Oliver shook his head and assured them they did not overdo anything. "You know you can't really help but be *very* feminine---even if you had worn potato sacks!" They giggled and held his arms closer, squeezing him between them as they walked.

After a long silence, Lena asked, "Oliver, why haven't you ever kissed us?"

Oliver smiled and said simply, "When I figure out how to kiss you both at the same time... you shall be properly kissed."

Again they giggled and put their heads on his broadening shoulders, contented to be together, joyous in the knowledge they were loved and respected by the young man they had always adored.

The daily activities of the *Celtic* were as various as they were in any small town. They enjoyed shuffleboard and quoits and spent hours in the billiards rooms. Sitting in deck chairs outside their cabins and reading was also a very pleasant distraction. Harold had to remark a few days into the journey, "Do you three ever separate? I have yet to see you apart for any more than a few minutes at a time."

Lena answered seriously, "We do not bathe, dress, sleep nor poop together... we are apart constantly!"

She kept as straight a face as she could manage, as did the other two until Harold finally laughed realizing she had just tried to be humorous and accurate at the same time---and had succeeded. He let the topic alone. If they wished to always be in their own company, more power to them; it was going to be difficult enough at college without their being forced apart for any reason now. Chloe had made some mention of their penchant for each other's company a long time ago; he had just presumed it would wear off with age... it didn't.

At breakfast the final day before arriving into port, Harold began a conversation about what each of them were intending to ultimately study. Oliver said he would very much like to pursue a medical degree and either work in a general practice, or become a ship's physician. Mia and Lena responded by saying that while they were leaning toward the medical sciences also, they were equally drawn to the craft of naval architecture. Harold had not expected any of those responses and sat silently with this new information. At last he asked, "To what schools, then, would you apply after your undergraduate work is complete?"

They answered at almost the same moment, "Liverpool Nautical College and University of Liverpool---the Victoria University." After some chuckling and giggling, "We will be in Manchester, or Liverpool for a few years after Malvern. If we study hard and schedule everything carefully, we will be graduating at the same time and shall embark upon our careers---and with luck, will still be--- together."

Harold raised his brows, "Well, it seems you have done your research and are set for the next several years, at least." He mused over the notion that they were setting their sights on Liverpool, and thought aloud, "I wonder if Salford, Greengate is still owned by old man Waterhouse? I'll have to do some checking..."

Chloe and Hannah were waiting at the docks when the *Celtic* arrived and passengers began disembarking. Hannah was slightly taller than her mother and the twins were the same height as Hannah. They held each other at arm's length after initial embraces.

Hannah remarked, "You two look exactly like MamaKat! And look at my little brother---who doesn't look so little anymore!"

Oliver grinned and hugged his sister and his mother, again. "It is good to be here, it really is. We have so looked forward to this, I can't tell you how much!"

Harold directed the trunks to be loaded onto the trolleys for the station across the tarmac and went in to arrange ticketing to Redditch. When he rejoined his family, Chloe was just saying, "...so we have been at Clive House this summer, father and Olivia are so excited to have the next generation of Livingsons at their home, they are just beside themselves. We actually live practically next door, so it is up to you whether to stay with them or at our home for the few days before you leave for Malvern."

Oliver surprised his mother by saying that 'they' would be happy to stay with Grandpapa and Olivia over the next few days and that "...We really look forward to spending all our holidays at the Bessamer House." Chloe instantly realized that the three of them were still an inseparable trio as much as they were as children. The twins and Hannah began their own conversation about Malvern Girls' College, its buildings, the classes, the other students, the teachers, the clubs...

Harold was pleased to say that he'd checked in withthe headmaster and found that Oliver would be in Number Four, "...The blue and white---just as I was. Traditions are so refreshingly British at times. It has been a revelation to your mother and I just how much we took for granted when we were growing up here. Now we look around and wonder at all the curious habits and traditions of the people and institutions... everywhere we turn. Well, at least some of them are good and most are harmless in themselves."

A rumbling vibrated through the benches upon which they were sitting and a whistle split through the cacophony of the station and platforms. "Here we are, this is our train," and they boarded for Redditch and their home away from home. Mia and Lena were holding Olly's arms throughout their welcome and it was apparent to Hannah that nothing short of stuffing her brother in a closet would keep her dear friends from his side. She smiled and sighed. They were her sisters too, after all, and now they would all be together again, here in Redditch, there in Malvern and everywhere in between."

"Well, this is a curious turn of events, but it takes all kinds..." the young host remarked. His guest looked at him with an interested shift of her eyes.

"In what way *curious?*" she inquired.

He wondered if he'd spoken out of turn or something, "I mean about the twins and Oliver... that they are... well, a trio, not a couple---but three behaving like a couple---It's just unusual is all... you know, not what most people think of as normal."

"That's silly! Do you know *most people?* Or what those 'most people' *actually* think?" She asked candidly.

"No, of course not. I neither know 'most people,' *nor* even what the relatively few people I think I know---I don't know what they think..." He made a quick review of why he'd made the comment at all. "I suppose I meant that..." and he couldn't put any reason to what he thought he meant either. "Did I just repeat what I've heard from someone else? Is that how it feels when one actually examines an assumption? That if it trips off the tongue so easily, like 'conventional wisdom,' or what 'they say,' it is likely to pale in the face of reason?" He was a little sheepish about this subject because the more thought he gave it, the more he realized how very saturated he was with it.

She asked a few questions in response, "Why is lying considered to be sometimes necessary, but always a 'sin'? How can something actually necessary be an error? Why does one society or culture feel absolutely certain a given action is taboo, while another perhaps even neighboring society or culture not give the same action a moment's thought? How can what is 'good' and 'bad' be so relative depending upon whom you ask?" She had posed some basic ethical and moral conundrums, which could be debated ad infinitum, but she continued, "Objectively, there is good and bad. However, it is not the same as these presumed ethical and supposed moral judgements would seem to be. Good is what advances our work, bad is what impedes our work---and each of us make subjective determinations about that objective criteria. The rest of what occurs around us, well, *it just is...* all will be shown for its true worth in time."

When she said it that way, he had to wonder why that wasn't generally accepted as obvious. Then he considered that objectivity itself wasn't generally available because most people functioned without the benefit of knowing how they themselves were constructed and were supposed to function. That without an objective measure, verifiable and capable of repeatable experiment and practice, all that anyone was left with was: speculation, conjecture, hearsay and guess---superstition, blind faith---personal abdications of the efforts necessary to know, to be able to be and to do.

She watched him as he was thinking and a small but perceptible smile was just rising at the corners of her mouth. He noticed and asked, "What? Oh... I think I see what you are saying."

"It is a boon *to be able* to actually think; is it not?" she began, "Probably a good practice to employ... actually thinking, I mean."

He had to smile in return at that. "I'll get there. Someday..." he promised himself that. Then he remembered the question he wanted to bring up before his 'that's curious' statement. "Earlier you said 'nature abhors a vacuum,' and even before that I remember when you were talking about influences and how to deal with them... you talked about filling the space intentionally. Would you speak to that a bit more?"

She responded genuinely. "Certainly. How about another experiment? Are you up to that?" He nodded and said aloud that he was. "Good, I could just tell you but it will likely be of more benefit if you actually learn it for yourself." She paused to be sure they were in agreement. "Take a piece of paper, and you'll make a list." He did so, waiting with his pencil poised. "Write down in a few words or a couple phrases, a description of each of the *most* memorable *and* powerfully inspiring instances you can remember encountering in your life to date. Now, it doesn't matter how long is the list, what matters is that *each* of the events you briefly record on that list are *potent* for you *personally*. That just thinking about each of them, helps you to relive it and invigorates you in the present. Do those sound like clear enough directions?"

He finished writing the instructions, reread them aloud and agreed that he did, in fact, understand what he was to do. "And this experiment will help to answer the question I had about what you meant by filling the space?"

"It will be a good first step in that direction... Shall we pick up our story after your assignment? I don't want to inhibit your getting the answers you seek..." She looked solicitously at him.

"I would like that, thank you." He jotted his first entry on his list and she rose to leave. "Will you be back tomorrow then?"

She said reassuringly, "I will return when needed." He smiled, satisfied and turned back to his list.

J. L. LAWSON

8

Equipoise

*"The man who has sufficient power over himself to wait until his nature has recovered its
even balance is the truly wise man, but such beings are seldom met with."*
---Giacomo Casanova

The afternoon's brief warmth was breaking the grip of the morning's chill and he rose and stretched from his seat on the porch. The afternoon and evening before had been productive and this morning proved no different. The list he'd compiled was rather extensive, but as he looked over it then reviewed each event, he was invigorated and satisfied that he had indeed done as requested. When he came out on the porch that morning and she had not shown up as usual, he was anxious for only a moment or two until he picked up his list and went over it again thinking he might be able to add to it. He was still reviewing his life and making changes to the list when he reached for his coffee cup and realized it was empty. Then he noticed that it was well after noon and that the few pangs of anxiety he'd felt much earlier hadn't plagued him in the least since then.

When he came back out, with a glass of iced coffee, he heard a familiar tune being whistled and getting louder from the lane to town. In no time there was his guest walking at a brisk pace with her shoulders back, ringing out a melody in the high pitches of a whistle that from her sounded like an instrument of some kind and less like just her lips and air. His foot tapped along with the tempo, at first without his realizing it, then he was happy to let it tap... it was an evocative tune after all.

"Welcome," he said as she stepped onto the porch. She smiled and nodded in return as she assumed her seat. He jiggled his glass and asked if she would like some as well, which she accepted.

"I have quite the list and I must say it has been very worthwhile to review my life finding them." He handed her a glass and continued. "I unearthed some very troubling memories as well, some tragic, some for which I have a great deal of remorse... all in all, a good exercise. Now what?"

"What you have been assembling are the constituents of your own 'objective prayer.' It's purpose is to raise your state of being the same way that..." and she stopped suddenly, realizing he hadn't been told of the 'other' exercise. "I was about to say: in the same way that the exercise called, 'Where am I on a scale of one to ten,' allows a person to raise their state of being, but I suddenly remembered that I don't think you were told about that..."

He was instantly interested, "No, I haven't. What is that one?"

"Pick a number between one and ten, where one is the least 'together' you have ever felt---the least collected if you will, and ten is the greatest experience of wholeness and unity you have ever felt. The number you choose is actually rather immaterial, it's not a measure of your worth or anything... it's a starting point. Let's say I am at a 'five,' for the sake of explanation. The task for me then is to get to a 'six.' What must I do in my inner world to raise my state to the next level?

Very often a change of posture, a few deep breaths and a realization of my purpose and my intent will suffice to make me more collected, more re-membered than I was a moment before. Once at a 'six,' the question becomes: do I try for a 'seven'? Then further efforts must be made. I might have to look at myself and my inner participation... Is all of me involved? Are there 'I's that do not think they also need to participate? I find I must be the master of my own machine and call all of myself into participation, from my little toes to my ears, from my idle thoughts to my most deliberate mentations, from my blandest moods to my most piercing emotions. Then with all of me in concert, and directed at unity... I reach a 'seven.' And the question arises again: do I try for an 'eight'? What now must I do to achieve this next step?"

Her words had gradually gained the force of the content she was conveying and when she paused, the air was almost electric. "So your objective prayer can assist you in this raising of your state. What you must do, however, is to arrange the experiences you have recorded into a series which will provide the most impact when recalled in a certain order or arrangement. Therefore you will want that list to be pared down to only the *most* potent, the *most* beneficial for the task at hand. Can you reduce it to a list of say, six or seven truly memorable and potent instances. Those which elicit in you a thorough participation of sense, feeling, thought and even posture?"

He looked over his list and began reviewing it from this new perspective. As she had explained the 'one to ten' exercise, he had silently enacted it for himself as she did and he was also in a much higher place in himself than even when she arrived... and that had been pretty collected---for him at least. She gazed across the pond, and marked the flight of a pair of hawks as he worked on the challenge. She hummed softly to herself and was, it seemed, quite satisfied to sit there all day, quiet and patient if need be.

After almost an hour, he said aloud, "Okay, here are six which for me are the most personally involving... as you suggested.

She said, "Now that you have them, practice them in various orders until you hit upon an order that really resonates; that when repeated produces the most 'bang for the buck,' so to speak. You will find that by intentionally occupying your mind---filling the space that is going to be filled anyway, whether mechanically or otherwise---you shall begin to return again and again to wanting to fill that space yourself and not allow just anything to occupy it. You will develop a *taste* for intention that will not be satisfied in any other way."

He was empowered and would have begun at once to pursue this exercise, but she asked, "We have but a little left of this part of our story, for today that is, would you like to continue and explore your newfound experiments after while? 'With every push there comes a pause'."

He looked at her with sincere affection and answered, "I would be delighted to continue. Thank you very much!"

"Very well then..." and she picked up the story once more.

"After three years of very constant sailing, and even though her skippers were especially diligent in her upkeep, the *Victoria* was due for a good repainting and refitting. The harbormaster recommended a very good and thorough company to do the dry docking and prep work, knowing the young mariners would want to do most of the work themselves. A couple months off their busy schedule was a small price to pay for the maintenance due the old girl. That was the spring before the Malvernians would be Leavers at the end of summer and head on to graduate studies in Liverpool as they'd planned.

Harold *had* made contact with the Waterhouse firm and asked after the Greengate house, "We're sorry Mr. Bessamer," they apologized, "If you had solicited for that residence just a few months ago, we might have come to equitable terms, but we're afraid it has been purchased..."

Harold began the search for other suitable quarters for his University-bound charges. All the girls were leaving Malvern Girls College with the honors they had dutifully earned, and Hannah was ready to pursue medicine just as Olly intended to do. The Commemoration ceremonies arrived mid-summer as scheduled and surprises all around lay in store.

Lawrence and Miranda came up from Venice, leaving the Inn in the capable hands of Gio and Varrissa. They were determined to add their cheers to those of Harold and Chloe's at the graduation of the young Bessamers and Livingsons. During the pre-ceremony events, and most specifically the ball the evening before, Hannah and the twins threw themselves into fully looking the part of grown women fresh from a long college career. They arrived at Malvern College's Pavilion as the stunning young women they intended, gone at last were the days of uniforms. The young men of the college were likewise attired and were set to make a final bid at impressing their female counterparts of the Girls' College. Olly was spared the angst of his peers; there had never been a hint of a doubt whose attentions he would have to himself that evening. The families who'd arrived for the mid-summer's events were ranged round the great hall, occupied with the discourse befitting proud parents of graduates while the young men and women mingled and socialized in a separate sphere of activity all their own.

One young man, dressed as his contemporaries but oddly aloof around them, simply surveyed the assembly of accomplished people, enjoying it appeared, the parade of couples and ladies passing around him. Until his eyes fell on one young lady flanked by two other gorgeous women and a nonchalant gentleman. He instantly, though unobtrusively, moved to within range of their conversation. After what seemed an eternity, he was close enough to have touched her sleeve and he listened to the topics they pursued unaware of his eavesdropping. The young lady who had so captured his attention was just answering the young gentleman's inquiry regarding her choice of specific medicine, which she was evidently intending to pursue.

"...You may very well relish a general internal medicine practice, but I am intent upon caring for children and addressing childhood diseases."

The young man and the two ladies nearest him looked at each other knowingly and one replied, seemingly speaking for the group, "You don't suppose that decision has anything to do with a certain family member so close to lifelong debilitation when he was a toddler?"

The children's physician answered evenly, "I imagine it has a lot to do with Oliver's incapacity as a child. I wasn't there by his side, and felt more helpless than anyone. It would be silly for me to dismiss that influence on this present course of study..." The young gentleman who had made his way to her side at last spoke up.

J. L. LAWSON

"Excuse me for overhearing, but did I just understand you to say that you are intending to pursue a medical profession?" he asked in a subtly inflected Italian accent. Hannah, startled that someone was suddenly speaking from over her shoulder, was careful not to wheel around upon the speaker too abruptly.

She turned her shoulders just enough to face the young gentleman, "If you are speaking to me, sir, then you *over-heard* correctly. And to whom am I offering this confirmation?" Hannah was pleasantly surprised at the young man's solicitous expression; nothing haughty or arrogant about that face, just humble curiosity and that he was handsome didn't hurt anything...

"My apologies, again, beautiful lady, I am Jon..." at least that's what it sounded like when he said his name, "I only meant to comment that any child receiving your ministrations would undoubtedly recover at once."

Hannah had nothing to say. The young man in formal attire in front of her wasn't the least bit impeded by her silence. He continued his statement, "The mere presence of the divine, I am told, works miracles upon the insufficiency of the soul and thereby heals the physical from the inside, as it were..."

Mia and Lena took Oliver's arms as they were wont to do when they were emotionally touched by something around them and this young gentleman had certainly touched their sense of justice. That a stranger should recognize their Hannah for the wonderful young woman they knew her to be, proved sound judgement on his part. The trio looked to Hannah waiting for her response.

"Sir, while that may be so, and I can not verify it at this moment---that you should ascribe to me, a stranger to you, these extraordinary powers I have more than a few qualms at accepting at face value. For all *you* know I am merely disguised as an angel of light and have in my heart the darkest of designs..."

He replied quickly, "Miss... I can now see you clearly. If there are any dark designs hidden in your heart of hearts they are most assuredly for the enemies of mankind; for the woman I see before

418

me I have judged rightly to be divine indeed." With that said, he bowed deeply, reached for her hand and kissed it. When he rose again, he asked her to dance. Hannah accepted graciously. The trio merely watched them walk to the dance floor with their eyes wide open.

"Who *is* that young man?" Mia asked at last and the other two nodded in symphony at the query.

'Jon' guided Hannah to the floor and they danced in smooth movements to the waltzing tempo of the piece of music the little orchestra was playing. He wasn't finished with his questions, "Miss... where are you planning to take your studies for the noble profession?"

Hannah was liking this gentleman more each minute: first he surprised her, next he flattered her, then he acknowledged her, now he was solicitous of *her* interests and future *and* he stared into her eyes not at her breasts... "I hope to be studying at the Liverpool School of Medicine in the autumn; I am merely awaiting the course offerings, my acceptance to that institution was registered over a year ago."

His left eyebrow raised slightly, "Indeed, I have a situation in Manchester and am to be enrolled in the Liverpool Mechanics' College, as you say my acceptance has already been granted in the study of marine architecture..." Hannah gasped. "Did I say something wrong, Miss?"

Hannah recovered, "Not at all, it's just that that course of study is precisely the aim and purpose of my cousins' enrollment at that very institution," and she inclined her head toward the trio, looking back at them from where they still stood.

Jon replied, "Ah, that *would* be cause for a slight shock. What would be the odds that a stranger should become your servant and also be in pursuit of similar goals as your own cousins? It is remarkable," and he glanced again at the trio, "But are you saying that one of those lovely young women with that gentleman is to join the naval pursuit?"

"Not just one of them, both of them. The gentleman is my brother and he also is studying medicine—as you overheard---as I am..." replied Hannah with no small tone of pride in her voice for her twins and brother.

"Again, beautiful lady, I must admit this is remarkable..." and the handsome young man guided her through a spin and a turn; Hannah now danced forward as he was in the reverse. Hannah was certain she liked this fellow very much indeed and wouldn't mind continuing any conversation into which he might wish to engage. Then she caught a glimpse of her father and mother moving toward the trio, with another couple in tow. She had to look again to see who were the other couple, but the crowd blocked her view. The orchestra finished the selection, Jon bowed deeply to her and escorted her back to her brother and cousins' sides.

As they just came to within the circle of their company once more, Harold and Chloe approached and were grinning broadly. Harold began, "Hannah darling, you dance beautifully; as do you Jon..." Harold made it sound more like Sean. Hannah looked from her father to the young man, just as Lawrence and Miranda stepped to their side; at once hugs were administered all around with smiles and laughter to boot.

Miranda opened with, "I see you are getting on famously with Jean Baptiste!"

Mia and Lena instantly threw their arms around the necks of Grandpa Lawrence and Miranda. "PapaLawrence, MamaRanda! Ooh... we are going to cry!" They then disentangled themselves and administered hugs to their Uncle Jean Baptiste.

Jean looked at Hannah again and she at him. They both looked at their parents, then at the trio's grinning faces. "You mean this is *little* Hannah?" he began.

She gasped, "This is *baby* Jean Baptiste? Sir, you are not a baby, my apologies, I only remember seeing you as an infant..."

He cocked his head at that last enigmatic comment, but slowly accepted that this beautiful lady in front of him, whom he'd sought out among all the ladies in the Pavilion---was Hannah Belle. But not 'little' Hannah any longer, this was a ravishing and very intelligent woman before him.

As the two of them were still shocked into an awkward silence, Oliver reached out a hand and introduced himself... "I am Oliver Henry Bessamer, near former Malvernian and soon to be medical student," he bowed. "Jean Baptiste this is a most welcome happenstance," Oliver continued, "Uncle Lawrence, what brings you all to Malvern of all places?"

Miranda answered, "For *your graduation*, of course! And the passing of the torch to these elegant young women here..." she squeezed the hands of Mia and Lena which she was still holding in greeting. "The other reason is to install Jean in University..."

Hannah turned to her cousins and quickly reiterated their conversation from the dance floor; the twins were delighted. "Lena, did you hear that? A study mate!" Mia crowed.

Oliver smiled broadly, "Thank goodness! I was truly afraid I would have to learn both medicine *and* marine engineering! Bless you Jean, bless you!"

Harold again spoke up, "And *this* is why I was unable to secure Greengate... Lawrence had snatched her from under my nose just a few weeks before! How's that for a coincidence?" The young people looked at each other all around as the realization of what was about to transpire sunk into their present state of surprise.

Miranda picked up from there, "You *will* be willing to *share* Greengate, won't you all?" Hannah gazed into Jean's eyes and his gaze met hers. The growing smiles and rising blush in their expressions were as inconspicuous as the Emperor's new clothes.

"Shall we settle at a large table and have a bite to eat; we have some catching up to do..." announced Harold and he took Lawrence's arm.

Once seated, Jean took a photograph from his wallet and stared at it and the young ladies. "I have been at the University of Munich the last three years with barely any time in Venice; this one picture is all that I carry to remind me of my family in America..." Hannah, seated next to him, looked over his shoulder. "I suppose..." he began looking between her face and the picture of all the family on the hanging deck at the home on the hill, "...there is some resemblance here, but honestly, I have a real difficulty translating *these* two faces into the visages of those two elegant women there," and he gestured to the twins.

Hannah giggled for the first time all evening and acquiesced to the real difference between herself as a child and the woman she knew from her own mirror every morning. "You are allowed this faux pas, but let's not have surprises like this repeated... agreed?"

He nodded, sighing as he did so, "Mia and Lena, my nieces..." he shook his head in the astonishment which he had still not entirely shaken.

Oliver offered a challenge, "Jean, if you can tell which is Mia and which is Lena after a few weeks getting to know them better, your study time with them will go far more smoothly... but if not, do not be disconsolate. On this side of the Atlantic, I'm afraid I'm the *only* one to whom they answer honestly."

Hannah jerked her head at her brother, saying, "Oh, nonsense! I haven't gotten them confused for a moment their whole lives..." and she looked over at her near-sisters. They were very shy about meeting her gaze, and she reiterated, "Mia, tell my brother he's mistaken!"

Lena, to whom Hannah had just spoken and inadvertently called Mia, had to admit what they preferred not *ever* to admit to *anyone*. "Sweetheart, I'm Lena; we do not correct people when they get us confused... We're just not that invested in our names. However, *Olly* is correct, he *is* the only one besides father and mother who has *ever* *always* been accurate... that *is* when he calls us by name at all, anyway."

Hannah wasn't so much crestfallen as she was intrigued by her 'sisters' ability to abandon their personal identities so easily and had for the length of their lives it now appeared. Jean made a like comment aloud, echoing Hannah's thoughts, "That is utterly amazing. So you have *never* made it clear to *anyone* else which of you is which?"

Mia replied looking at Hannah, "Well... *once;* when we were two years of age---actually the first and only time until now---it was *also* with *you* Hannah: when we were at our first play, remember? You were introducing us to Mr. Goodman and you got us backward and Lena said something about it?"

Hannah admitted she did not remember the instance, although she remembered the occasion quite well otherwise. Lena continued, "I felt so bad. Mia looked hurt and you seemed embarrassed... well... we just decided then and there to not bother with our names ever again."

Chloe had been listening and was now very interested, "What about in the case of someone calling for one of you by name to lend assistance or to deal with some task or some such thing?"

Mia answered, "If I'm the only one standing there, I'll do it; just as if Lena's the one nearest, she'll do it. It's really not a burden in the least. Actually, we were *most* surprised when we started school and heard other children hoping not to be chosen by name to do something or other... usually unpleasant in their view."

Lena enjoined, "That was a real eye-opener. People are *so* attached to their name-as-their-identity---whilst most of them *really* don't have much of an identity to even attempt to protect in the first place. That was the amazing aspect of it... for us anyway."

The four adults made quick personal reviews of their acquaintances and even of their own lives before meeting the twins' father and they had to agree with Lena's assessment... unless it was Mia who had spoken? They were far wiser than most but then the apples don't generally fall far from the tree in the Livingson family and that was a fact.

Oliver sat quietly after his initial challenge-suggestion to Jean, but now spoke again to Mia and Lena, "I didn't mean to push you into admitting anything... really! I didn't *actually* realize just how completely indistinguishable the rest of the world *really* finds you. I am *so* sorry." They put their arms around him and kissed his cheeks.

"*You* can't hurt us, Oliver Henry, we're immune!"

After a pleasant repast, Hannah asked Jean for the next dance and the twinkle in her eye made it quite apparent to her intimate family and friends that Jean had lit a fuse---they each hoped he was up to the daunting prospect of Hannah Belle Bessamer's attentions. Her expectations, where she had any, were *very* high---a trait she acquired no doubt from Harry and MamaKat, her surrogate parents. As they rose and advanced to the dance floor, Mia held silent council with Lena, who then stood and invited Oliver to dance as well. He instantly looked to Mia and she smiled and nodded, "Don't worry I'll cut in before too long---*If* it appears you actually *can* dance, that is."

Oliver could dance *well*. Each twin in turn was a flowing addition to his own poise and grace. Harold and Chloe were smiling the smiles of very proud parents when Miranda asked quietly, "Do both the girls so adore Olly, or is this an unusual display?" Chloe turned to whisper to her dear friend and behind her hand related all that the adults in their lives had gathered about the curiously strong attachment between the trio.

Miranda's eyes widened and at last simply said aloud, "Well good for them!" and she raised her glass in a toast to her husband's granddaughters. "To Love and to those who bear it!" That was answered by the others and the evening had finally become a most auspicious inauguration of the rest of not only this weekend's events, but for the events of the not so distant future as well.

The next week was a transition. The Bessamers and Spelmans accompanied them to Salford and Greengate, having already decided that the 'kids' should furnish their house at their own pace and with their own finances. There were beds ordered for all the rooms and the basic sticks of furniture ordered for their fundamental needs, but outside of stocking the kitchen with only the necessary equipment, they kept their hands off. Jean yielded the master bedroom and bath to his nieces to which they at last agreed only after many well-conceived arguments in protest. He actually had to 'pull rank' to get them in the room. He reminded them they were conceived within those very walls and therefore *obviously* had the *only* legitimate prior claim. Hannah took the room across the hall from them and the fellows both took the room overlooking the garden. Neither had ever had a roommate before college, but each had become so accustomed to sharing quarters it was near second nature to them now.

After settling the simple logistics of house holding, they went on a weekend trip to Redditch to visit Chloe's folks. (Harold's parents had both passed away a few years before.) Samuel and Olivia were the happiest of grandparents and doted on all of the 'children' equally. They made sure each of them understood explicitly that they were always close at hand for support, advice, encouragement and hospitality. After they returned to Greengate, and although there were still several weeks before classes would begin, they made a trip to the bookstores to gather all the texts they would need for the coming term. Naturally the galleries and museums weren't spared their interest. They were especially interesting to Mia, Lena and Olly who had not *ever* had access to so many wonderful places of collected art and beauty. Jean and Hannah had been to many across England and northern Europe, but that didn't jade their appreciation through the fresh eyes of their younger family.

When their first evening alone in their Greengate residence arrived at the end of that day, it was Jean who went to the kitchen and began preparing a meal. He didn't ask, nor did he particularly notice that he was alone in the kitchen making preparations. He was a highly trained and qualified chef and really didn't even expect any assistance. When Hannah wondered in she at first simply marveled at his efficiency and flair. After a few moments she asked, "Well what may I do to help?"

"If you will please..." he answered as he continued his present task, "...we need eight or nine cloves of garlic and the salmon would be better without its head and tail..."

She set to it at once. When the trio arrived they went to the cabinet and began to set the table. Olly went to the stove and Jean had him continue stirring a sauce while he turned his attention to setting out the spices for a fish rub. Once those were selected, Mia intuitively began combining them into a bowl and passed it to Hannah for the filets. Lena gathered goblets and after placing them at the table, went down into the wine cellar wondering if there were still any bottles left from all those years before when her father and mother lived here. She was more than in luck, in fact she had to call up to Jean and get his advice about the selections. With everything simmering, or in the oven, he took a moment and went to see what she'd picked out so far. After a very brief lesson in vintages and a few other aspects Lena would have to have repeated later, she brought up the 'ideal' bottles for the meal... according to Uncle Jean.

He uncorked one, poured out a little into one of the wine glasses and savored it as he leaned back waiting for the meal to cook itself. Olly held out a glass and it was likewise filled. They tapped the glasses together and toasted the beginning of a new era in Greengate cuisine. The ladies weren't to be left out of anything so momentous and followed suit. Oliver began singing a scottish air and the twins added harmony. It was a tune they had learned at the piano back home and their rendition was a haunting echo of both boldness passed and an invigorating promise of greatness to come. Hannah and Jean applauded then shooed them out of the kitchen and into the dining room. There were so many stories to share; all those years apart and such very different lessons learned along the way. They each began to realize how fortunate they were to both have a common understanding of each other and to have such diverse lives to bring to the table, as it were. Oliver raised his glass for another toast, "To Love and to those who bear it!"

All present knew the origins from the family history of that particular toast and at the same time truly appreciated Oliver for offering it for *them* at this gathering. Hannah looked to Jean and he back to her. Mia and Lena's eyes were for Oliver's alone, as his were for them. "What's for dessert?"

"I thought once the kitchen is put right again, we might amble down to a coffee shop and enjoy the free evening while we still have a free evening. I suspect that condition is likely to change in not too long..." offered Jean and the others recognized the import of his observation.

"To the kitchens!" Hannah exclaimed and grabbed up some of the plates and platters nearest her.

The August evening was balmy and soft; they took a long stroll through a nearby park before attaining the patisserie. Away from disapproving eyes and under the nominal cover of dusk, the twins and Oliver walked with their arms around each other, and even Jean and Hannah had gone so far as to hold each other's hands. They sat out under the rising stars, sipping the coffee and nibbling the pastries. Silent for all intents and purposes, not one of them feeling the need to fill the silence with sounds other than those of the street and cafe. The glow of the city center and the lanes leading off in various directions hindered the complete view of the star-filled sky, but every now and again one of them would ooh or aah at a streaking meteor passing low toward the horizon. "The Perseids..." Jean said aloud.

The ladies looked at each other and chanted, "The Tears of St. Lawrence..." and laughed.

Oliver and Jean weren't sure whether to ask or laugh. Mia said, "There was a catholic girl in our dormitory and she would *always* correct *anyone* who used secular names for anything for which there was *obviously* the 'right' name."

Oliver rolled his eyes, "There was a fellow in our room in Number Four House who did something similar, except he wasn't catholic. For him it was baffling that anyone would use colloquial or common names for creatures which were already 'quite plainly and accurately' labeled in Latin according to a given taxonomy. Fortunately he kept his outbursts to alpha taxonomy..."

Jean sneered, "How tedious!"

Oliver accepted that, but added, "Of course as Hannah and I head into med school, I think I might appreciate his encyclopaedic vocabulary..."

Jean had to admit that he'd been a little rash to so quickly label the fellow, "But it does sound tedious still."

Oliver admitted that the fellow did get on everyone's nerves from time to time, "...*especially* at mealtimes." That elicited a round of 'Ews' from the ladies, and with their noses squinched they requested a change of topic.

Silence again reigned. Jean made a movement to pay the check and Oliver interrupted him, then Hannah said she could pay her own way and the twins suggested they would be more than happy to pick up the tab. Jean heard them all and after they stopped grabbing for the chit, he opened a pressing topic. "Well this won't do at all. We shall need to decide how to handle this as a family. We are not strangers after all---who need to impress or otherwise take care of our acquaintances. Any suggestions?"

Hannah said, "Perhaps we should have a 'community bank' for just these occasions and for groceries and the other mounting drains on our household economy?" Jean nodded approvingly at that, as did Oliver and the twins.

Lena asked, "Okay, what do you think? So much per month like maintenance, or pool our resources and elect a treasurer?"

There was silence for a little while as each person weighed the alternatives. Oliver spoke first. "The money I have is not mine; it was given me as an allowance from father." Hannah nodded agreement, that was her situation as well.

Jean admitted as much, "While I do have some sum that is my own from years working in the *Final Concession*, I have no idea what that sum is nor would I ever need to find out. Like you my father has provided an allowance, a very generous allowance to be sure, but limited."

Lena spoke for Mia in saying that "We don't have an allowance per se; we have been given the keys to the city, after a fashion. Father simply turned over one of the family accounts to us and told us, if we needed more in a crisis, how to get more."

Oliver suggested that they write down what their allowances amounted to and if the twins could make a viable estimate of their historic monthly expenditures, then perhaps the community bank idea might suffice. He produced a napkin and a pencil and scribbled an amount at the head of the list and passed it to Jean who did the same, and on around the table the napkin passed until all the sums were in a column. He quickly tabulated a total and whistled, "We are extraordinarily well off for unemployed students!" They all had to chuckle at that, knowing that their parents had indeed seen to their finances very, very well.

"Alright, what do we propose? Cash in a bowl by the door? A secret safe under the wine cellar? A mattress?" Oliver opened the discussion.

Lena made a softly spoken suggestion, "Can we just keep a box and ledger on the kitchen table with the understanding that whatever goes in is recorded and whatever comes out is recorded? I don't think we have to initial it or anything, just keep a balance sheet..." Mia nodded hopefully.

Jean and Oliver looked at Hannah. She added, "Perhaps for occasions like this, which I hope are not infrequent, we might should have a bursar or treasurer. Any volunteers?"

Jean nominated Oliver, who paled, "Whoa, just because I made the suggestion first doesn't mean I was volunteering..." But it was too late, the rest of them voted him into the position and the motion was carried unanimously.

Hannah then asked, "Is having all our funds in a box in plain sight a good idea?"

Jean chuckled, "I remember asking my mother about that very thing when I was five or six. She and father have always just kept the Inn's monetary assets just sitting in a little bag under the concierge desk---right out where anyone could reach over and walk off with it."

Hannah had to ask, "What did she say?"

"She said, 'I pity the poor sap that attempts to take from your father what is not their own.' I didn't really understand what she meant until my seventh birthday. After spending countless hours in a boat with him, rowing 'just so,' and 'shifting' without end, then scrubbing, sanding, painting and cleaning the entire Inn from stem to stern---I had to ask 'why?' I spent the next hour protecting all my favorite body parts from the staff in my father's hands. Then I figured out why my mother didn't mind leaving the money bag under the desk..." The others laughed out loud at his description which so closely mirrored their own experiences. Jean concluded with, "So, I'm confident a box on the kitchen table shall be quite safe enough... 'I pity the sap who tries to take it'!'"

Hannah had to follow up on that story and with tongue in cheek, she asked, "Which parts was he aiming at that were so precious to you?"

He opened his mouth to respond, but Lena answered, "His ears of course; doesn't he have the cutest ears!"

Mia said quickly, "Don't be silly, he had to protect his lovely hands and wrists; aren't they the most perfectly formed..."

Then Oliver couldn't help but add, "You two! Really. Obviously he was protecting his feet; just look at his fine shoes, there must be some *very* pretty feet in those shoes..."

Jean was now visibly blushing, and Hannah, who had merely made the simple inquiry to have him acknowledge that his whole body had been a target---that the peril to 'his favorite parts' was precisely how *she* would have assessed MamaKat's attack on herself all those years ago. So she spoke up, "Stop it! That's not what I meant..." and the others looked between her and Jean.

Oliver commented, "Brother, we were ribbing Hannah more than you just now," and he looked at his sister, "Hannah Belle, *we* love him *too*. We won't do anything to hurt his feelings or yours just to watch either of you squirm... We promise." At the words *love him too*,' Hannah blushed to her toes.

Lena said, "Well at least you two match now."

Oliver then commented that at least the others assembled there had been on terra firma when they were forced to suddenly use their newfound strengths in mortal self-protection, "I made the mistake of waiting until we were out on the Tahoe to ask the inevitable question. Uncle Harry didn't wait until we got back to shore to proceed to 'inform' me as to what 'the point' of my endeavors had been. He was everywhere at once... so I had to be *nowhere*!" They all winced at the image of a boy having only the confines of a sampan in which to avoid the masterful, near invisibly quick blows which Harry was capable of delivering.

Once all was said and done, Mia pointed out the obvious. "Have we settled who's paying the tab this evening?"

Jean's comments after their first dinner were close to prophetic; they didn't have too many free evenings over the next few months *or* years. Between classes, studies, meals, housework, laundry and sleep the house was relatively quiet until they at last settled into the new rhythms of University and home life. The parlor, as had been employed during their parents' residence of the house, was given over to drafting and model-making; while the library-reading room was the exclusive domain of the physicians. The first two terms for both groups were the most intense it seemed in retrospect: the new languages to assimilate, the digestion of concepts, the processes and principles of the disciplines occupied their every waking hour.

The holidays were the only true rest any of them experienced and the time spent in Redditch was priceless--especially for the twins and Jean. Samuel Allcock had connections with certain key Canadian suppliers of whom the ship-builders truly wished to take full advantage. The task of building a 'project' was a tacit requirement for their future graduation, but they decided to be pro-active. In addition to an elaborate scale model, they were aiming at something a bit *more practical*. With Grandpapa Samuel's agreement to import the materials they requested, the next step was to find an available warehouse or other suitable 'shop' for construction.

Upon returning to Greengate from the break, Mia and Lena set about to scour the Liverpool port district for the ideal establishment, preferably vacant, electricity was essential. Jean tracked down a former classmate from his college days in Germany---a Dutch fellow with loads of experience in welding virtually anything. Their searches came to fruition before the end of February and by spring the three of them were spending more time at the boat shop than they were at home. This naturally prompted Oliver and Hannah to shift their schedules a little and bring their own studies with them on weekends to see their loved ones for at least some of the time during the week.

Their boat design was a truly novel conceptual development. No one had ever built a trimaran of that size and definitely not in metal; the cabins and decks of the ship appeared more like a split-level home than boat cabins. At sixty feet in overall length, with a beam of near fifty feet, the anticipated draft, even with the metal hull, was about three feet. Once the framing of longitudinals and transverses was completed, they were able to direct the welding of the copper-nickel hull plating. The initial process had been time-consuming, but once they were merely waiting on the welder to complete his part, they were able to spend more time at home. As each panel was added and each hull was completed, they drew closer to being able to finish out the interior, the deck spaces and prepare for the rigging. In the meantime, they produced a tenth scale model both for reference and for submitting as the school project dictated; they had no intention of presenting the full-size ship as their final submission.

Jan DeVott, the dutch welder, wasn't taken aback by either the design or the size of the project; he simply gave them a firm estimate of his material and labor costs, set up his gear and set to the task. He complemented their choice of metals for the alloy's longevity and maintenance-free nature. It seemed he could weld anything; his seams required only the slightest brushing and no grinding once complete---and there wasn't a gap or breach to be found in any single inch of the vast number and lengths of the welds required. It was a masterpiece and inspired the three builders to apply the same level of craftsmanship to the rest of the ship.

By the time Oliver and Hannah were interning, Mia, Lena and Jean were nearing graduation. Their model project had received mixed reviews from the faculty experts. The progressive engineers of the College praised its innovation and material construction. The conservative members at least appreciated the application of a proven sail plan for the 'gangly' craft. *Gangly* was the general consensus of its appearance, but when the specifications and tank trials proved the soundness of her hydrodynamics, even outperforming every other student-produced design, gangly became 'exotic.' That was a satisfactory label and both the twins and Jean accepted the epithet with pride.

The full-scale 'exotic' ship's interior and rigging, which their project model hadn't needed, was still being completed as their time allowed. If the trimaran's hull design was radical, the mast itself was revolutionary. Jean spent a lot of time with Mr. DeVott while he was welding and one of the conversations they had had led to Jean investigating applications of aluminum. He sat down with the twins and they sketched out what could be accomplished with the rigging if the mast were hollow metal. They explored wire ropes for halyards, guy wires and tensioners for shrouds and stays. Mia made a leap of thought:

If they installed aluminum pipes over the head stays, and were able to attach the jibs' luffs to the pipes, even if only at the head and tack, the head sails could be reefed or furled by the same person handling the mainsail---a *wrapped furling* sail. Then Lena made an insightful comment about the amount of lateral space they had with the multi-hull design, and why couldn't they rig the staysail to tack between two blocks, or even on a track for that matter. "That would allow a second headsail, say a wrapped furling flying jib to be handled manually with the main and we get beaucoup sail area but won't need more crew to handle it." After spending more than the first year and a half on the boat's fundamental construction with such intense time and labor, Oliver and Hannah insisted they scale back their time invested daily so that a more comfortable home life could be managed.

It had been over six years since the twins had been back to Tahoe and their family back home decided to take matters into their own hands. Jamie and Will had been of invaluable assistance during the San Francisco earthquake and fires, ferrying survivors to the East Bay and safety. They estimated later they made nearly as many round trips to the other wharf in those four days as they had made in one year of pleasure excursions. Aaron and Hipolyta had opened up the Booklove house and their own extra rooms to as many refugees as could be comfortably housed. They all spent a good deal of time cooking and serving at the additional soup kitchens set up to keep the inundation of involuntary visitors fed. Once the Bay got back to some modicum of normality, they retreated to Tahoe.

The Livingson family in Tahoe was enduring their own 'shake-up.' The *Concession* and the Lodges were barely able to maintain profitability, due in large part to the success of Mr. Bliss's Tahoe Tavern. The good side of that story was: they still owned the land and the years of full activity had made them very well off and able to afford facing the inevitable closures. The *Concession* would remain available to the School and Theater, but could not serve the public--- when there was no public to serve. The Bungalows were sold off individually as summer cottages and moved to the buyers' properties all around the north shores. Interestingly enough, once the last lodge was sold and removed, the Livingsons saw a *sizable* profit over their initial construction costs... let alone all the years of rental income with virtually no overhead to speak of. So when Aaron and Poly arrived with the Captains another family meeting was called to discuss any near future plans they might have.

Harry opened by reading an excerpt from Mia and Lena's last letter.

"...We hope Jamie and Will don't resent our suggestions for changing their sail plan. The Bermuda rig for the main mast simplifies the pilot's job of handling that sail and steering at the same time. It also, as we said at the time, allows for more points of sail---downwind in particular. The sails we sent to replace the Victoria's old ones are of our own invention. They are a kind of canvas, but we have contracted to have them woven with heavy preshrunk silk adjacent to strong cotton fibers for the warp, with a weft of linen. The resultant sailcloth is slightly lighter, but also slightly stronger than cotton or linen alone...and it's pretty. But you'll have noticed that the most ingenious aspect of those sails is the way they were assembled; we have made sure that the stitching enhances the sail's filling. The jibs are radially stitched, and the main and fore sails are stitched in such a way to provide for the stresses of their use...

...Oliver and Hannah are to graduate at the end of May next. Jean Baptiste and ourselves have only to launch and set the masts and rigging and the Hannah Belle *will be ready for cruising. She's a beautiful, although exotic ship; she'll sleep eighteen very comfortably, and as our fairing instructor noted, 'she looks like a floating apartment, not a boat,' so we took that to mean we succeeded in making it just as comfortable inside as she is winsome on the outside.*

It shouldn't be too startling that both of us have gained our Captaincy licenses...Uncle Jean has already had his for several years now. Oliver is relieved that he can focus on doctoring and won't have to do the tedium of navigation in addition to those other duties. We promised to take care of him and we're holding up our end of the bargain as well as he has held up his. Both he and Hannah are top in their class, and have already had to decline positions to some of the most prestigious institutions in Europe to make this journey. Jean and Hannah have agreed to join us on the maiden voyage, of course if they hadn't we'd probably have shanghaied them anyway. Besides why wouldn't Hannah want to have her honeymoon on a ship named after her and co-designed by her own husband?

Our best estimates place us in Venice by no later than July, and from there the main voyage begins: through the Suez, and on to the Indian Ocean. While we hope to be in the Filipines perhaps by winter, we won't feel like failures if we only get as far as the eastern British Raj or the Dutch East Indies. These are the regions where, historically, the resources have been more valued than the people. Our main purpose is to bring much needed medical assistance to victims of local epidemics, unsafe water, natural disasters, and the like---to generally provide effective aide in the most neglected corners of our world. So if our schedules slip a bit here and there, it'll still be worth it to us. Dr. Olly is stocking supplies and Dr. Hannah keeps adding more to the lists, so it's really fortunate that the Hannah Belle *is so accommodating..."*

"What's this boat look like?" Will wanted to know, although Jamie asked.

Harry reached beside his chair and pulled the drafts of the project from a tube. "Have a look for yourself, but I warn you, it's not like anything you've seen on the water before..." They took the plans and spread them on the floor for all to see.

PapaGeorge whistled, "Wow, she's enormous!"

Will and Jamie looked over her specs and sail plan, "She's probably the fastest sailing vessel in any waters. Look at how easily even one person could handle the sails, unlike the *Victoria.*" Jamie looked up at Uncle Harry, "Is this the actual sail plan? Are these numbers right? With a boat just slightly longer than the *Victoria,* she has more than half again as much sail area from a single mast! Whew...you weren't kidding: *fast.*"

Jameson and Aaron went for a little walk while their sons were looking over the plans inside. "...so it may be *that* time at last..." Aaron was saying.

Jameson answered, "Tania and I have tied up all our loose ends."

Aaron went on, "Harry and Kaitlyn agree that Alouette and George Lawrence should absolutely finish *all* their education before taking to the seas even for a few months and they will naturally keep on giving them a wonderful home life."

Tania and Poly wandered into the garden and joined the

discussion. Poly gave an estimate of when she thought their own provisions could be ready.

Tania added, "The skippers will have finished the hull and sail renovations by when the twins say they wish to launch, so it's conceivable that we can catch up to them in the Philippines easily, maybe even in the Indian Ocean. We'll just need to establish with them a series of prearranged checkpoints, so we can find them..."

Poly added, "If we wire Lawrence and Miranda, the *Hannah*'s crew will have our input and checkpoints. No matter how big the ocean, we *will* find them one way or another."

The same week that the *Hannah Belle* would reach Venice, the *Victoria* would reach harbor at Kaneohe Bay in Oahu. George Lawrence was deciding between the different Colleges and Universities which had offered him admission and Alouette was trying to influence his decision with her own informed preferences for future academic residence. They bid bon voyage to their families after their summer term in Berkeley.

Kaitlyn had an idea, which gained momentum: to take an expedition by the Atchison, Topeka, Santa Fe through the Arizona and New Mexico Territories, then back through Colorado and on to Reno and Tahoe---the Grand Tour. This suited both George Lawrence and Alouette. George Lawrence was leaning toward the New Mexico Normal School because it was the only U.S. College offering courses on anthropology and archaeology, *and* it appealed to Alouette because she had been following George Lawrence around for her whole life and wasn't going to stop now... especially if he might be staying in Santa Fe for the same schooling she wished to pursue. She had very similar interests in the tracing of cultural roots to their source, of tracking the nuances of societies which when viewed from a greater perspective revealed more of similarity than difference. The University at Berkeley had just initiated publications of 'ethnology,' and so was rapidly also becoming a viable option for both students.

Uncle Aaron, Alouette's father, had been quite influential in this regard for the aspiring collegiates. His persistent determination to recover the cultural identities of long passed civilizations---the oral traditions of the ancient world from the nordic to the semitic---had enlivened their curiosity to also investigate other aspects of those peoples of the distant past. For George Lawrence and Alouette, that meant searching back through the threads of tradition which bound them to their own journey's origins and its fulfillment. A noble quest to be sure, but first they needed the proper tools of research to begin the 'excavation,' as it were. The New Mexico Normal School counted among its faculty and courses one: Dr. Hewett, of some note and experience in the very disciplines they sought to master. Decisions, decisions...

Harry and Kaitlyn were left to manage the two houses in Berkeley. The Booklove House, which was still owned by Harold and Chloe, was on the market for sale---although at present it was serving as an income property by annual lease to the University for visiting lecturers, professors and other dignitaries. For the summer, at least, they had stayed in Aaron and Poly's so that their children could take courses over the summer term at the University. When they were at home in Tahoe, Kaitlyn would see to it that it was always cleaned and the grounds landscaped by the same house and groundskeepers who had been responsible for the Booklove House over the last several years. By late August, Harry received an inquiry for purchase of that home. A husband and wife with two children had made application and an appointment was arranged for a walk-through.

George Lawrence and Alouette were at their morning classes when Harry and Kaitlyn met the interested family for the viewing. Alfred Arastu and his wife, Dashi, arrived at noon. "Welcome to the Booklove House, I am Harry Livingson and this is my wife Kaitlyn," Harry announced as they ushered the couple into the great room. Mr. Arastu introduced himself and his wife and Harry couldn't help noticing the thick British accent.

"Oh yes, no doubt our college years have thickened our tongues beyond even the accent of our Indian birth," Alfred responded.

Dashi added, "Alfred did his undergraduate studies at Malvern and I met him at Cambridge... we were both in the Union you see," and she smiled up at her husband in fond recollection.

"But that's marvelous," Harry began and held out a hand, "Leaver of '86..."

Alfred's smile grew broader, "Leaver of '89, School House!"

"You don't say. As was I!" Harry gripped his hand tighter.

Alfred's brow furrowed, "But then you're not THE Henry Livingson?" and he beamed in admiration, "You were nearly revered, you know..."

Kaitlyn joined in, "*I* like to think of him that way, of course..."

Dashi decided she liked this woman already, "I understand you implicitly Mrs. Livingson. Truly I do." The ladies walked out of the great room arm in arm to look through the house, leaving the men to discuss their college adventures in England and to further continue their other mutual interests.

"The Cambridge Union... hmm... my brother-in-law was a celebrated member of that fellowship: Aaron Backhouse, now Professor Backhouse of U. C. Berkeley, presently on sabbatical in the south Pacific," Harry added.

Alfred was fascinated at the small world they inhabited, and Harry said, "It may be smaller than you think, I designed and built this house for another brother-in-law Harold Bessamer---another Malvernian."

"*You* designed Booklove House? It is very attractive and inviting from the street; the views from here are fabulous..." Alfred commented as they too began to amble around the rooms and out into the gardens. The conversations turned from the house and terms to their families and histories. Their children, at present were in classes at the University, they admitted and were to join them here at two-thirty. The family was staying at an Inn near the docks until they could settle into a home. Alfred was a physician and had accepted a position at the University, in their hopes of advancing their fledgling Medical School. His first term would begin in the Spring Term, allowing his family to become settled and ready for their new lives in the States. "We began our family at home in Hyderabad and decided our children should experience all that we have enjoyed of a world-wide education... so here we are."

The ladies were also chatting more about their families than the house and were just about to rejoin their husbands in the kitchen when the front door opened and four young people entered unannounced. Kaitlyn and Dashi both smiled at once, each welcoming their children home, then they looked at each other and simply laughed out loud. "Well it seems we have even more in common than we at first thought..." Dashi said aside to Kaitlyn.

Alouette rushed to Kaitlyn, "MamaKat! This is Lila and her brother Aria, they are in our classes at school, but we hadn't *really* noticed each other until we were all walking the same direction after our discussion groups... and here we are!"

Aria interjected, "At first I thought we had left our notebooks or something behind... why else should they be following us? I thought. And one thing led to another... Oh father, I treated at the soda fountain; here's the change," and he returned what was left of the monies Alfred had given him that morning before school.

Alfred turned to Harry and admitted they weren't actually on a budget, but his children were still acquiring a proficient understanding of U.S. currencies, denominations and the widely various costs for the same items depending upon where one procured them. "This is a *most* commercial society!" Alfred moaned.

Harry nodded his condolences, "I wish I could say it'll get better... but I'm afraid that would be only wishful thinking."

Dashi and Kaitlyn announced they would be going down the street to the other residence and begin supper, the youngsters opted to linger and look through this house a bit longer, as Harry and Alfred sat down to terms for the purchase of Booklove. That settled, they herded the kids toward Alouette's house and supper. Each father noted the early signs of the bonds of friendship in their children, beyond the acquaintances and colleagues they were already. George Lawrence was fascinated by Aria's stories of his family's roots and traditions, as much as Aria was intrigued by George Lawrence's anecdotes of his own family. The girls were two peas in a pod---neither strayed far from the young men's sides and both were wholly interested in what can only best be described as 'girl things': the strong women of their families, their cousins and the relationships each maintained, their aspirations for their own young men, fashion in general and in whispers---inside information on the two young gentlemen with whom they were currently keeping company...

After dinner the topic arose of the Livingsons' plans for 'the grand tour,' which elicited instant interest from the Arastu family.

"That is exactly what we need to do at some point," Dashi was saying to her husband, "see this vast country from the great mountain ranges to the deserts and plains... I suspect it is very much like home in a lot of ways, but it is *our new* home and bears touring."

"Very well," Alfred conceded and turning to Harry, asked, "Please keep a good record of your travels and costs, so I ll have something to go on when I plan our own journeys? That would be ever so helpful."

Kaitlyn interjected, "Why wait? Once this term is over next week, what else will you have to keep you in Berkeley for several months? The contracts for the maintenance and upkeep of this house can just as easily be extended for the Booklove House..."

Aria and Lila were grinning their approval in concert with the smiles of George Lawrence and Alouette at the idea of taking the tour with their new friends. Although from Harry and Alfred's perspectives it was difficult to determine just which of them were grinning at whom, and vice versa.

Dashi decided for them, "Indeed, we shall plan upon it and begin at once." Applause and cheers arose from the younger members at the table.

Harry added, "Well Alfred, shall we head on down to your hotel and remove your things to Booklove House, so you can at least get some things settled yourself before the ladies whisk us off on tour?"

Alfred's eyebrows were as far in his forehead as they could stretch, "I'm right after you, sir..." and they motioned their sons to follow as they left for the Inn.

Kaitlyn admitted after the men were gone, "It appears that our houses function in the same manner... what else shall *we* decide *for* them for the near future?" Both women giggled at that as the girls got up and began to help pick up after the meal and choose desserts. Lila asked Dashi could she stay with Alouette this night and Alouette pleaded her case with Kaitlyn. Neither mother was indisposed at the idea and the girls went off to Alouette's room to conspire further about the upcoming 'tour.'

A few days before their train was to leave for the first leg of their journey, Aria and George Lawrence had finally decided on certain 'must see' attractions along the route. The Yosemite Valley and King's Canyon, of course, then the Grand Canyon, but that's where their ordinary interests departed from the mainstream. They would study the Mesa Verde and the Chaco Canyon ruins, Adolf Bandelier's excavations near Los Alamos, and the Pecos Pueblo which both he and Dr. Hewett were studying, then if the schedule permitted, they wished to spend as much time as possible visiting the pueblos between Santa Fe and Taos. Alouette and Lila were equally adamant about some of the same places, but for the purpose of recording petroglyphs and architectural features.

As the *Victoria* and *Hannah Belle* headed closer to the Indian Ocean, the Livingsons headed off for the Indian Country of the great southwest with their newest East Indian friends, the Arastus. Besides the boys' inclinations, each of the other travelers had researched the route and so every hundred miles, it seemed, there was the opportunity to take a side trip to see some natural wonder or archaeological site.

"We should expect to be here five days at least..." Alouette insisted when they reached Flagstaff and the junction toward the Grand Canyon. Aria had been supporting Alouette's choices since they left Yosemite... as well as maintaining her closest companionship. That was fair enough, Lila and George Lawrence were seldom seen without each other as well... and their parents had given up any illusions that the new relationships were merely passing interests on their children's part---they had to finally face the realization: those four weren't children. At one of their early campsites, Dashi overheard Lila and Alouette discussing their young men in *very* explicit terms of endearment and she immediately passed that knowledge along to the other parents so everyone would be on the same page, as it were. That is what prompted them to open the discussion of family traditions not generally open to conversation.

The Arastu's family was as richly gifted with a deeply spiritual ancestry from the Naqshbandi sufis to Bappa Rawal and Guru Gorkhanath. Harry and Kaitlyn listened with rapt attention as both Alfred and Dashi candidly described their families' traditional training and devotional practices developed over many generations. Harry returned their candor with a narrative of their own family origins and traditions. In the wee hours of the next morning they were still huddled around the fire swapping tales of their ancestors' exploits, when Kaitlyn and Dashi at last yawned and announced they would try and get a few hours sleep at least. Alfred and Harry bid them sweet dreams and pulled their wives' abandoned blankets over their own shoulders and began a new round of tales. The men were still talking as they made coffee and breakfast the next morning. The children rose and joined them enticed from their slumbers by the aromas of the camp meal. Dashi and Kaitlyn wandered out of their tents well after sunrise looking for all the world as if they'd just stepped out of the finest hotel---immaculately dressed and ready for the day's arduous adventures along the canyon's rim. With their mothers as inspiration, the young ladies made sure they were attractively groomed and dressed as femininely as possible, though the rugged terrain dictated accommodation to the contrary.

The ancient ruins of Pueblo Bonito held all of the future field scientists' attention for days upon end, then the cliff dwellings, petroglyphs and kivas of the other sites along their journey made similar demands of their time and studies. Until at last they were at La Fonda on the plaza in Santa Fe and enjoyed a respite from their archaeological-anthropological-ethnological endeavors. They sat around a dining table in the hotel restaurant and tried to compile their notes and drawings into an organized tome of reference. It took Dashi and Kaitlyn to literally drag them from their chairs and kick them out of the Inn for them to see the culture and sights of one of the oldest cities of north America. They hardly knew what to do with themselves at first, but youth and curiosity will overcome almost any obstacle---they tramped all over the place hand in hand and often arm in arm.

Kaitlyn made inquiries among the locals at the market concerning herbs and dried plant vendors, which didn't actually go anywhere until she mentioned: 'for medicines?' Then she and Dashi had a longish list of the most reputable vendors from all the obscure corners of the county to visit---which they attempted to do. Mrs. Arastu was well familiar with the herblore of her native subcontinent and was most anxious to expand her understanding to the indigenous plants of her new home.

"When we get to Tahoe, I'll introduce you to MamaBelle---then you can learn from someone who *really* knows... I am just a dabbler compared with her," Kaitlyn admitted.

Dashi and Alfred were indeed looking forward to the near end of their tour by visiting the Livingson home in Tahoe. Of course there were innumerable pueblos, natural monuments and vistas which had to be documented before then.

When they at last transferred to the narrow gauge train leaving Truckee for Tahoe City, the sights and smells of their beloved Sierras awakened their senses to the home they had for so long been absent. George and Belle walked with them from the Tavern station up to the home on the hill and listened with open hearts to the narratives of both the tour and their new friends' lives and backgrounds. Meanwhile George Lawrence and Lila, Aria and Alouette fetched their horses from the high pastures behind the house and went for a leisurely ride along the lakeshore before the first snows kept them mostly indoors for the winter. The Spring Term wouldn't start until after the holidays and the Arastus were persuaded to spend them in Tahoe occupying the Connor's cottage. Alfred and Dashi were overwhelmed by the hospitality shown them and in repayment, they offered to host George Lawrence and Alouette in Berkeley, should they decide to continue classes at that institution. All of the parents surely hoped they would, as it appeared wherever one went the other three were sure to go. Maybe, they speculated, it was just a phase or merely the thrill of travel and so would wear off as the semester picked up and stretched on. It wasn't, and it didn't.

Dr. Alfred Arastu began his classes with a healthy enrollment and his schedules weren't too awfully off sync with the young scientists' in his house, much to Dashi's satisfaction. She had intended to assist at the department of Literature in whatever capacity was required at the time, but managing the household began to occupy her days far more than anticipated. She and Alfred had also elected to oversee the Backhouse Residence---Alouette's house---for Harry and Kaitlyn, since they were only a block or so away and the Livingsons would require a train trip to accomplish the same tasks. As it turned out, Alfred and Dashi were very nearly as capable a couple of people as any of the Livingson tribe and both George Lawrence and Alouette felt right at home with them.

As May crept toward the summer break, Harry got a wire from Jameson and Aaron that indicated they would perhaps be back in American waters as early as the year following September. He passed that information along to Berkeley when next they visited.

"What have they been doing and where have they traveled?" Dashi asked Kaitlyn as they strolled the docks and markets near the bay.

"Hmm. Well, I suppose the best way to put this is to give you a bit of family history regarding our daughters..." She reviewed the careers of Mia and Lena, of Dr. Olly and Dr. Hannah, her half brother Jean Baptiste then the maritime career of her nephews. "So when Jamie and Will were set for their long-awaited circumnavigation, their parents were ready to go as passengers... and participate in the humanitarian exploits of the *Hannah Belle*, naturally."

Dashi was wholly rapt during the tale and agreed that the western imperialism of the last centuries had indeed left those populations bereft. "There are pockets of well-meaning and helpful western people on missions of humanitarian assistance, but they are few and far between. The advent of western technological progress has surely made a lasting impact *on* south Asian peoples, without I'm afraid lending much in the way of benefit *to* them. Your daughters were right to say that the resources have received far more attention than the humanity of those regions." She walked in silence for a little while, then added, "Did I hear you correctly, Mia and Lena designed and built this huge ship?" Kaitlyn proudly assured her she had heard rightly. "And your 'nephew,' Dr. Oliver Bessamer, is he... uh... How shall I ask this..."

Kaitlyn saved her the anguish of forming the words to the question which was left hanging from her story about her daughters. "They are a trio it seems."

Dashi simply nodded her head in receipt of that tidbit. "Do you suppose their decision to minister to the needs of people so far away from their familiar culture and society has any bearing on that relationship? Or rather, I mean that the other way around."

"Yes, it is an interesting situation... the chicken or the egg conundrum..." Kaitlyn mused absently.

They had gathered all the items they intended from the market and just turned to head up the avenues to home when George Lawrence and Lila came running down the street toward them. "Thank goodness we found you!" Lila panted.

George Lawrence continued, "You won't believe this... hurry!"

446

and they took the packages from their mothers' arms to hasten their progress.

"What is it?!" both Dashi and Kaitlyn were anxious to know at the same time.

"It's Aria and Alouette..." Lila began, "They had a quarrel and aren't speaking to anyone!"

Harry and Alfred were in San Francisco and wouldn't be home for hours. "They haven't hurt each other have they... I mean physically wounded one another?" Dashi asked hurriedly as they picked up their pace.

"Well... not exactly..." George Lawrence began sheepishly, "but the back garden is a mess that will take quite a while to organize again..."

"What on earth are they at loggerheads about?!" Kaitlyn insisted.

"Honestly, MamaKat, George Lawrence just got home as they were storming off in different directions. Alouette won't tell me, and Aria won't talk to George Lawrence... We don't have a clue. We just thought maybe they'll tell you..." answered Lila.

They entered the house and called aloud. No answer. They peered into the back garden as they went from one room to the next looking for them. George Lawrence had understated the condition of the garden. It appeared that a cyclone had blown through it. Limbs were broken off the trees, shrubs were flattened, the vegetable patch wasn't recognizable as such, the fence was busted in places with pickets and rails dangled sadly and the turf looked as though a herd of large animals had stampeded through. Alouette was in one of the bathrooms sobbing in a corner. They found Aria on the edge of the roof in just as bad a shape. After quite a bit of coaxing, they at last assembled in the kitchen and tried to sort out what happened.

"He... he... said... I... I... we..." Alouette stammered and fell into a silent whimper.

"She said that if... I... and then she..." Aria couldn't bring himself to say the words. Kaitlyn and Dashi looked as perplexed as their children.

"Alright, let's start with the garden. Not that it matters in the least that it appears a natural disaster struck, but can you relate *how that* came to be?" Kaitlyn tried.

Aria looked up at her and his mother, wiped his sleeve across his eyes and nose and tried to master his voice. "We sorta got carried away..."

That was gross understatement, but it was a start. Dashi asked in as soft a voice as she manage, "Carried away with what?"

Alouette tried to reply, "It was my fault..." she involuntarily gasped for air as she uttered the admission, but made the effort to continue. "I forced him... into it..."

This wasn't clarifying anything. Kaitlyn took a stab at it. "Would one of you tell me: What is 'it' that we are talking about?"

"Our training..." Aria at last spouted.

"My virginity..." Alouette exclaimed.

Every one else at the table rolled their eyes in frustration---for a second it seemed as if it was going to make sense... then it went south. Dashi tried again, "Okay, How did the garden get between your training... and your virginity?"

Lila and George Lawrence nearly doubled up with laughter at that point and even the disconsolate ones couldn't help but look up in wonder with glimmers of self-conscious smiles.

"George Lawrence? Lila? What is suddenly so hilarious?!" Kaitlyn had to ask.

Gasping, Lila answered, "It's obvious isn't it?! They are in the throes of a ridiculous sexual tension!"

George Lawrence added between breaths, "Lila and I have been through the very same arguments... first her, then me, then what if we... or maybe we could decide by combat..."

"By flipping a coin..." Lila added.

"By reason, logic... chess..." George Lawrence listed.

"A race, a sparring match..." she continued.

"Darts..."

"Archery..."

They went back and forth, as the others' heads turned form one to the other as they listed all the challenges in which they had engaged.

"Memorizing the most lines at a sitting..." he contributed, and everyone looked at him oddly.

Lila acknowledged, "We probably should not have chosen *Romeo and Juliet*..."

They went on enumerating all the ways they'd devised to try and arrive at a decision they were too unwilling to decide for themselves, between themselves every time their impulses drove them in that direction. At last Aria and Alouette were actually giggling and laughing at the images introduced by the 'other' couple. Dashi and Kaitlyn tried to imagine how to counsel their children from here. They weren't sure whether to be relieved, or even more concerned as a result of this little powwow. 'When faced with the lesser of two evils...' Dashi commended them on not seriously injuring each other. Kaitlyn applauded George Lawrence and Lila's creativity. Harry and Alfred came in the front door.

"Anybody home? How was your day?" Alfred called and came into the kitchen followed by Harry. They glanced passed the breakfast nook, where their families were sitting, through the window into the back garden.

Harry commented, "I didn't notice any other damage in the neighborhood! Was this a local phenomenon?" Their families erupted into laughter and he and Alfred went out the back door to investigate. Quickly, while Harry and Alfred were out, Kaitlyn and Dashi cautioned their children to continue their... uh... *extraordinary efforts* for just another couple years. "...then a long sea voyage to the

South Pacific will be in order. You can visit Easter Island or plot the populating of the Pacific rim... or whatever scientific adventures are calling you all these days... Okay? Do we have your words on this?"

Dashi added, "And no more destroying the garden... but thank you for not starting in the house!"

Alouette said sheepishly, "It kinda did but Aria ran outside..." She took Aria's hand, "I'm sorry I tried to undress you."

Aria replied sincerely, "I'm sorry I said we were too young..."

Alouette stiffened, "*We*... Meaning ME!" and everyone at the table tensed.

Aria said reassuringly, "No, I mean *WE*."

Alouette repeated, "*We*," and she visibly melted, "I love *you* Ari."

"I love *you* too, Ally." Aria took Alouette's hand, "Come on spitfire, we better start repairing some of *our* mess." They walked away from the table as if they were just going to wash dishes after a meal.

Their fathers weren't as uninformed as Kaitlyn and Dashi led their children to think. Harry and Alfred had almost seen this coming. Perhaps not to *this* extent of damage, but the tensions in the house were palpable and they had attempted to at least be sure someone older was *always* around lest an outbreak erupted that might cause some emotional or physical damage to those involved. Thankfully it was just the garden.

Harry sighed, "Ah, Alouette---That red hair was no lie."

Will and Jamie's estimated return wasn't too far off from their actual arrival date; they passed through the Golden Gate over a month before they anticipated. Their return was greeted with the fanfare appropriate to family heroes. They had not yet made the circumnavigation; all two years had been spent in a supporting role to the *Hannah Belle* and once they were restocked with medicines and special equipments, they would be heading back to Melanesia. Some of the vital supplies were in transit via rail and some had already been procured locally. The equipment needs which had been ordered by the doctors from port in Manila, were already waiting at the Backhouse and Arastu's homes upon their arrival. So Berkeley was the scene of a rather largish family gathering. George hadn't been well for many, many weeks; Belle and Becky were at home tending to his needs.

"I really think that with the newest cameras we can document the migration of those first intrepid colonists who left the Guang for Formosa, or Malay for Borneo and then into the islands of the South Pacific," insisted Alouette.

"From what we were able to see, you may have something there..." Jamie confirmed, "Even if you simply document petroglyphs and such, you'll likely find the threads for which you four are searching."

George Lawrence tried a different tack in determining the language roots. "What were the words for 'sea,' 'rain,' 'pig,' 'house,' on each of those seventeen islands?"

Will simply rolled his eyes, "Ask Mom and Auntie, they were the ones who spent the most time ashore... Or better yet, ask Dad; he listened to more stories by toothless storytellers than even the natives probably could stand..."

"Really..." Aria stood and went to the great room with the intention of encouraging the Professor to share his notes from those encounters; George Lawrence was right behind him. Although the *Victoria* had spent two years in the south seas nominally reconnoitering for the *Hannah Belle* and assisting with resupply along with the other logistical requirements of the *Hannah's* mission, Aaron had made time to carry forward his own cultural investigations.

"Who knows when anyone would ever get to have those interviews..." Alouette's father was saying, "Some of the storytellers were already ancient and the majority of the next generation, who should be the recipients of that legacy, aren't interested in traditional ways. Then of course there's the disease, poverty and malnutrition... nobody is interested in 'stories' when they need to eat."

451

Aria asked to look over the professor's notes and Aaron was only too pleased to oblige. George Lawrence and Aria were soon joined by the girls; they all sat and methodically categorized and studied the field work done. The next day, having already decided what they intended, Aria and George Lawrence approached their fathers and Jameson and Aaron.

"Here's the proposition in a nutshell: Will and Jamie are perfectly willing to have us aboard---since we can also crew---and if we are able to have even half the time in documentation that Uncle Aaron had, we shall be able to compile all the data necessary for water-tight theses upon our return. Alouette and Lila are preparing for all the archaeological artifacts and specimens, just as Ari and I are set up for the anthropological side." The four men hadn't interrupted, which they took as an encouraging sign.

Ari picked up from there. "To perhaps be able to trace the migration of not only the Polynesians but their forebears, and their forebears... as far back as we can document, is a truly once in a lifetime opportunity. If what we have discovered thus far, and if our hypotheses are even partially correct, the results of this expedition could yield some answers to the very questions which have plagued mankind for thousands of years."

Alfred looked at Harry and nodded. Harry replied at last, speaking for all of them. "What each of you are hoping to find, hoping to unravel is at best searching for needles in haystacks. The trail of conscience doesn't leave breadcrumbs. Our own lineage, until Papa George, was only ever father to son---no artifacts, nothing *ever* written down..."

George Lawrence interrupted as delicately as he could, "Yet that's the point of our investigation: Our working hypothesis is that it was due to *those very men and women of conscience* that any successful migration occurred at all---the concerted efforts organized by effective leaders who were in touch with objective reason. Just as the earliest migrations into Asia and Europe must have had similar adept leadership."

Again Aria added, "While it would be stupendous to find *some* artifacts which indicated directly the involvement of highly conscious individuals, it will be enough that we can first establish to a high degree of certainty the migration routes they must have taken."

Alouette and Lila had crept into the conference while Aria was speaking and Lila joined in, "It is not enough to *suppose* that all of humanity arose from one place, as Darwin stated, 'There is a grandeur in this view of life, with its several powers, having been originally breathed into a few forms or into one,' and then over tens of thousands of years made the inevitable march across continents: the presumed peopling of North and South America from Berengia, the conjectured coastal migrations along the Indian Ocean's shores all the way to Australia, on and on---all of these suppositions are a house of cards unless we can find *evidence.*"

Allouette couldn't *not* say something and she put her hands on her hips, threw back her red curls and faced the elders of their family. "If Mia, Lena and Olly, Hannah and Jean can minister to the present ills inflicted upon the peoples of this world---*We can at least* attempt to clarify humanity's singular origins and perhaps head off the perpetuation of these insanities due to the most basic of misunderstandings: *That we are not many peoples---we are all one people!*"

Kaitlyn and Dashi, Titania and Hipolyta had followed the girls into the conference and now the whole family was gathered for the deliberations. Whelmed by their children's compelling case, Kaitlyn replied, "You will need an infrastructure of support in this endeavor, not unlike any corporation must have to further its aims in a rather hostile commercial environment. Should your investigations go inland, overland and on to the ends of the earth---you shall need support."

Dashi whispered to Alfred, Kaitlyn made the particulars of her wishes known to Harry while Aaron and Poly conversed with Jameson and Tania... the results of all the considerations were essentially this: Alfred and Harry would set up an international humanitarian fund for the express purpose of establishing accessible financial and legal support both for the *Victoria* and her expedition and for the *Hannah* and her ongoing missions. The vast network of contacts required was well within the families' range of resources. Harold and Lawrence would be tapped for Europe and the near East, Alfred and his relatives for the subcontinent and Southeast Asia. Central Asia would still require some investigation, but it was entirely possible Lawrence had contacts where nobody even suspected.

Jamie and Will, sitting aloof from the serious deliberations but interested in so far as the *Victoria* was one of the flagships of this expedition, added only, "The Aussies have strong banks and are very tight with the banking interests of England and the U.S.---all you need is an affiliate contact and funds can go anywhere in that part of the world."

Will added, "Believe us when we say: you do not want to carry large sums of cash with you anywhere, let alone in the south seas... Piracy is not altogether a non-issue, it just doesn't get headlines. Oh, and it'd also be a good idea to brush up on your Spanish, Portuguese, French, German and Dutch..."

Lawrence and Harold were contacted by wire; the expedition's purposes and the ongoing mission of the *Hannah Belle* were made clear. Both men in Europe were so persuaded into action that within a few days Alfred and Harry had more contacts and specific institutions to approach than they ever expected from the outset. The *Victoria* was laded with the supplies for which she had initially returned and waited now for the ethnographers to complete their packing.

It was the last week of August 1910; back in Tahoe City, Becky sat at the table with Belle and George eating lunch. She no longer wished to stand idly by and watch as her former students---her family---made the journeys of a lifetime. At the same time, she was loathe to abandon Papa George in his illness and of course her responsibilities to the Tahoe School.

Belle proposed an alternate perspective: "Dear, George is either going to recover as fully as possible, or become weaker..." George nodded in agreement and had a coughing fit as if to stress the obvious. "...and I will either outlive him by a many years, or succumb to the infirmities of old age as well. What is important at this moment is that you decide for yourself---What will Becky do? The school committee will find a suitable replacement for the short term until a truly qualified teacher is found... your students shall be in good hands one way or another."

Becky mulled over MamaBelle's words and a tear ran down her cheek, "You have been my family for these many years... I wasn't this torn up inside when I left my own parents more than two decades ago..." she suddenly realized, "Oh my! I have been here over twenty years! You two *have been* my mother and father longer than my own parents were..."

Belle smiled and patted her hand. "Sweetheart, if I've learned one thing about you over that time... it's that you are one of *the most capable* women in this family... Don't you think it's time to fly the nest?" and she kissed her adoptive daughter's cheek. "Where ever you go, *whatever* you do, you will *always* be our daughter and we will *always* be proud of you."

Becky's tears were now freely flowing and her voice was thick with the emotions of decision. Belle put an arm around her shoulders, stood her up and walked her to her room. "Darling, perhaps you should pack only a few personal items; I think the South Pacific requires quite a different wardrobe than what you have here..."

Becky smiled in spite of herself. Belle continued, "If you hurry, you can make the afternoon train and be in Berkeley by tonight. The *Victoria* will not sail without you. That I promise. Now wash your face, run a brush through your hair, pack a few things and *get on that train!*"

Becky was welcomed in Berkeley that night with the jubilation normally given a newborn daughter. Aaron and Hipolyta made their sister know just how especially glad they were that she had decided to make the voyage. Those sentiments were repeated all around the family as each offered her reassurance and praise for her decision---just tribute and reward for the years she had invested in their own children's lives.

Kaitlyn and Titania made it crystal clear, "You have given your entire life to the service of this family and as we cannot go on with them, please consider yourself: our collective representative in this new chapter of our family's story."

Those parents who had been on the two year voyage to the south seas took Becky aside and went over the particulars of what she might anticipate and how best to prepare for the journey. Tania and Poly spent the near entire next day helping with her clothing choices---most of which came from their own wardrobes collected during their voyage. Aaron and Jameson passed along everything from recipes to maps and pocket knives.

"You'll be surprised, we're sure, at how much these folks are capable of *and* how much they still rely upon a voice of reassurance in times of difficulty---but don't we all. Thank you so much for accepting this charge on our behalf... Truth be told: all of us have been a bit concerned that we should be so absent from this episode of their lives. That you shall be there with them is the icing on the cake for our hopes and plans."

Becky could not have imagined in the least that her own wish to go---and *that* at Belle's insistence---would have the impact it was having upon her family. What had seemed a selfish *desire* on her part, 'to just not be left out,' was rapidly becoming an apparent *imperative* that she participate... as if it were somehow expected of her to make this journey; that it really wasn't her own wishes or decisions which drove her to this step. It was feeling more and more like she was a vital part of this family and should to the best of her ability, fulfill her *ever-changing roles* within it. When she tried to explain all this to Harry and Kaitlyn, he chuckled.

"Rebecca Jane Backhouse, from that first moment that you sent me to fetch pastries, up to the moment you decided to go on this journey... how could you have *ever* considered that your life wouldn't *always* be tied inextricably both to mine and to this family's future. You have been our partner, friend, sister, teacher and daughter. The roles we assume may change, but our commitment to fulfilling them never wavers. You have been and always shall be: a Livingson and we are most blessed for that reality."

Kaitlyn held her hands as Harry spoke and both women were now in tears. Kaitlyn tried to add, "That 'girl behind the mask' from so long ago is the strongest of women and the dearest of sisters to me..."

The last of the supplies arrived and were duly laded. The Arastus, Backhouses, Connors and Livingsons stood arm in arm on the dock as the *Victoria* raised sail and carried their hopes and dreams for the future to the unknown shores of a vast and potent tomorrow."

Then his guest said quietly, as a conclusion to this last installment, "And that is how this next generation came to be away from North America for the duration of the first World War—They were on the other side of the world from the conflict, attempting to secure a peaceful future for the rest of their human family. That same family of man who were at that moment in time yielding yet again to their historical tendency to destruction and domination, suspicion and hatred—the supreme ignorance." The young man sat in his chair on the porch unable to move.

"This leads us to a new chapter in the Livingson family's story and so it's as a good a place as any to pause and allow you the time needed to practice your new exercises..." she concluded.

He smiled, "Actually, I'm glad you mentioned that; I have a few more questions about my work that I know you'll be able to resolve..." He almost said, 'resolve for me,' but he caught himself in the realization that it would have to be himself who resolved anything, if he was to benefit in any way. He rephrased, "I'm sure you can point me in the right direction."

She sat waiting for his questions and comments, her eyes expectant and her expression comfortingly gentle. "I hope to think so."

"When you spoke of 'active reasoning,' it seemed to me at the time that it was a recourse for pausing before reacting... allowing time for an appropriate response to arise instead. Is that the gist of it, or is there some broader application or use which I missed?"

She gathered her feet under her and began, "You are correct to say it is tool used against simply reacting, and at the same time it's more. Active reasoning is just what the label suggests: the intentional use of our highest faculties. We should become used to the efforts of right mentation, to the flavor of deliberate consideration, the taste and aroma of good judgement. So that when we fall into habitual reactions and mechanical desires and inclinations, there is a palpable distinction sensed and felt throughout our whole being between the two.

Another aspect of this activity beneficial to us is the sheer practice of *thinking* itself. *Really* thinking along a line of inquiry or investigation and following it through to a reasonably arrived upon resolution. The process of the enneagram we discussed has much to do with this type of real thinking and should be practiced often and in as many applications as possible. To question one's own thoughts, to interrogate yourself concerning the attitudes and assumptions under which you have lived is of preeminent value and is precisely what Socrates meant when he said: *the unexamined life is not worth living.* We are the creatures of this planet who have risen to the station of being capable of receiving directly the divine advent of reason---to ignore that access is to not only turn our back upon our birthright, but to disregard the efforts of all who have had a part in its arising--- as far back as it goes.

'Active,' because passively or mechanically is not only useless but meaningless. 'Active,' because it is an act of Will... a small beginning perhaps, but of Will none-the-less. 'Active,' because we are called to action by the journey itself; it is a living thing after all, composed of a membership stretching from the earliest of those first initiates in the mists of epochs passed, all the way to farthest reaches ahead, up to the end of time." Her eyes had become fixed on an undetermined place seemingly past the horizon itself. She made a little gulp and her features softened again. "Anyway, the more we practice..."

He finished, "...the better we get at whatever it is. Thank you, that does help. If you aren't annoyed with my lack of understanding yet, I have another question..."

She nodded, "Ask away."

"Well, this has more to do with the structure itself. Very early on in these dialogs, I was promised an explanation of the MI-FA interval and why it is a stumbling place, a gap which the octave must have assistance to pass. Am I ready for that explanation yet?" He really didn't wish to have more information if he couldn't make use of it and thus far every time some new bit of knowledge was entrusted to him, he not only made sense of it but he also had a clear vision of where it belonged in the 'big' picture.

She raised one eyebrow and answered, "I think you may almost be ready to fit that piece into puzzle... soon, very soon..."

J. L. LAWSON

Manuscripts Currently Published by
J. L. Lawson

---The Donkey and the Wall Trilogy---

Book One: An Honest Man
Book Two: The Thief
Book Three: The Tiger

---The Curious Voyages of the Anna Virginia Saga---

First: Weigh Anchor
Second: Harbor
Third: Storms
Fourth: Locks & Gates
Fifth: Tidal Bore
Sixth: Beyond the Littoral
Seventh (final): Red Sky at Night

www.ingramcontent.com/pod-product-compliance
Lightning Source LLC
Chambersburg PA
CBHW020827030726
47496CB00001B/129